For Mum, Dad, and Ian

Acknowledgements:

At the time of writing, the following people wrote a nice Amazon.com or co.uk review of my last book, or sent a kind e-mail. Thank you so, so much. As someone new to this game, those meant everything. I'm only using the names you put on your Amazon reviews, as these will be ones you're happy to have associated with my work ... I hope:

Paul C. Gomez, BonFire, Amy Glavasich, Malika H, Shelly Olmstead, Sharron, Janet Farley, Huwbat, adamb1980, Miss Sl Orr, VB, Bloodrush 78, mstlh, F. Hughes, scrooby1, Spiritman "unicorn175", chrisinamsterdam, Daisy, Chezisme, VAN, Guy Beauchamp, T, Russell Jones, against nat, Suzan J, purplejuice, D. Maccauley, Neil Harris, Mr Keith J Lawrence, Red, Fishtoys, Sarah, and A King.

Sincerely, they kept me going with this. Hope you like this one too.

The Stone Man

By
Luke Smitherd

All men are frightened. The more intelligent they are, the more they are frightened.
—George S. Patton

Every single person I was with would have done what I did.
—Sal Giunta, on receiving the Congressional Medal Of Honour

One thing you will discover is that life is based less than you think on what you've learned and much more than you think on what you have inside you from the beginning.
—Bret 'The Hitman' Hart, quoting Mark Helprin

He'd never stood one single time to prove the county wrong
His mama named him Tommy but folks just called him Yellow
Something always told me they were reading Tommy wrong.
—Kenny Rogers

When the danger is far away, or at least not immediately imminent, the instinct is to freeze. When danger is approaching, the impulse is to run away. When escape is impossible, the response is to fight back. And when struggling is futile, the animal will become immobilized in the grip of fright.
—Bruce Schneier

Before you accuse me, take a look at yourself.
—Bo Diddley

Table of Contents

Part 1:
All the Time In the World

Chapter One: Andy at the End, The Stone Man Arrives, A Long Journey Begins On Foot, And the Eyes of the World Fall Upon England

***

The TV is on in the room next door; the volume is up, the news is on, and I can hear some Scottish reporter saying that it's about to happen all over again. I already knew that, of course, just like everyone watching already knows that 'The Lottery Question' is being asked by people up and down the country, and around the world. *Who will it be this time?*

That was my job, of course, although I won't be doing it anymore. That's why I'm recording this, into the handheld digi-dicta-doodad that Paul sent me after the first lot of business that we dealt with. *To get it all out if you need to*, he'd said (he knows I find it hard to talk to people. He thought talking to the machine might be easier. Plus, *getting it all out* now gives me an excuse to use it after all; feels strange holding one again, as if my newspaper days were decades ago instead of just a year or so).

I didn't really know what he was talking about, back then. It had hit him a lot harder than me, so I didn't really understand why I'd need to talk about it. Eventually I got it, of course ... after the *second* time.

That was worse. Much worse.

This room is nice anyway, better than the outside of the hotel would suggest. I actually feel guilty about smoking in here, but at this stage I can be forgiven, I'm sure. Helps me relax, and naturally, I've got the entire contents of the mini bar spread out in front of me. I haven't actually touched any of it yet, but rest assured, I expect I shall have consumed most of it by the time I finish talking.

I just thought that I should get the real version down while I still have time. Not the only-partially-true, Home Office approved version that made me a household name around the world. I'm not really recording this for anyone else to hear, as daft as that may sound. I just think that doing so will help me put it all in perspective. I might delete it afterwards, I might not ... I think I will. Too dangerous for it to get out, for now at least.

I'd obviously had to come here in disguise (amazing how much a pair of subtle sunglasses and a baseball cap let you get away with in summer) and it's a good job that I did. They'd already be up here, banging on the door, screaming about the news and telling me what I already know. Thanks to my disguise, I can sit quietly in this designer-upholstered, soft-glow, up-lit, beige yuppie hidey-hole, with Steely Dan playing in the background on my phone's speakers (sorry if you aren't a fan) and remain undisturbed, until … well, until I'm done. And it's time.

This is for you as well, Paul; for you more than anyone. You were there for all of it, and you're a key player, not that you'll ever actually get to hear this.

Well, *actually*, you weren't there at the start, were you? I often forget that. Which, of course, would be the best place to begin. Heh, would you look at that; I just did an automatic segue. Still got all the old newsman moves. Slick …

Sorry, I was miles away for a moment there. Remembering the first day. How *excited* those people were. Everybody knew it was something big.

Nobody was frightened. Not at first.

***

It was summer. Summer meant more people out shopping, eyeing up the opposite sex, browsing, meeting friends, having outdoor coffees and watered-down beer. In Coventry, the chance to do this (with the sun out, and not a single cloud visible in the sky on a *weekend* no less) was as rare as rocking-horse shit, and so there were more people out and about in the city centre than at pretty much any other time of the year. I sometimes wonder if this was the reason that particular day was picked; attracted to the mass of people perhaps? Or maybe it was just sheer chance.

I was stuck indoors for the earlier part of that day, and that was just fine by me. One, because I've never been a person who enjoys being out in harsh sunlight (makes me squint, I sweat easily, I burn easily, I can't stand it when my clothes stick to me … need I go on? Sun worshippers doing nothing but sitting in sunlight; I'll never understand them) and two, because I was interviewing a local girl group ('Heroine Chic'; I shit you not) who were just about to release their debut piece-of-crap single. And it was *awful*, truly awful (I don't mean to come across as someone's dad, but it really was an assault on the ear drums. Middle-class white girls talking in urban patois. Exactly as bad as it sounds) but, at the time, I was still just on the right side of thirty-five, and so considered myself in with a chance of charming at least one of the trio; a stunning-looking blonde, brunette and redhead combo in their early twenties whose management were clearly banking on their looks to get them by, rather than their output. None of us knew it back then, but even that wouldn't be enough to help 'Get Into Me' (again, I shit you not) crack the top forty. Two more non-charting efforts later, Heroine Chic would find themselves back in obscurity before fame had found them; of the six of us in that room, including their enormous security guard and their wet-behind-the-ears looking manager, only one of us was destined to be known worldwide. None of us could have ever guessed that it would be me.

Not that I didn't have high hopes of my own in those days, lazy—but earnest—dreams of a glorious career in my chosen field. Obviously, the likes of Charli, Kel and Suze weren't going to land me a job at *Rolling Stone*, but I was starting to get good feedback on freelance pieces that I'd written for the *Observer* and the *Times*, and was listed as a contributor at the *Guardian*; I'd finally started to believe that in a year or two, I'd leave behind the features department at the local rag and then make my way to London to start shaking things up. I actually said that to colleagues as well: *I'm gonna shake things up.* That's how I often find myself talking to people, using sound bites and stagey lines to make an impression. As the interview drew to a close, and their manager started making 'wrap it up' signals while looking nervously at his smartphone, the girls and I posed together for a brief photo by the office window. They pouted, and I grinned honestly, enjoying the moment despite receiving zero interest from any of them. I made myself feel better by putting it down to the age gap.

They left with an all-too-casual goodbye, their bouncer blocking them all from view as they made their way to the escalator. I was done for the day—I'd only come in for the late afternoon interview, with it being a weekend—and it was approaching five, so the temperature would soon be dropping nicely into that relaxing summer evening feel that I actually like. I had no plans, and flatmate Phil had his brother over for the weekend. He was a good guy, and his brother a good guest, but I didn't particularly want to be stuck at home listening to the two of them endlessly discussing rugby. I decided that I'd maybe find a beer garden and have a read for an hour or so. In my twenties, this would have been that magical exciting hour where you'd text around and find out who was available for an impromptu session. No one was anymore.

I grabbed my bag and headed out of the building, thinking about possibly getting a bite to eat as well—although I intended to have something healthy, as lately the gym hadn't really been graced with my presence, and it was starting to show—and for some reason, I decided to stroll towards Millennium Place.

It used to be a big open-air space, a modern plaza designed for concerts and shows of all kinds. None of it's there anymore, of course; after the Second Arrival they dug it all up and put a small lake in its place, to see if it made any difference.

For some reason I was in a good mood and—in the words of the song—having 'no particular place to go', I thought I'd take a look at the summer crowds at Millennium Place, and then decide my destination from there, giving me time to work up an appetite. I people-watched as I went, passing barely dressed young couples who made me feel old and think about past opportunities of my own. I realised that the tune I'd been humming was 'Get Into Me'. I laughed out loud—I remember that distinctly—as I turned the corner and saw Millennium Place fully. When I saw what was going on, the laughter trailed off in my throat.

I suppose that I must have heard the commotion as I'd drawn closer; I'd been so lost in thought that somehow it didn't really register, or possibly I just subconsciously wrote it off as the usual summer crowd sound. But this was different. Around two hundred people were gathered in a cluster near the centre of Millennium Place, and there was an excited, confused buzz coming from them, their mobiles held out and snapping away at something in their midst. Other people were hanging back from them, getting footage of the crowd itself. That was the other reason I wanted to get into the big leagues, of course; *everyone* was a reporter in the digital age, and local print was shrinking fast.

I couldn't make out what was in the centre of the crowd, standing at a distance as I was, but I could see other people on the outskirts of the plaza having the same response as me; *what's going on, whatever it is I want to see it*. Don't misunderstand me, at this stage it was surprising and intriguing, but nothing really more than that; a chance for hopeful people to capture some footage that might go viral. You have to remember, none of us knew what it really was at that point. I assumed that it was somebody maybe doing some kind of street art, or perhaps a performance piece. That in itself was rare in Coventry, so in my mind I already had one hand on my phone to give Rich Bell—the staff photographer—a call, to see if he was available to get some proper photos if this turned out to be worth it. Either way, I walked towards the hubbub. As I got closer I could hear two people shouting frantically, almost hysterically, sounding as though they were trying to explain something.

The voices belonged to a man and a woman, and while I couldn't yet make out what they were saying, I could hear laughter from some listeners and questions from others; my vision was still mainly blocked by the medium-sized mass of bodies, but I could see that there was something fairly large in the middle of them all, rising just slightly above the heads of the gathered crowd and standing perfectly still.

I reached the cluster of people, now large enough to make it difficult to get through (to the point where I had to go on tiptoe to get a clear view) and that was the moment that I became one of the first few hundred people on Earth to get a look at the Stone Man.

Of course, it didn't have a name then. I'd like to tell you that I was the one who came up with it, but I'm afraid that would be a lie. As you may know, I was one of the people who *really* brought it into the common parlance worldwide, but I'd actually overheard it being used on a random local radio station as Paul and I raced through Sheffield later on (obviously, more on that to come) and thought it perfect, but I'd never actually intended to rip it off. By the point I was in front of the cameras, I'd used it so often that I'd forgotten that it wasn't a common term at the time.

It stood at around eight feet tall (to my eyes at least; the Home Office can give you the exact measurements) and it made me think then, as it does now, of the 'Man' logo on a toilet door, if someone were to make one out of rough, dark, greyish-brown stone and then mutate it so the arms were too long, and the head were more of an oval than a circle. The top half of its body was bent slightly forward as well, but the biggest departure from the toilet picture was that this figure had hands, of a sort; its arms tapered out at the ends, reminding me of the tip of a lipstick.

The most intriguing thing was, there was also an extremely quiet sound emanating from it. The best way I can describe it is as a bass note so low as to be almost inaudible. They still haven't figured that one out.

Now that I was closer, I could hear what one of the ranting people was saying. It was the woman, stood about ten feet away from me on the inside of the circle of gathered people. Based on the distance between the crowd, herself, and the Stone Man, it looked to me as if she was the reason they were hanging back from the hulking figure, and not swarming forward to touch and prod it.

She was patrolling back and forth in front of the Stone Man, wide-eyed and breathing heavily. If she wasn't keeping the people around her at bay deliberately, she was still doing a damn good job of it. The mass of bodies on the other side of the Stone Man seemed to be getting an identical treatment from someone else; I couldn't see them clearly around the bodies of the woman and the Stone Man itself, nor could I hear what they were saying over the general noise, but it sounded like a man.

The woman was about fifty, well-dressed, and clearly at the end of her rope. She was very red-faced from her efforts, and sweating. Her smart white summer blouse and beige skirt were in sharp contrast to her flustered appearance, giving her a temporary air of great visibility. The people on the very inside of the circle looked uncertain, wondering if this was some kind of show (which was probably another reason that they were hanging back, not wanting to either spoil or become part of a public performance) and some of them were smiling nervously at each other. As I drew within clear-hearing range, she was taking a moment to try and get her air back. She'd obviously just finished her rant, and was now struggling to compose herself before continuing, deciding that an attempt at a more rational demeanour might better help her cause.

She closed her eyes slowly, and took a deep breath, lifting her chin. She reminded me slightly, in that moment, of Yoda, just before he tries to lift Luke's X-Wing out of the swamp. When she started speaking again, her eyes remained shut.

"I'm not crazy," she said, quietly but decisively, her voice shaking slightly. "I'm not making it up. I'm not some loony, and I'm not the only one here that's saying it. This isn't a, a ... I don't know, some kind of bloody *play* or anything, this is what's happened. It's real. Any of you who were here earlier, did you see anyone bring this thing over? Look, look how much it *weighs,* for God's sake!" she suddenly cried, shouting this last part as her composure gave way and she struck at the Stone Man, first with her purse and then with her balled up fists. She moved up close to it and began to push against it with her shoulders and full body weight. It didn't move a millimetre. I always remember the crowd's seemingly subconscious reaction when she first hit it; everyone responded in the exact same manner, without really noticing that they'd done it. They'd all flinched away slightly.

I think at that point someone might have moved in to calm her down, but I didn't see if they actually managed it because that was when the young guy— the one who'd still been shouting at the people on the other side of the circle— suddenly flung his arms in the air and pushed his way out of the crowd. I could see him clearly now, dressed in a dark hooded top and overly baggy jeans. The people parted to let him out, perhaps relieved—the human urge to treat public displays of volume as if they were contagious coming into full effect—and I broke away from my side of the circle to pursue him. I'd seen enough for now, and I wanted to find out what the shouting was about without having to deal with any interference. More and more people were arriving and joining the circle, and I knew that if I was going to speak to him, it would have to be now if I were ever to stand a chance of getting back into the crowd and regaining a decent vantage point.

I dashed around to the opposite side of the pack and saw that he hadn't gone far, stomping along with clenched fists and shaking head. He'd pulled the hood of his top up over his head as well, so I couldn't get an idea of his facial appearance from the angle that I was approaching at, but it was clear by his body language that he wasn't happy. I could at least see that he was shorter than myself, and of slight build. I decided to open a dialogue by appealing to his righteous anger; in my experience, angry people warm to you very quickly if you agree with them. Running around him so that I was several feet ahead, I stopped, looking past him to the crowd, pretending that an idea had just occurred to me. Waiting until he drew near, I tutted loudly.

"What the hell is wrong with all those idiots, eh?" I asked him, speaking as if I was just making conversation. I probably wasn't very convincing; small talk has never been something that I'm comfortable with.

"Fuck 'em," he muttered, not looking at me as he went to walk past. From this new angle I could see that he was in his early twenties at most, with crew cut hair and a face that was only just seeing off the last ravages of acne. His cheekbones stood out, giving him a drawn, wiry look. He started to fish a packet of cigarettes out of his pocket, and seeing the opening I pulled out my lighter to accommodate. I don't smoke myself, but I often find that carrying a lighter has its uses, especially in this job. He stopped—still not looking at me—and clearly wasn't really thinking about what he was doing, still lost in his fury as he fumbled out a cigarette and put it in his mouth. I flicked the wheel and a plume of flame appeared. Lowering his head towards it, he gave a non-committal grunt of thanks as he took a drag on the cigarette and let out a sigh that was more of a hiss. Straightening, he clenched his jaw and looked back at the crowd, still shaking his head. Whatever they'd done, they'd really managed to offend him.

"Ah saw it. Ah fuckin' *seen* it, man," he said, staring angrily at the crowd, shaking his head gently. He paused to take another drag, let it out. "*Twats*," he said, drawing out the *s* longer than was necessary.

"What, the statue thing?" I asked, pointing at it, the head still slightly visible above the growing crowd of people. He nodded, not turning around to look, inhaling again instead. The cigarette was calming him, steadying him, soothing his ego. I decided it was safe to press on. "But ... haven't they all seen it as well?"

He suddenly whirled round to face the same direction as me, face screwed up in disgust at my stupidity. He looked like a rat that had smelt something it didn't like.

"No, ya fuckin' ..." His words trailed off, as he realised that not only did he not know me well enough to talk to me in such a manner, but also that I could probably pound him fairly comfortably. I'm not a big guy, or even a tough guy by any stretch, but it was clear that taking down this spindly specimen wouldn't prove to be too much of a challenge. He looked me up and down quickly, and his angry eyes dropped slightly, although his expression didn't change. "No ... all those arseholes *seen* the fucker, man. Ah saw it *first*." He stared at me, waiting for me to comprehend. I shrugged slightly, confirming that comprehension wasn't coming anytime soon. His face screwed up further.

"*Ah* saw it *turn up*. No one else was looking. Nah, ac'shully, dat woman was looking, she was looking, but she fuckin' ..." He paused for a moment, waving his hand in the air dismissively. "She fuckin' *blah blah blah* and no-one give a fuck, but ah was *tellin'* them that ah *fuckin'* seen it, and they all just standin' there like *errrrrrrrrrr* and ah'm tellin' 'em and *tellin'* 'em and they don't fuckin' *geddit*. Fuckin' jokers, bruv, jokers." He took another drag, and wagged a finger at the crowd. "And some of 'em start *laughin'*, man, fuckin' bitches ... fuckin' nearly *battered* 'em, man, *boom*," he finished emphatically, punctuating the word with a short, aggressive air punch that said that he meant it, unaware of how ineffective he probably would have been. His anger was so genuine that I suddenly wanted to know what he had to say, despite my normal loathing for this kind of chavvy little twat.

"Look," I said, reaching into my bag for my Dictaphone, "tell me. I want to know, I'll listen." He saw the Dictaphone and started to back away, staring at it.

"Fuckin' *what?*" he said, drawing out the *t* in the same way he'd done with the *s*. Though my first instinct was to smash him over the head with the Dictaphone, I merely waved it dismissively, smiling.

"I write for the paper. Just want to get an idea of what happened. Won't even use your name if you don't want me to."

He didn't reply at first, just carried on staring at the Dictaphone with that screwed up face of his, smoking. He turned to look at the crowd for a moment, and then faced me again with a snort and a little shake of the head, gesturing me towards him. I bet Straub still has the recording. I'll never forgive her for taking that Dictaphone off me. I bet it's valuable, too; it's probably the first eyewitness account of the first human sighting.

***

(Faint sound of crowd noise. By now, there are around three hundred people in the background, plus constant traffic sounds from the cars driving past Millennium Place. The first sound is a large post-exhale intake of breath from the interviewee. I can be heard telling him that it's now recording, and then asking if he wants to give his name.)

"Nah, bruv, nah ..."

(There is a long pause while he possibly considers what he's doing, but then thinks better of it, clearly keen to be heard. He's smarting, still angry and feeling

humiliated with that brand of indignation that only the young can muster.)

"Ah was on da phone, like, just talkin' an' that, and dere, over dere like?"

(The sound fades as he turns away to gesture to where the crowd is standing.)

"There were no one dere, right, and maybe like ... some people dere, and dere, and over dere, and dat's it—"

("How many people?")

"... thirty ... 'bout thirty innit, like spread out? But ah was the only one near dere 'cos ah was on me phone, like. So ah fuckin' saw. Dey's like, like ..."

(He pauses, holding his hands apart, seeing it again.)

"Right next to me ... it was like, cold, like fuckin' freezin'. And ah'm like, fuckin', shiverin' an' dat, and everyone else is like la la la, fuckin' warm, and it's all sunny but ah'm lookin' round tryin'a see where the fuckin' cold's comin' from, but dey's just ... nuthin."

(He breaks off and takes another drag on his cigarette. His hand is shaking.)

"And then ma phone is just like WEEEEEEEEE in ma fuckin' ear! Like ah can hear Donna and then it's just this fuckin' ... noise, like the speaker's fucked, and ah'm like fuck dis an' hang up like, and then ah look and just like, dere—"

(He gestures to a spot about two feet in front of himself, implying distance.)

"—it's dere, and it weren't dere before, man, it weren't-fucking-dere, but it's not dere properly, like ah can see troo *the fucker."*

(Another pause as he stares at me, almost daring me to say anything. I don't respond at first, not understanding. He continues.)

"Ah mean, like, it was fast, *man, like ah could see troo it for like, a second, then* brap, *it's there totally, and ah'm all 'ot again innit, and it's dere, but it's just fuckin', just ..."*

(His eyes are wide, his expression manic, looking into space with his hands splayed as he sees it again.)

"... bing! DERE. Outta fuckin' nowhere. And ah'm looking at this fuckin' stone thing dat's just fuckin' poofed, appeared like, and ah'm lookin' and no-one's noticed, and ah just ... ah just ..."

(He searches for the words.)

"... ah fuckin' ... man ..."

(There is a long pause as he almost visibly deflates, shaking his head. I think he is starting to feel sorry for himself. When he continues, I think that he has forgotten who he is talking to, this adult stranger with a Dictaphone, an adult who thinks he might just be interviewing a smackhead. I almost turn it off and put it away. Later, I will know that he would have been genuinely traumatised by seeing the impossible, the materialisation of a solid physical object out of thin air,

and was simply having an emotional release. But now, I just think he's off his tits. I carry on recording anyway.)

"... I just, like ... ah dunno ... ah just started fuckin' ... like...shouting, or somethin', and then ah can't fuckin' breathe an' ah'm shakin' and ah fall on ma arse, but ah'm still shoutin' an' pointin' at it, 'cos ... 'cos ... it shouldn't fuckin' BE dere, y'know? An' then ah fuckin' honk up a bit, and other people are comin' over an' ah'm tryin' to tell 'em but den dey's walkin' away quick, but den dat old woman come over an' she's shoutin' too like AH SAW IT AH SAW IT TOO and some people are stayin' and some are fuckin' off and some fuckin' pricks are laughin' ... an' ah can hear people saying it's a statue, it's a fuckin' ..."

(He waves his hand, searching for the word. "Sculpture?" I say, offering it up.)

"Yeah, scupter. Dat. And I'm like, it's not a fuckin' scupter! An' ah stand up and start fuckin' shoutin' an' that, an' ah'm fuckin' shoutin' at 'em for ages, then ah just ... ah fuck off out of it."

(There's a long pause, and a faint sound as the cigarette is flicked away into the gutter. "So the woman saw this too?" I say.)

"Musta done. She said the same stuff. 'Ohhhh, it was see troo and then it fuckin' popped up ...'"

(I mentally register this statement in particular, as it is the first time I feel some real confusion. The woman had looked too well-dressed to be a crazy person jumping on the bandwagon. She'd looked like a teacher, or someone's Mum. Another long pause, as he stands looking back at the crowd, shaking his head. I don't speak either, rather bewildered at this point as to what the hell is going on. He suddenly speaks.)

"Right, fuck it, the end. Safe."

(He turns to leave, finished just like that, and holds out his knuckles for me to put mine against. I do so. "Are you all right?" I ask. He responds without turning around, still hurriedly walking away and not even looking at the crowd.)

"Yeah, safe, man. Safe."

***

I stood there for a moment, watching him go, and starting to think that maybe this really was some kind of annoying performance piece. I turned back to the crowd, looking for the woman and thinking that I'd try and have a word with her as well, maybe get a few crowd reactions for an opinion piece or something, but I suddenly realised that the woman couldn't be heard anymore. That was when the first of the police cars arrived. They didn't have the sirens or lights going; they just quietly turned up, presumably to check that there wasn't some kind of trouble occurring, or maybe brought there by somebody reporting the shouters. Either way, they'd arrived, and so I headed back over to the source of the hubbub. I don't really remember what I was thinking at this point; I was more intrigued than anything else, I think. I certainly didn't believe what the chav had just been saying, but it was all interesting regardless.

As I was walking over, everyone in the crowd suddenly let out cries of varying volumes—there were several screams—and jumped back a foot or two. I stopped walking and started running. So did the police.

I reached the crowd about as quickly as the cops did, and snuck in with them, following in their wake as they pushed to the front while asking people politely to back up and let them through. I was looking at the Stone Man and the crowd, trying to see what the hell had happened to make everyone jump at once like that. Most people were now giggling nervously, embarrassed at their reaction, but I couldn't tell what they had reacted to; a quick inspection of the Stone Man didn't give anything away. As far as I could tell, nothing was any different. The police were talking to some people at the opposite side of the inner circle, too far away for me to hear, so I tried to pick up on the conversations of people around me. I didn't get any clues at first.

God, feel my heart!

I was like, oh shit!

You elbowed me in the ribs when you jumped!

I was just about to ask the couple to my right what had happened, when I suddenly saw the evidence for myself; I'd been wrong. There *was* a difference to the Stone Man.

It was no longer bent forward. It had straightened up, and its head was now tipped backwards towards the sky. The arms seemed to be held out at a slightly wider angle than before as well. Everyone must have jumped when it switched position, but were simply excited now that it was perfectly still; already the police were smiling again and talking to the people, most of whom were now looking amused and expectant, phones out once more. It seemed that the general consensus was that this was definitely some kind of unusual, intentional show, and everyone was waiting for whatever was going to happen next.

I, however, kept seeing the teacherish woman in my mind as she leant on the Stone Man, as she struck at it. I hadn't seen any movement from it in the slightest. There was clearly real *weight* to the Stone Man, real solidity. I couldn't see any hinge or break in the rough stone surface, any point of articulation. So how the hell had it now straightened up like that? I looked around for the teacherish woman; she appeared to have left, just like her chav counterpart. One of the police was on his radio, sounding as though he was calling in more officers or support of some kind—there were still people turning up to see what was going on—but he looked more amused than anything. I decided to stick around. I wasn't massively hungry yet, the temperature was just nice now in the late afternoon, and there looked like there would be further developments.

As the next hour passed, police barriers arrived, along with two more officers who good-naturedly spread the now four-hundred-strong crowd back a few feet—receiving a chorus of playful boos as a result—and set up a low retractable tape barrier at a radius of about eight feet from the Stone Man. A gentleman from the council turned up at one point, asked the police a few questions, and then moved back to the outside of the crowd, where he remained on his phone for the rest of the time that I was there. It filtered back through the crowd that he was trying to find out who was responsible for it, if they had a permit, and so on. Eventually, he apparently moved on to trying to sort out its removal.

I'd gotten a few bits of audio from the people around me, a lot of them all too eager to talk into the Dictaphone, describing how it had suddenly moved without a sound (the silence of it was confirmed by all of them, which again struck a chord with me. How could something with so much weight move silently? Unless the teacher woman had been an excellent mime) and a few opinions (*I think it's representing the death of Coventry's industry/I think it's a marketing stunt/I think it's shit*) but was starting to grow a bit bored, to be honest. Rich Bell wasn't answering his phone either, so all I had image-wise were a few shots I'd managed to grab on the digital camera that I kept in my bag; my phone's own camera was far too primitive. Even those who had been there all along were starting to look at their watches and think about dinner.

I couldn't blame them. I would have liked to have sacked it off myself by then, if not for the fact that the teacher woman's story corroborated the impossible account of the chav ... it made me think twice, or at least give me enough desire for an explanation to warrant me staying longer. My stomach rumbled, and I began to think about where the nearest chippy was that I could dash to—even though it meant I would lose my place at the front of the crowd—when the temperature suddenly dropped by about twenty degrees.

Everyone there suddenly started chattering, and looking at the sky, even though the sun above was still blazing down. It was *freezing*, impossibly cold under that still-blue sky, and I was more covered than most of the other people due to my jeans. I hate to think how cold the summer-dressed people there would have been. Goose bumps covered my entire body, and I saw couples and friends suddenly and instinctively huddling together for warmth, some laughing, some looking confused. Even the cops shared a concerned look. I found myself remembering what the chav had said about the cold, how the temperature around him had inexplicably dropped, and suddenly I had a brief flash of belief; *he was right.* I tried to remind myself that this was the age of people like David Blaine, street performers who prided themselves on their ability to freak people out by making them believe the impossible, and took a deep breath. I noticed that my heart rate had still picked up dramatically, though.

Then the cold suddenly cut off just as quickly, and almost unnoticed in the moment of relief—everyone around me breathed an audible sigh and started to laugh, delighted that the heat was back again—the Stone Man took two steps forward and stopped.

Everyone who was directly in front of it, albeit eight feet away, shrieked and leapt backwards. One or two people at the back fell over. The steps had not been quick, or slow; they were about normal walking pace. The Stone Man had come to a stop with its feet side by side, like it had only meant to take two steps and no more. It was now completely still again, and nervously giggling people had already started to step back into their original position. The police inside the barrier had backed away, but one had already gathered his wits and was politely taking charge, telling people to calm down. The council man was impotently demanding to be let back through the crowd, but no one was paying any attention.

Then the Stone Man began to walk.

***

Time to crack open the mini Jim Beam here, I think. I don't really like it, but then I'm not mad on half of these, and I've decided to polish them all off. Bollocks to it. I'm even tempted to turn on the TV and watch it all live for myself; I can pretty much hear everything from next door's TV anyway. In fact, let me turn it back on so I can properly describe it to you.

There. Not much has changed since I started this. There's the lake, there's the barrier, there's the vehicle blockade beyond that. That barrier must be, what ... three or four hundred metres in diameter? Pretty pointless, really, but I guess it's just to mark out the extra-restricted area. The soldiers are only there now to stop any approaching people from interfering, should any idiots try to get inside the barrier, but that would just be a precaution. The evacuation would have begun some time ago, and hell, it wouldn't have taken long. There's hardly anybody left in Coventry now anyway, except maybe on the outskirts, but I guess they're taking no chances. There's also the *very* slim chance—to their minds—that someone might get through, someone who might be ... you know. Needing to be put down, for obvious reasons. Slim odds, as I say, but they have to take that precaution. That would be a turn up, eh?

Even the helicopter shot that they're showing on screen is clearly being taken from a great distance away, an obvious fact even though the camera is zoomed in as much as it can be. You can only just make out the lump in the middle of the lake, the hulking figure at the heart of it all. The tanks outside the barrier seem a bit pointless; they're only gonna move anyway, and the soldiers alone would have kept any people back.

There's people watching this who must get a real kick out of it. Probably the majority. They all know what it means, and it's still a circus to them. Fuckers. *Fuckers!* I owe them nothing. *Nothing.* Geez, I've only had one slug and I'm already getting maudlin and bitter ... hardly a surprise though, eh? Ah, I can't handle my booze anymore. I'll just turn the sound down.

That shot is so far back it's almost pointless. Nowhere near as good as the one during the Second Arrival, the one from the roof of the Old Fire Station building. They showed that one over and over. Of course, after the Second Arrival, the Old Fire Station isn't there anymore; ditto most of the surrounding city centre. No one was allowed to inhabit buildings around that space, no one ever rebuilt the ones that got demolished, and then they flattened them all anyway. Safer, they said. They paved it all over. There was a square mile in the centre of Coventry that no one was allowed to enter for a whole year, unless they had high-level military clearance. I was allowed in, of course. The ban was officially lifted once they figured out was going on, but the lake and the barrier around it were guarded more closely than the White House. And I mean that literally. I can still get inside that if I want to, as well. Heh. Still makes me feel smug, amazingly. Paul might have said I was a nice bloke, and I'm not sure that I agree (you hear that? Nice bloke, someone said) but it can't be said that I don't have an ego. Here's to you, Pauly-boy.

So, Millennium Place, when it was still Millennium Place. The Stone Man, beginning to walk. Everybody excited, oohing and aahing ... and for a moment, it was something great, like everyone knew that the world would be wanting to know about this, one of the most amazing street tricks ever, pure YouTube fodder, and in Coventry of all places! I felt the same, that I was lucky to be there; everyone was immediately caught up in it all. For a few moments, it was just a great thrill. Then the guy in the green vest got involved, and suddenly, we all knew different. It all went to shit from there.

***

Immediately, a cheer went up; I cheered too. It just looked so incredible, how the stone before us could move and bend without any visible joints or creasing. It seemed like it somehow compressed when it needed to, and then stretched out afterwards without any sign of *how* it could bend; you could almost guess that it was some kind of rubber, if not for the complete lack of rippling and the way it hadn't had any give at all under the woman's blows. It was *stone*, you could see it was *actual stone* ... and yet there it was, 'knees' bending as the legs moved, the arms swaying slightly at its sides with no visible lines where they met the shoulders. It walked with its head up. Hell, you could *feel* the weight of it as each of the tree trunk sized legs came down. I remember that vividly. It may sound weird, but the Stone Man walking was one of the most incredible things I, and the people around me, had ever seen. Everyone was looking at each other, open-mouthed, laughing and gasping and shaking their heads, all thinking the same thing; *how the hell do they make it do that?*

I remember seeing clips of a street performance in ... I want to say Barcelona. I don't know. A giant egg in the middle of a town, which later 'hatched' to give birth to ... was it an elephant? I can't remember, but I do remember the footage of some woman riding on it, and everyone there just being amazed. And it *was* amazing, no sign of puppeteers or wires. It even spewed water over the people, for God's sake! I think it went on for a few days, meeting up with different aspects of the show that were planted across the city. It was wonderful. All I could think though, while seeing the Stone Man walk, was that by comparison the puppet elephant looked like a piece of shit.

Everyone in the Stone Man's path jumped back to let it pass, even before it had reached the edge of the barrier. The police looked a bit dumbfounded, and moved forward uncertainly, half expecting it to stop once it reached the tape. But it didn't. To everyone's surprise, it just kept going, pushing into the barrier and dragging it forward like it wasn't even there. Everyone started cheering again, expecting the whole barrier to be dragged along with the Stone Man or for the police to stop it somehow. The former would have happened, too, if not for the quick thinking of one officer. Perhaps he thought that whichever performer was inside the Stone Man couldn't see what they were doing, or was thinking that the barrier was only going to become a hazard if it were dragged across the square, or even that he didn't want to ruin a potentially good bit of public performance; either way, he unclipped one end of the barrier tape, sending it retracting back rapidly into the opposite pillar that it had been drawn out of and effectively ending the problem. The crowd cheered again, the officer smiled sheepishly—there was no law being broken, after all—and the police followed after the Stone Man to see, like everyone else, what was going on.

It began to pass through the crowd, who moved with it, and the people on the opposite side of the circle surged in to follow. It was setting off in the direction of the huge transport museum that lay at one end of Millennium Place, and I assumed that it was heading for the entrance. I snapped a quick picture of the scene, then scurried after the Stone Man myself, following the incredible walking statue and the laughing mob that walked alongside it.

People were actually keeping a safe distance from the Stone Man when I drew alongside them (managing to snap a few pictures over their heads as I did so, some of which came out very nicely) creating a gap of four feet or so; despite the fact that we could all see it walking easily and freely, everyone could feel the weight in its steps, and didn't want to risk getting caught under one of those feet. And they all probably would have gone on this way for the next few moments if it wasn't for the guy in the green vest.

Out of nowhere, this guy who had been with a couple of girls, drinking out of little hip flasks that they could keep out of sight of the cops, dashed forward from the pack, laughing. The girls who were with him cheered. He couldn't have been more than eighteen, wearing a pair of deck shoes with half-length combat trousers and the aforementioned green vest. He started to shout something, but couldn't get the words out for laughing as he ran alongside the Stone Man, avoiding its legs. He then suddenly leapt sideways, grabbing onto its shoulders and hoisting himself up as the girls cheered again. A yell of dismay went up from the crowd, thinking he was going to ruin the spectacle somehow, but it turned into a scream as Green Vest immediately went totally limp and slipped off the Stone Man's back.

He landed like a sack of wet meat, not even attempting to break his fall. I can't decide which was worse; the sick thud as his head hit the concrete, or the audible snap as his leg broke under his own bodyweight. Three quarters of the mob screamed again—the loudest came from his female fan club— and stopped, turning to look at the fallen boy. The remaining quarter gave him the briefest of glances, then carried on after the Stone Man, most of them still actually laughing. The police immediately rushed over, one already calling on his radio for medical assistance and one kneeling next to the boy, asking if he knew his name and where he was. I moved in close myself, stunned but concerned. Amazingly, the boy was still conscious, and not even crying out in pain. His eyes were open but far away; not wide eyed, just distant, and his lips were moving rapidly. As other people began to crowd in, the other two police were ordering everyone back, and one, thinking ahead, radioed for backup to follow the Stone Man. Even in all the chaos, he'd realised that something was off. The boy hadn't simply fallen; something had happened to him.

There was nothing I could do for this kid, and the ambulance was on its way. I knew that I'd only be a hindrance anyway, and better trained men than I were already looking after him, so I decided to head back after the Stone Man. As I turned, however, I caught a bit of what the boy was saying. There were no words; just an endless stream of syllables, non-stop gibberish over and over that I then realised were individual letters. He wasn't even slurring them either, as you would expect after a blow to the head like that; he was enunciating them perfectly, and in extremely rapid fashion.

"*GCCAATTGAATTTGGCCCGTTAACTCAGG....*"

I barely had time to register this before one of the police came aggressively close to me, asking if I were deaf. I didn't bother to respond, turning to chase after the mob along with everyone else who had stopped to look at the boy. I would later find out that the boy never regained awareness.

The Stone Man was continuing towards the transport museum, and the people inside were clearly visible through the large, thirty-foot-high glass-and-metal latticed windows that covered the front of the building, almost pressing against them to see what was causing the commotion and crowd. A couple of them were laughing in astonishment, amazed by the wizardry of what they were seeing. Presumably, like me, they thought the Stone Man was heading for the transport museum entrance. This was not the case, of course. As we all drew closer it suddenly became apparent that, on its current trajectory, the Stone Man was going to miss the entrance by several feet, and was in fact in direct line with the glass frontage instead. As it drew a few feet closer, this was apparent to everyone, and a murmur of uncertainty began to emanate from the surrounding mob; nervous laughter and a few comedy *Uh-oh!* sounds as the Stone Man came within eight feet of the first window.

Seven feet, six feet ... the murmur became a swell of laughter and excitement, people thinking *Surely not, but* ... I found myself caught up in it, laughing, feeling the thrill of imminent destruction but knowing it wouldn't happen. Five feet, four feet ... the laughter became laughing words, people hooting and whooping as the Stone Man marched on without any sign of slowing whatsoever.

Three feet, two feet ... the crowd stopped following at this distance, faced with a wall of glass, and the screams started; fun screams though, like people approaching the first big drop of a roller coaster, frightened and excited but fearing no real harm. The people on the other side of the glass suddenly started backing away, the same mix of uncertainty and excitement reflected on their faces. A foot away now, and the screaming suddenly pitched into sudden, genuine shock as everyone realised that the Stone Man *wasn't stopping at all,* the people on both sides of the glass freezing as hysteria took over. This was happening so fast, and no one had to consciously process the excitement that turned into horror as the walking statue smashed straight through the glass wall of the transport museum without missing a step, effortlessly snapping the metal frames that held each enormous pane in place.

Everyone inside scattered like ants, gasping or crying out in surprise as they staggered or leapt backwards to get out of the Stone Man's path, as well as to avoid the spray of glass and metal that skittered across the floor. The people outside stayed frozen in place, stunned and silent now, as the three remaining police (one had stayed with green vest) ran past, radioing for assistance and shouting at us to stay outside. As a reporter, I admit my first instinct should have been to follow, regardless of whatever the police had said; the path of the Stone Man was where the story lay, but if I'm being honest here (and why the hell not?) I was as stunned and frozen as the rest of them, unable to comprehend what I was seeing. If this was really a performance of some sort, it had just gone *way* further than a mere piece of street art. My mind whirled with attempts at an explanation; perhaps the transport museum was in on it somehow? Impossible, I thought; this was far too uncontrolled and dangerous. Or maybe something had just gone wrong? That seemed more likely, but if so, then it had gone *very* wrong.

The Stone Man was now several feet inside the atrium, and to my astonishment I saw it bounce aside an on-display Jaguar XK8 as if it were made of Styrofoam. The side panel, where the Stone Man's leg had struck it, crumpled like tinfoil. Understand, the Stone Man hadn't *kicked* the car; it had just kept on walking like the car wasn't there, and had hit the car en route as a result. As the Jag bounced to the right, it struck a middle-aged couple who had moved behind it when the Stone Man first smashed through the glass. The car hit them with a heavy thud, and both of them went down with a cry of pain. Two of the police, obviously just reacting without thinking—wanting to prevent further destruction and injury—ran in and leapt onto the Stone Man, perhaps intending to weigh it down, but both their bodies immediately went limp upon impact and they also fell, just like Green Vest. Again, they made no attempt to break their fall, and landed heavily and mercilessly onto the tiled atrium floor. Anyone who hadn't seen the strange effect that touching the Stone Man had upon Green Vest saw it now. The synchronised physical reaction of both men made it far more clear and disturbing than before. At least they hadn't broken anything on impact, unlike Green Vest, even though one of them had slightly caught the backward motion of one of the Stone Man's legs and had been bumped several feet away. Almost certainly, he would have suffered internal injuries. They lay there as several people unfroze and rushed over, along with the third cop who had turned up—presumably help had arrived for Green Vest—and was shouting about ambulances, but I could still hear the two downed officers; they were speaking quietly, rapidly and precisely through the noise, just like Green Vest.

"*AATTGAATTTGGCCCGTTAACTCAGGCCAG ...*"

Everyone else still stood around, struck dumb, stunned beyond cognition as the world went mad before their eyes. I looked away from the fallen cops to see the Stone Man reach the opposite wall of the atrium, and smash straight through it without slowing. The noise of the impact was deafening, made worse by everyone screaming again as plaster and chunks of breeze block rained down on the Stone Man's departing shoulders. Plaster dust billowed out, temporarily obscuring it from view, but screams were heard from inside whichever area it had just entered.

The remaining cop, with a shaking voice, stood up hurriedly from his two fallen associates, and raised his arms.

"Everyone out of the building! Everyone back outside, it's not safe here! Police backup is on its way! Everyone outside, *NOW!*" he yelled, making gathering gestures with his arms to both the new arrivals and the workers and visitors that were already in the atrium. People began to hurriedly stream for the exit, casting glances toward the hole that the Stone Man had made in the wall, and a scream went up as another deafening crash was heard from farther inside the building. The Stone Man had passed through another wall. The stream of people making their way out suddenly became a dash, and I was caught up in it and swept outside. I was relieved, in a way; if the Stone Man had gone through two walls like that, I wasn't sure of how stable the building would be, even with it being as large as it was. My main thought though, was *What the fuck is going on?* I'd just seen a walking piece of ... well, what *looked* like stone smash through a solid wall as if it wasn't even there. Was this some kind of protest? *Terrorists,* the old woman in me said, and I almost dismissed it ... but then thought again, as this was so unprecedented that nothing could be discounted.

As I lurched out into Millennium Place, hearing more crashes from inside and wondering what the hell was going to happen next, I suddenly realised that I needed a photographer down here immediately, as I could well have a national-level story on my hands. The thought energised me, woke me up, and I pulled out my phone to ring around some contacts to find *anyone* that had a decent camera and could take a half decent picture; worst case, I had my own reasonable camera, but obviously better quality pictures meant better media exposure. Rich Bell was missing the assignment of a lifetime. I turned back towards the museum at the sound of the next crash, and saw the lights inside go out. There was still plenty of daylight, so the difference was marginal in terms of vision, but it still sent up another scream. Shocked and terrified-looking people were still trickling out of the museum, some covered in plaster dust, people who had been flushed out of the building by the Stone Man's entry like ants staggering out from under a freshly overturned rock. Clouds of dust were now starting to pour out of the museum, and I could hear sirens coming from the ring road as other members of the emergency services rushed to attend the scene.

Old instincts kicked in at the sound, making me realise that soon, the area would be cordoned off, and I would probably be removed. Thought was starting to trickle back into my stunned brain, and all it was saying was *Money, don't lose the MONEY*, and I knew I had to think fast. Another crash came from inside the building, along with fresh, distant screams. This time, there was one that didn't end. At least one person was hurt, and badly. I registered this, but my thoughts didn't stray from a possible career-making scoop. Something big and crazy was happening, and I was *right here* at the heart of it; I had to stay on top of the action. People were coming from all sides of Millennium Place now, attracted by both the sounds and the sight of the glass-fronted museum smashed inwards. Two ambulances began to pull up.

Then it hit me; the Stone Man wasn't stopping, clearly, for the time being. That meant that, unless its destination was a point inside the transport museum, it was bound to pass straight out of the rear wall ... and out onto Cook Street. I didn't hesitate. I pulled out my camera, snapping off a quick shot of the ruined museum as I ran, and sprinted across the square, heading round to the right of the museum and onto Chauntry Place. I ran up the gentle incline of the street, past the several houses that ran along the right-hand side of the building, and I could see another person up ahead of me, a woman, running as well and clearly having the same intentions as me. I wondered with a sinking feeling if anyone *else* had the same idea, and was already waiting around the rear of the building. My lack of exercise came into play, as I was already puffing and panting; I'd have breezed the same run only five years earlier. If you don't look after it, you lose it.

Before I reached the top of Chauntry Place, I heard a huge smash from round the corner and a screech of tyres. This was followed by a loud metallic bang, combined with the sound of breaking glass. After a brief pause, there was another, similar bang, and then silence ... except for a continuous hissing noise. The woman up ahead had already reached the top of the street, and had stopped, staring at something. I caught up a few seconds later, turned left and saw it for myself. Immediately, it was clear what had happened.

Cook Street was a narrow, single-lane road, hemmed in on either side by industrial looking buildings (the rear of the museum was certainly a step down from the impressive, modern front) with a high metal fence running along the buildings on the right-hand side of the street. It wasn't one of the city's more pleasant looking streets, and now it was even less so; a gaping hole lay in the centre of the museum wall on the left, with rubble strewn in front of it across the street. Skid marks in the centre of the road led to a dented lamppost on the right, although there was no vehicle on the end of them; that lay a few feet away, wrapped around the crumbling, twisted mess that was a combination of waist-height wall and metal fence. There was a mangled gap in this fence where the Stone Man had passed through, kicking aside the crashed car (for a low-traffic street, the driver had been extremely unfortunate with his timing) and continued on its path, crushing the car, wall and fence together as it went by. The vehicle was now around half of its normal width, the front end pressed almost to a point, and the hissing sound was coming from the remains of its engine. I couldn't see, from the angle I was at, what the deal was with the driver. There was a fresh hole in the wall of the building beyond the fence; I had more running to do.

I felt numb to all of this, like my mind had already adapted to the situation *(OK, enormous stone man walking through everything. Got it)* and was already in its usual assessment mode.

Incredibly, I later found out that he had lived, and made a full recovery. Two people had died from the Stone Man's passage through the museum, however; one had been unfortunate enough to be directly in its path as it came through the third wall, and the other had been crushed between two exhibits.

My lungs were burning as I ran around the left of the second building (turned out to be a car rental depot. That, along with the whole transport museum thing, was the reason for all the wild speculation that the Stone Man was somehow related to cars, drawn to them somehow. It made more sense that a lot of the other early theories) and came out at the T junction of Tower Street, faced with the huge looming mass of the post office depot. I didn't like the idea of running through freshly smashed buildings after it. God knows what might have fallen on me, or which live wires might have been exposed.

Tower Street was busier with traffic than Cook Street, but not by much, due to the time of day. There was a handful of people walking past, and one or two had actually turned to point at something above the rental depot; I turned to where they were pointing to see a plume of smoke rising in the near distance, from what I assumed was the transport museum. That was the moment the Stone Man smashed through the wall of the rental depot with a bang, covered in dust, but seemingly unaffected by anything in its path so far. Even though I'd seen it only a few moments earlier, I was stunned by the thing all over again.

Most of the small handful of people on the street screamed and ran, but one or two just stood there, frozen with shock. A car braked, hard but safe, mere feet away from the Stone Man as it crossed out into the road, heading directly for the post office depot wall.

"Get back!" I shouted. "Don't touch it!" I don't know why I said that. It didn't even look like anyone was thinking about doing so. I just couldn't stand the idea of having to hear that staccato stream of letters again, and seeing those glazed eyes. I don't think anyone even heard me anyway; they were too shocked by the sight of the moving stone before them. It was the weirdest sensation, watching the Stone Man walk towards the wall of the post office depot in its steady, almost casual manner, and knowing that it wouldn't just stop short of the red brick wall. Looking back on it now, I can say it was more exciting than anything I'd ever known. I even had my camera ready to get a shot of the moment. I kicked myself later for thinking like an old-school newspaper man; I never took any *video* footage. Stupid, I know. My only defence is that I wasn't really thinking properly at the time, and fell back on old habits.

That was when I heard the sound of rotary blades, and looked up to see the helicopter hovering above. I wasn't sure if it was police or news (I hoped to God it wasn't news) but the answer became clear when the loudspeaker started blaring:

"PLEASE RETURN TO YOUR HOMES. DO NOT APPROACH THE STATUE. POLICE ARE ON THEIR WAY TO DEAL WITH THE SITUATION. WE ARE EVACUATING THE AREA. PLEASE RETURN TO YOUR HOMES."

People almost immediately started to obey, staring at the hole in the wall of the post office depot as they hurriedly departed. I was running on instinct as it was, but at least I'd had time to get used to the idea. What the hell those people made of what they were seeing, I'll never know.

All hell sounded as though it was breaking loose inside the depot. I decided to stick with the outdoors policy, and after snapping a pic of the outside wreckage, I sprinted round to the left of the building and up the hill of Bishop

Street, the top of which met four lanes of ring road. At least, to the police, this would look as if I were evacuating the area.

There was a pedestrian flyover that went over the top of the ring road, and although I didn't want to risk being on top of it when the Stone Man went by (in case its path took him through the supports of the flyover) I decided it would be best to get across the ring road now and maybe be ahead of it for once. I raced up the flyover steps, casting a glance at the police chopper to see if it was doing anything. It turned out it was; turning and heading in my direction, probably having the same idea of getting ahead of the Stone Man. They were no doubt feeding back reports to their own base, so they could sort out their plans to do ... what, exactly? I didn't fancy being the guy stuck with figuring that solution out. Solid walls couldn't even slow it down, just the same as metal couldn't. I couldn't see a line of police riot shields or patrol cars proving to be much of a problem for the Stone Man, based on what I'd seen.

I'd just reached halfway up the steps to the flyover when I heard the boom, then the deafening sound of crumbling brick as the Stone Man emerged through the rear wall of the post office depot. I didn't know it then, but the death toll had already reached four people. If it had been a weekday, God knows what the count would have gotten up to. I panicked, realising I'd overestimated the time that I had to get ahead of it, and as I reached the top of the two flights of steps up to the flyover, thirty feet above the road, I ran to the railing to look down.

I breathed a sigh of relief for two reasons: from this height, I could instantly see that the Stone Man's path was several feet away from the flyover, (the first thing I ever learned about the Stone Man was that it was undoubtedly set in its path) and that the small back alley behind the post office depot—and therefore the point at which the Stone Man emerged—was seven feet below the level of the ring road, with high black metal railings running along the top of the alley wall. Effectively, the Stone Man would find itself stood at the bottom of a concrete cliff. I doubted even this thing could plough through endless amounts of solid concrete; maybe it would finally stop?

This idea was immediately rejected as, without missing a step or even moving its head to 'look', it swung its nearest arm in an overhead arc and plunged it into the concrete wall. The other arm followed, and in two or three more short movements the Stone Man had effortlessly clawed its way up the wall, pulling itself up using its arms alone. Once it was on top of the wall, it got its legs underneath itself once more and stood, walking again without any pause and smashing through the metal railings that fenced off the drop, which gave way with a deafening, screeching wrench. The concrete beneath its feet continued to crack as it walked. I stood and watched, mouth agape, struggling to comprehend it, yet fascinated by seeing this incredible walking object carry out a new series of movements. Behind him, the railings remained splayed outwards where he'd smashed through (sorry, where *it* had smashed through, must remember that) and looked like the wall of a burst metal stomach after some kind of horrible, monstrous pregnancy. That might sound like an odd way to describe the scene, but I can remember it clearly; standing on the flyover, staring down, and feeling an immense sensation of unreality. It felt like this was happening to someone else, or that I was dreaming. In that moment it finally hit me, the crazy undeniability of what I'd actually been seeing, and when I think about it now I wonder if—from the moment it began walking across Millennium Place—I'd been in shock up until then. I don't know. But watching it cross the pavement towards the edge of the ring road, all I could think was *This is fucking insane! This is fucking insane! This can't be happening, it CAN'T be happening!*

As the sound of the chopper drew overhead, barking orders that I was no longer listening to, I realised that there was a lack of any other nearby sound. In my temporary state of delirium, it took me a moment or two to understand why, but then I had it: no cars on the ring road. The police had already closed it off, a response carried out at a speed which astonished me at the time, but in hindsight I imagine it would have been quite easy; get on the radio, send out the units, and park them at entrances and exits. Quick, simple and effective. I realised I could hear more sirens in the distance, and another, deeper sound starting to join them. More helicopters. Military, I wondered? They hadn't tried out the less extreme responses yet by the looks of it, so at least they weren't about to start dropping the major explosives. The fog of growing crisis still hung over all of their options, after all; they didn't have a fucking clue what was going on.

I watched the Stone Man crash through the railings on the central reservation, and realised that I'd better get a move on if I actually wanted to get ahead of the thing. I didn't have a plan, but I did have enough awareness at that point to grab a quick shot of it from above. I even fumbled my Dictaphone out and made a verbal note (*straight line from transport museum, through Cook Street and Tower Street and post office depot, onto ring road*) then began to run across the flyover, intending to reach the other side some way ahead of the lumbering figure below. I never made it.

***

Better have some water. Gentleman Jim is making his presence felt already, and I feel a little warmer. I didn't realise I was such a lightweight these days … I'd better pace myself for a bit, at least until I get nearer the end, otherwise this'll end up even more of a rambling waffle than it no doubt already is. Actually, I might as well have some of the mini bar's bottled water. Heh. Something I normally avoid out of principle. Principle … that's what's gotten me to this point in the first place, the principle of the thing. I blame the sergeant. Henry, that old bastard. Why couldn't he have just …

Sod it. I'm having another bourbon. The last thing I need is to start thinking about that guy.

So anyway. The flyover. I could tell I'd been out for a good few hours, as the sun had dropped considerably. The sky was displaying that beautiful early summer evening haze, the kind that casts those warm shadows that I love so much. Of course, I didn't stop to appreciate this, as I was too busy freaking out over what had just happened.

Wait, wait … I'm getting ahead of myself. I'd passed out, did I mention that? Sorry, don't think I did. Yeah, one minute I'd been on the flyover, running across, then bam, next thing I knew it was several hours later and I was lying on my side on the floor of the flyover with a headache, hearing nothing but sirens and helicopter blades. When I realised what had happened, and the shock hit me, I did just about the worst thing I could have done; I jumped to my feet, panicking, and not thinking about any possible head injuries that I could have just made ten times worse by jerking myself upright.

I was breathing in short gasps, almost hyperventilating, as I tried to work out what could have happened. Was it shock that had caused it? Had I been hit by something, attacked maybe? The other thing that was rattling around frantically in my head was the thought of being scooped, that the biggest story of my entire career—a story that would possibly be the biggest of *anyone's* career—had slipped through my fingers while I was having a nice nap on a ring road flyover. I rushed to the railings. The Stone Man was long gone, and it was clear that he had indeed stayed on the same trajectory; the small unit of apartments on the other side of the ring road was partially collapsed, with several people sitting by the roadside wrapped in blankets. The chopper was gone too, obviously prioritising its observation mission over collapsing men on flyovers. Two ambulances were at the scene though, and a few people in fluorescent clothing were picking through the rubble, waving handheld devices. When I saw the headgear they were wearing more clearly, I realised that their bright clothes were yellow hazmat suits. Beyond all that, in the distance, the sky was filled with smoke, and I could see several choppers hovering near the black haze in the sky. There was so much *noise* coming from that direction, a cacophony of different chaotic sounds that I will never forget.

I pulled out my phone as I felt gingerly along the back of my head and the sides of my face; there appeared to be no bumps on my skull, but there were what felt like small scratches on my left cheek that stung when I touched them. I paid them no heed and unlocked my phone, going straight to my contacts book. I'd always stored the relevant numbers for national news outlets in the hopeful but unlikely belief that I might come across something on a national news level (and had even submitted pieces to them from time to time, but had gotten nowhere) but even though I had a hollow, sickening, sinking feeling in the pit of my stomach because I knew it was probably too late, I thought I'd try anyway. If nothing else, I had the pictures, and they had to be worth something. I dialled the *Sun*, and when I just got a beeping sound, I looked at the screen. *Call failed*. I tried again, and got the same result, and again with all the other numbers. I had full signal on the handset, yet I was getting nowhere, just as if I were trying to place a mobile call at midnight on New Year's Eve. This was getting bigger by the minute, and I was missing the whole damn thing. I decided to head towards the smoke.

As I ran across the flyover and down the steps on the opposite side of the ring road, my thoughts raced back to the fact that I'd passed out like that. Why the hell did that happen? I wondered wildly if the military had tried some sort of gas, or a new kind of weapon to halt the Stone Man that had somehow had an effect on me as well. I didn't like the idea of that. Plus, the headache was worrying. I had no painful spots or bumps on my skull, so I didn't think I'd damaged my brain significantly, but it was a deep, *full* headache, unlike anything I'd had before. Not more painful, just a feeling like it was surrounding my whole skull. It made my eyes squint slightly, darkening the already gloomy buildings around me even further. The sun was dipping fast.

I ran around the ruined apartment building, trying not to catch the eyes of the people sitting on the kerb. One was covered in dried blood, staring straight ahead, glassy eyed, while another was weeping hysterically. From what I could see in the air up ahead, it didn't look like the destruction was stopping anytime soon; there would be more of this. I think of that moment often, seeing the looks on those people's faces as I sprinted away, as they cried for their loved ones and their ruined homes, as I ran after the story and worried about getting beaten to the punch.

I don't remember much about that sprint towards the smoke, as so much of it was simply more carnage and rubble. After a while, it lost its shock value, and I had a job to do. I have certain stand-out images from those chaotic few hours in my head, of course, but they are only there as glimpses.

Memories: a fire engine freeing seven or eight people from a tree that they'd jumped into to get clear of their ruined building, the lower floors partially destroyed and blocked. A nursery completely flattened, the children fortunately all gathered safely on the lawn, already over the shock of the destruction and trying to play as staff counted heads and told them to stand still. A beautiful Porsche squashed down the middle, its owner sitting and sobbing helplessly by the side of the road in the arms of his girlfriend. A bus that had been concertinaed by a Stone Man-sized object that was no longer there, people still trapped on board as rescue crews cut an exit into it with an oxyacetylene torch. Bloodied people. Exposed wires fizzing and giving off sparks. Traffic, so much completely stationary traffic, horns blaring and filling the air and adding to the siren sounds and helicopter whirrs. And worst of all, at two separate locations, TV news crews. I'd missed it.

I was absolutely devastated, even moaning out loud as I pulled up at the sight of the first OB van, but already my mind was ticking over as usual, shutting down in the mechanical process of analysis rather than feeling. Going over the ways this could be salvaged.

At this stage, no one would have *stills* of the Stone Man in early motion as I had, or at least as many. Most of them there would have gone for the standard mobile phone mp4, shooting *moving* video. Good for TV, yes, but I had stills of a higher resolution that would look far better when blown up on the news. Stations would still be interested in both. *Here's some early footage ... and here's a clear close-up.* It wasn't the strongest argument, but it was relevant.

One thing I do remember is feeling completely and totally physically fucked. The running became a jog, the jog became a wheezing walk, and the walk became a stop-start, hobbling, sweating farce. My fitness, as I suspected earlier, was a joke. I'd also had some time to do a bit of maths as I ran, and I'd come to a rather worrying conclusion. It was now some time past seven in the evening. I'd reached Millennium Place sometime before five, and it wasn't long after that the Stone Man had started walking; it was only a few minutes after *that* I'd passed out. Simple maths said that if the Stone Man had been travelling at normal walking pace—which to my knowledge was about three miles an hour—and I'd been unconscious for at least two, then it was already good six miles away. Although I might be able to catch up if I had the endurance, it was clear that I didn't. Plus, by this stage, I think it was safe to assume that it now had a fairly heavy police or military tail of its own, and I wasn't going to get close enough to get any good footage. I was out of the loop.

I stopped and dropped my head to my knees, both to gasp in more air and as a gesture of extreme frustration and disappointment. I'd been there at the start. I was one of the first to see it, and the only one of those who were there to properly follow it. Now I was playing catch up with everybody else. Why the fuck had I passed out? At least if it had been my fault I could have *accepted* it as being my fault, but this was just ridiculously unfair. Another potential career break, foiled by the Fates. I stood there, gasping in air, and felt the sweat pouring down my back and legs. To say the least, I was pissed off.

"*Fuuuuuuckkkk!*" I screamed to the sky, catching only the briefest and mildest of attention from those around me; I would not have been the only person they had seen screaming or cursing in dismay that day, and many of those people would have had far better reasons than I did. I was in the middle of an urban residential area now, and by now the sun had dropped even farther in the sky. The light was at dusk level, but I could still very easily see the various people stood in small clusters in the street as they frantically swapped witness accounts and discussed theories.

As I stood there, angry and wondering what to do next, the injustice of undoubtedly being scooped hit me afresh, and I balled up my fists I looked for something to throw. Perfectly, a foot or two away from me, there were some bricks lying on the kerb, formerly part of the now-ruined garden wall behind them. I seized one and, without really thinking, threw it straight through the cracked windscreen of a nearby partially flattened car. It obliterated the glass with a deeply satisfying smash. The satisfaction only lasted for a moment, however, as a kid across the street pointed my actions out to one of his friends. The friend looked at the windscreen, looked at me, then immediately flew towards the nearest house shouting *DAD! DAD!* I decided it was time to get out of there as quickly as possible. Summoning the last reserves of energy I had, I sprinted off down the street.

***

Once I was at a comfortable distance from my previous position, I found myself in a similar street with a convenience store on the corner. It had a small wall outside, which to my exhausted, embarrassed body looked like a heavenly place to rest after buying a much-needed drink. I was, by now, ridiculously thirsty. I definitely had cash on me—I'd been aware of my wallet banging against my hip with every jogging step—so I went inside. The place was clean, small, and wonderfully cool thanks to the air-conditioning. The young Asian guy behind the counter briefly turned and nodded as I entered, then went back to staring at the TV on the wall, which was of course showing the news. You can probably guess what the story was.

I was still not even close to being over losing the biggest break of my career (this despite having long ago learned an almost unhealthy level of cynicism where my career was concerned) and seeing the distant helicopter images on the screen stung me deeply, but I pushed those thoughts aside and asked the shop assistant if he could turn the sound up. Like everyone, regardless of anything else, I wanted to know what the hell was going on. I'd tried my phone repeatedly during my run, and every time the result was the same. Dead network. Even now I wonder if someone had seen to that, and that maybe it wasn't because of frantic callers jamming the network. I don't know. I'm generally a lot more suspicious of that kind of thing these days, since I saw the way they handled things after the Second Arrival. The guy behind the counter didn't take his eyes off the screen, or even acknowledge that I'd spoken, but he did pick up the remote and increase the volume.

The image was distant but unmistakable. In the centre of the screen, the Stone Man could clearly be seen making its way across a field. By the looks of the area, it seemed that my roughly-six-miles-ahead prediction was about right; the Stone Man seemed to be some way out of central Coventry by now, heading across rural land that the TV confirmed would lead into Nuneaton. It was bizarre, seeing the Stone Man relentlessly plough onward via the tiny TV screen, after seeing its miraculous walking up close. As we watched, it smashed effortlessly through a large fence, and then the shot cut to footage of a crushed JCB excavator in an urban setting. Apparently, they'd tried to pick the Stone Man up in the scoop. It hadn't worked; it was evident from the way the JCB was flattened into the ground, scoop and all, that the Stone Man had been somehow too heavy (how much could a JCB lift? Surely the Stone Man wasn't that heavy; surely pavement couldn't support that kind of weight without shattering entirely?) or had basically walked straight up and over the machine. I leaned on the metal counter as the report continued, thoughts of tiredness or thirst temporarily forgotten. Across the bottom of the screen there was a tracker bar, relaying snippets of the media frenzy that had begun while I was sleeping through what would soon become the biggest news event of the decade, and would later become the biggest occurrence in human history. But even I had temporarily stopped thinking about my own heartbreaking career miss; the revelations in the report were just too big to let me dwell on such things.

The military had apparently calculated its trajectory, and (although they were currently keeping its actual estimated path secret from the media so as to avert panic in the areas the Stone Man was heading for) police were evacuating populated areas in its immediate line of approach with, they said, an extremely large window of time to clear further areas should the need arise. The relatively low speed at which the statue (they called it a statue; this lasted until I cemented the Stone Man name with the media) was moving, they said, allowed for plenty of time to react for any changes in trajectory, and to 'allow for any necessary further evacuations should our preventative measures, currently being implemented, fail at this point in time'. These were all quotes from earlier statements by various authorities. No interviews were being granted. These quotes were taken before the first 'preventative measure' had been implemented. As it then turned out, the timing of my arrival at the shop couldn't have been any better.

Later, I would see the whole footage from the actual fighter jet's camera, but on that day all I had was the video that was being shown to the rest of the world; from the TV's speakers I heard the sudden roar of the jets as they performed their first pass at breathtaking speed (loud even over the sound of the news helicopter's rotors, a roar even at such great distance). Obviously the government were taking this extremely seriously; they'd hadn't wasted time in despatching the air force. Immediately after the scream of the jets, there was the near-simultaneous boom of the just-launched Hellfire missiles as they ploughed into the Stone Man's back, exploding with a devastating flash and an eruption of earth and debris that suddenly obscured the Stone Man from view.

Both myself and the Asian guy behind the counter jumped. This feed was live now, and the attack—presumably the first 'preventative measure'—had been unannounced. Neither of us said anything, and so we stood in silence as we stared at the cloud of vaporised earth that hung in the air where the Stone Man had been. We waited for it to clear, wondering if there would be nothing left but a pile of rubble, or a still-standing Stone Man. Before the cloud dissipated, we had our answer; the Stone Man became visible as it walked out from behind the haze of dirt, still travelling at the same pace, apparently completely unhindered by the strike. It didn't even appear marked, other than the bits of earth and grass that stuck to its back, blending in nicely with the plaster dust that still adorned its surface here and there. Neither of us seemed to notice the reporter's frantic commentary. We were too stunned, or at least I was. This was starting to look more serious than anyone had previously thought.

Without taking my eyes off the screen, I fumbled around with my right hand until I found the handle to open the fridge next to the counter. I grabbed the first can I could find, pulled it out, and reached into my pocket with my left hand to fish out a coin. I put it on the counter with no idea what denomination it was; the shop assistant picked it up and put it on top of the cash register without a word. He hadn't taken his eyes off the screen either. I popped the can's ring pull and took a swig. It was fucking Dr Pepper. It would have to do.

The tracker across the bottom of the screen changed, and now it showed a statement from the US. The Americans wanted to know what the UK's next response was going to be to contain 'this threat', and offered their assistance and support, as well as echoing the UK government's request for whichever individual or group was behind this to come forward and make themselves known. Pointless grandstanding from the Yanks, but it brought on that sinking feeling yet again; that sensation of somehow *knowing* that this was the beginning of something very big, and very bad. I started to glance around the store. I decided that I wasn't going anywhere for a while, and, thirst now quenched, I wanted a proper goddamn drink.

As I looked on the shelf just above and to the left of the counter, where the harder stuff lay, I noticed the footage on the TV had changed. Presumably due to a temporary lack of action on the live feed, the news had switched to a quick recap montage of the story so far, presumably for people coming to it fresh. A lot of it was footage I had seen firsthand; grainy footage of the Stone Man walking through the transport museum (another fist of bitter resentment slammed into my guts) followed by shots of the aftermath of its journey through the post office depot and the car hire company. Then there were shots of other damage it had caused. That was when I nearly fainted all over again, and this time I would actually know the reason. Shock. My knees actually started to buckle, but I grabbed the counter to support myself, making the shop assistant jump again.

Given the rough direction that I knew the Stone Man to be taking, I'm amazed when I look back on it that I hadn't even considered the possibility. I'm a pessimist at the best of times, and this was a worst-case scenario that even the average man in the street might have thought about, given all that was going on around him ... but it hadn't even crossed my mind.

The TV was showing footage (clearly taken by a professional news crew this time) of another flattened apartment block. It was a far bigger one this time, many floors high. The destruction, according to the reporter, was total, due to bad dumb luck. The Stone Man had happened to not only strike the eastern wall, but continue directly along and through it, utterly removing any support for the eastern side of the building. It had taken twenty minutes to fall fully, and incredibly, the handful of people inside at the time (most of them elderly) had been evacuated during this period by fire crews, but the building itself was no more. The shot, taken from behind a line of police tape, showed the faint remaining haze of dust and plaster hanging in the air. The familiar betting shop was visible next door, and the edge of the Dominos outlet next to that was also just in shot.

That had been my apartment building. I was now homeless. It was not the last thing that the Stone Man's arrival meant I would lose.

***

Chapter Two: A Very Different Kind of Broadcast, Andy Heads North, And Paul Shakes Hands

***

I remember the arsehole laughing. He actually laughed when I told him that had been my home. *Unlucky mate!* Son of a bitch. I was almost too shocked to say anything, but then he took down the bottle of Sambuca from the shelf and handed it to me, still chuckling, and said that it was on the house. I was still so shocked and confused, both by what I had seen and his reaction, that I dumbly took the bottle from him and staggered out of the shop without a word.

I stood in the street with the sun now nearly completely below the horizon, trying to work out both what was happening and where I was so that I could get back to where my building had been. I don't know why I wanted to go back. I just did. Some kind of dumb hope that I might be able to salvage something from the utter wreckage maybe, or perhaps just a need to see it for myself so I knew that it was really gone. At this stage I wasn't thinking about insurance or possessions. That would come shortly after. Right now I just wanted to get back.

In absolutely typical fashion, now that I no longer wanted to get hold of anyone in the media, I found that my phone's network was suddenly stable again. All of the few local friends that I had lived in the suburbs of the city, and mostly behind the starting point of the Stone Man's path, so they would be safe. My parents had both died some years back, so I didn't have to worry about calling them. Perhaps some people would be concerned about me, given that they may have seen the ruin of my apartment building thanks to national TV, but at that time I didn't give a shit. I just wanted to get back, and phone signal meant that I could use the GPS and map function on the device.

A quick check showed that I was almost an hour's walk away from home. I was very tired, and it would soon be fully dark. I had a bottle, and I was feeling sorry for myself. I walked up the street until I found a bench, and sat down. I sat there, I think, for around two hours.

The streets were fairly deserted now. Most people were presumably indoors, glued to their TVs to follow the Stone Man's progress. Indeed, why should they not be? When had there ever been such a genuine marvel portrayed live on TV for all the world? A real-deal, miraculous, tangible thing of wonder not provided by CGI or puppetry, but by something far, far more magical; a mysterious, unknown creator. The only thing in this world more irresistible to human beings than greed is curiosity, and the need to know the answers. I was no different. I simply had concerns of a more practical nature to deal with at that point, as I staggered, rather tipsily, through the streets of Coventry. Passing cars, too, were few in number, both due to the TV attraction at home and the scare factor of the earlier traffic chaos. The city seemed to have a settled feel to it as the night fell; although there had been destruction and death on a scale not seen since the wartime bombings, and the fact that Coventry had been at the very heart of an event that held worldwide fascination, the initial impact of it was over. For those with still-standing homes, the aftermath could be dealt with and cleaned up tomorrow. The people wanted to rest. I knew the feeling. Every time thoughts tried to push in (*what about clothes? What about ID? What about the computer? What about the TV? What about*) I simply took another swig.

Everyone's phone was going straight to their answering service. Even now, other people, normal people, had loved ones to call, families to check on, friends to ring and gossip with, people that they hadn't yet called for their opinion. I would have exhausted all of my close-enough contacts within an hour of the story first breaking, had I not been in hot pursuit. This realisation made me pause for a moment, and a sadness washed over me that was far greater than any feeling I'd had about the destruction of my flat.

"Andy? It's Andy, isn't it?"

I jumped out of my skin, and leapt up off the bench. I hadn't heard the speaker approach, lost as I was in self-pity. A man was standing in front of me, a freshly bought loaf of bread and a packet of toilet rolls in his arms. He'd clearly just been to the same shop that I had.

"Andy? It's me, Shaun, Phil's mate?" That did it. Of course. Shaun. One of Phil's mates ... and then I immediately felt an instant pang of fear for Phile himself. Phil, my flatmate, and his visiting brother. I hadn't even thought about the two of them. Shaun must have seen it in my face, as he held up his free hand quickly to placate me, drawing closer.

"No, no, don't panic; it's okay, they're fine," he said soothingly. "They were actually round at mine earlier, they're both fine. They'd gone out to have a look at the damage in the city, just being nosy, and stopped in at mine when they found out they couldn't get anywhere. Then we saw your building on the news ... I'm sorry about that mate. I took them to a B and B for the night though, don't worry. We managed to get them into one, so many are full. It took ages to find one."

I remembered Shaun well. Nice guy. He'd been round the flat a few times; he was a workmate of Phil's who happened to live nearby. He was a few years younger than me, only just into his thirties, and still in enviably good shape. He hadn't long been married, and I'd met his wife briefly too; gorgeous. It wasn't surprising, as Shaun was good looking and outgoing. By rights I should have hated his guts, but the fact was that the man was just naturally likeable. Shaun held out his hand, smiling with sympathetic eyes as he stood in his beach shorts and T-shirt. I took his hand and shook it. I also realised that, after working my way through most of the bottle, I was drunk. I hoped Shaun didn't notice.

"Glad to see you're all right," he said. "We were wondering what the hell had happened to you. Phil tried to call you a few times earlier, and all he was getting was your answer phone. We didn't think you'd been in there, as you were out when they left and the fire crews had managed to check a few flats before it came down, yours included. But still …" he shrugged. "Send the guy a text if you can get signal, eh? Let him know you're okay."

"I will," I replied, and meant it, but I didn't think Phil would be too worried. We liked each other, but we weren't close. "I've had no signal for most of the day, to be honest, but I don't think I'm the only one."

"No, everyone here's been saying the same thing. Did you … did you have anything in there that was important?" Shaun asked, wincing theatrically.

"Nope. Laptop here in my bag, phone here, everything else was just clothes, food, a few pictures," I said, slurring my words now and waving it off with a flapping, uncoordinated hand. "I had contents insurance, but I don't know where the hell this fits into the policy. You want some of this?" I asked, offering the bottle of Sambuca. Shaun looked at it, thrust towards his face as it was, and started to refuse, then suddenly raised his eyebrows and took the bottle, unscrewing the top.

"Yeah, sod it. Listen, have you got a place to stay tonight?" Shaun asked, taking a swig. He screwed his face up slightly at the aftertaste, and continued. "I offered Phil and his brother the spare bed and the sofa but they didn't want to impose. Stupid if you ask me, the offer was there, but hey. Anyway, leaves more room for you. You want it? If you don't mind me saying so man, you look like hell." I took the bottle as he offered it back, and considered the question.

"Thanks, Shaun. Thank you," I said, meaning it and suddenly feeling emotional again. "That's a very, very kind offer of you … from you … of you. Of you. Okay," I finished, taking a deep breath and standing upright, looking around. A moment passed, and Shaun didn't seem to know what to say next. Nor did I, really. I was very touched by his gesture, but I really *was* drunk too.

"Ok buddy, ok," he said, suddenly tender, perhaps thinking of the loss of my home and feeling a need to reassure. "It's like a five minute walk from here." He took my elbow as I swayed a little on the spot – I guess would have noticed the lack of fluid in the bottle, no matter how good my performance - and we set off.

As we walked, he filled me in on the latest developments with the Stone Man that they'd shown the TV. I saw actual footage later myself, much later; they'd tried using nets. Not to stop the Stone Man—even at the time they'd realised that trying that would be laughable—but to lift it up. The idea went round very quickly that, yes, obviously it couldn't be destroyed, but if it could be *lifted*, removed from the ground, then any further progression would be impossible. But, as with many things regarding the Stone Man, the result was baffling. They couldn't pick it up. They'd laid an immense steel-cabled net, attached to four choppers, one on each corner, and placed the whole thing in its path (another field if I remember right) and waited. Once the Stone Man had stepped onto the net, the choppers had taken off ... and yet the Stone Man had just carried on walking. The net had gone taut, and yet the part of it that had been under the Stone Man's foot at any single time remained anchored to the earth. As the Stone Man stepped forward onto the next part of the net (obviously raised up at an angle due to the upward pull of the choppers) that part went down under the Stone Man's heel also, actually dragging the choppers slightly downward with it. The bit that the Stone Man had just stepped off sprung upwards, taut as a drum. The really, really crazy thing, that they still don't understand even now, is that apparently it was nothing to do with weight.

When I saw this footage later on, it was accompanied by scientific analysis. apparently the amount of weight it would take to hold down four choppers of that model (whatever the hell it was) especially when placed onto a point the size of the Stone Man's foot, would have left a small impact crater under each footstep many feet deep. I don't remember the numbers. But the marks left on the field were, while still much deeper than that of a normal man, only several inches deep. Obviously, no civilians knew anything about this until later, when the footage came to light, but at the time the military and government absolutely freaked out. Even after all the staggering destruction and ease with which the Stone Man had flattened entire buildings, it was still at least vaguely within the realm of our understanding; we understood physics, and the laws of greater forces acting upon solid objects. Walls collapse, buildings fall down. Everything the Stone Man had done so far obeyed those laws, even though we had only vague ideas how such a creature, or machine, could be created to carry these actions out with such force. But this was the first sign that we really were unquestionably dealing with something far, far beyond our understanding; at this point, the men and women at the top started to become very, very afraid. Later, the rest of the world would catch up. But that was later.

On that first day, before any of us knew *anything,* Shaun and I eventually arrived at his terraced house. Shaun called out *hi* as we walked in the door, and a corresponding cry emanated from behind the kitchen door at the opposite side of the living room.

"I'll go tell her you're here," Shaun said kindly, and he headed off into the kitchen to explain to his wife why he'd brought a drunk man home. As I struggled out of my shoes, I looked at my surroundings. Shaun's living room, at least, had the air of a house designed for resale; Magnolia walls, stripped of paper and painted over, with small, carefully placed shelves on the wall bearing miniature coloured candles. I headed towards the kitchen, feeling unsteady on my feet and becoming more and more aware of the need for some water. As I pushed the door open and found myself in the kitchen, the harsh, unshaded light from the spotlight bulbs hurt my eyes and my head. If the living room was magnolia, the small kitchen was white-white-white, with the odd cheap reflective surface here and there. Shaun was turning on the LCD TV on the countertop, while his wife turned to see me as she paused halfway through loading the dishwasher. To her infinite credit, she actually smiled.

"Hi Andy," she said, "long time no see." I thought that was a bit of a strange greeting considering we'd only really met once or twice, but hey.

"Thought we'd watch telly in here, keep up with things while we get you some food," he said. "Anything you want?"

"I think I'd better have some water, to be honest," I said, and meant it.

"Good idea," said his wife (I still couldn't remember) as she went to the cupboard, still smiling, and took out a pint glass to fill at the sink. "We haven't got a lot in, but have a look in the cupboards and the fridge; help yourself to whatever you want. Seriously, I'm going shopping tomorrow, so go nuts." She crossed the room to hand me the glass, and I was struck by how right my original, hazy memory had been. She was indeed gorgeous.

She looked a few years younger than Shaun perhaps, in her late twenties, and tiny. Short enough to come up to the bottom of my neck, which isn't normally my preference. As she looked up at me, offering the glass, I looked in her brown eyes and took in all of her beautiful, high cheek-boned face, framed by a mess of long, light brown hair, and found myself caught for a second. I was speechless. Maybe it was the booze, but I don't think I'm exaggerating. She was beautiful. However, I wasn't gone enough, or drunk enough, to miss the slight creasing of her forehead as I stared for a moment too long, and made a comedic show of shaking myself 'awake'.

"Sorry, I was miles away there! As soon as you mentioned food, my brain just went, you know, 'Mmm … *food!*'" I laughed, unconvincingly, and took the glass, but it seemed good enough for her; her expression relaxed and a more genuine sounding laugh of her own escaped her lips.

"I'm not surprised, I can smell the booze on you … but if anyone's got an excuse after what's happened to your poor flat, it's you. Really sorry to hear about that," she said, with genuine sympathy in her expression as she reached out her arm and rubbed my shoulder.

"Ah, all the important stuff is still here with me," gesturing in the direction of the bag I'd left in the other room, "And it might have even been worth it, who knows? Got some decent early shots of the statue thing, and some close-ups other people weren't around to see—"

I didn't get to finish my sentence, as Shaun was already out of his seat.

"You're kidding!" he said, moving closer, "Where? On your camera? Have you got it with you?"

"Yeah, sure," I replied, heading back to the other room and actually feeling slightly annoyed, in my drunken state. I just wanted to drink my water and eat. Couldn't this wait? I staggered over to my bag and fished out the camera, then swayed back to the kitchen and handed it to Shaun. "Knock yourself out, buddy." I turned to his wife, wishing he'd refer to her by name so I could find out what the fuck it actually was. "Sure it's okay to help myself?"

"Of course, of course," she said, but she was only half-paying attention, already moving to Shaun's side to get a closer look at the shots on my camera. Giving up on the cupboards and rummaging in the fridge, my eye fell on a packet of cheap, budget brand sausages. They would do perfectly.

"Okay to have these?" I asked, straightening up, sausages in hand. Shaun's wife barely looked around.

"Mmm? Oh, yeah. Go for it," she said, waving her hand, and went back to perusing the camera photos. The pan and oil were already out on the side, so I turned on the stove, my mouth already beginning to water. Normally, when I've been drinking, I forget all about eating, but right then I was ravenous. At that moment, as I put the pan on the heat, a number of very odd things happened all at once.

I heard Shaun and *Laura*—I remembered then, of all moments, that her name was *Laura*—rush over to me, heard them saying my name and asking me what had happened, felt them kneeling down and trying to hold me still, heard Shaun telling Laura to grab a wooden spoon for some reason.

Externally, I was all chaos, but strangely, inside, the stunned feeling gave way to a sensation of calm. It was possibly the single strangest sensation of my entire life, up to that point at least. I could feel my body's spasms and the way my teeth ground against each other, could feel the way my knuckles pushed up, against, and into my face as my feet rattled against the vinyl tiles; yet at the same time, it was as if I was only aware of them as if they were happening to someone else, and that they were of no consequence. It was like I suddenly had more important things to think about, and that sense of purpose was so all-encompassing that it made me feel like I'd found my place in the universe. In that moment I was comforted entirely by knowing that all I had to do was wait. I know, it sounds insane, doesn't it? The droolings of a hippy shaman. But that's the only way I can describe it.

Here it comes, my body seemed to say, and it was right; an image began to emerge in my mind. The only way I can explain it would be to ask you to imagine letting someone else imagine *for* you. I don't know. That's the closest to it. But anyway, there it was, someone's face appearing before my mind's eye. A blur of a face, at least, but a face nonetheless.

A man's face, I was certain. You might think I would be going crazy with confusion at this point, confronted with the insanity of an unknown visage appearing in my head, but not then. All I felt was calm, calm enough to consider the image before me. A blonde-haired man, thin in the face, but the image wasn't clear enough to determine his age. I tried to focus, but I was suddenly distracted by the feeling of Shaun trying to shove a wooden spoon between my jaws. They were trying to stop me swallowing my tongue.

Abruptly, the image disappeared and my body relaxed. The sense of total mental calm was instantly replaced with a strong sense of the absurd, as I found myself on the floor of a relative stranger's kitchen with him and his wife trying to jam a cooking utensil into my mouth.

They realised I'd stopped fitting, and relaxed themselves, pulling away the spoon and slowly lowering my head to the floor. I lay there, and stared up at Shaun and Laura, who were breathing heavily.

"Can you stand?" Shaun said, and I nodded, holding out my hand. He helped me up into one of the dining chairs, and then sat down himself, as did Laura. There was a moment of quiet aftershock, and Shaun slowly took a deep breath and blew air out of his cheeks. "You're ... epileptic, or something?" he asked, cautiously, not knowing me well enough to feel comfortable asking. Does that normally happen?"

I heard him, but my head buzzing with a million questions; whatever had done this was whatever had laid me out on the flyover, for certain. And the question I wanted an answer to most of all was: what the flying fuck was the face I'd seen in my head all about? I wish I had the words to explain the sensation of seeing it, and as someone who writes for a living, the fact that I don't would, once upon a time, have embarrassed me beyond measure. Nowadays ... pride is not much of an issue. But the one thing I knew beyond any measure was that it was not a hallucination. It had been too ... *artificial*, is the only way I can describe it. There was relief in that; it *wasn't* just some sort of radioactive side effect or whatever, something that had damaged my brain ... I *knew* it, I was *connecting* to something. I could hardly speak. And there was, of course, still fear. *What the fuck was I connecting to?* What was happening? One thing was certain, at least. I was now sober.

"Well ..." I started, then broke off to swallow as my throat was now very dry. I inhaled through my nose, resettling myself, and continued. My hands were still shaking a little, through shock I think ... but I was starting to form an idea that I wasn't entirely comfortable with. "No. It happened earlier. Well, I think it did. I passed out." I filled them both in on the story of my pursuit of the Stone Man, concluding with my passing out on the flyover.

"Oh my god ..." Laura said when I finished, her hand to her mouth. "And that never happened before you were near that ... the statue thing?" I saw her looking slightly nervous. I didn't blame her. I could be contagious ... but I didn't think I was, because already, a theory was forming.

I found myself reluctant to explain my thinking for some reason; whether it was because it *was* just a theory at this point, and probably a bit of a leap of logic, or whether it was because it was yet another fantastical idea to get one's head around on a day filled with enough of them to last a lifetime. Whatever the thinking, one thing I definitely *didn't* want to say to these to was how I'd just have a vision of a blonde-haired man while lying on their kitchen floor.

"No, never ... well, not since I was a kid," I added, lying through my teeth but seeing a way to make her feel better. If I had fits as a kid, they could happen as an adult and be a result of stress rather than an alien encounter. It worked; I saw her shoulders relax a little. "Must be the stress, I think," I added.

"Yes, yes, of course, you've had a hell of a day," she said quickly, embarrassed. "Sorry, we've just never seen that before."

"No, no, don't be silly," I said, forcing a smile. "Sorry about the mess, by the way," I said, gesturing to the oil and sausages on the floor. I took a breath, and stood up. "I'll clean it up. It's all right, it's all right," I added quickly to Shaun, who was starting to protest, "I'm fine, don't worry. Plus this place looks pretty clean, and those sausages should still be fine after a good frying. I'm still starving." Shaun chuckled at this, and ran his hands through his hair, pulling a 'What a day!' face. I was glad of it. The levity of my remarks was purely for their benefit, and for a reason I couldn't put my finger on, I was beginning to get a real sinking feeling in my stomach

But wasn't this whole day absolutely insane, crazy beyond all recorded human experience? We'd seen a seemingly living statue start to walk and lay waste to a good portion of a town, a miraculous moving object that was impervious to missile attacks and apparently capable of anchoring its own selective and variable points of gravity. Perhaps that's why I wasn't freaking out more after seeing visions in my head; this day had battered my sense of normality so much that I was more accepting of the bizarre. Even so ... there's only one thing people hear when you talk about seeing visions in your head, and it starts with L and ends in oonybin. It was a step too far, at least for now. I grabbed some kitchen roll and began to wipe up the oil, picking up the scattered sausages and putting them back in the pan on the floor. That much was sincere, at least; I was still going to cook the goddamn sausages. I could think and still *cook*.

We've seen it do some unbelievable things already, I thought. And one or two things that I'm not even sure are physically possible. *So it's not out of the range of possibility that it could do other things that we haven't really noticed yet.*

I began to think that the Stone Man was sending out some kind of signal. Or one that I was getting feedback from.

Shaun leant back in his chair so that he could reach the fridge door. He opened it and pulled out a bottle of wine.

"One way or the other," he announced, "this is all some crazy shit, and it's been a fair old headfuck of a day. Darling?" he asked, grinning at Laura.

"Hell yes," she said, and he laughed and went to get some glasses out of the cupboard.

"Andy?" he said, holding one out to me. "Top up?"

"No thanks," I said shaking my head and forcing a smile for Shaun's benefit. Inside, my mind was racing, trying to make sense of it, and turning over that image of the blonde-haired man's blurry face. I wanted to sober up, I also wanted to eat ... but I realised that the best thing I could do would be to sleep as soon as possible. Everything else could wait until tomorrow. My head was *fried*. But I *was* a guest. "But I will sit with mine hosts while I finish this sandwich, and then I'm hitting the hay before I can have any more disasters today," I concluded, forcing another smile – I really didn't feel like being social, but I wanted to be polite - and joining them at the table. My remark about disaster was supposed to be a joke, but they didn't know whether they should laugh. In the end, they half laughed awkwardly and poured two glasses of wine.

"Oh, don't sulk, Andy," laughed Laura, leaning over and rubbing my hand.

THE STONE MAN

***

The next morning, I awoke to find that Shaun was already up, though, in the kitchen. As I shuffled into the kitchen, buckling my belt and blinking my eyes to get them to wake up, I was dimly aware of a strange pulling sensation in my scalp. At the time, I was still half asleep enough to dismiss it as the remnants of a hangover. Shaun obviously wasn't feeling too bright himself, hunched behind the paper—you can guess the headline—and raising a hand without looking up as I entered. I realised that it was Sunday, but was still mildly surprised to see him instead of a key and a note asking me to lock up. Shaun worked at a car dealership; Sunday could still be a workday. As if he'd been reading my mind, he spoke.

"Work's closed. Apparently, lots of places are. Some government team taking samples of the surrounding area, so lots of roads in town are blocked off for the day. Laura's round at her sister's. Kettle's just boiled, help yourself."

"Anything on the news about the statue?" I asked, eyeing the boxes of cereal lined up on the side and deciding which I was going to go for.

"It's just passed Derby," he said, looking up. He looked a lot less cheery today. Maybe hungover himself. I'd left them drinking in the kitchen, and I noticed three empty bottles by the sink. "There's still been more deaths, believe it or not. People who deliberately avoided evacuation, even though they were in the firing line. I guess it's because it's so damn slow; some people are just thinking it'll be all right. Weird, really. When it's just one thing, and so easily avoided, if you know it's coming ... you'd think it would be the easiest thing in the world to prevent any more loss of life. The people killed at the start, the biggest amount, they had no idea. But I guess when it's just this one, slow thing, people get complacent. I dunno. People are stupid," he finished, sipping his tea.

"No disagreement there," I replied, with a forced chuckle. My head was starting to annoy me. It was like my hairs were trying to gently pull themselves out at the root. I scratched at my scalp, wrinkling my nose and gritting my teeth. I had more immediate concerns as well, like calling the insurance company and finding out what the hell I could claim, if anything. Plus I had to find somewhere for that night, and more importantly, for the future. I didn't know these guys well enough to stay here more than one night. My social anxieties meant I would rather sleep rough than do *that*. However, there would obviously be a lot of other people on the market today, other residents of my block that would need to rent immediately, and it was ... what? I looked at the clock: 10:13 a.m. I was behind already, no doubt. *Fuck it*, I thought. I'd get something to eat on the go.

"They've closed a lot of motorways as well," said Shaun, lowering the paper. "People are kicking off because a lot of the closures are nowhere near the statue, but the government are saying they don't know what it might suddenly do, and if it got onto a busy motorway the consequences would be blah blah blah. So much is unknown at this stage, that's the problem."

"Can I turn on the TV?" I asked, wanting to get a visual update before I left.

"Mm, be my guest," he said, and lifted the paper again. "What time you off?" he asked, slightly more airily and casually than necessary. My time as a welcome guest was clearly up, and I didn't blame him. He wasn't being nasty; he was just hungover and wanting to be alone, while doing a poor job of hiding it. He'd offered me a bed for the night, and his obligation to me was over.

"I'll just have this and be off, mate," I said, raising the mug that was about to contain some tea. "And listen, thanks again for putting me up. Big deal to me, that."

"Our pleasure. What have you got sorted for tonight?" Subtle meaning: *once was enough, I'd like my living room back.*

"Oh, I've had a text off a mate, he's got a spare room going permanently, so that'll do for the foreseeable future," I lied, forcing a smile and clicking the TV on. He looked more relieved than he probably realised, and gave me a thumbs-up. The ad break finished on the screen, and the live feed came back. The news shouldn't even have been on then, but the breaking news tracker bar that was scrolling across the screen gave me the impression that it wasn't going off any time soon. Blanket coverage. The picture showed the Stone Man making its way through a well-to-do looking estate, walking along a street at an angle that would take it through a nearby house. It was surrounded now (presumably due to being in an urban area) by a squad of armed soldiers, keeping pace with it in a circle that stayed around six feet away from it on all sides. Moving slowly behind them was a jeep. I didn't really take in any of this properly at the time though, as the moment that my eyes fell on the Stone Man, the top of my head felt like someone had poured cold water all over it and I became very, very awake.

It was as if something inside had just screamed *THERE*, and connected with the image onscreen. I felt a pull inside me, not a physical pull but just a kind of ... urge. I was picking something up, there was no doubt about it. My fingertips and toes felt slightly numb, and my heart raced, both with shock and something else, that other force, as if I was having a mild panic attack. It was a physical and mental connection.

Wide eyed, I looked at Shaun. He was still reading the paper, unfazed. I managed to get my breath, and speak.

"Shaun?"

"Uh-huh."

"Just … are you seeing this?" I needed him to look too. I had to check. He turned, lazily, and looked at the screen. He stared at it for a second or two, blinked, then turned back to his paper.

"Yeah," he said. "Once you've seen it go through a few buildings and flatten a few cars, the appeal wanes a bit."

So it was just me. I was the one who'd passed out, I was the one who'd had a fit, and now I was the one who was connecting with it. But why me? Sure, I'd effectively been at ground zero with this thing, right there when it 'woke up', but I didn't think that was it; or at least not that alone. There'd been a *lot* of other people there too, and if enough of them had been having the same experiences then that would be news too.

Your theory, I thought. *The one you had last night.*

I wasn't going to tell Shaun, but I'd been thinking about it a lot during the night, and the more I did the more I was convinced I was correct.

Lots of people there when that thing switched on … but how many of them were like you?

 You see, when I was twenty-five years old I was diagnosed with Asperger's Syndrome.

As you probably know, Asperger's is a mild form of autism, so mild that generally you wouldn't really know unless someone told you … but you might notice that something was a little *off*. It's defined as having a lack of social awareness (sentences are literally interpreted and nuance is unnoticed) a lack of empathy, and often a reduced ability to take pleasure in what should be pleasurable activity. We're generally clumsier, and can be obsessive over particular things. We're supposed to like routine, but that one doesn't apply to me. Yes, these days, everyone is apparently '*on the spectrum*', but mine is actually Asperger's, as opposed to some fucking yuppie who can't understand why his wife doesn't think he's funny.

I've worked over the years on various techniques so I can function better in 'normal' society (don't stand too close to people, don't reveal too-personal details or ask too-personal questions, and learn which situations do and don't warrant such conversation, learn appropriate and expected behaviours, be aware that you might be boring someone and talking too much) but it doesn't change the way I think. These days, I just generally avoid conversation with strangers full stop. In my adult life, it's turned into quite a bitter view of other people; I tend to see them as insincere, indirect, and guarded. I used to get upset by not quite understanding the way they work, but now I hold their 'knowledge' in contempt; the things you 'just don't do' and the things you 'just do', in my eyes, are the actions of sheep. Act the way you feel, not the way you're expected to. Say what you mean. But apparently *I'm* the weird one. Anyway, it's probably the reason that my circle of friends has always been small and selective, and why most of my past relationships had been difficult; I read often in online forums about other Asperger's people who were married with kids and so on (it's actually very common) but I don't work that way. It's not who I am.

I'd accepted it anyway, and was fine with it. *Their* ways were not my ways, and even though I knew I was the one that had the 'problem', I thought that the way I viewed the world was one hundred percent correct. I still do. Regardless, Asperger's isn't the sort of thing you open conversations with. What would be the point?

My theory, as regards to my condition and the Stone Man, was that perhaps it was something to do with having my brain wired slightly differently. The first jolt had straight-up knocked me out, although the second one hadn't done so and had instead merely caused me to have a fit. But I didn't think other people with Asperger's around the country were having the same experience as me. As I say, by the time the Stone Man 'came to life', there had been a few hundred people standing around it; I thought that the odds of someone else in that crowd having Asperger's like me *and* being so close to it for a sustained period of time were surely pretty slim.

Regardless, if my theory was correct, I was unique, and that meant I was picking up on something in a way that no one else was, or would. Whatever the cause, the effects of it had downgraded the second time, and any after-effects seemed to range from nothing to a minor sensation; it had been reduced to a low-level buzz in the head, except for when I looked at the Stone Man onscreen. Maybe the more dramatic hits were some kind of *initial* side effect, a result of connecting to whatever it was just for the first few times. Perhaps it was like drinking the local water on holiday, with the first few drinks giving you the shits before you built up a resistance. Either way, I now seemed to be more conditioned to the effect of the Stone Man.

I had to sit down for a second, genuinely shaken by these possibilities. I thought I was definitely in the right ballpark, if nothing else. I wanted to blurt it all out to Shaun, but not only was he not in the mood, I didn't think he would have bought it anyway. He just wasn't the open-minded type.

That sense of urgency, that physical tug, was still ticking away, even though I was no longer looking at the screen. It wasn't anything to do with visual input, then; something to do with mental focus? Maybe seeing it, and thus giving it my full attention, had strengthened the connection in some way, and now I was thinking about nothing else, keeping the connection strong. No faces this time, though.

I took a deep breath, and began to concentrate as hard as I could on thoughts of the Stone Man, remembering being close to it. I remembered its rough surface and colour, seeing it begin to walk, feeling the deep thuds it created with every step. I tried to relax (difficult with my heart pounding the way it was) and closed my eyes. Shaun didn't notice a thing, still deep in the paper and probably assuming that I was just taking my time drinking my tea. Slowly, I felt the buzz increase in my scalp and fingers, felt that pull in my head grow ... but still no face, not this time. But that pull ... a pull towards where?

I leapt out of my seat as I had the revelation, spilling my tea and causing Shaun to jump in surprise.

"Jesus, you scared the crap out of m—" he started but I whirled round to him, cutting him off.

"Shaun, I need a road atlas. D'you have one? It's important."

He stared at me for a second, cocking his head with an '*Are you kidding me*?' expression, but then decided questioning it would only keep me hanging around longer.

"Yes, Andy. Yes, I have a road atlas. I have a road atlas for sudden, jumping around emergencies just like this. Drawer on the left, over there. If you decide you want something else, if it's just possible you could avoid scaring the shit out of me first, that'd be great." I didn't reply, and was already making my way to the drawer. My revelation hadn't been where the pull was drawing me towards, but what I thought the pull might *be*. It wasn't telling *me* where I was supposed to go ... but I thought I was picking up wherever the *Stone Man* was supposed to go. And if connection to the signal, or whatever it was, was just a matter of focus ...

I was making a leap, but I didn't think it was that much of one. I could feel that the pull had a direction, so it surely had to have a source, or a goal. My mind was racing, not stopping to analyse what was going on (extremely rare for me, a sensation that I would have enjoyed if not for being so immersed in what I was doing) as I pulled out the atlas, noticing it was several years out of date. That didn't matter for what I had in mind. I carried it back to the table and spread it open, turning to the front few pages, where the overview image of the UK was laid out. I took out my iPhone, and swiped across to the compass app, planning to use it for probably the first time ever. I waited until it found north, and turned the map so its northward point matched the same direction as the compass.

I stood up straight, feeling excited, hopeful, and a bit stupid at best. It was very possible that I was wrong about this, but I didn't think so … not now I could feel the connection in this way. It just seemed to make sense.

I closed my eyes again (just as I saw Shaun regarding me suspiciously from the other end of the table) and tried the same focusing trick that I'd used a few moments ago. That electricity in my fingers and scalp intensified, and my heart rate picked up; it was like a first date, that fluttery combination of the mental and physical, but colder, more clinical. Goose bumps broke out on my forearms. *It's working, it's fucking working!*

Opening my eyes, and still trying to keep the connection strong, I held my hand out over the map, more excited than I'd ever been in my entire life. This was the stuff of magic, *and I was doing it.* I couldn't fathom the truth of that, couldn't begin to comprehend it, and perhaps it was a good job that I didn't; I would have stayed sitting there all day, stunned by it and not getting to the bottom of what was going on. As it was, I managed to stay focused on the actual job in hand.

Where had Shaun said the Stone Man was? Just past Derby; I held my palm over the corresponding area of the map, trying to link the visual with the mental. *It's there*, I told myself. *This is the whole country, laid out on the table before you, and the Stone Man is right* there. *You're looking at it from above, and you can feel the same pull that* it *does. It's going north; you know that. But where? How far? Where is it going? Follow the signal. Find the source.*

Shaun started to speak, but I shushed him. Right now, I couldn't care less about pissing him off; this was desperately important. I was full of electricity, and he did not matter. I heard him put his paper down, but he didn't move. He was not a man that would challenge another, even in his own home.

Slowly, something began to happen. The sensation in my fingertips began to fill my hand, now flowing up past my wrist, my elbow, up to my shoulder. The pull became more physical, stronger, *drawing* me, and in my mind's eye I saw the Stone Man walking on the map, the map that became lush and three dimensional as the flat blue of colour representing the sea began to churn and flow, the grass covering England blowing in a breeze as the Stone Man made its way north and my mind created a frighteningly vivid picture. It was like watching a film. My body leant forward, pulled towards the map, and the electricity reached my shoulder and the arm attached to it began to travel upwards.

My heart was hammering even harder in my chest, my amazement increasing my excitement as my eyes widened and bulged, but I managed to keep focus; I was locked into something else, and the feed felt so strong that it was almost impossible to lose. It was *in* me. I watched my hand travel, looking possessed—which, in a way, it was—moving upwards along the map, watching it pass Sheffield ... and then stop. Dead.

I looked at the area my hand covered; the distance was huge, but I knew the Stone Man was moving in a straight line. Unless there was a sudden detour, I could narrow down its movement horizontally, at least. At some point under my palm (an area that covered, at this scale, hundreds of miles) the Stone Man would apparently stop, but that wasn't good enough, wasn't *precise* enough. In a panic now, worried that I might somehow lose it suddenly, I flipped to the index at the back and found Sheffield, trying to maintain the connection's current level of strength in my mind, even though the visual aid was temporarily gone. I flipped over to the Sheffield page, but I could feel the intensity of the mysterious input begin to drop back down to where it was before, even when I moved my hand up and down across that area.

Over the next few minutes, in a near panic, I tried different pages that showed close-up versions of the areas along the line that my hand had drawn, but I couldn't get any more of a handle on the signal. I even went back to the original UK map page, and after a minute or two, once I'd achieved the same effect as before—the map coming alive in my mind as I saw the Stone Man's avatar stomping its way across the UK—I tried using my finger instead of my palm, hoping the smaller area of my fingertip would give me a more accurate result and whittle the options down. It didn't work; all I found was that the Stone Man's goal was somewhere in or near to Sheffield, my finger simply wavering up and down around the same area that my palm had previously covered. Whatever I was picking up, it couldn't give me a more accurate reading at this point; perhaps distance was also a factor. Well, that didn't matter. I, too, would now be going north for certain, and I'd find out first hand if being any closer made a difference.

My blood rushed in my veins. This was exciting beyond measure (barring the possibility that I was having some sort of mental episode and imagining the whole thing) and in the same moment I realised how long it had been since I was truly, genuinely excited about something before today, let alone to this extent. It had been many years. The thought made me stop for a second. And then the process was complete, and my thoughts moved onto the next practical thing to deal with, the next item on the unending list.

First things first; leave.

I closed the atlas, and looked up at Shaun, who was looking at me with a very wary expression. I realised how bizarre the whole experiment I'd just conducted must have looked to him, and briefly made the effort to think of an explanation. I failed.

"Trying a bit of an idea, experimenting with the … y'know …" I made beaming-in gestures with my hands towards my head, and tried cracking an aren't-I-daft grin. I thought it was an utterly fruitless attempt at making light of it, but Shaun's mouth actually curled up a bit at the side, forming a smirk.

"Yeah? Any joy?"

"Afraid not, buddy," I said, quickly swigging a mouthful of tea and then walking to the sink to pour the rest away. "But it was just a crazy idea that I had to try out, then and there, got a bit too excited. Never mind, sorry if I made you jump." Shaun chuckled slightly at this, and shrugged. I think he could tell that I was preparing to leave. "Anyway," I said, "I'd best shoot off. Thanks again for putting me up, man, especially when I'd had a skin full. Most people would have brushed their hands of me, but you didn't, and I needed it. Thank you." I held out my hand for him to shake, and felt pleased with myself. That had actually sounded believable. Sometimes I really could do polite, it seemed, even when I didn't give a shit and just wanted to get going. But there were some empty social gestures that even I was programmed to observe.

Ah, judge me all you want. Hell … oh, fuck it, you'd be right to do so. You'd be right. I'm sorry. I'm sorry for everything.

Shaun smiled, and stood as he shook my hand.

"No worries, mate, couldn't leave you out on the streets, could I? You're not safe for decent people to be around," he added with a wink and a grin, as he led me towards the living room and the front door. I picked up my laptop bag, slipped on my shoes, and opened the door. The sun was bright again, and it was already getting hot. The day was going to be another scorcher, and I realised that the clothes I was wearing weren't at their freshest after all the walking and sweating yesterday.

"Tell Laura thanks too, okay?" I said, stepping off the front step and turning to face him. "Sorry I missed her this morning."

"Will do, buddy," said Shaun, looking noticeably more relaxed now he knew that he was going to have the house to himself. He probably didn't get it that often. "Got far to go, have you?" He meant to my fictional mate's house, and he knew I'd have to walk. I thought about the BMW parked on his drive to my left, and noted that he wasn't offering a lift. I couldn't complain—no mistake about that—but it still burned me a little.

"Nah, besides, I could do with the walk actually. Nice to get out in the sun. What are you gonna do with your day off, grab a beer and sit in the garden?"

"Mate, if it stays like this, I think a whole six-pack and a barbecue might be in order!" he said, grinning. "Missus is away, no visitors coming round, so it's

Shauny time. Have a good 'un, mate." He raised his hand, still smiling, and I returned it as he closed the door. I began to walk up the street, pulling my phone out of my pocket and dialling for a taxi. I hoped (correctly, as it turned out) that I could at least get a cab out here, road restrictions or not. I needed to be taken somewhere for a proper breakfast. I cursed myself for not asking if they'd had an iPhone charger in the house; I was down to half battery. As I listened to the phone ringing on the other end of the line, Shaun's last words came back to me. *No visitors.* That was exactly what I thought I was about to become; a visitor. Because I didn't think that the face in my vision was random, nor did I think that it was anything other than extremely important in terms of finding out more about the Stone Man. I thought that when and if I got to where the Stone Man was heading—whether it was being called or had been sent, whether it was expected or not—I thought that there would be a person waiting on the other end, and that person would be a man with blonde hair. And I was going to do my damnedest to make sure that I reached him first.

***

Getting hungry. All this talk of sausages and breakfasts is actually bringing my appetite back, as much as I thought I'd never get it back again. There's a couple of those shortbread biscuits here in a little dish, next to the packets of sugar, tea bags and single-serving mini-tubs of cream. They'll do for now. I'd like to avoid ringing room service, if possible; the less human contact the better. I really, really want to be on my own right now. Still, it might be unavoidable. I've started thinking about bacon.

I've also been eyeing the little bottle of Sambuca here, and realising that I haven't had any since that first night. Not by choice, just one of those things. I think I'll start on that one next. You know what the irony of this whole story is? I hate to travel. I find it a real pain in the arse. Some people love it, and to an extent I understand that; new places, new people, new experiences. I get all that, and sometimes I could even go in for it myself. But then I think of the way time slows to a standstill when you're in the *process* of the actual *travelling* itself, that interminable boredom that seems to operate on its own set of laws regarding time and space, and decide I'd rather not bother than go through that. But since the Stone Man came, it sometimes feels like I've done nothing else, for one reason or another.

Gonna keep the next bit brief. Travelling stuff. Boring. Paul comes in after that, so gonna get to it quick. Your bit's coming up, Paul. This is where I slag you off like I've always wanted to. No, no, kidding, kidding.

***

The cab driver had taken me to the nearest McDonald's, a journey that would normally have taken about five minutes. Today it took twenty. The roads were still crawling, whether due to structural repair and the resulting bottlenecks, or government interference, I didn't know. I kept my eyes peeled for men in hazmat suits, but the only workers I saw that day were men in high-viz waistcoats, busy in the beginning stages of the rebuilding process. They *were* there in Coventry though, the government spooks; I found out later. Hell, I met the guy that *ran* the spooks. A lot of people at the time complained about the extreme protective measures that the government took during this period—shutting down roads and cancelling train travel anywhere within a radius of fifty miles from the Stone Man's position at any time—but I thought they were right to do so. Nothing like this had been seen before; how could they not plan for the worst? The whole country was gripped. Apparently, over seventy-five percent of the country were glued to their sets that Sunday.

Everyone wanted to know what the hell it was, what the hell it was doing, where it was going, who'd sent it. The radio in the taxi talked about nothing else, in between songs, and there was a constant flow of new information to go with it. You might think not—how much can be said about something just walking?—but there was always another flattened building to report, another avoidable death for the blame game to be played over, another interview with the family of the person who had met with said avoidable death, another international message of support, another theory from a leading physicist, professor of chemistry, religious leader, another rebuttal from a prominent atheist, another vox-pop, studio discussion, analysis of earlier footage, another complaint about transport disruptions, another mini riot in the next town from which the government were reluctantly announcing temporary evacuations. Flight paths were altered miles away from the same area as the Stone Man, lest some unknown signal disrupt an aircraft's instruments, causing air traffic chaos and resultant pandemonium at airport terminals up and down the country, organ transplants not reaching destinations on time or at all, more deaths, and so it went on. That's what people always forget, when they express amazement at the body count that the Stone Man racked up. They think the numbers only meant people crushed in their homes, in cars. They forget about all the ripples it caused, ripples that caused waves that swept so many lives away.

The dilemma I'd had, on the way to my takeaway breakfast, was deciding the best way to get up to Sheffield and beyond. Trains were a nightmare, so that route was next to impossible. Roads were a better bet, but from the radio traffic reports it was clear that not only would I be looking at extremely lengthy tailbacks—hours, in some cases—but also having to deal with last-minute road closures that might mean getting stuck again in the rush to get back the other way. I needed to be able to ignore traffic if it arose; I needed a motorbike.

I knew how to ride, and had both my CBT and full motorbike licence, having owned a 750cc cruiser for about four years before I'd realised I just wasn't using it anymore. Plus, not having a garage meant storing it outside, and it was heartbreaking to see the chrome begin to rust. It had been time to sell. Which left me currently up the creek.

Long story short, I made a few phone calls to old biking acquaintances I still kept in casual touch with over Facebook. Out of five people, I got no response from three of them, one told me he'd sold his, but Dan (a big, fifty-three-year-old mechanic with permanently dirty hands and a dirtier laugh) had a very small collection, and was happy to take me up on the offer of a hundred sheets to borrow one for two days; the only condition that any damage was 'coming out of your ass, with interest', and that all I could have was the 125cc Suzuki Marauder. I wasn't too surprised. The Marauder had been his son's, and the other two were a Triumph and a Harley. I didn't expect to be lent one of those. The Marauder was like a mini version of the Harley in looks—and a micro version in terms of power—but it would do sixty fairly comfortably, and that was all I needed.

Forty-five minutes later (more than enough time to sort out temporary insurance online via my phone) Dan rode up to the McDonald's car park on the bike, followed by his wife in the family Hyundai. He'd brought with him his son's helmet (a little too snug, but it would do) and a leather jacket that was about two sizes too big for me. I thanked him profusely, and asked him to follow me to the nearest cashpoint, but he waved me off.

"Nah, I trust you," he said, wagging his sausage finger with a grin. "Plus ... I know where you live!" he finished, laughing at his own joke and clapping me on the shoulder. I hadn't told him that where I lived didn't exist anymore. He'd obviously missed it in the media frenzy, but regardless, I had every intention of paying him. "Anyway, there's about twenty quid in the tank, so make sure the fucker comes back with about the same amount in it," he finished. I assured him that the fucker would.

"Why you want to be off on that piece of shit anyway?" asked Dan, as he climbed into the driver's seat of the Hyundai. His wife had already gotten out of it and had been waiting patiently in the passenger seat. There was a woman who was used to playing a certain part in Dan's life. "History's on the TV! If there wasn't a soft hundred quid in it I wouldn't have moved off the settee. Why pick today of all days to start missing the bike? You're not one of the end-of-the-world-crowd, are you? Those guys going nuts on TV. More riots!" he cried, waving his hands theatrically above his head and still grinning.

"Mid-life crisis," I said. "I've already bought the leather trousers. I just needed the bike." Dan roared with laughter, and got into the car, shutting the door. As I clipped on the helmet, I looked through the Hyundai's window and could see him repeating the exchange we'd just had to his wife, who was smiling pleasantly. I swung the laptop bag over my shoulder, feeling its weight compress the gap between the too-big jacket and my back, and swung my leg over the Marauder's leather seat. I found myself enjoying the feel and weight of the bike as I settled onto it, discovering that I'd actually missed it. It was, I realised, perfect for the job in hand; the same riding position as my old bike, which meant that I could get back into the swing of things pretty comfortably, but still small enough to easily wind through endless lines of traffic. Keys in the ignition, I pushed the starter button and the Marauder roared into life, albeit with a less audible roar than I was used to.

I felt comfortable almost immediately, my feet finding the gears nicely and actually enjoying the experience. It probably helped that the sun was out, as being on a bike is one of the very few things that I personally find are improved by high levels of heat. Try biking on a cold day, with very few layers on. The wind gets around you like an icy fist, but on hot days it creates a delicious breeze.

I won't bore you with the journey, as I say; there was a LOT of traffic, more than I'd expected, but thanks to the Marauder I made relatively short work of it, albeit at a fraction of the traffic-free speed I would have liked to have been doing. The one thing I hadn't expected was the religious element. Large groups were clearly visible in the service station car parks that I passed along the motorway, carrying fluorescent banners proclaiming that it was 'Time to repent' and singing songs that I couldn't hear over the Marauder's straining engine. Though one Stone Man was hardly enough to bring about Armageddon, I figured they'd seen it as a sign, a harbinger of things to come. These displays were obviously coordinated in some manner, as once I got through the first hour of the journey there was a different group at every service station. A fight had even broken out at one of them, between one of the singers and a guy who looked like a truck driver. Not everyone agreed with their interpretation, it seemed.

By the time I reached Sheffield it was around one in the afternoon, and I rode into the city centre under the now-blazing sun. The bright light, as it did with Coventry (as it does with anywhere) made the place look glorious, and on a normal sunny Sunday like this there would have been people everywhere, going about their business between the concrete buildings, but today there was hardly anyone. Even though I'd stopped to refuel, when I pulled up in the main train station car park and swung my leg up and over the seat to dismount, my hamstrings twinged heartily to let me know they weren't happy about being stuck in position for so long. Walking like John Wayne, I shuffled round to the front of the bike and clamped on the disc lock, and took in my surroundings.

I don't really know why I'd picked this central point; Sheaf Square just felt to me like a good place to get into the heart of the city and then try to feel my way outwards from there. I already felt that I needed to go farther. That low-level pull was still there, and the closer I'd gotten to Sheffield, the stronger it had become; even now, it was trying to take me somewhere else, merely lacking the strength and the grip to carry me off my feet to wherever it wanted me to go. No, not *me*. Where it wanted the *Stone Man* to go.

I went back to the bike, and after slipping off the ridiculously oversized jacket and pulling my sweat-soaked head out of the helmet, I dumped them on the seat and opened one of the saddlebags. Inside was an atlas of my own that I'd bought when I stopped for fuel, and this one was at least up to date. I'd already started to breathe slowly, to try and relax and prepare my mind for the new trick I'd learned, hoping it would be easier now I'd already performed it once; now, of course, that I was closer to wherever the Stone Man's exact destination was.

I was flicking through the index, managing to miss 'S' twice in my rush, when I suddenly became aware of something else. A new sensation, one just out of reach. The pull was still there, no doubt, but there was another ... something. It was like trying to hear if you've left the TV on in another room, without turning off the volume of the one you're watching; barely there enough to be noticeable, and just when you convince yourself that you're imagining things, you pick it up again. It was like the pull, felt very similar in fact, just smaller, and different.

The more I concentrated, the more sure I became that I wasn't imagining it, and the more sure I became, the easier it was to pick the signal up. It was definitely there, and it wasn't even really a *pull* as such. The best way I can describe it would be to say that it was like a beacon, pulsing, letting me know it was there. I remember standing still, becoming drawn in to the hunting sensation (that's what it was now, a hunt, instinct taking over for what seemed like an hour; although I found out afterwards, when I checked my watch, that it had been about ten minutes. Anyone could have stolen my stuff; I wouldn't have noticed) and as I felt that keenness, that almost predatory desire to track down this new quarry, I realised there was a reason a new urgency was descending upon me. It was because the source of *this* signal was *close*. And I could feel it getting closer.

Barely pausing to grab the jacket and helmet (and the bunch of keys that were still in the disc lock, thus ensuring that nothing would be coming out of my ass, at least not courtesy of Dan) I started to run. I wasn't even thinking—I remember the sensation clearly—but simply loving the experience of not having to analyse every single thought that popped into my head.

The few people that I passed stared at me as I dashed by, running along the streets of Sheffield city centre, panting and gasping and unaware of my own discomfort. I barely felt the sweat that had already begun to pour down my back and bead on my scalp. My earlier observation that the place was pretty much deserted stayed true for the most part, but there were still one or two people around as it turned out. Most would be at home, glued to their TVs for more Stone Man news and to find out whether or not they were in the path of destruction, to find out if they had to evacuate. Some would have already have been on the motorways, and some would be stubbornly refusing to go anywhere, wanting to stay to see it. I actually ran so hard that at one point I tripped over my own feet and nearly went sprawling on the pavement, snagging the shopping bag of a middle-aged lady with my flailing hand in the process.

I don't know how long I ran for. Perhaps a few minutes. I was aware of travelling through an unfamiliar city, my eyes registering the different buildings and outlets and recognising chain stores from my own hometown, but my brain didn't care about them. It only wanted to seek and complete a goal. And so it was that when I began to feel myself closing in—feeling the source grow nearer and nearer, and realising that at this range, this newer pulse was an equal force to the pull—that I rounded the last bend in such an insane, gleeful rush that I ran headlong into the source itself, barely getting my arms up in time to protect my head and nearly getting knocked out for the second time in as many days.

There was dull thud that clattered my senses as I collided with the forearm and chest of another human being at running speed, briefly drowning out both pull and pulse. I sent the jacket and helmet skittering away for the second time that afternoon.

I say forearm because the source appeared to be another human being, one with either the foresight or rapid reflexes necessary to get *his* arm up in time, covering his face. The fact he was six inches taller—and I was bent at a run—meant that I'd collided head first with his raised forearm just above the elbow. It had hurt him, but had caused me considerably greater pain. As I sagged against the wall of the nearby building, I waited for my now-blurred vision to clear, moaning and panting. Sweat dripped into my eyes and stung them, making sight even more difficult, but I could make out an outline, and a fairly big one at that.

"Bloody *hell*," I heard the outline say through gritted teeth, hunched over slightly, and in that moment I became aware of the pull and pulse again; the pulse was everywhere, it seemed, and it began in the man in front of me. My vision started to clear, and I felt a slight disappointment (I hadn't really expected him to be blonde, as I thought that guy was elsewhere, but what did I really know about the rules of the game at this point?) that he had dark hair. He was definitely a big unit, too.

I blinked the last of the sweat out of my eyes. I could see clearly now, my head apparently resettled. He looked to be about my age, but with a more weathered face; his bulky frame seemed to back up the idea that he was an outdoorsy type. It wasn't all muscle, though; he had the same build some rugby players do, several pounds of fat on top of a barrel-like physique that just created an air of mass. Despite our similar ages, his fine brown hair was already thinning quite a bit, at odds with his strangely childlike face.

He held up one thick finger (a finger like Dan's, maybe bigger) and pointed it at me. He held it there for a second, still wide eyed, and then cocked his head slightly, raising his eyebrows.

"Yeah?" he asked, nodding slowly. I knew what he meant. I nodded back, still breathing hard.

"Apparently so," I said.

"Did you ... you were coming to me?" he said, realisation creeping across his face, now shaking his head slowly in disbelief. "I was coming to you!" he said, now starting to smile. I returned his grin, confused but pleased. I wasn't nuts, after all. And here was someone who was as connected as I was, somehow, even though I couldn't yet tell if he had any more of a clue as to what the hell was going on.

"How ... how did you find me? What brought you here?" I asked, in between gulps of air. I was also becoming aware of just how wet my clothes were from sweat, and felt them sticking to me. I hated that sensation with a passion, but right now there were far more important things to worry about. The pull and pulse were booming, screaming in my brain.

He screwed up his face at this, pulling an almost comical *Eh?* expression.

"What brought me here? I *live* here. I take it you don't, from the accent," he replied, pronouncing *don't* as *dun't*. I shook my head.

"Coventry," I breathed, "Came for something else, though ... then I just ..." I waved my hand, trying to find the right phrase. I ended up shrugging "... picked up your, I don't know, your signal," I finished. The big man's response was to screw his face up even more. He flattened his big paw of a hand against his chest.

"*My* signal? I was following *your* 'signal.' It's coming off you like a speaker," he said, his thick accent coming through clear as a bell again (*Your* as *Yaar*.) "I nearly honked up this morning, then a couple hours later, it happens again and here you are. What the fuck have you been *doing*?" he asked, spreading his hands wide and suddenly looking a bit pissed off. This was not a guy you wanted to get on the bad side of, clearly. I held up my hands, head down, and made the let's-calm-down gesture, bobbing my hands downward. I coughed slightly, clearing my throat. I was steady again.

"Whoa, whoa. Hold on. Looks like ... looks like we're each getting the wrong end of the stick here. I'm not sure either of us knows what's going on. Let's start again." I straightened up, and held my hand out. "Andy Pointer."

He looked at me, and dropped his arms after a second, his face unknotting. As his face relaxed, I was struck by how bright his eyes were, which may have also had something to do with the fact that he'd just stopped squinting. Even so, they were a younger man's eyes, I thought, now appearing to take years off him, making him look almost like a boy. As I would later find out, when he was excited, that he had the enthusiasm of one, too. That was very much a part of who Paul was. Is. Sorry, Paul.

"Paul Winter," he said, quietly nodding his head in an okay-let's-be-reasonable kind of manner, not looking me in the eyes. He took my hand to return the shake—my hand felt tiny in his—and I saw his eyes jerk open in utter shock, just before I felt the electricity slam into me as well. The pull consumed all of my senses and overloaded them.

Everything around us disappeared in an explosion of white light.

***

Part 2:
Making the Most of It

Chapter Three: Paul's Story, Driving Under the Influence, The Weaker Points of Double Glazing, and A Meeting With a Blonde That Does Not Go Well

***

The room is dark, but it isn't night time. The venetian blinds are drawn; blades of sunlight creep through them in a slatted pattern, striking the sofa. The rectangles of light sit just above the face of the sleeping man, and create just enough illumination to make out his surroundings. On the large, expensive looking coffee table are several empty microwave dinner trays, each one slightly less fresh than the last. There are several items of clothing strewn around the floor, and propped against the radiator is a large, broken picture frame. Surrounding that are shards of the glass that once were inside it, and the picture has fallen out. It shows the sleeping man in a different time, not so long ago, smiling and holding a certificate of some sort.

Right now, he is naked except for a pair of navy blue boxer shorts, and his sleep is clearly troubled. He mumbles constantly, and now he cries out incoherently, shaking his head in a twitching manner. He doesn't wake.

He looks very different from the picture on the floor; he is now unshaven, haggard even, with dark bags under his eyes. He is, however, very recognisable to you; see the blonde hair. He doesn't look like someone who has slept properly for some amount of time. Suddenly, he begins to whimper and thrash around on the sofa, striking at his head with the heels of his hands, harder and harder—

***

There was moment of strange visual static, followed by whiteness again, and then the street I was currently stood on snapped back into view. I would have no doubt have taken a moment to regain my senses, and then internally register my amazement and verify my surroundings (stunned by the fact that I was no longer seemingly stood in a stranger's living room and immediately back on a street corner in Sheffield) were it not for the sudden realisation of blinding pain in my fingers. Paul's monstrous paw of a hand was clamped on mine so hard that his knuckles were white; my fingers were literally about to break. One look at his glassy, vacant eyes and clenched jaw told me that he was still in the other place, wherever that was, but that was no good to me. I had to save my hand. I shouted out in pain, but he was beyond hearing me.

In a moment of panic, helpless to think of anything else to do, I kicked him in the balls as hard as I could.

Paul blinked. His mouth then gaped as his eyes darted left and right, trying to get a handle on where he was, then looked at me and started to speak frantically.

"Did you—" he started, then immediately stopped as his brain caught up with physical reality. His eyes screwed up, and his hands flew to his genitals as he gave a low moan and slumped to the floor. He curled up into a ball and stayed there, breathing hard and making little noises.

That's when I became aware of something; the pull was now stronger than ever, but the pulse was now gone. The pull was *everywhere though*, and yet somehow still only taking me in one direction. That's the best way I can describe it. Something had changed. Connecting with Paul seemed to have completed part of a circuit, or broken the pulse's hold, or changed our receiving frequency, or *something*, but whatever had happened had intensified my connection to the pull. Operating normally while the pull was that strong was like trying to think with a marching band playing in your ear; you could do it, but you really needed to concentrate.

I realised I had more immediate concerns, and focused on Paul lying on the floor. I stood over him awkwardly for a second, as a car drove past with a female passenger staring at the foetal giant lying on the pavement. I gave her a *What are you looking at?* gesture, and she hurriedly looked in the opposite direction as the car drove on. I crouched down to Paul, uncertain of what to do, and touched his shoulder. I couldn't see his face. It was buried under his arm.

"You okay?" I asked, nervously. The response was muffled, but it sounded as if he wasn't impressed with me asking such a stupid question. Thinking it wouldn't be a good idea to have a man of his size—and one who I would probably need to work with—severely pissed off with me, I thought that a little creative diplomacy was in order.

"I had the same thing happen to me when I came back," I lied, but with a tone of sympathy that was genuine. "I came to, and then suddenly it just felt like I'd been kicked in the balls. Once I got my breath back, I could see that you were just standing there. I mean, you were clearly still seeing that other place, so I shouted at you and you woke up. Did you see it? Did you see the room with the guy?" There was a long pause, and I began to feel very nervous indeed, but then there was a quiet noise of affirmation from Paul.

"I'll give you a moment. Try and ... try to get your breathing under control," I said, not being very helpful, and stood, rubbing my eyes. That had been a vision on a whole new level; not merely a face, but a complete scene, and furthermore one that I very much thought was happening right now. I was certain of it. That had been like a live feed, just like the ones I'd been seeing on the news of the Stone Man, albeit without the production graphics. The concept was incredible, but by this point I found it far easier to push the lunacy of it to one side and concentrate on the task at hand. Clearly, Paul was the key here. He'd found me, I'd found him, and when we'd physically connected, whatever force or signal that I'd been latching onto previously suddenly went haywire. It was like I was an antenna, and Paul was some kind of ... booster pack.

The question was, what the hell was it that we were picking up? And what did the blonde-haired guy have to do with it all? Whatever it was, he certainly didn't look happy. Either way, I knew that we were close; the Stone Man's destination, as far as I knew, was a point in or around this city, and I thought that with Paul onside—and the pulse now being stronger than ever—finding the blonde-haired man was going to be even easier.

I was right, of course. God forgive me, I was right.

Paul was stirring now, holding out a hand with his head down, wanting to be helped up. I grabbed his arm and pulled, doing my best to offer assistance despite having almost no effect on his upward movement. Paul is a big man. Once he was standing, he patted me on the shoulder as a gesture of thanks, still not making eye contact, and then stood with his hands on his hips as he took heavy, regular breaths. I didn't say anything, and let him breathe as I quietly thought to myself. I needed him to work with me, and by my reckoning, a ten-minute recess to get ourselves in order and see what Paul knew (if he knew anything) would be a good idea.

He suddenly began looking around again, as if he was hearing something. Turning on the spot, he finally looked back at me, confusion on his face.

"What ... what the bloody hell was ... wait. Do you ... d'you feel that?" he asked. "That's ... that's different." So he was picking it up now too. The circuit had connected, and there had been a reaction for us both.

"Yes," I said, nodding, "I know what you mean. Look, I reckon we could both do with five minutes to debrief as best we can. I'll try to give you as much of an explanation as I've got, including what you've just mentioned, and you can tell me what your side of it is. We can also explain to each other who the hell we are. Then we can plan the next bit."

"What's the next bit?" he asked, furrowing his brow further. I scratched at my forehead.

"I think if we want to get to the bottom of all this, we both need to go and see the gentleman we both just saw. He's the reason I'm here, he's tied up with the statue thing somehow, and I think that you and me can find him. More quickly than I could alone, at least. Let's get a pint somewhere close by—I think we both need it—we'll rattle through it all and you can tell me whether you're in or not. Yeah? I know this sounds like a lot in one go, I mean, we don't even know each other, but I think that's the best plan of action right now?" I held up my hands, palms out, giving him the choice. He sighed, and nodded.

"Oh, I'm definitely in," he said, scratching at his own face now, "as if I couldn't be. All this shit ..." He trailed off shaking his head, silent for nearly a full minute, head down. He then shrugged, and gave a humourless chuckle. I knew what he meant. It was so unbelievable, so ridiculously immense and impossible to get your head around, that you just found yourself accepting it, bemused.

"Nuts," he said, with a sad smile. "Absolutely nuts. If you weren't here, I'd have thought it was all in my head." It came out *Ah'd of thaat it weraal in me ead.* In time, I'd find myself subconsciously picking up bits of his accent myself, using more flattened vowels and saying *Aye* instead of *Yes.* "But I do wanna hear your side. Tell me everything. All of it. This is just ..." he trailed off again, and waved the sentence away. He shook his head, and jerked a thumb over his shoulder. "Nearest pub's two minutes down the road, we can walk it. You can buy." He turned and began to walk in the direction he'd pointed, so I wasn't really sure if that last bit was a joke or not. I decided to play it like it was.

"Okay, but you can get the next one," I called after him as I followed, trying to lighten the situation further.

"Nope," he said, without turning round, "that's yours too." This seemed less of a joke, and I wondered if I'd gotten the whole thing wrong.

"How's that then?" I asked with false jollity.

"Tell you what," said Paul, putting his hands in his pockets and striding ahead, still facing forwards, "you get the beers in like a good lad, without any fuss, and we won't have to have a little chat about you kicking me in the balls. How's that sound?"

I stopped dead for a moment, and wondered if my heart might just have done the same.

"Fine," I said softly, and began following again, now maintaining a slight distance between us until we were at the pub.

***

The shouting has started on TV. I know, even without looking, what's happening. They've arrived. Now it really starts. And I've just been proved totally right.

I'll carry on in a second, there's something I have to do first.

Right, back. I don't know how much time I have now. Where was I?

***

"Okay," said Paul with a sigh, gently flattening his hands on the table, "I'm forty-three, married, no kids, benefits officer for the council, been having horrific bouts of nausea since yesterday that seem to have something to do with you, and the guy I saw when I shook your hand has the same face that was in my dreams last night. Not really happy about any of that, apart from the married part. But you're going to explain all of it now anyway, aren't you, so it shouldn't be a problem, should it?" He raised his eyebrows and his glass at the same time, not taking his eyes off me as he drank.

We were sitting in the sort of pub I didn't like; one room, one bar, tiled floor. I like a cosy pub, built like a rabbit warren, a place you can sink into. This was too bright, with too little upholstery and upkeep. At least it was quiet; the Stone Man effect was destroying bar takings and attendance as well as property. A cheap radio was playing music, perched on a shelf, which helped; otherwise, the aging barman and the two equally silent drinkers perched on barstools would have been privy to our conversation. Even if we lowered our voices, sitting as we were by the window, I think the things about to be discussed would have, even if overhead slightly, drawn further attention.

"I'm afraid that's not really the case, Paul," I replied, trying a thin smile. "I have some ideas, and some personal experience of what I think is at least the *source* of what's happening to us, but in terms of concrete facts ... I only have speculation. Let's just put our stories together before we do anything, just so we don't screw anything up that could have been avoided." I sipped at my own pint, feeling nervous. I'd only met Paul about four minutes ago, and already things didn't seem to be going well. He drummed his fingers, examining them

"O-kay..." he said, quietly, before continuing, "well I think you should probably go first, as you've just heard the main beef of what I have to tell you. That's everything I know in a nutshell, and it sounds like you have a bit more on this than I do."

So I told Paul everything I'd been through since the Stone Man's arrival, as well as the varying theories I'd had along the way. This part was immensely frustrating for me, as even though we both seemed to be feeling the more intense pull now, it was Paul that turned out to have the most to learn here. He was the one with the reason to be sitting here learning new things, and not me, which was extremely disappointing; all I was doing was repeating old hat. If what he'd just said was right, then I really had already heard his most relevant info, which wasn't much. I began to wish we'd just set off to find the blonde-haired guy straightaway and not bothered exchanging stories first. We could have found out along the way, I realised; both how and where we fit and into the Stone Man's origins and purpose. I've never been the patient type, to be honest, and was annoyed with myself for suggesting taking time out. I hadn't been thinking straight when the pub idea came to me, shocked and wanting to get on this guy's good side.

By the time I'd finished, Paul's shoulders and general body language had softened slightly, hopefully because he'd seen that I was someone just like him; someone who just happened to be involved, and who was trying to find answers. I wasn't the cause of it, and I wasn't a threat. Hopefully, he now saw me as an ally.

"Well, I didn't have any of that business, the passing out and the fits and what have you," he said, rubbing at his cheek thoughtfully, "but I *had* seen that bugger before, the one we both saw in the room. The vision, you know. Seen him a few times, since yesterday."

"Seen him how?" I asked, suddenly intrigued, despite my annoyance that he hadn't mentioned this before. Did he not think this was important information?

"Almost like ..." Paul's sentence trailed off, trying to think how to describe it. He stared at the ceiling, thick neck straightened out as he found the words. "You know when you think you've seen something out of the corner of your eye, and you turn to look and it isn't there? Like that. I'd be washing a cup at the sink or something, and then it'd be like ... like his face was in the cup, not looking at me or anything, but just there. Then it'd be gone, but it had been there *enough* for me to know I'd seen it. Or that I was going crazy and thought I'd seen it. But either way it was there."

"Did you tell anyone? Your wife?"

"Nope. I was really worried about it, and wanted to see if, I dunno, if it passed or something. I had ... well, there's a reason I was worried about it." He shifted in his chair uneasily, and stared at the backs of the guys sitting at the bar for a moment. When he spoke, his voice was softer, and he talked to the table, not to me. It was unusual, seeing him suddenly uneasy. I already had the impression that Paul was not someone who was easily made nervous or shy. Not because of his size, either, although that probably didn't hurt. He had ... charisma, presence, call it what you will, and it clearly stemmed from an innate, easy confidence. I envied that, but also knew that I was about to hear a weakness. This would clearly be the reason he didn't mention seeing the face before.

"About two years ago, I was involved in an accident," he said. "It wasn't my fault, but that doesn't matter when you're being cut out of your car and you realise you can't see. The vision came back eventually, obviously, but not for some time afterwards, along with certain motor functions, memories, and feeling down the left-hand side of my body. Face is still totally numb on this side," he said, and pulled on his cheek to prove it. "There was brain damage, anyway. They said I was lucky to be alive, all that jazz, and that I should keep a close eye on myself. They said ... if I experienced episodes later ... blackouts, dizziness ... hallucinations. They said that might mean that there had been further, unforeseen complications. And when you start seeing blonde-haired, middle-aged men staring at you from the bottom of your pint pot, you also start seeing yourself drooling down your shirt while you shit your pants and wait for the nurse to come and change your bloody nappy."

Paul swigged from his pint and plonked it back on the table, mouth set in a grim pout. I thought his eyes might have been a little more shiny than they were a moment ago, but I didn't want to stare. I waited for him to continue.

"I didn't want to say anything to Holly. She'd been through hell before, and I wanted to see if the, you know, visions ... if they carried on. To be more sure. I was absolutely fucking shitting myself, truth be told. Having to work my way back once before, getting back to being myself after the accident ..." He lifted a hand and stared off into space, then snorted briefly, a humourless laugh. "And it wasn't all that at all, was it? It was all ..." He snorted again, and this time there were definitely tears in his eyes. He curled his lip, wiped a hand across his eyes, and let out a theatrical sigh. "It was nothing to do with that. Fuck it, fuck it ... anyway, you were seeing them too. And it all looks, according to you, like something to do with that stony bugger smashing its way across the country. And that Blondie has something to do with it. But where the hell do you and me fit into all that?"

"Well, I've got a theory about that, too," I said, staring into my glass and swilling its contents around the bottom. "We're obviously picking up something, a signal of some sort, I think that's clear enough, right?" Paul nodded. "Now, whatever form that signal takes, whichever way it goes in terms of source to target or vice versa, it's leading the statue to 'Blondie' as you put it, because it's leading us, too. Your accident, what it did to your brain, I think ... I think whichever knock it's taken has tuned it in to the right frequency, although being so close to the target here in Sheffield probably helped as well. And again, whether it's me to you or you to me, I think being locked into it and nearby to one another somehow made us *aware* of each other. We picked up the glitch, and followed that too. You didn't have the signal like I did, you were just catching part of it—and I think I might be the only one who can, alone at least—but you caught *me*, and then we came together. We're like ... bits of a circuit, parts of a system that works better together. When we touched, we closed that circuit, and now it's like adding extra aerials to a receiver. It's stronger, clearer. To me, at least. You can feel it now too, can't you? A different pull to the one before?"

"Hell, yes," said Paul, emphatically. "It's in my goddamn fillings. They feel like they're vibrating. Weird thing is, I can kind of feel it in the numb side, too." He held his jaw, seemingly unaware that he was doing it.

"And when did you pick up the feeling? The one that took you to me?" I asked.

"Hmm ... about an hour or two ago, maybe?" he said, shrugging.

"Which would have been roughly about the time I arrived in Sheffield, or at least got close enough for you to pick me up." I spread my hands, and sat back in my chair, giving him a moment to digest it all. Paul pursed his lips, and nodded gently. He then drained his pint, and sat staring at me in silence, his expression curiously blank. This went on for a while, and I began to feel rather awkward, until eventually the penny dropped and I went to the bar. When I came back with two more pints, Paul grinned and slapped me gently on the arm.

"Okay, you're off the hook. Except you'll be driving shortly, so I'll have yours," he said, sweeping the other pint across the table towards him. I didn't protest; he had a point. We had a journey ahead of us, and even as short as it was likely to be, the last thing I wanted was to miss an event of world importance (and the story of my career) because of getting breathalysed by the cops. "So," continued Paul, mood now considerably lighter, "the million dollar question. What the fuck *is* it?" I didn't have to ask what he was referring to. I shrugged again.

"Who knows, is the only response at this stage. Maybe Blondie is the creator? It's connected to him in some way. Maybe he's a military guy or something, and it's an escaped experiment." I felt stupid as soon as I said it, but to my small delight Paul merely nodded sagely, considering it as an option.

"Mmm, could be, could be. Maybe, y'know ..." He stopped, and pointed upwards, raising his eyebrows. "Looks pretty much beyond anything we could possibly make."

I had to agree on the latter part, at least. As outlandish as the idea was, I struggled to see the Stone Man, or the statue as I was calling it then, being made in a lab with even the most advanced of mankind's technology. The best we could do at the time was that Asimo robot, the one that everybody went crazy over because it could run up some stairs. A technical marvel, absolutely no doubt, but the fact that it took our absolute best tech to create a humanoid figure, one capable of handling the hundreds of tiny factors and constant calculations that went into something as simple as walking? Knowing that made it very hard to imagine a human creating the same that could not only smash through entire buildings as if they weren't there, but that could anchor itself to the ground in such an inexplicable way that it could resist the pull of four military grade helicopters.

"Also possible," I said, "but we could sit here all day and speculate, and we won't know anything for definite. We've got some time before our stony friend hits town at least, but the more we have, the better. Have they started evacuating any areas yet?"

"Kind of. The government is talking about working on the basis that it's not going to stop, and is just gonna stay in the same line as it goes across the country. The initial, wait-and-clear-each-area-as-it-approaches, dumb-arse tactic isn't working, that's for sure. There's been too many deaths, apparently. People panicking, people not getting the message in time, and worst of all a combination of the two ... panicking when it's too late. Over ninety deaths so far. The home secretary's all over the news, trying to justify the initial plan, how they'd wanted to avoid panic and hysteria until they knew more about it. To be fair, I kind of feel sorry for the fella." Paul swigged his pint wistfully. "I can understand why they kept the path officially secret for now, even though home-created versions are all over the Internet from people who've pieced it together. Problem is, they all contradict each other so much that no one can trust them. But imagine you're the government and you release the official path to the public, and everyone on the line panics at once and gets out of Dodge. Roads are blocked, the country grinds to a halt, and the emergency services can't get to where they need to be to save the lives of the people who either got caught in the chaos, or stuck inside a building when that stone thing obliterates it. Damned if he tells everyone at once, damned if he tries to take the steady approach. Anyway, they haven't released the official one yet, so they're advising people to stay at home and wait for further instructions. It's a few hours from us, at least."

"Right, so there's nowhere around here that we can't go to yet, at least, and that's good," I said, feeling hopeful. "You up for a little journey then? How far from here do you live?"

"About a twenty-minute walk. Should still leave us plenty of time. Where's the bike, Easy Rider?" Paul said with a friendly grin. I smiled back, despite the playful jibe.

"Chained up at the train station," I said, "Should be fine where it is, barring a parking ticket, and I'm not going to worry about that. Finish up and let's go." Paul nodded, and drained the rest of his pint in one go as he stood. The other one stayed on the table, untouched. He looked at it, and sighed.

"Waste," he said, and then looked at me thoughtfully. "Come here a sec?" he said, beckoning me forward. He then held out his hand. I did the same. Our fingers touched. Nothing.

"Just checking," he said, and we left.

***

We got back to Paul's house (a terraced three-bedroom affair that they'd made very nice inside from the little that I saw) and picked up his keys. I was briefly introduced to his wife Holly as a mate from work; Paul was going to help me with some DIY apparently, and I watched as Paul effortlessly spun a casual series of lies that would nicely cover our absence until the early hours of the morning if needed (something about a home cinema installation, and that we might reward ourselves afterwards by utilising said home cinema with some beers) that she accepted easily and without question, to my great relief. Holly was busy herself anyway; tonight, as luck would have it, was one of her friends' hen nights, and she had a little black dress to customise in the next two hours or risk being 'the odd one out'. We left her sitting in their living room, surrounded by small plastic tubs containing sequins, iron-on letters, and glitter. On the coffee table was a box of drinking straws shaped like penises.

"Have fun, love," said Paul, bending to kiss her, and I watched her return it in a brief but loving way. He flicked one of the curlers in her hair with a smile, and she slapped his hand away and pinched his arm.

"Don't you try to sabotage me, Paul Winter," she said, threatening him with a sewing needle. "I'm going to look ridiculous enough in all this as it is."

"Yes, and then what would the men of Sheffield think of you then?" replied Paul, holding his hands to his cheeks in mock terror. "Who will buy you lambrinis and pinch your arse and hump against you on the dance floor? The horror—" He cut off mid-sentence as a plastic bottle of fabric glue bounced off his chest, and he skipped away towards the door, chuckling to himself.

"Don't wait *up*," hissed Holly, gesturing him away with her free hand. He blew her a raspberry and she blew one back, then smiled and shook her head as we left.

"This is us," said Paul, as he headed towards a blue Ford Focus parked just outside on the street. He stopped and looked back at the house as I made my way around to the driver side. "She's a great girl, Andy," he said wistfully, still looking at his front door. "I don't like lying, but ..." he shrugged, and turned to me. I nodded. What else could he do, for now at least? Time was of the essence, and we couldn't afford to delay while we explained the impossible-to-believe situation to her.

Once we were seated in the Focus and belted in, I started the engine; other than its quiet hum, silence now descended. The car smelled reasonably new, and it was clean. Paul had clearly looked after it. I pulled out into the street, and Paul didn't need to ask if I was heading in the right direction. We were both running on the same internal Sat-Nav, and we could both feel it. Houses went by, and even though the pull seemed to be directional on an as-the-crow-flies basis, I took lefts and rights through the streets on instinct. Paul only had to correct me twice, knowing that certain roads would be dead ends.

It was strange, those first few minutes. If you'd asked me (and Paul would say the same, I'm sure) I'd have told you that we were about half an hour's drive away from our destination. We both knew it, and though that alone was a concept utterly mind-blowing in itself, talking about it seemed incredibly awkward, to me at least. I assume Paul felt the same, as he didn't make any attempt to make conversation either. We were strangers, after all, bound only by something entirely beyond our comprehension, and while one might think that bond would make any social barriers more insignificant, small talk seemed flippant, and talking about what we were actually doing seemed taboo. It was *insane*, this mission, with only the knowledge that we weren't alone stopping us from thinking we had lost our minds. We'd seemed to have made a silent agreement that we'd just get on with it and see what happened next.

Of course (and this, I would realise after more time in his company, was a mark of the man), after a while Paul found the perfect conversational balance. Not glib, not directly addressing the fact that we were, in fact, chasing a man using our newfound psychic abilities and racing a walking statue at the same time. He asked about what we were going to do after it was *over*. (Of course, we didn't know that we weren't even *close* to it being over.)

"Listen, this arsehole. Say we find him and he spills his guts, tells us the facts, maybe even how to, you know, shut it down or whatever. Or he knows nothing, and he's just the destination for whatever reason. If we have answers and a solution, or no answers at all ... this might be a stupid question, but do we try to go to the authorities with this? I mean, I know they probably wouldn't even listen, but do we try to find a way to convince them we have a link to this thing and see if they can do something with it?"

It occurred to me in that moment that Paul didn't yet know I was a reporter—not wanting to lie, yet not wanting to make Paul doubt my motives, I'd just said I was a writer when I was giving him my backstory, and he hadn't pursued it further—and seemed to think I was here purely motivated by the mystery, in a Richard-Dreyfuss-Close-Encounters kind of way. He hadn't put two and two together and realised that I had my own reasons; career and fortune being the first two (although not necessarily in that order.) My heart sped up a little, but I wasn't *that* nervous. Socially awkward I may be, but I have always been a great liar. I think fast. Hooray for me. Plus, dammit, I was excited, *thrilled* beyond measure to be on this. I didn't even want to *think* about a buzzkill, about Big Brother's possible involvement. *We* were going to solve this!

"We'll play it by ear," I said, keeping my eyes on the road. We turned onto a dual carriageway, taking us away from the city as we headed further north. Several police cars passed in a convoy going in the opposite direction, their sirens and lights off, moving in a quiet hurry. They were almost the only cars we'd seen on this road so far, and the drivers stared at us as we went past. The evacuations and roadblocks were beginning. "Who knows what might turn up in the meantime? Hell, they might even find out for themselves. I mean, we don't know what they've managed to figure out already. But obviously, if we can help, we'll help."

Paul was silent for a second.

"I just can't help thinking ... ah, sod it, what the hell would we tell them anyway, right?" said Paul, raising a big hand and turning to me. "It means nothing until we actually have this geezer, and then we can hopefully back up our story. Until then, we'd just be a couple of bloody loonies. I just wish there was a way to let them know *now*, you know? Get them to believe us. It might mean ... well ... no more deaths."

"I don't know about that," I said, wanting to avoid this line of conversation. Here was something I hadn't even considered. Would letting them know they needed to clear a line all the way to Sheffield sooner have saved more lives? Maybe a few, I thought, but human nature would always play a part. The religious element, the rioters ... and anyway, as even Paul said, how the hell would I have gotten them to believe me? "People have never seen *anything* as incredible, as straight-out-of-a-comic-book incredible and ... well, magical, if you like, as this in their entire lives, in the entire *history* of the human race. They're shocked by this like nothing ever before. And that percentage of the population that are less capable of dealing with it are doing very, very stupid things. I bet there's been suicides too, right? End of the world stuff? I haven't seen much news."

"Yeah, there's been three suicides so far, reported ones at least," said Paul, looking thoughtful.

"There you are. I'm telling you, Paul, that thing is killing some people just by *existing*." A beeping horn filled the air as a car full of laughing twenty-somethings passed, heading in the opposite direction, of course. "No, even if we could have let them know the instant that thing showed up, and they'd cleared the path, you'd have had the same effect. They can't stop it moving, so they can't stop it destroying, and that means they couldn't keep it quiet, not with the Internet."

I believed it. I'd been speaking initially to convince him, but in my stream-of-consciousness speech I'd convinced myself. (I saw things later on that confirmed my thinking was right.) Paul sat silently for a second, mulling it over. "Mmm. Yeah, I see your point. I suppose then, for now at least, it really is just you and me ..." He stopped, and rolled his eyes theatrically. "*Jesus*, that was Hollywood. Sorry, sorry ..." I laughed, both amused and glad of the change in mood and subject. Paul settled back in his chair, smiling slightly, then blew out his cheeks. He jabbed at the car stereo, and Radio 2 came on, halfway through the latest middle-of-the-road female singer-songwriter that they were championing. No Non-Stop Oldies on a Sunday either. I was disappointed. The song finished, and I noticed the DJ talking with a more sombre tone than usual. I remembered when I'd heard something similar before, on 9/11, when Radio 1 ran constant news updates while keeping the DJ links very brief, and just played music. All the usual light-hearted talk and bullshit had been gone, and they'd only relayed the latest news with brief explanations and reminders as to why they were doing things differently that day, out of respect. The same thing was happening today.

The report explained the Stone Man's latest movements (this was the first time I'd heard the phrase used, and Paul and I looked at each other upon hearing it. We found ourselves referring to the Stone Man by that name from that point on) and that it was now approaching the outskirts of Sheffield. Relevant evacuations were beginning, and roadblocks were being set up, so people outside of the evacuation area were requested to stay in their homes unless members of the police or military came to remove them. Farther south, in the capital, there was apparently a growing religious gathering in Trafalgar Square, which had developed into clashes with the police after other religious denominations had become involved, causing the biggest riot yet. The police's initial intervention had caused it to escalate, and things were worsening, increasing the growing calls from some quarters for a temporary curfew while the Stone Man was walking. Sixteen people hospitalised in the riot so far, one fatality. Paul hissed air through his teeth at this last announcement.

"Another one," he said, then pointed at a passing exit sign. "You're taking this one, right?"

"I wasn't going to."

"Yeah, I know why, but this will be quicker."

"Okay."

I became aware of having pins and needles in my fingers. This was new. Goose bumps broke out on my forearms and I saw Paul sit up in his chair, looking at his hand. He then looked at me, eyes wider than before, and broke into an excited grin.

"Getting close, eh?" he said, breathing slightly faster. I returned the smile as I felt the goose bumps spread across my chest and shoulders, making the car suddenly feel colder.

"Northeast, still," I said, nodding, "We're still far away enough to keep it that little bit vague, but this is really strong. I know what you mean about the fillings, I only have a few but mine are starting to buzz." Paul tapped his cheek in response.

"I got loads, to be honest," he said. "Fat kid. Probably why I got that sensation early."

"Well, I think pretty soon we'll be getting even more," I said, and then an unpleasant thought occurred. "It might get painful, you know." And then another, worse. "Jesus, what if we can only get so close? What if we can't take it right at the source?" I felt the blood drain from my face, and it wasn't because of the pull. It was because I realised that I had no idea how high in strength the pull went. I stared at Paul, aghast.

"All right, Dad's Army, don't panic, easy," said Paul with a smile, but it didn't reach his eyes. He was trying to calm me down, but the idea had clearly rattled him too. "We'll just have to wait and see. Worst case, we tried, right? Day off wasted. The answers will come out soon enough."

I nodded—even though I knew he didn't mean it at all—but Paul had no idea what I *did* have to lose. To have the golden ticket for your entire life dangled there to grab, in a way so few people ever get to have, and then have it snatched away ... I decided right then and there that I didn't care if my veins started rupturing, I was going to get to Blondie, on torn knees and scraped knuckles if necessary.

However, over the course of the next fifteen minutes, the pull *did* intensify as predicted, and heavily so. You know the feeling you get when you're on a waltzer, that sense of shift and extra weight as it suddenly changes direction?

The way your whole body is drawn along in the previous direction, even your skin? The pull became like that, but in our bones, too. That sounds more painful than it actually was, as pain was not, to my intense relief, yet present. But we were being pulled from the very *centre* of ourselves now.

The thing that did become a problem was light-headedness, as A roads became rural B roads and we headed across the eastern side of Barnsley. I found myself having to squint and breathe slowly in order to concentrate on driving; by now I was used to the intensified pull inside, but I was unaccustomed to this new, added difficulty.

As we pulled onto what was apparently called Stonyford Road, we saw, through squinted and shaking eyes, a sign that said 'DARFIELD 1 MILE'. Paul pointed a limp hand as we went past, and I nodded as much as I could. We were only a mile away, I knew, and heading in the right direction. Our man was in Darfield, then. I felt no surge of excitement though; it wasn't possible. Every nerve ending was already firing away, my heart pounding, my balls already shrivelled and my skin as cold as the grave. I couldn't *be* any more wired. I looked at Paul, hunched forward in his seat, eyes squinting and panting like a dog.

Darfield was small, one of those places that has an odd blend of the rural and the urban, changing suddenly from one to other. Someone's garden had a horse in it. A few buildings we passed were boarded up, which seemed out of sorts with the pleasant look of rest of the place, but then everywhere has its sad stories. The pull suddenly ratcheted up a small, extra notch, and we both knew that it had peaked. We were going to make it.

We were moments away from our goal, we knew, when Paul suddenly sneezed and sent a small spray of his blood up the inside of the windscreen. I whipped my head round to look at him more clearly, but he was already waving me away with one hand, wiping his face with the other. Blood was trickling out of his nose and pooling around his upper lip.

"Doesn't hurt," he said breathily, opening the glove box with a shaking hand and pulling out some tissues. "Bit ... bit of a relief, actually. It's ... one of these, isn't it?" Paul was pointing to a row of houses that began on the corner of East Street, running along the strangely named Nanny Marr Road. In my mild delirium, I thought they'd named it after the guitarist from The Smiths. I then remembered that was Johnny Marr.

"We'd ..." I began, then became slightly more dizzy as I pulled the car to a stop along the kerb. My body wanted to keep moving, my bones still pulling forward as the car slowed. That was probably the worst of it, looking back. I thought I was going to be sick.

"Take a sec," said Paul, leaning his own head back on the seat and taking a deep breath. "No rush, no rush. We've ... got hours yet, I reckon." He was right, but I'd waited long enough.

"I was ... I was going to say," I said, struggling to speak. I managed to unbuckle my seat belt after a few unsuccessful attempts to negotiate the clip, "We'd better be ... absolutely certain we both have the same house. We can't show up on the wrong person's doorstep ... looking like this. They'd call the police, and then the whole thing's ... shafted. It's one of these three houses, but I'm going to hold my hand behind my back with a number of fingers extended. You say which one you ... think it is, and if it matches the one I'm thinking of—"

"The first one," said Paul, opening his eyes and looking at me with a tired expression. "It's the first house. You know it, I know it. Let's not ... piss about, eh? Come on. Let's go and say hello." He'd picked the same house as me, at least.

We staggered our way out of the car, me looking drunk and Paul looking like he'd been on the losing end of a fight. As we looked at the house we'd picked, I was glad that it was semi-detached. Only one set of neighbours to worry about. In fact, it was even better than that, with the nearest residential building being about twenty feet away; there was an expanse of grass between the left wall of the house and the row of fenced bungalows that would be its neighbours. Some sort of sheltered housing, perhaps. The house itself wasn't anything to be embarrassed about, either; a nice little driveway to the left, leading to a garage set back at the rear. I hadn't expected this. From the way Blondie had looked in the vision we'd had, I'd been half-expecting some kind of crack den. Paul looked mildly surprised, too.

"Guess he ... bought this round about the same time that broken picture of his was taken," he said with an effort, sniffing and wiping his still-bloody nose as he echoed my thoughts. "You knocking, or me?" he asked, gesturing towards the door. We were still stood at the edge of the concreted front garden. I looked at the windows, and noted the drawn blinds. It was mid to late afternoon, and the sun was still high in the sky.

"I'll do it," I said, and staggered towards the door, Paul falling into wobbling step. It occurred to me how unnatural the silence was around us; no passing cars, or even the constant, airy drone of distant ones. It's funny how we never notice that, and even class it as silence. This country is never silent. Even on top of our mountains, there are distant motorways below and passing planes above. The Stone Man had silenced us all with its presence, a nation in awe of how such a thing could be amongst us.

I reached the doorstep, and knocked in the door.

The knock was weak, but loud enough. Even so, there was no response from inside, the only sound being Paul's laboured breathing as he leant on the wall for support. We waited for another twenty seconds or so, and then I knocked again. Time passed, and still nothing.

"Fucker's ... in there," breathed Paul, the words slightly muffled by his hand stemming the blood flow from his nose. "I can almost *see* him, can't you? He's in the front room, right there." I knew what he meant; if I concentrated, the awareness of Blondie's presence was so strong that I could almost conjure a vision of his outline. I tried harder, leaning on the wall myself so that my efforts could be totally focused, trying to home in on our quarry. The outline became clearer but still vague, like watching someone through extremely bad thermal imaging.

"Bloody hell, Paul, you're right," I said breathing hard myself. "He's on the ... other side of this wall. He's ..." Something wasn't right. The outline seemed squashed, misshapen. I concentrated as hard as I could, but it didn't change. It was then that I realised there wasn't anything wrong with the image, it was the just the angle that I was 'seeing' it from.

"He's ... low," I said. "Isn't he? He's low down. He's lying on the floor ... he's asleep on the floor?"

"Nope," muttered Paul, grimly. His eyes were shut and his forehead was knotted in concentration. "That's not someone asleep. That's someone hiding. He's hiding and hoping we'll ... go away. He doesn't want us to find him."

Opening his eyes, Paul straightened up, swayed for a moment, and then moved to the letterbox and bent down. He pushed it open with his fingers, and spoke loud enough for his voice to carry inside the house but not out in the street.

"Hello?" he called, gently. "My friend here has ... come a long way to see you. We know you're in there, so there's no point in thinking ... we're gonna assume you're out. This all gets done a lot ... a lot quicker if you just come and open the door like a good lad, and we're not ... here to hurt you or do anything nasty." His struggling voice softened slightly, and he took on a more reassuring tone. "Seriously, we just ... want to talk. But listen, this looks like a nice house, and I'm ... sure you want to keep it that way, so it's probably best that you come and open up, 'cos one way ... or the other we're coming in. Trust me, mate. And hell, I honestly don't want to break anything to get in, as ... uh, you know, I'd feel bad about that. Really. So do us both ... a favour and stop pissing about on the bloody floor, up you get now." When he stopped speaking, he turned his ear to the open letterbox and waited, closing his eyes again and rocking on his heels slightly as he got his breathing under control again. After a while he looked up at me, raised his eyebrows and shook his head. He then turned his mouth back to the letterbox.

"Okay," he called, "but I've got to say I'm not ... happy. Don't worry, I still won't do ... anything when I get inside, but you've made this into far ... more of an all-round ball ache for me than it needed to be. Not good to make a man's day ... harder for no reason. Poor form." He waited for a moment for a response, then let the letterbox shut and straightened up. He let out a weary sigh, shivering slightly as it left, and then shrugged slowly at me. "Right, fuck it, we're gonna ... smash a window in round the back. I'm not pissing around here all day. Silly sod. I can't take much more of this ... need this shit to stop. Come on," he said, beckoning me to follow as he stepped down from the door and made his way round the back on shaking legs. I didn't reply, and meekly followed instead. What was there to say? He was right. We were going in one way or another, so we might as well have been getting on with it. I did wonder, however, how he planned to smash in double-glazed windows without any heavy blunt objects, or at least alerting the neighbours.

The answer to the first question was fairly immediate; Paul checked the garage door at the end of the short driveway, found it to be unlocked, and disappeared inside. I leant on the house, breathing slowly while I waited, and he shortly returned carrying a small hammer and wearing a satisfied smile.

"Neighbours ... neighbours will hear you," I said, shaking my head.

"Aha, not true," he said, pointing at the rear of the house that I couldn't yet see from where I was standing. I peeled off the wall and staggered towards him, resisting the pull that was trying to drag me through the brick wall and towards our target. The garden at the back was small but neat; again, a sight at odds with what I'd expected to find here.

Paul was pointing towards the back wall, or rather the section of the back wall that stuck out about seven feet from the rest of the house to create a small, one-storey extension. Embedded in the wall there was a door with a large glass panel, and to its right was a small double-glazed window.

"The trick with ... double glazing," he breathed, pointing with the hammer now as well, which swayed left and right as his wavering hand held it, "is to get it in the corners, you see. It's extremely strong in the middle, but in the corners ..." he tapped his nose and grinned, pleased with himself.

"How do you know?"

"Friend of mine. Builder," he said, staggering over to the window, "and this baby ... here is small enough so that when it shatters—and it *will* shatter, into lots of little bits—it won't be that loud. We could both go through ... door panel, but the sound of that ... size of breakage *would* attract attention, so we'll do the window."

"You'll never fit!" I exclaimed.

"No, I won't, but you will. And I'm sure you'll ... find a key back there." A thought occurred to him, and he rattled the door handle. Locked. "Just ... checking," he said. He closed his eyes once more, took a few breaths in through his nose to steady himself, and then went to work.

I felt a jolt of fear pass through me as Paul took aim at the bottom corner of the window and gently drew the hammer back a short distance. Not fear of alerting the neighbours—I thought Paul was right about the window being small enough to make minimal noise—but of the idea of me having to go through solo. We knew nothing about this guy and who he might be. Yes, he was currently hiding from us inside, but that didn't mean he was defenceless. If he were linked to the Stone Man, the possibilities were endless. What if he were hiding not for his own safety, but to avoid a situation where he might have to kill us? It was a crazy thought, but compared to the last two days it was well within the realms of reality. It's embarrassing to admit, but I had no problems breaking in when it meant a: I'd be breaking in with a large man as backup, and b: Paul was going first. Now it was me going in alone, with no guarantee that I'd be able to get Paul in, and certainly not in a hurry if I needed to.

Paul struck a corner section of the glass with the hammer and it shattered beautifully, making a noise but certainly nothing to attract attention from neighbouring families undoubtedly huddled round a TV in the house next door. He dragged the hammer's head around the edge of the frame, clearing any remaining jagged bits, and then leant his head through and looked at the opposite side of the door.

"Ah, good. Key's ... in the lock this side. Can't reach it from here though." He looked at the room. "Back porch and utility room or something. Washing machine here ... nothing exciting." He stepped back and laced his fingers together, palms up at stomach height. He fell back against the wall for support and bent his knees slightly, breathing in heavily through his nose again to steel himself.

"This is gonna be ... harder than normal," he said, and jerked his linked hands upwards briefly, beckoning me. "Come on then, good lad."

The only other option, of course, was to walk away, and that was impossible. I moved forward, stood facing the squatting Paul, and gripped the window frame with hands that felt as brittle as the glass that now lay all over the floor inside. I wasn't even sure that I could do it, but I was going to try. Without a word, and after a brief glance into Paul's eyes, I put my foot into his linked hands and boosted myself through the window frame.

It was a reasonably tight fit, but I could still make it through without too much trouble. The problem was on the other side; Paul was right about it being some kind of rear entryway that doubled up as a utility room, with two wash baskets and a washing machine on the right, and some coats hanging from a rack on the left-hand wall. A small row of men's shoes lay underneath them. There were two doors leading out of the room, one on the left wall and one in the wall directly ahead of me; the latter was the one we wanted. Blondie was farther inside the house. I went to stretch for the washing machine to prop myself up on while I pulled a leg through—one hand holding the window frame as I reached with the other—and I could just about get a hand to it. The shakes made it nearly impossible, but I slowly managed to squeeze through.

I staggered over to the door and turned the key. As the door opened and Paul came through, I whipped my head round to look towards the other side of the house. Paul started to speak, and I held up a hand to shush him. I wanted to listen.

After a moment, I was convinced no one was coming. Plus, I could still feel that Blondie hadn't moved. Or had he? Not from the front room at least, I was sure of it, but had he moved round, perhaps now facing our direction? I thought that he had. He was conscious, then. If so, he definitely knew that we were now inside the building.

"You all right?" whispered Paul. I gave him the thumbs-up, and he nodded his head while gently patting me on the shoulder. His concern was sincere, and touching.

"I'm fine," I whispered. "You can go first the rest of the way though." Paul smiled briefly and nodded again, accepting the suggestion without question and moving towards the door at the opposite side of the small room. His response wasn't a display of bravado, but simply that of a man getting on with things. I found myself wondering how much—or at all—he'd considered the unknown quantities here, the strong possibility of danger. I wonder now who would be the better man if it turned out that he hadn't.

The door wasn't closed all the way, and when Paul pulled it, it swung inwards silently. Beyond it was a dark hallway; the only light inside this part of the building came from the small glass panel in the front door at the other end. The wallpaper was covered in a raised pattern, and was some kind of shade of white, adorned with several small picture frames whose images couldn't be made out in the darkness. On the right was a staircase, and there was no light from the top of it either; presumably the bedroom doors were shut on the upper floor as well, shut like the single door in the left-hand wall; this was the door that Blondie currently lay behind, hiding. Or waiting.

***

Later, someone told us Blondie's name was Patrick. Patrick Marshall. We didn't get to find out at the time, you see. Of course, we'd have known eventually anyway. It wasn't long until the whole world knew his name.

***

Paul went in first, as requested, and slowly made his way towards the door in the wall, moving very quietly for a big man; he'd even managed to slow his erratic breathing. He turned his head to see if I was following and, embarrassed, I realised that I wasn't. I held my hands up, nodded quickly, and began to follow. Paul shook his head a bit, then turned back and carried on walking. In a few steps he'd reached the door. He grabbed the handle, looked at me, and then raised his eyebrows. *Ready?* I wasn't anywhere near ready. I could barely even stand, and I felt like my eyes were burning, but I gave him a shaky thumbs-up. He nodded, turned the handle, and slowly pushed the door open.

The room beyond was as dark as the hallway, but even in that dim light, the effect on us both was overwhelming; unless you've ever had a vivid dream that later appeared in front of you while you were awake, you won't know what it was like. This was the room from our shared vision, as expected, but to see it in front of us—to be about to step into it—was mind blowing. After the last two days, to be amazed was quite a feat.

On the floor against the wall, ten feet or so away, was the same shattered picture frame, showing the same image of a far-neater Blondie clutching his certificate proudly. The same clothes, strewn everywhere. And bits we hadn't seen before, as the angle had been different; a glass cabinet against the back wall, tucked into the left-hand corner and full of various corporate-award-looking trophies. These were the usual engraved, cut glass affairs given to regional salesperson of the year and the like. To the right of that was another door that presumably led to a kitchen—unless this house had the extremely unusual feature of an upstairs kitchen—and to the right of *that* was another picture frame, this one intact, full of photographs taken at various tourist locations. It was too far away to see, and we weren't really paying attention to it, but I thought I saw Blondie posing with different people in each one. Blondie was a sentimentalist, it seemed.

I stuck my head further in, looking around Paul as my curiosity overwhelmed me. I could now see the empty TV dinner trays, strewn everywhere (including the top of the large, expensive looking coffee table that we'd previously seen) but accompanied in the flesh (or foil, as it were) by the unpleasant smell of leftover food and sauces developing a life of their own. The TV itself, a large plasma one that stood in the corner, was off. It faced the large leather sofa that, in. stark contrast to our previous vision, was now empty.

I looked at Paul, giving him an exaggerated expression of puzzlement. *Where the hell is he?* Paul started to shrug, and then seemed to think of something and held up a thick finger. The finger went higher in the air, and then the hand arched and the finger moved downward. *Up and over*; Paul thought Blondie was hiding behind the far end of the sofa. He tapped the side of his forehead. *You can feel it, can't you.* In the excitement—and the fact that the pull was almost unbearable at this range, so overwhelming that you actually had to focus to find its true direction—I realised that he was right. If I concentrated, I could feel that it came to a sudden stop point, right at the last inch, and that point was behind the far left arm of the sofa. I took a deep breath, and my skin seemed to ripple spastically across my back. I gave Paul another thumbs-up. He returned it, and then something took a chunk out of the wall to the left of his head.

I jumped a whole foot in the air, crying out, and Paul jerked away in response, losing his footing and falling over. There were two heavy thuds, one after the other; the flying object hitting the floor, and Paul's head connecting with the door. I suddenly couldn't get my breath—everything in my body was already running at maximum, and this was too much—as my wide and searching eyes scanned the room frantically, looking for more incoming projectiles. I saw that which had narrowly missed Paul's head; it looked like a bookend in the shape of a horse and rider, made of metal. It had been thrown.

"Fuck!" shouted Paul in pain, holding his head with one hand and grabbing the door handle with the other, pulling himself to his feet. "You little twat, you could have fucking killed me!" I stood there dumbly as Paul brushed me aside and strode angrily round the settee, hearing a voice shouting weakly in response as he did.

"Get out!" the voice cried, sounding cracked and fragile. "This is my house! You're intruding in my house! *Get out!*" Now Paul was bending down, and hauling someone to their feet, someone who was babbling and cringing at the same time. That someone was Blondie, wearing only a dirty white vest and underwear, covered in food stains. He was shorter than Paul—possibly slightly shorter than me, even—and although he was gaunt in the face, he still had the remains of a belly. His eye fell on me, and although Paul had a hold of one arm, Blondie pointed at me with the other.

"*GET OOUUUUUUTTT!!*" he shouted, having found his voice. His eyes bulged from their sockets, showing yellowing teeth that hadn't been brushed for many days. "*LEAVE ME ALOOOOONNNEE!!! YOU SHOULDN'T BEEEEEEEE HEEEEERE!!*" It was the cry of a lunatic. Blondie was clearly at his breaking point, if not already past it. Sorry ... not Blondie. That was just what we called him. Patrick. His name was Patrick.

"Shut up," said Paul, firmly, shaking him. He didn't seem to have too much trouble restraining him, being a lot larger, but Patrick wouldn't stop shrieking and babbling. "Shut *up*. Shut *up*," repeated Paul, shaking him by the arm over and over. Patrick kept on bellowing, and I suddenly thought about how all the commotion might be attracting attention.

"Paul," I said, "the neighbours." Paul looked up at me, anger still on his face, but he got it after a second. Paul paused, looked at the screaming man, and then pulled Patrick towards him, wrapping a thick bicep around his throat. He then slipped his other forearm under Patrick's shoulder and up behind his squirming head and pushed, hard. Patrick's voice immediately dropped to a squeak as his air cut off, but he still tried to curse us out. He made desperate rasping sounds that came in regular bursts, and flailed his arms fruitlessly backwards.

"Ssh," said Paul, effort etched across his face, "ssh. Calm down." Looking back, I think normally this wouldn't have been too hard for Paul, but keeping the sleeper locked on as well as keeping himself upright, while standing this close to the heart of the pull—touching it—must have been a superhuman effort of will. I was impressed.

Patrick started to tire, and as his struggles lessened, Paul lowered him forward towards the sofa, finally dropping him slowly down so that he lay on the side of his face. At first I panicked—I thought he was dead—but then I saw he was breathing gently. I looked up at Paul, who had his hands on his hips now, taking in heavy breaths through his nose and pushing them out through his mouth. His face was covered in sweat. I stood there like an idiot, stunned not only by what had happened—and how *quickly*—but by my own lack of action or decisiveness. I had frozen, and furthermore I'd come up with no suggestions or contributions of my own since we'd arrived here. Sure, I'd gone in through the window and gotten us into the house, but that had been Paul's idea. He'd done *everything* else, while I'd stood there and waited to be told what to do. I'd been full of ideas until now, running out of them when *action* needed to be taken, and quickly. Frankly, it was embarrassing.

"You okay?" I asked Paul, sheepishly. He nodded, not looking up from where he now sat the floor as he breathed. The effort of restraining Patrick had wiped him out.

"Uh," he said in further confirmation, "just give me a sec. Room ... room's spinning." His left hand felt the air around him blindly, and found the back of the sofa, which he then used to pull himself up. As he did so, I heard a faint whimpering; Patrick was already awake. He obviously hadn't been as completely out as we'd thought.

I looked down at him to see tears running out of his screwed up eyes, his hands balled up into fists. He was muttering something as he cried, but in such a high-pitched, desperate whimper that I couldn't make out what he was saying. Realising both that Paul would need a moment, and that this was *my* moment, I made my way over to the sofa and sat next to Patrick's head. He didn't seem to notice, which was just as well; my mind had gone blank. Totally fucking blank.

I tried to steel myself; I needed answers. A reporter gets answers. I had to do my job, had to *think* like a reporter, get past the weirdness and find out the truth. I suddenly thought that I should get my Dictaphone, so I could have a record for important future reference. That did it; just like that, the spell broke. Suddenly, it was work, and I was in work mode. Unfortunately, like an idiot, I'd left it in the car along with my bag and laptop, but a shift had occurred in my head and I was capable again.

"Paul?"

"Mmm. Just give me a minute."

"No, it's okay. I'm just going to the car. Can you keep an eye on him?"

"Uh-huh."

"You sure?"

"Uh."

"Just sit on him if he moves, okay?"

"Will do."

That would have to do. I quickly got up, nearly fell over, then straightened myself and staggered into the hallway. I shut the door behind me to slow any sudden bolting that Patrick might attempt. Walking to the front door, I popped the latch and opened it. Wobbling out to the car, I retrieved my bag from it and returned inside.

Pulling my shoe back out from under the front door, I kicked my other one off as well—we were guests here, after all, unwanted or otherwise—and shut the door behind me, making sure the latch was shut. I dumped my bag on the small table by the front door, fished out my Dictaphone, and brandished it in front of me as I opened the living room door.

"For future reference," I explained to Paul, expecting him to be impressed by what he would see as simple forethought, not knowing my job. He was sitting on the arm of the chair now, looking at Patrick, and looked up.

"Oh, yeah, yeah of course," he said, as if suddenly woken from a daydream. He waved a hand at me to say *carry on, all yours.* I switched it on, and sat down again next to Patrick, who hadn't stopped crying or whimpering. I pressed record, the little red light came on, and I was away. I would listen to that recording a lot in the hours to come, during the waiting. If you asked me to back then, I knew it so well that I could probably have recited it word for word. I couldn't manage that now, though.

But not because I don't remember it.

***

(Sound of faint crying, and creaking leather as I shift on the sofa, moving closer to Patrick. I am the first person to speak.)

"Can you hear me?"

(No response.)

"We're not here to hurt you. We're sorry we had to break in, but you wouldn't answer the door. We didn't have a choice. We just really need to talk to you. I've come a long way to do it."

(He says something now, but it's barely audible.)

"Sorry? I couldn't hear that?"

(He says it again, and it's still hard to hear, but it sounds like 'Lies.')

"Lies? No, we're not lying. We just think you might be able to help explain a few things. People are dying."

"Please ... please ...leave me alone. I'll do anything."

(The voice is dripping in fear. It's like he's pleading for his life.)

"What are you so afraid of? What do you think we're going to do?"

(There is a long pause, but the crying has stopped. When he next speaks, it's in a harsh, broken whisper.)

"Something awful. Something terrible. Knew you were coming, felt you coming for days. Locked the doors. Couldn't go outside. Couldn't go outside. Had to be safe. Secure."

"You ... you knew we were coming? Like ... I mean, the same way we knew how to find you?"

"Knew disaster was coming. Some disaster. Knew running would only make it worse. Had to hide. Had to hide. Had to get secure."

(There is a pause again at this point; he opens his reddened eyes and looks at me. They stare into mine for nearly a full minute, his head trembling, and then he looks me up and down. When he speaks again, his voice is slightly clearer.)

"It's … it's not you, is it? You're not the … disaster. You're not it. And … he isn't either, is he?"

"Try throwing something else at my head. Then you'll see disaster."

(That voice is Paul's.)

"I thought …"

(Patrick breaks off suddenly, wide eyed in terror. There is a sound of rapid movement as Patrick bolts upright, and grabs my arm in a painfully tight grip.)

"The window! You broke the kitchen window! It's not safe!"

"It's okay, it wasn't the big one, it was just the little one—"

"No, no, it has to be fixed, has to be secure—"

"Okay, okay, we'll let you fix it, but please, you have to answer some questions first—"

"But it's not—"

"That's the deal. Okay? Quicker you answer our questions, the quicker the windows gets covered. I'm sorry, I know it's your house, but there's some really bad stuff going on that you might be able to help stop. Okay? So calm down."

"PLEASE!"

"Sorry, pal. That's the deal." (Paul again.)

(There is a very long pause, then a slumping sound on the leather, followed by heavy breathing.)

"Come on then, come on come on come on. Quick."

"You said this 'disaster feeling' started a few days ago? Wait, what's your na—"

"At work. I was at work. I was sitting at the computer, preparing the contract for the Anderson shipment, and then suddenly I knew that I had to go home immediately because total disaster was coming. It was COMING. I wasn't safe out in the open. I looked around the office, and no one else knew it. Thought about telling people, but no time. I just grabbed my keys and left. I think someone asked where I was going. Didn't stop. That was Monday. Haven't left this room since, except for food and toilet."

"This was Monday? Has it gotten worse since then?"

"No. I know it's coming. That's enough. I thought it was you. Can we fix the window now? Please? You said you'd help me!"

"What kind of disaster?"

"I don't know, I told you. I'm not crazy. It's coming. Just because I don't know what it is doesn't make any difference. If it finds me ... something terrible will happen. Something ... TERRIBLE. I ... I have to stay here, and be secure. I'll be safe in here. I'll wait. I'll wait it out."

(There is a pause here, as I look at Paul. He returns my gaze, and I know we're thinking the same thing. This house will not protect this man. Paul suddenly looks confused, and it's him that speaks next.)

"Monday? But the Stone Man didn't arrive until yesterday. That doesn't make any sense."

"The what?"

"The statue thing."

"What are you talking about? Help me fix the window, you said you would."

(The voice is pleading, desperate again, almost like a child. Paul speaks next.)

"The bloody statue thing that's been smashing up half of the country, it's the only fucking thing that's been on the TV!"

"Haven't had it on. Didn't want to risk attracting attention. I've been very, very quiet ... had to be SAFE!"

(There's another pause, and I remember the confusion Paul and I shared here. We did not expect this. I speak next.)

"There's ... there's something very big going on right now. And we think— well, we know—that it involves you."

(There's a loud intake of breath. I can still see his wide, terrified eyes. He doesn't say anything.)

"We thought ... you could tell us ..."

(Silence.)

"You don't know, do you?"

(Silence.)

"When you say 'disaster' ... do you mean for you? Or do you mean disaster for ... everyone else?"

"Don't know. Don't know. Please ..."

(There is a loud, slapping sound of hands on thighs, caused by Paul slapping his own and standing. There is a stomping sound as Paul moves, and he speaks next.)

"THIS thing, THIS fucking thing—"

(Sound from the TV is suddenly heard as Paul turns it on, the steady sound of helicopter blades interspersed by occasional remarks by the on-the-scene commentator. The live feed is from high above, as always, although initially there is no visual other than an immense cloud of smoke in the middle of what could possibly be an urban centre. This goes on for a while, as evacuation updates pan

across the tracker bar that runs along the bottom of the screen. The camera zooms farther suddenly, and although it is still shown at a distance, the unmistakable shape of the Stone Man appears from the smoke, unmistakable and unstoppable.)

"WHAT do you know about THAT thing—"

(There is a loud crash, so loud the audio distorts, as the glass coffee table goes over. Patrick has just leapt to his feet, striking it hard enough to upend it. He doesn't even notice. He speaks next, his voice barely a whisper, strained and soaked in horror.)

"What ... what ..."

"It's okay, just talk to us, and we—"

"It ... it walked through a building ... what is ... the building didn't stop it from ..."

"Okay, calm down a second and we—"

"I'M NOT SAFE! I'M NOT SAFE! I'M NOT SAFE! I'M NOT SAFE!"

(There is flurry of movement followed by a popping sound on the recording, and it ends.)

***

The Dictaphone flew out of my hands as Patrick smashed past me. I was unprepared, surprised, and off-balance, as well as being barely able to stand as it was; I tumbled aside like a pathetic bowling pin as this half-starved, older man knocked me down. Paul lunged over to grab him, but his foot connected with the corner of the upended coffee table as he did so, and he tripped, slamming onto the floor for the second time in five minutes. Patrick flung open the living room door, fled through it, and was out of sight along the hallway, still gibbering. We made it to our feet as we heard the front door opening, and reached the hallway ourselves just in time to see Patrick's pale body disappearing out of the house and onto the driveway. We lumbered after him, jostling against each other in our efforts to catch up, and reached the front door at the same time as Patrick was halfway across his driveway. In a second he would be out of the gate.

As it turned out, that didn't matter. As he ran through the gate and out onto the street, we saw Patrick jerk upright suddenly, as if he'd been shot. His whole body then suddenly went utterly limp and buckled sideways, like a marionette with all of its strings cut.

Paul and I stood frozen in the doorway, shocked, and then Paul half-ran, half-limped over to Patrick's unconscious form on the concrete. I shook my

98

temporary freeze off and followed, but even close up I couldn't see Patrick thanks to Paul's bulk blocking him from sight. I suddenly had a very bad feeling indeed; this was all very familiar, and I couldn't think why.

"What ... what the hell ..." said Paul, looking down at Patrick in amazement. I started to ask what was wrong, and then I heard it, and remembered where I'd seen this before.

"*GCCAATTGAATTTGGCCCGTTAACTCAGG ....*"

Patrick's eyes were open but vacant, devoid of thought, and in this too he was exactly like the guy in the green vest I'd seen jump on the Stone Man back at the transport museum in Coventry. The same staccato, rapid-fire gibberish over and over, coming from Patrick's mouth this time, low and steady. Paul looked up at me in confusion.

"What the hell is this? Is it the bang on the head?"

"No ... I'm afraid not. Something else is at work here, I think. And it's pretty worrying. This is long-range stuff."

"This is to do with the Stone Man? It must be twenty miles away still, at least."

"I know. Look, let's get him inside, then I'll tell you all about it. We can prop him up in the living room; I don't think he's going anywhere for a while. Then we'll have a cup of tea and try to figure out what's what. We need to calm down." Paul nodded in response, then looked down at Patrick and sighed.

"Poor bugger," he said. "Something's messed him right up. Sounds as if he didn't even ask for it either." He paused, then touched Patrick's arm, surprisingly. The touch was quite tender. "I shouldn't have put the TV on. I was just ... so frustrated. Being like this, and him freaking out, and not even knowing a bloody thing about the Stone Man, when all those people have died ... I just snapped. This is my fault."

He was being hard on himself. While I agreed that putting the TV on was a dumb move, I could understand his frustration. I squatted down opposite him, and hooked my hand under the still babbling Patrick's shoulder.

"Done now," I said. "He might still be fine, we don't know. At least we don't have to worry about him doing anything stupid and hurting himself, and hey ... it leaves our options open, doesn't it?"

Paul stopped in the action of putting his hand underneath Patrick's opposite shoulder to help pull him upright.

"What do you mean?"

"Well, I just mean that we have to decide whether we're going to try to take him to the Stone Man, or sit here and wait. And this way, with him like this, well ... it means we have a choice, right?"

It made perfect sense to me, but Paul just stared at me for a long time, his eyes examining my face.

"What?" I said, tersely. I wasn't having any more of this. What I'd said was absolutely true; we did have a choice to make, and regardless of anything else, Patrick being like this made it easier. Fact. We had a job to do, and Patrick was in no state to make choices now (not that he exactly was before). The responsibility was now ours, like it or not. Why couldn't Paul see that?

Either way, he suddenly waved it off with his hand.

"Not yet. You're right; tea. We both need a cup. Let's get him inside and have some bloody tea."

***

I badly wanted to shut the kitchen door for two reasons. One, in the unlikely event that Patrick was in any way aware of our presence, I didn't want him to overhear this conversation, and two, more importantly, it would drown out the now incessant drone of his constant babbling in the living room. It was maddening, every syllable clipped and fully enunciated. It was obvious to us both why it wasn't an option though, as we had no idea if Patrick might suddenly come to at any minute and attempt to run away again. Basically, we just wanted to keep an eye on the guy.

Paul stood by the boiling kettle, looking out of the window onto the small rear garden. He seemed to be examining the lawn bric-a-brac that Patrick had presumably set out himself; there was no evidence so far of anyone else living here, or of an immediate family. Neither of us said anything, using the pause in proceedings to try to get ourselves under control and breathe easily for a moment (getting Patrick back inside in our physically depleted state had been a considerable effort) as well as to avoid our first mutually thorny argument. Eventually, the kettle's button clicked back into place and the steam stopped.

"Take sugar?" asked Paul with his back to me, picking up the appropriately labelled jar nearby and removing the lid.

"Two," I told him, "Not a lot of milk."

"Uh-huh."

I wondered how this was going to go. His reaction outside was clearly one of disagreement, but he hadn't committed to it; he was either open to suggestion or one of those men who needed their tea to fortify them before an unpleasant task. I, however, was resolute. I had too much at stake. I was prepared, my mind ready.

Paul handed me a mug, and leant back against the opposite counter. The silence continued a moment as he took a small sip from his mug, closed his eyes appreciatively, and then gestured towards me theatrically with a free hand. *Go on then.* It signified reluctance, but willingness to have it out, because this was a matter worth going through the hassle over.

I thought I knew one other thing, though; I was getting an idea of Paul's style, and this was part of it. To him, letting me go first was a passive aggressive move. Letting me go first was his way of both giving up and establishing control; granting permission to speak. I'd obviously pissed him off, and he wanted to win. I usually missed this kind of thing, even when it was at its most obvious, but unfortunately for Paul, I'd seen this exact behaviour nearly every day for a whole six years under a former editor of mine. So far, Paul had been running the show, I felt, and that had been fine. I didn't think he'd been doing it on purpose, but here he was. Now he was potentially going to derail my plans, and had just made it clear—unwittingly—that he was going to actively *try* to do so.

"No, no," I said, "after you. The floor is yours." Paul looked mildly surprised, and I knew my guess had been right. He hadn't expected me to see his hoop, hadn't expected me to refuse to jump through it.

"Right. I say we wait," Paul said, flatly. "He's clearly locked into the Stone Man in some way, same as we are, and he knows that something bad is gonna happen. We take him to it—even if we can—and we hurry that 'disaster' up, whatever it is. We have no idea whether moving him out of here might actually make things worse; you saw what happened when he tried to leave the house, or the immediate area at least. We came here for answers, and there are none, not yet anyway. If there was some obvious way that we could help, fine, we could then do that. But there isn't, and we've been told quite clearly that the one thing we *could* do will cause 'disaster'. We wait it out, and our consciences are clean; anything that happens is out of our control." He finished speaking, stared at me, and sipped from his mug again. It was a convincing argument, but I wasn't worried. I had a few of my own.

"Okay," I said, returning his gaze, "well, we both know we can't take him farther away—take him up to Scotland or whatever—as that just prolongs all the destruction and draws the Stone Man farther across the country. This guy is the source, and the Stone Man will follow him. But we take him to it—risking this vague and possibly made up 'disaster' that he's foretelling—and that destruction stops. And we're still there to get our answers."

"*If* there are any. And you're assuming the destruction *will* stop."

"What do you mean?"

Paul shrugged, and pointed out of the window.

"Say we take him to the Stone Man, and whatever happens, happens. Presuming that it doesn't bring about the end of the world, how do we know it's not just going to head off to another target? How do we know somebody else doesn't automatically become the source?"

"That doesn't even make any sense. If *anyone* could be the source, then why would it pick someone halfway across the country?" I asked, feeling myself starting to become a bit angry. I don't really know why; something about the guy was rubbing me up the wrong way, but the last thing I wanted to do was be the first person to lose it while letting him keep that passive expression on his face. I wanted to see it break, to see that practiced composure fall away. It was obviously something he'd mastered, but I thought I could crack it.

"Maybe he was the first one it found. The first ... I dunno, appropriate person."

"You don't think it might try a bit harder to find someone a bit closer?" I asked, adding a bit more scorn than I felt to my voice. Was I winning? I thought I might have been.

"Why does it need to hurry?" said Paul calmly, not biting. "It's got all the time in the world. It can't be stopped. It must know, or whoever sent it must know. A hundred miles, ten miles, it's gonna get there in good time. Plus, look at what just happened; this guy tried to run away and the poor bastard is a babbling vegetable in the front room. He couldn't even run to the other side of the street, don't you see? He's trapped. He got shut down when he made a bolt for it. So why should it need to hurry? *Blondie wasn't going anywhere.* Distance doesn't matter to the bloody thing, time doesn't either. They only matter to us."

A good comeback, too. But I had the trump card.

"You do realise, though, that if we just sit here and wait ... any deaths that happen between now and the time it arrives? On our heads. Our heads, Paul. We could have stopped this early—"

"You don't know it would stop—"

"And you don't know it *wouldn't*," I carried on, refusing to be interrupted as I'd let him have his say. "As I was saying, if it turns out that we could have stopped this early, but all we did was just sit back and wait while it smashes through umpteen more buildings, causes umpteen more riots and heart attacks and religious suicides and fights, then when people ask us why we didn't do anything and we say 'Well, we had no guarantee that it *would* have stopped it,' they'll lynch us. Because I tell you for a fact, and you know this, if we do nothing it definitely *will* keep coming. If we take him to it, it *might* stop."

It was my turn to shrug now, this time as if to say *You tell me which makes the most sense.* Paul was still staring at me without a word, so I pressed on.

102

"Plus, what happened to all this talk about saving the day? That could be us. We'd be the guys that stopped it in its tracks."

"Or the guys that brought about disaster. We don't know what it wants!" There it was; the first trace of annoyance. I was getting to him.

"But we know what it's doing," I said, putting my hands in my pockets, leaning more now, relaxing. "Wrecking the country. Causing people to die."

"And what will it do to him if we try to take him towards it? Look at him now. That happened when he tried to move thirty feet. What happens if we take him more than that?"

"He's already gone, Paul."

"Are you kidding me? What the hell do we know about it? We don't know if that effect lasts, or anything. You'd risk doing him damage on an assumption? What the fuck is wrong with you?" asked Paul, putting his mug down now and looking openly pissed off. "He didn't want that thing to find him, he knew it'd cause something bad even if he didn't know what that might be, and you want to take him right to it?"

"I'm trying to save *lives*, Paul—"

"What about his?" said Paul, his voice rising. "He's already nearly had a seizure because of us. You want to go the whole hog and risk killing him by pushing him even farther out of the area?" Paul's hands were spread now, and he was gesticulating rapidly as he spoke. I realised again how much bigger than me he was, and how I didn't actually know very much about this man, or what he was capable of. Still, I was angry now myself, and I wanted my goddamn answers. What he was saying didn't even make any logical sense.

"It's coming here regardless," I said. "We can't take him farther away, and *we know it's coming here*. The end result will be the same; it will get to him. One way takes longer, and risks lots of lives. The other way is quicker, and risks just one. His. Plus, Jesus, I mean we could even keep an eye on him on the way. Check if he gets worse or whatever. Paul, you know what I'm saying makes sense. Why are you arguing with me on this?"

Paul didn't respond, and instead stood there with his jaw set, and then looked out of the window again. He then turned back, and I was a bit taken aback. He knew he didn't really have a point to argue, and was angry about having to admit it ... but it was clear that he was really just angry with me in the first place.

"When he collapsed just now," he said, voice dangerously even, "you didn't even think about him, did you? Straight away you were on to the next stage, the next best thing we can do to get pissing answers or whatever. You almost seemed ... glad. You knew he had nothing for us, and so him ending up like this was clearly a, a, a blessing or something, because you could get him to the Stone Man. You didn't even think about *him* for a second." He took a deep breath, suddenly, and I wondered if it was him trying to keep himself upright again or whether it was his way of keeping himself calm. I hoped it was the former, and even began to try to see, in my peripheral vision, anything I might need to grab as a weapon that I could defend myself with.

"Hold on, Paul," I said, realising something and holding up a finger, "I didn't hear you saying 'Oh, I hope he's all right' when we were getting visions of him sprawled out on his sofa. You wanted answers yourself, and that's all you thought about. So don't give me the good Samaritan routine. *You* turned on the TV, *you* made him run out in the street." I was on a roll. "I think this is you feeling guilty. I think you feel guilty because you caused this, and so even though what you're proposing makes no sense, you're saying it to try make up for your guilt. You want to keep him away from the Stone Man for as long as possible because he was scared of it, even though it's just delaying the inevitable. Well there's more at stake than your conscience here, and I'm not gonna let other people die because you feel guilty for—"

I didn't really see Paul move, because I'd been lost in the euphoria of my own steadily growing realisation for a second. To my eyes, he was just suddenly on me, grabbing me by my collar with both hands and bending me backwards over the countertop, face pressed right into my own. His breath was right against my mouth, pushing out between his gritted teeth.

"Listen to me, you little twat," he spat, shaking me slightly as he spoke. I couldn't move, as his superior body weight had me pinned in place. "You don't have a fucking clue. I don't like, I *really* don't like what I saw outside. You'd have fed him into a fucking cement mixer if it meant you'd get more information. You were like a hungry fucking dog. And I'll be damned if I'm gonna let you do that. That's a man in there, a *man*. Remember that. Remember ..." As he trailed off, I thought he was struggling to find the right words, but when the silence continued, and his eyes began to dart slightly around my face, I thought he looked lost for a moment. Suddenly, he let go, and stepped back, not taking his eyes off mine. There was a long pause. I didn't even straighten up.

"That ..." he started, and then looked at the floor. I still didn't move. He didn't speak. There were a few moments of silence. "Sorry. Sorry. I'm sorry. That was too much. I didn't mean all that. It's been a fucked up day, and feeling like this, my nerves, they're just ... I'm just ..." He trailed off again, and I wondered what the hell was going on. He suddenly looked up.

"I'm sorry, yeah? I'm sorry. You just ... don't forget that's a human being in there. That's all," he said, and then turned and grabbed his mug, turning the tap on to rinse it out. I didn't know what to say, but I knew something was expected. I slowly straightened, corrected my clothes, then felt my neck for any scratches. I'm not a man used to violence—I hadn't been in a fight since school—and that had been shocking.

"Well ..." I began, lost now myself for words. "Okay, fair point, but ... Jesus ..."

"No, I know, there's no excuse," said Paul, back still turned. "It's just I'm, I'm stretched so *thin* by all this. I just want it to be over. I can't stand feeling like this, my body's just ..." He clenched his free hand into a fist, tight, shaking.

"I know, mine too," I said, and it was true. I could almost understand, to my surprise. But that was too much, and I would tell him so. "But I did ... I suppose I did forget that. I just got carried away, and we're so close to the truth, but ... no, you're right. Look ... don't worry about it, okay? Just don't do that again, okay? You're a lot bigger than me. Not very fair."

"I know, I hate that shit. It's not right. My temper sometimes ... I'm sorry. Look, you *are* right. It's getting to him one way or the other, and we might as well try to shorten it and save some lives. You're right. You're right. The needs of the many and all that. But like you said ... we keep an eye on him on the way, okay? If he starts to get worse, we bring him back. We don't kill him, trying to save others or anything, I'm not going to kill a man. Fair?"

"Fair."

"Right." And with that it was done, and we both knew it. Maybe not better now, but almost. He put the mug on the drainer, then turned off the tap. He still hadn't turned around, and now he put both hands flat on the edge of the sink and leant his weight on his arms, looking into the garden. He sighed. "Poor fucker, eh?"

"Well ... we don't know what's going to happen. He might be all right once he meets it."

"Mm. D'you believe that?"

"I don't know."

The babbling from the other room filled the silence.

"Let's get him in the car then."

***

We made it five minutes down the road before Patrick was sick, and then his body began to spasm. That was enough. To this day I have no idea what would have happened if we'd gone further. Hell, it all might have turned out totally different if we had, when I think about it. But I can't think about that. Everything that happened afterwards, happened. The sergeant. The Nottingham woman. Sweet Jesus. Fuck it, I'm opening the Sambuca.

We turned around, and took Patrick back to the house. To wait.

***

The next few hours were strange. We didn't want to watch the TV—all it was showing was Stone Man reports anyway—and we didn't need to. With the Stone Man this close, and with the amplified connection that Paul and I had created, we could easily feel it making its way towards us. We deposited Patrick back on the sofa, and Paul fetched a deck of cards from the car, holding them up without a word for my assessment of the idea. I nodded, and he opened the pack. I rooted around in the kitchen drawers for some matches, found some, and suggested Blackjack. Paul gave me a silent thumbs-up, and we played for the next few hours, switching dealer every time Blackjack was dealt. I even found a few cold beers in the fridge, and with my hangover long forgotten, we cracked them open. The only sounds in the room were Patrick's babbling, and occasional double taps on the now-upright coffee table to signal a hit to the dealer. It wasn't awkward, despite the way it might sound; in a way, it let us both know that we were closer already. Silence was acceptable now, and to have time to sit and wait after such constant stress was almost relaxing, or as relaxing as things can be when your whole body is freaking out. I guess it's true what they say about people bonding in crisis situations. We weren't quite picking out curtains together yet, but we had taken a step forward, at least.

Sometimes Paul got up to stretch his wobbling legs, and went out into the garden for some air. I found myself listening to my Dictaphone recordings in these breaks. They made me feel strange.

The light from outside dimmed further as the hours passed—we hadn't opened the blinds, didn't see any need to—and the late afternoon turned into early summer evening, the sun sitting lower in the sky. Shadows lengthened, and Paul's pile of matches steadily outgrew my own. I liked playing Blackjack as a rule, but Paul seemed to have a better handle on the tactics than I did, sometimes sticking when I thought it insane and hitting when I thought it meant his certain downfall. More often than not, he turned out to be right.

I was deciding which way to go on a hard sixteen (Paul was the dealer on this one, with an upcard of nine showing) when we both became aware of a sound from outside. It was low and steady, but still sounding far away. We strained to listen, but couldn't quite make it out over the sound of Patrick's constant chatter. I moved to the window, and Paul joined me.

"Helicopter," Paul said. "News or military, but either way ... everyone's coming."

"Yep," I said, looking over at Patrick's wide-eyed and unseeing face. Were we responsible for that? Would it have happened eventually anyway? "It's, what ... at least an hour away yet?"

"I think so."

"So I think we'll be getting a visit soon. There'll at least be people close enough—authority people—that we can try to talk to. Didn't the Home Secretary say that they'd be doing house-to-house checks well in advance of each evacuation?"

"Something like that. He's danced about on it so much, I can't really remember *what* the plan is supposed to be," answered Paul, picking the remote up and turning the TV on. The picture showed the Stone Man, surrounded again by a circle of soldiers walking in step with it, standing at a distance of about ten feet on all sides. It was crossing a field again; it was apparently back in a rural area once more.

"Well, either way, they'll be here long before the Stone Man is," I said, sitting back on the sofa. "And that's the time we'll need to convince them that this guy has to meet it. We can't leave him in the house, because it'll be flattened with him inside it ..."

"And if they take him, they'll put him in the hospital and that could be disastrous," finished Paul, nodding. "I've been sitting here assuming you have some kind of genius plan lined up to convince them that we're on the level. Any time you feel like sharing said genius plan, I'm all ears." I smiled slightly, and reached for my bag.

"Well, I had an inkling of an idea earlier, and I've been thinking about it while we were playing ... and I reckon I might have something," I said, opening the bag up.

"Never doubted it for a second."

"It's not even particularly complicated. I think ... if we do this and it works, they'll at least give us a chance to talk to one of the higher-ups. And then it's just a case of whether it's enough to convince them completely. As well as a few little bits of bullshit, but that's just a risk we're going to have to take. You can bullshit, right Paul?" I smirked at him, but it was friendly.

"Like a pro. Okay, sounds like a winner. I love it when a plan comes together. Talk me through it."

I did. It wasn't much, but we didn't have anything better.

***

Chapter Four: Persuading Private Pike, Facts About Patient Zero and Radiation Spikes, and Andy Discovers a Very Different Point of View

***

Ten minutes or so had passed when we heard what sounded like—after the last day of abandoned roads—an almighty noise coming up the street. Two days ago we wouldn't have even noticed it; the sound of several large vehicles moving at once, which before today would have just been background noise. We moved to the window to watch. Army personnel trucks, about eight of them, parked up in a line about three hundred metres away from the house, and soldiers began to pour out of them and make their way to houses on either side of the street. Many more trucks continued on down the road, on their way to clear the next area. The soldiers were only carrying sidearms strapped to their legs, and I saw only one carrying any kind of heavy automatic weaponry; the guy standing nearest to the trucks. I got the impression they didn't expect any issues from the residents other than perhaps a reluctance to evacuate … but they weren't completely certain.

"Here we go," muttered Paul, and patted me on the shoulder. "It's up to you, old boy." And then, out of nowhere: "What did you say the day job was again?"

"Writer," I said, cursing internally. Now, of all times.

"Oh?" Paul seemed genuinely surprised, despite the urgency of the situation. "Anything I might have read?"

"Not that kind of writer," I said, and changed the subject. "Stay in here when he comes to the door, okay?"

"Why?"

"Just extra pressure if you're watching. If this works, you'll be in the mix soon enough."

"Okay, okay. Your play."

I nodded, and then went to the front door and opened it. I looked out into the street and saw people heading towards the trucks, some complaining, some carrying pre-packed suitcases, some hurrying children along. There weren't many; I wondered if some were simply refusing to answer their doors, or were hiding, or had already left. The evacuations could have simply been the authorities' way of making sure houses along the path were cleared.

A soldier spotted me standing in the doorway, and raised his hand. He then began to beckon me over. I shook my head, and then beckoned him in return.

The soldier seemed taken aback, then annoyed. He turned around and shouted something to another soldier, who looked at me, and then shouted something back to the first soldier, who shook his head and then ran over to me. He was young, a lot younger than me, which I thought might help things. It was all dependent on how big of an authority kick the guy was on.

"Sir, you have to leave the area, sir," the soldier said once he was at the end of the driveway. He didn't come any closer. "It's only temporary. We're taking everyone to a holding centre, and it should only be for a few hours until the Stone Man has passed, or we know it's safe to come back. If your house isn't fit for residence afterwards, we will arrange temporary accommodation for you and your family. If there is anyone else in the house with you, please get them and bring with you only essential items." This was said automatically, clearly learned from a prepared statement, and recited with the air of someone who is sick and tired of repeating it. He wasn't in the mood for any complications, which was unfortunate for me. Even so, I couldn't help but notice him calling the Stone Man by its media-given name. That just sounded unusual.

"I understand that, Private," I said, instantly regretting it. He could have been a goddamn officer for all I knew, and if so I'd just insulted his rank massively. I'd just assumed he was a private because of the way he seemed to ask somebody else if it was okay to come over. I carried on speaking anyway, and he didn't correct me, so either I was right or he was just too sick of all this to care. "But I need to speak to your commanding officer, please. It's extremely important." The soldier nodded, and gestured towards the trucks.

"That's fine, sir, I'll make sure he speaks to you once we're back in the trucks, but we have a lot of ground to cover today so if you'll please get your things then we can go. Is there anyone else in there with you?" he replied, doing a reasonable job of hiding his impatience.

"Yes, there is," I said, "But I'm afraid I need to speak to the officer in charge before we get in the trucks. I've got something that I need to show him."

"That's not going to happen, sir," replied the soldier, testily now. His voice was very flat, and it was clear that this was someone who had just decided that they'd had enough crap for one day. "I'm sorry. I'll make sure he speaks to you on the truck. But we do have the authority to move you, sir, if you make things difficult. I don't want to do that, so why don't you just come along nicely and we can get this over with as quickly as possible." *Jumped up little shit*, I thought. I didn't have a problem with him carrying out orders, but when someone at least ten years younger than me tells me to 'come along nicely' it's never going to get on my good side. Even so, I kept my cool.

"I tell you what, then," I said, trying to keep my voice sounding pleasant, "why don't I show you? You won't even have to come in the house. Then you can decide whether it's worth bothering him with, but I think you will. I don't want to be removed forcibly either, and it'll only take, literally, about a minute. If you want me to go once we're done, no problem, I'll go." I smiled, and raised my hands and eyebrows in a *Waddya say* manner. The solider started to shake his head, but hesitated. He'd obviously been told what to do when met with resistance, but not what to do when presented with a deal; especially one that would end with it being his choice as to whether I went in the truck or not. If I'd asked him to go in the house, it might have been different; that would have been more suspicious. In this instance, he clearly decided that it was easier to humour me than force me to enter the truck at gunpoint.

"Can you come to the end of the driveway to show me then, sir?" he said, sighing slightly and stepping back a few feet. I didn't know if his moving away was to show me that he wasn't going to grab me, or to demonstrate that he wanted me to come out of the house.

"Nothing funny now, eh?" I asked, trying to make a joke with what I hoped was a winning smile. It wasn't returned.

"Sir, our orders are to evacuate any residents as peacefully and pleasantly as possible, and to only use force as a last resort. I'm taking you at your word that you're going to show me whatever it is you have to show me, and then you're going to get in the truck nice and easy. I'm trusting you on that, sir. So the quicker we get this done, the easier it is all round, right? Obviously, 'nothing funny' goes for you as well." He was trying to be reasonable, at least. I appreciated that, but not enough to forget *come along nicely.*

I nodded, and started to pick up my bag.

"Leave the bag on the floor please, sir. Take out whatever you've got," he said, and I noticed his right hand straying towards his sidearm.

"That's okay, that's okay," I said, holding my pale and shaking hands out as I bent down to the bag. I fumbled around in it for a second, found my camera and held it above my head. As I made my staggering way over to the solider, he glared at me impatiently, clearly thinking I was some kind of mental midget out to try to get a piece of the bigger action. He was half right, thinking about it.

I drew closer to him and lowered the camera, turning it to indicate that I wanted to show him the viewscreen on the back. He took a very small step backwards, still keeping a preferred distance between us.

"I can see from here, sir," he said, holding up his hand, palm out in a *stop* gesture. "Just show me and we can get on with things." I didn't respond—there wasn't any point—and instead turned the camera onto play mode. The viewscreen pinged into life, and I pressed the play button embedded on the back. The last photo I'd been looking at appeared, which of course was the one I'd gotten ready while we'd been waiting for the military to show up.

The image was of the Stone Man, of course, snapped by me as it had stood waiting in the middle of Millennium Place. It was clear that, unlike all of the footage that had been plastered over the news for the last twenty-four hours, this one had been taken when it was standing still. The soldier's impatience vanished from his face, and he was intrigued. Not jumping in the way that I'd hoped, but I had his attention, at least.

"This was taken yesterday," I said. "I was there, at the start in Coventry. I've no doubt other shots of this time are out there—I wasn't the only one with a camera, or camera phone—but you can have this shot checked. I'm sure your superiors have a copy of every available Stone Man photo that's online, so they'll know whether I downloaded this or whether it's a photo I could only have taken in person. They'll know I was there. That's the first thing. Okay?" I waited for him to reply, but he didn't, so I took it as a cue to carry on. "The second thing—and I'm taking a bit of a gamble here—is that I'm sure you've been briefed, to some extent, on the Stone Man. After all, you're here to evacuate, you're potentially going into the danger zone, and they've no idea if that thing can suddenly speed up or something, right? So they'd tell you, I think, the limited number of do's and don'ts that they've been able to work out when it comes to 'Best Stone Man Practice'. And one of those don'ts, just in case you found yourself in close proximity to it, would have been *don't touch it*. And they'd have told you why. They have, haven't they?" The hook line had been used; if he didn't take the bait, we were going to be loaded into the trucks and that would be that.

"That's restricted information, sir," said the soldier, but he suddenly looked as young as he really was, his weary attitude now replaced by deep confusion. The awkward customer that he'd been dealing with had suddenly produced something utterly unexpected, and he was rattled, so much so that it was clear my hunch was right. He obviously knew what had happened to the kid in the green vest that jumped on the Stone Man's back, as well as the two cops at the scene.

"It's okay," I said, trying to sound as sincerely reassuring as I could. I might have had the idea, but I realised that Paul should have been the guy to do this. I'd a feeling that he could do Man-to-Man better than I could. "You don't need to tell me anything. *I'm* the one telling *you* stuff, aren't I? Right. They didn't have to tell the general public not to touch it, specifically. They'd already told them not to approach it, and enforced that as best they could. But *you* guys ... you could well be close enough to touch. I saw what happened to the first guy who touched it; I was there, see? And I think they'd have shown you what can happen, and what to look out for in case anyone shows any of the signs. Did they take video of him? Or is there already video out there, maybe from someone else who was there and got some and put it online?"

The soldier shook his head gently, more unsure than ever, but he didn't speak.

"Did they tell you about him instead then? Told you what happened to the people that touched it, and what they looked like as a result?" I asked, and then thought that I might be pushing it. "Never mind," I quickly added, "here's the third thing; I know that the path of the Stone Man will take it *directly* through this exact house. You might not, I don't know—you might just have orders to clear this street, and others like it—but your superiors will. I know that the government hasn't *released* an exact list of threatened buildings along the path, but *they'll* have worked out its exact trajectory, and they'll know precisely which buildings are in line." Paul and I had managed to get online before the army arrived (by now, our phone networks even had 3G coverage back) and check the now-released government version of the Stone Man's path. They hadn't listed exact buildings, or shown the trajectory as a straight line; even calling it a path was misleading. What they'd done is show a list of 'projected future areas' for evacuation, listing streets by city that should be 'prepared to leave their homes for a few hours at short notice.' It made sense. Naming buildings that were potentially about to be demolished gave idiots too much chance to try and follow the fucking thing, to try to get a glimpse of it in action, along with many other problems. This gave Paul and I an edge; a chance for credibility.

"They'll have a list somewhere," I continued, pointing back at the house, "and this building will be on it. How I know that is another story, and one for— no offence intended at all—the person in charge. So, for now, here's the fourth thing; inside that house is a man who is in the exact same state as the guys in Coventry who touched the Stone Man, the ones you know about. Except *this* man hasn't been within twenty miles of the thing. You might think he could be faking it, but trust me, show him to your superiors and he'll show you that he isn't. Again, how he's in that state is a story for another time, but I'm telling you this to convince you that the man who owns this house—this place directly in the Stone Man's path—*is special.*"

Still nothing in response from the soldier ... but I thought that was still a good thing. "I'm telling you all this to convince you that *the man who owns this house* is what the Stone Man is heading for. He's what it's all about. And my friend and I ... we're connected into all of this as well. But we need to explain this to the guy in charge. Because none of us can leave yet, you see. That's the important thing." Before he could dismiss these last parts, the biggest, hardest to swallow bits with the potential to convince him that this was bullshit after all, I turned back to the house and cupped my hands to my mouth. *"Paul!"*

On cue, Paul emerged in the doorframe, filling it dramatically, and looking even bigger with Patrick slung over his left shoulder in a fireman's carry. Paul carried Patrick across the driveway to where I and the soldier were standing. Again, it wouldn't have been hard for him normally; Paul was very strong and Patrick's frame was light. But in his current state, just standing up was hard enough for Paul, so carrying Patrick like this was a real chore. The soldier watched, mouth slightly open, but his hand didn't stray back to his sidearm. Both of his hands hung at his sides as he tried to figure this out. Paul reached us, and nodded at the soldier.

"Private Pike," Paul grunted by way of a brisk greeting, and lowered Patrick to the floor. I could have smashed Paul in the balls again quite happily for that one, then and there, watching him smirk ever so slightly as he straightened up and then dropped down to one knee to get his breath. The back of his clothes were soaked with sweat. Fortunately, the soldier didn't hear it, staring wide-eyed at the sight of Patrick's strung-out form. In the evening light, the clear deterioration of the man would have been enough to make someone pause at the sight of him; shadows and lines taking on even harsher tones in the long light of an early summer evening. But now, there were extras; the near-white pallor his skin had taken on since his failed attempt to flee, along with the dilated pupils and the frankly inhuman sounding stream of letters that flowed from his lips (so fast and unending, yet so clipped and pronounced that he sounded like the world's greatest speed talker) made him grotesque. It made him look alien.

That did it. The soldier backed away slowly, without seeming to realise he was doing it. A moment later when another soldier called to him, presumably to ask what was taking so long, he quickly turned to look in their direction, then back at us.

"Stay here," he said, looking pale now himself, and with a last, almost frightened look at me, he scurried over the road to his colleague and began talking rapidly out of earshot.

"Think you pulled it off?" muttered Paul out of the corner of his mouth, looking up at me from his kneeling position. His breathing was a little easier, but his forehead was still beaded with sweat.

"I don't know," I muttered back, watching the two soldiers talk. "This is only the first bit. They might even just cart us off for questioning and then take

Blondie off to hospital, unless our friend there manages to make enough fuss to get the brass interested."

"But all the stuff you said?"

"Who knows. It worked on him, at least, with Blondie here doing his bit."

"Wait until they find out I'm doing it all without moving my lips. Gottle o' geer, eh?"

"Not funny."

"No. Sorry. Bit hypocritical, that. Sorry. I'm just nervous."

"Don't worry about it. Hold on, they're coming over."

Private Pike, as he now was known, was heading back over with the other soldier, hanging back slightly behind him. The new soldier was slightly older, if not slightly shorter, with dark, Asian looking features. If he outranked the other guy, I didn't know how to tell, unless carrying a clipboard was a sign of rank. As he got close enough to see Patrick, he stared down at him as he walked in our direction. He didn't speak until he got to us, and even then he continued to stare down at Patrick, perhaps listening to his Morse code babble.

"How long has he been like this?" he asked us, without introduction.

"Since about three hours ago, I think," I told him.

"And what caused it?"

"He tried to run away," said Paul, wiping his forehead with his forearm. "He has to stay here. And so do we." The clipboard soldier looked at Paul, as if noticing him for the first time.

"Names, please?" he said, talking to Paul but addressing us both.

"Andrew Pointer and Paul Winter," I said. "We don't live here though. He does." I pointed at Patrick. "We came here because he's important. I can tell you all about it but we have to speak to someone higher up, and we can't leave." The clipboard soldier looked up from the clipboard he'd been checking.

"Neither of you are ..." he trailed off as checking his papers, "P. Marshall?"

"No."

The clipboard soldier scribbled something on his sheet with a pen.

"Okay, Mr. ... Pointer? You can tell me all about it, and I'll pass it on," he said, turning the top sheet on his clipboard over and holding his pen above the fresh page beneath. I took a deep breath.

"Sorry, but I can't. We want to talk to someone higher up. It's up to you, but I think you haven't got a huge amount of time to waste. You've got about ... fifty minutes, I think? Until it gets here? It'd be longer if it was travelling by roads, but as we know, the Stone Man prefers to travel as the crow flies, and I know it's coming exactly in this direction." The clipboard soldier stared at me, his face unreadable. The amount of confidence and unflappability spoke volumes; this guy clearly knew what he was doing. The extra experience was all over his face. The younger soldier still hung back behind him, looking at Patrick, when the clipboard soldier spoke.

"Can I see the camera, please?"

"You can see it. But I'll hold it."

"I could just take it, you know."

"You don't need to do that. I have copies, anyway," I lied, holding the camera up to show him the Stone Man picture. He examined it silently for a while, lips pursed, and then scribbled something else on his sheet. He flipped the sheet on top back over, and pointed at the camera.

"Hold on to that," he said, and produced a radio. "Henderson, report?" There was answering noise on the other end, which clipboard soldier seemed to understand, nodding. "Roger that, evac complete section 347," he said. "Vehicles one through seven rendezvous at section 348 and vehicle eight stays here with me. Send Branson and Carter over here." He turned back to us. "Stay here a moment please, sirs, I have a few things to deal with." He nodded at Private Pike—who saluted and stood to attention—and then walked away, talking into his radio as two others soldiers came towards us. He met them halfway and seemed to give instructions, and they then headed over to stand next to Pike as clipboard soldier headed back to one of the trucks. A few awkward moments passed while Paul and I stood face to face with them, none of the soldiers saying anything.

"Are you guarding us, or something?" asked Paul. They didn't reply. "It's not Buckingham Palace, boys," said Paul, leaning back on the floor and propping himself up weakly on his arms. "You can tell us. Plus, I highly doubt you're gonna shoot a couple of civilians for no reason, eh? We under house arrest now then, or what?"

"Just bear with us please, sir, and stay where you are," said Private Pike, but clearly with less confidence than he'd had earlier. He looked sick. I looked down at Paul, who shrugged and patted the ground next to him. Why not, I thought. It was all out of our hands for the time being, and besides, the longer we were here the better. All the time we spent sitting outside Patrick's house, the Stone Man was drawing ever closer, gaining on us like it had been all afternoon. Not that it was us that it needed to reach. The person with that honour was the gibbering figure to Paul's right, and he hadn't asked for any of this.

I sat down on the concrete driveway—which was warmed perfectly by the summer heat—and lay down flat on my back. Though my whole body was thrumming like a freshly picked guitar string, I was so glad of the break; I had no decisions to make, nowhere to run off to, no one to question. I could just lie here and wait. I looked up at the clouds above me as they slowly drifted overhead, and asked Paul if he was okay.

"All good," he said, and the tone of his voice sounded like he felt the same way that I did. Nothing more was needed, and in that manner we passed the next ten minutes or so. While we waited, I heard the army trucks—vehicles one through seven, presumably—drive away, and I thought that was probably a good sign, even if I had no idea what we were waiting for. A helicopter passed very close overhead, right through my sight line, and then hovered in the near distance for a time, giving me the impression of being inspected from afar. Right at that moment, I didn't care. The chopper then began to set down in whatever nearby area it had been hanging above.

Shortly after that, we heard the sound of a freshly approaching engine. I sat up, and to my surprise I saw an open-topped jeep heading up the road towards us. I was slightly surprised; I'd only ever seen these in films, in scenes set in military bases or warzones. Seeing one in a reasonably suburban area was out of place to say the least. Seated in the front of it were two figures in military uniform, and seated behind them were two armed military escorts, each carrying an automatic rifle of some sort.

"Here we go, look," said Paul, pointing at it as if I hadn't already noticed. "Looks like we got some bugger's attention." I nodded in agreement, and we both struggled to our feet and began to head towards the end of the driveway.

"Just wait there please, sirs," said Private Pike, not looking at us directly, and then all three soldiers standing guard saluted the jeep as it drew closer. In the near distance I saw Clipboard Soldier climbing out of the remaining truck, parked now with two rifle bearing soldiers stood at either end.

The jeep pulled up alongside the end of the driveway, and the soldier in the passenger seat got out, as well as the two armed soldiers in the back. To my surprise, and therefore very probably to the confirmation of my own sexism, the soldier in the passenger seat was a woman. At distance, in baggy uniform with hair either pulled up under her hat or worn short—I couldn't tell—and without makeup to help determine sex, I hadn't realised. (Maybe not sexism. Maybe more of a lack of awareness of the levels of equality in the British army.)

"At ease," she said, and the soldiers of course did as they were told. She turned to us, and I could see that she was perhaps in her late forties, and the shortest of the military members currently present. Her features were hard-ish, but in the same way that a marathon runner's would be. Now that she was closer, I could see that her hair was swept back underneath her beret, and that it was brown. Said beret had a different badge on it than all the others I'd seen, and adding that to the fact that Private Pike and the others had saluted her first—as well having a chauffeured jeep with her own set of guards—suggested to me that this woman was the higher brass that we'd asked to see. Clipboard soldier had arrived by now, saluting and introducing himself.

"Brigadier Straub, ma'am, I'm Sergeant Craddock. I'm the one who put in the—"

"Thank you, Sergeant Craddock," interrupted Brigadier Straub, looking very serious. Her manner was brisk, but not patronising; I got the strong feeling that she was extremely aware of the situation's time constraints. "These are the two men?"

"Yes, ma'am."

"Gentlemen," she said, extending her hand for me to shake, "I'm Brigadier Straub. I've been sent to have a talk with you both about any information you may have regarding the current situation." She repeated the gesture to Paul, after I'd released her hand. "You'll have to forgive me if I seem brusque, but time is of the essence and—pardon me for saying so—there is a very good chance that you're just wasting mine, so I need to get on with this."

"We understand that, ma'am," said Paul, politely, "but if you've seen the other guys, the cops and the young fella, or footage of them—I haven't, but he has—then you'll know that this guy, unfortunately, is the real deal." Straub looked down at Patrick for a moment, then nodded, more to herself than to Paul.

"Yes," she said, looking back at us, "yes, this is ... this is interesting. But again, as I say, we need to get on with things. Shall we go inside and talk, gentlemen? My men will take your friend inside for you; you two don't look in the best of shape, if you don't mind me saying so."

"He's not our friend, Brigadier Straub," I said, shrugging slightly, but realising as I processed her words further that we seemed to have acclimatised slightly to being this close to Patrick. Whether it was prolonged, close range exposure that was helping us to adapt, or just having the last few hours to just sit for a while, I realised in that moment that the physical stress wasn't quite as bad as it had been. Either that, or we'd just gotten used to it. Even so, we still looked bad enough for her to notice. "We've never met him before today, and even then it was brief before ... well, before this. But I think it would be better to keep an eye on him, yes."

"Agreed," said Straub, turning to the three soldiers behind her. "Privates, take this man inside and put him in the sitting room. Then you can return to the vehicle and wait for further instructions." As they got to work, Straub turned back to us and gestured towards the house. "Let's have us a quick talk then, gents, and I can decide what happens next."

***

Once we were back in the living room, Patrick was laid out on the carpet; Paul and I sat down on the sofa, while Brigadier Straub took the armchair. Two armed soldiers stood quietly by the door, watching us.

"Right, I'll get to the point," said Straub, leaning forward and lacing her fingers together. It was clear already what had helped her to advance so far in the military, overcoming whatever old-school bigotry might have attempted to block her path; she had an air of total confidence and efficiency. Already, she had no doubt that she would get what she wanted from us. She was probably right. "The gentleman in Coventry, the one you saw that first made active physical contact, we refer to as C.I. One, contact incident one. The policemen are referred to as C.I.s Two and Three, and will continue to be so for the time being. Eventually, we'll release their details, but you know that for now it's prudent to keep a lid on that side of things. Understand?" We nodded.

Straub nodded back, then held out a hand.

"Can I see the camera please?"

Paul and I exchanged a glance, after which I shrugged and handed it over. What else could I do? The two bruisers with the rifles looked more than capable of dealing with me, and probably with Paul, too. Plus we wanted to get on their good side. Straub took the camera, and had a quick flick through the photos. Everyone was silent while she did so. When she finished, she looked up.

"I'm going to keep this. All right?" It wasn't said in a threatening or intimidating manner. She was simply doing me the courtesy of the illusion of choice. I nodded again, dumbly. She held it out to one of the soldiers by the door, who took it and pocketed it. "Do you have any other recording equipment about your person? Either of you, camera phones, anything like that?"

Paul pulled out his old Nokia and showed it to Straub. "This thing doesn't even take pictures. Look," he added, turning it to show her the lack of a camera. Straub nodded after a second, seemingly satisfied, and then turned to me. "And you, Mr Pointer? Anything else?" There was something different in her tone and her stare, and as ever, it took me a moment to get it. Then it clicked.

She knew what I did for a living. They'd already run background checks on the names, and our jobs, and knew there was no way I'd be in a situation like this with just a camera. I considered lying for a second, but I'd already taken too long.

"You, your bag and your vehicle will be searched later, Mr Pointer," she said. "Best just be honest." I sighed heavily, and handed over my iPhone and my Dictaphone. As she passed them to the soldiers, I felt as if she was discarding the best opportunities of my career.

"Okay," she said, the previous task already forgotten as she moved onto the next immediately. "What I'd like to happen now is for you two to tell me your story so far, and I need you to keep it under five minutes. That's very important. Do you understand?"

"Yes, ma'am," said Paul.

"Just Brigadier to civilians," said Straub, holding up a hand, "I'm not the Queen, but thank you." It was a light-hearted remark, but her serious expression didn't change. She had business to take care of. "Right, off you go, and leave nothing out. Don't worry about anything illegal that might be in there, this is off the record for now. I just need the truth, most importantly."

We did as we were told, even though I did most of the talking because Paul didn't come into proceedings until later on, joining in when he had to explain his side of events before I arrived. Once we got onto the journey to Sheffield, Paul took over, with me adding bits to his story wherever they were appropriate. He was a more natural storyteller, which is embarrassing for a writer to admit. We ended with Patrick making a run for it, and our subsequent failed attempt to take him towards the Stone Man. They didn't need any details of the time after that; they knew what had happened from there. The whole thing, in our potted version, took only slightly longer than five minutes. Throughout our recap—even during the parts about psychic visions and following an unseen pull across the country to a specific house in Barnsley— Straub's expression didn't change. I could imagine how having a good poker face might help in an advanced military career.

Once we'd finished, Straub leant back, and rested her forearms on the chair's armrests. She let out a small breath of air, and seemed to be inspecting her knees. We waited patiently, feeling like schoolchildren wondering if *It was like that when I got here* was a convincing excuse. Eventually, Straub drummed her fingers on the armrest, and then spoke.

"Here's the thing," she said, holding up a hand in a gentle chopping motion from the wrist. "There's parts of your story that I *know* are probably true, based on information we have, parts that I *don't* know are true but sound as if they add up ... and slightly shaky bits that you could well be making up to stay on the inside of an international-level mystery. And no offence to you, Mr Winter and Mr Pointer—"

"Just Paul and Andy to brigadiers, Brigadier, we're not royalty," interrupted Paul, giving her a wink. Straub didn't smile, but did raise an eyebrow as she continued, and there might have been the briefest of twitches around the corners of her mouth.

"No offence to you, Mr Winter and Mr Pointer, but the last thing in the world I need right now are unnecessary and untrained civilians that may mean well but who, if they cause something to go wrong, can bring a ton of crap down on me and my superiors. So I need you to convince me of certain things, and quickly. Here's what I know about your story." She extended a finger on her left hand, and touched it with the fingertip of her right.

"Point one," she said, "about your man here bolting for the street—"

"Do you know his name?" asked Paul, interrupting again.

"Yes, if this is his house," said Straub, and carried on without addressing the subject further. "If you really wanted to know that badly, gentlemen, you could have rooted around for some documents or something of the kind. I assume you didn't feel the need to know that much." I bristled slightly at the statement, but she was right; once we knew that he didn't really know anything, what good would a name have done? We already called him Blondie at the time; that was enough for us. Straub continued talking.

"He bolted for the street and had some sort of physical attack, and ended up exactly the same as C.I.s One, Two and Three. You may not know this, but I'm told that the speed and unending nature of this speech pattern they're producing is impossible for the average human, without some sort of thorough cyclical breathing training. It's used by Gregorian monks and the like for their chanting. Neither any of the C.I.s, or this man here, were the type of people to be involved in that kind of thing, based on what we know. It takes extensive classical training. Regardless, you say that was a result of what happened when he tried to leave the area around the house. Correct?"

"Correct," I said. I wondered if this was going to be one of the points she thought was true, or if she was about to try to catch us out on one of the other parts. We hadn't even told any real lies. Yet.

"You gave the time of this incident as being approximately sixteen hundred hours?"

"About 4:00 p.m., yes," I said, and didn't know what to make of it when Straub nodded again slowly, not taking her eyes off mine.

"Something you won't know is that we've been monitoring certain aspects of Caementum since yesterday—"

"Aspects of what?" asked Paul, confused.

"Sorry," said Straub, "the Stone Man, you call it the Stone Man. Just the name the research team gave it at first. Latin. We've been monitoring certain aspects—the few that we can—such as radiation."

"It's radioactive?" I asked, suddenly thinking of all the time I'd spent close by it in Coventry.

"Very slightly, but only at a level that you would need some major exposure to if you wanted to have any issues caused as a result. I'm talking about hours and hours, Mr Pointer, and you couldn't have been near it in Coventry for more than two; it wasn't there long enough. Don't worry. That's not the issue here. The fact is that at 3:56 p.m., our men logged a comparatively huge spike in its rad levels, and one considerably higher than the other two spikes we'd seen before then. We theorise these were some kind of broadcast or signal boost, although we don't fully understand their purpose or how they work. But the time of that last spike adds up with your version, and you couldn't know that." I thought about the other two previous spikes she'd just mentioned, and thought about my passing out on the flyover bridge and fitting at Shaun's, but I said nothing. Paul and I exchanged another glance.

"All that," Straub continued, "plus the fact that no footage of the C.I.s has been leaked online yet—along with this man here having the exact same post-incident catatonia and appearance—says to me that he *is* probably connected with Caementum to some degree. How useful he may be to us is one thing, especially as he's a civilian and not currently one who can make his own decisions in the eyes of the law."

"Okay, so that's the good news," said Paul. "What's next?"

"The next bit is that yours are not the first reports of psychic visions and the like."

My jaw dropped, but Paul snorted slightly.

"Not surprised to hear it," he said, "I can only imagine some of the bullshit that's come out of the woodwork. But I assume you mean reports that actually check out."

"Yes," admitted Straub, "about five or six that have been accurate enough, and detailed enough, to warrant further investigation, but none that have actually led anywhere. But these people did know things that they couldn't have done by conventional means; someone in Scotland describing a victim that hasn't even been declared dead yet, and the exact manner and time in which they died. One person in Cornwall, and another in Newcastle, knowing—but only once—where the Stone Man would be passing through at a certain time, and knowing it *ahead* of time. Both of those referred to two separate incidents; both were visited after their report was proved correct and asked to reproduce it. They couldn't. The most interesting one, to us at least, was someone in Wolverhampton phoning the police three days ago and saying they were certain something terrible was going to happen in Coventry, and then spread north. They were adamant. We have him in custody now, but we think we're going to let him go. He knows nothing. But these have all been little flashes, people picking up little glimpses and finding themselves unable to do it again. But you two are the only ones with *any* kind of credibility and evidence to claim to have done it consistently and continuously ... and believe me, the evidence here is the important point with regard to me believing you in any way. Plus background, telephone and e-mail checks have shown it to be unlikely that you two have any prior knowledge of each other before today."

This time Paul's jaw dropped, and neither of us said a word. I thought I might have noticed that little mouth twitch again on Straub's face. She then continued.

"Basically, gentlemen, as you've probably guessed, what I need from you before we can continue is some kind of proof of this ... ability of yours. Let's be honest; you have the photos. You were there at the start, no doubt, and therefore probably saw C.I. One, at least. You wouldn't be the only one. And this house's resident is obviously connected to Caementum; again, there's pretty much no doubt about that. You two could have worked out its trajectory more accurately than others have; there's probably only one amongst the hundreds already online that's absolutely accurate, they just don't know it for certain. But it *is* feasible that you found your own way here through simple maths, and then somehow met Mr ..." she paused as she caught herself, "this man here, and then watched him have his incident, and put it together with C.I. One in Coventry and realised that you were onto something big. Why, you could have gone from house to still-standing house along the parts of the trajectory not yet evacuated until you found someone who was linked to it. It would have been an effort, but you've had twenty-four hours, after all. Other have tried it already, we know, they just haven't had the correct, specific line to follow. You wouldn't be the only newsman who realised what this could do for their career, Mr Pointer."

I stiffened as she said it, and silently cursed whoever had carried out my background check. Paul shifted in his seat next to me, and I made sure I didn't look at him; I couldn't. I found myself wishing I'd just been honest. Why keep it secret in the first place? What had I expected Paul to do? By worrying about getting called out on my motivations, I'd probably just lost the only ally that I had in all of this. I tried to console myself, thinking that hopefully it would soon be over and Paul, as helpful as he'd been, wouldn't be needed after that. I would have my story. Hell, had he even noticed what she'd said properly? Now wasn't the time to find out.

"So the question is," said Straub, holding up her hands, "can you prove it? Do that, and you have my full attention. If you can't ... well, that's a bit harder to decide. It's not like you wouldn't be findable if we needed you later, so I could just have you evacuated and take this man here to the military hospital to be examined. To be honest, there's benefits for me either way; if you can't prove it, I can get on with other things and I also have your details should I need you, but if you *can* prove it, then you might be useful here. I'd also be more inclined to listen to any potential advice you may have with regard to Caementum and this house's owner."

This last part showed a different side to Brigadier Straub; this was her dangling a carrot, and I thought it suggested that she'd rather I *could* prove it. Not out of personal curiosity—Straub was a practical woman, it seemed—no, I thought *she* thought I could help, if I were proved to be on the level. And why not? At this stage, the military and the government were helpless. They wouldn't even be here talking to us if they weren't. By this point, they'd be willing to try anything that might help to end the lunacy of the Stone Man. And the good news was, I *knew* that I could.

"Okay, Brigadier," I said, reaching down to my bag, "give me a moment."

It hadn't been too difficult the first time, and I had a feeling that, since Paul was nearby—and everything Stone Man-related had been more intense ever since we'd been with each other—it would be even easier now, or possibly a stronger, clearer experience. I pulled out the UK atlas, found Barnsley, and laid it out flat on the coffee table, after moving our abandoned playing cards out of the way.

"Need me to do anything?" asked Paul, quietly, staring at the atlas.

"No thanks," I told him, holding my hand out and closing my eyes, "I think you're already doing a lot just by being here."

"This the map trick that you said you used before?" I heard the brigadier say.

"Uh-huh," I said, concentrating. "Just give me a moment please, Briga—" My words cut off as I felt the connection take, almost like a clicking sensation in my head. I looked down at the map and, *knowing* it would work this time, and more easily, I closed my hand into a fist and extended a finger. Opening my eyes and watching my finger move like it was attached to someone else, I saw it trace its way over the Barnsley area, finding a spot in between two roads and stopping dead; then, impossibly slowly, it began to move upwards.

"There," I said, trying to read the names of the roads my finger was in between (my finger was pointing to a coloured area that possibly signified a field or park). "It's right there, and heading this way. Check it with someone; you know I've been nowhere near a TV for the last fifteen minutes, and I know you'll also find that it's still exactly on the same trajectory as it's always bee—"

And then suddenly, I wasn't seeing the map any more.

I was seeing dust, and blackness, and then I winced as I saw bright daylight; I'd just walked through a wall. I was now on a deserted street, and suddenly, from my left and right, came running soldiers, who had been forced to go around the building that I'd just passed through and were now catching up to reform the circle of walking bodies around me. I could hear a helicopter above, and, farther away, I could hear several more, spread out across the sky around me. Between the gaps in the soldiers, I could see cars parked along the side of the road that crossed horizontally in front of me, a road with a few shops, including—

And then I was back in the room, staring at the map. I blinked a few times, then my legs turned to water and I fell backwards onto the chair. I'd been riding inside the Stone Man.

"Andy? Andy?" asked Paul, leaning over and gently taking my shoulders.

"I'm okay, I'm okay," I told him, and, haltingly, sat up and faced Straub, who was now stood, having moved to see where I'd been pointing.

"Radio the men who are walking with the Stone Man," I asked, my throat feeling suddenly dry. "Ask them if, right in front of them, is a blue Land Rover and a red … I think it was a red Fiesta. And a shop named 'Timmins', or something like that."

"What? How did you …" asked Paul, incredulously.

"That's where they are right now," I said, ignoring him and addressing Straub, "and what's more, that's what's there. There's no way I could know that. How could I know what cars are there? It's not far away now either. About half an hour, I think."

"I know," said Straub, and stared at me for a moment. She then turned to the two guards at the door.

"Stay here, and keep an eye on these two, please," she said, and turned back to us. "No offence, but I'm sure you can see why I need to make sure you stay put." She then walked towards and out of the door without waiting for an answer, leaving Paul and I, once again, in a room where the only sound was Patrick's nonsense stream.

"Did you see it?" said Paul, not looking at me.

"Yeah," I said. "Well … I was *in* it. I was seeing things from its point of view."

Silence from Paul.

"Jesus …" he said, after a moment.

"Uh-huh," I said, forgetting completely about Paul's potential reaction to finding out about my job. "It didn't even feel that strange, it was just like watching through a webcam or something, only clearer." I paused for a second, thinking. It really hadn't felt odd at all, and certainly no stranger than seeing maps come to life and forming a psychic link with a man made of stone. Like Straub, I was all business, as time was short. "The thing is ... that's just given me an idea. Well, not an idea as such, but ... what I mean is, if I, as someone that probably wasn't *supposed* to be able to connect with it or whatever, can quite literally get inside its head ..." I trailed off, thinking of the best way to put it.

"How did you do it? Could I do it again, do you think?" asked Paul, gesturing at the map on the table.

"Maybe," I said, shrugging. "Probably. Would you want to, if you could?"

Paul stared at the map, thinking.

"Actually ..." he said, "call me a pussy, but ... no. I've yet to link up with that thing in the same way that you have, and who knows what might happen? Who's to say I wouldn't end up like our man here if I did?" He looked at Patrick, and shook his head. "God ... no thanks. I'll leave that to you."

"Fair point," I said, already thinking again about what riding along with the Stone Man might mean. I thought I was brushing the edge of a bigger idea, like an archaeologist uncovering the tip of some long buried monstrosity. I thought I might have just seen the edge of something that should make me very nervous. "I just wonder ... if I can ride inside it, and see what it sees, or what it's near ... who's to say it wasn't designed so someone could do just that?" Paul stopped looking at the map and turned to me, brow furrowed. I carried on.

"It just feels like ... if there's a remote feed from it, then there's reason for that. Someone, or something, somewhere far away wants to be able to see what's going on. It's like ... it must have a master. Or masters." Paul didn't say anything.

"I mean, it doesn't stop," I continued, feeling like the room was now that bit darker, "and as far we know, it or whoever sent it knew that Patrick wouldn't be able to run away. So why would they need to be able to control it remotely? They wouldn't. They could use whatever barrier they put in place to keep Patrick in one small area, and then just send the Stone Man here. Set it off, and wait. And watch."

"What are you saying?"

"I don't really know, to be honest. It just implies ... implies intelligence, forethought, planning, I don't know. It's almost like ..." I went a little bit cold as I brushed a big bit of sand off the buried bones, a huge chunk. I had no idea if I was right, but it *felt* right.

"It's almost like ... it would be the only way they could see what was happening. Or know that the job had been done."

"But ... of course they could see it. It's been on the TV constantly," said Paul, confused. "It's hard to police the skies over an area that keeps moving. Plus, satellite feeds, all that stuff." He'd missed the point, I knew, but before I could explain, Straub came back into the room, the two guards saluting as she did so.

"All right," she said, her hands behind her back. "We believe that your stories are pretty much on the level; the important parts anyway. We're going to introduce C.I. Four into the same area as the Stone Man and see what happens." So Blondie was C.I. Four now.

"And you're telling us?" asked Paul, surprised, and then pointed at me. "Even him?"

I winced slightly. He'd not missed her reveal, then.

"Well, I see your point, Mr Winter," she said, tilting her head slightly, "but Mr Pointer and yourself are considered essential personnel now. We're operating under near-total fog here, gentlemen, and so far you're the only consistent insight of any kind that we've had since this whole thing started." She sighed. "I've been ordered to grant you high clearance. Some of my superiors are on their way right now, along with several more units for backup should it be needed, and for securing the immediate area. The science teams will be here almost immediately."

Paul and I shared a glance. This was very, very big. I couldn't believe they were taking us seriously.

"A few things, gentlemen, and these are very important, so listen to me. One, this is very much a case of speak only when you're spoken to, unless you find that you have some sort of insight that we don't. Efficiency is key in any kind of operation, and although we might need you, you absolutely *cannot* be underfoot. Understood?"

We nodded.

"Two, you are to stay with me at all times from now on unless otherwise instructed. Under no circumstances are you to attempt to get involved with proceedings in a physical way, and you don't go anywhere unless told to. Understood?"

We nodded again.

"Three, any information about the operation will be on a need-to-know basis. Basically, don't waste time asking questions about what's happening, as you'll be told everything you might need to know. Anything else, you don't. Information will be coming one way, from yourselves to us. Understood?"

More nodding.

"Four, as I say, a lot of our science chaps will be here shortly as well. They might have a few questions of their own, and if they do, you will give them your full cooperation. Understood?"

"Yes, but what—"

"I'm not finished," said Straub, cutting me off. "Five—and I don't like to play this kind of hardball if it can be avoided, but time is short and I can't take any chances—everything you see and hear is restricted information. There's only so much media restriction we can get away with these days, but in terms of this operation, what you know as an insider, and everything you've told me about your experiences of the last twenty-four hours, *all* of it is to be kept under wraps, under penalty of treason and—quite frankly and off the record—anything else we can think of to bury you for the rest of your lives. Or worse." She looked at Paul and me, one to the other, back and forth, her face totally blank. She let it sink in.

Another hammer blow to the chest, and this one was the worst, most final one yet. I could barely process the concept, but in a nutshell, she had just taken away the best chance I would ever have at a dream career; a dream career that had seemed to have been sitting in the palm of my hand throughout all of this. I opened my mouth to protest, but she carried on.

"I know that's the last thing you wanted to hear, Mr Pointer, but let me quickly assure you of one thing; the lockdown is a temporary thing, as far as you're concerned."

"How temporary?" I asked, sounding more desperate than I would have liked. It was like having my head in the hangman's noose and thinking that I'd seen someone coming towards me, carrying a pair of scissors.

"Until this is over, and we know what the hell is going on. Once it is, and we do, you'll be rewarded for your services to Queen and country and given full, exclusive rights to the truth ... or our version of it. You'll be edited by us, but we'll work with you, not against you, and you can even admit that you'd cooperated with the military to help bring this threat to an end. Someone has to take this to the press, after all; the overall facts can't be covered up. The public already knows about Caementum. The world knows. They want answers, and they will have them, even if they're only the ones that we deem appropriate. And, as a sweetener—and to make sure that you are, in turn, working with us throughout all of it and not against us—I've been ordered to inform you that you'll be our voice on this. You'll be a hero, Mr Pointer. We need you fully onside; this is our way of ensuring your cooperation while keeping you happy." She looked at Paul. "And you'll be paid too, don't worry." Paul raised his eyebrows at me. It wasn't an entirely unfair deal.

"What if I'm scooped in the meantime?" I asked, feeling intense relief but wanting to check all of the bases. I knew that it was unlikely, and as I stood there and thought about it, it occurred to me that this offer could potentially be an even better result. The same story, but with endorsement by the military, and at the highest level? And access to exclusive information, even after it had passed through the army PR filter, would add an extra element to the whole thing.

"Highly unlikely," answered Straub, looking at her watch. "Anything anyone could possibly put together so far would have nowhere near the insight that you already do, and even if something happens in future that you're somehow outside of, we'll make sure that you have enough extra juice to blow away anything that anyone else might have. Trust us." I didn't have much choice. "Either way, gentlemen, that's just the sweetener. Go against us, and unfortunately you won't have much of a future. I can't stress that enough. Understood?"

We nodded again, but more quickly this time.

"Right," said Straub, "here's what you need to know about the plan. I'm telling you this so that you can just focus on keeping track of Caementum and telling us anything that we might need to know, rather than worrying about what's going on. It's this simple; we are going to put C.I. Four into the path of Caementum, or rather, *near* to it. This is being done with his full cooperation, as far as you or anyone else is concerned." She paused for objections. At that moment, we didn't dare offer any. "If it passes him by, then we, and you, will continue to monitor it, while we examine C.I. Four alongside One, Two and Three and try to make any connections. Being perfectly frank, we'll also be running some tests on you two at some point. Nothing painful, I promise, but our boys will have a lot of ideas they'd like to try out on you both, I'm sure. You understand, we *have* to stop this thing." Outside, we could hear the sound of engines, and running feet. There was also a light clanging of metal; something being unloaded. We didn't look, our attention riveted on Brigadier Straub. "If it doesn't, well ... then we wait and see." That statement in itself raised a lot of questions, but neither Paul nor I said anything just yet.

"We know from tests on C.I. One that doses of adrenaline should get C.I. Four physically mobile—" she said, but I interrupted her.

"He's awake? I mean, he's aware?" I asked, shocked. Perhaps there was hope for Patrick—or Blondie as he was to us then—after all.

"No, no," said Straub quickly, shaking her head and looking towards the window. Her radio crackled, and she lifted it to her mouth. "Straub here, I'll be there in a moment. Just get everyone in position, and let me know when the remote centres are up." She placed the radio back on her hip, and carried on talking to us. "I said he's mobile. He's not aware, but can stand, and be led. Imagine someone with extreme autism—or similar—so much so that they were lost in their own heads. You couldn't really communicate, but you could take them by the hand and lead them to where you wanted them to go. Temporarily, we can recreate that—only for a few minutes or so—using an adrenaline injection to give us that option."

The autism/brain pattern link again, I thought.

"As far as the world will be concerned, he's a member of our team, and a volunteer," said Straub. "We can sort the details out later. No one will know that he wasn't of sound mind." She stared at me, daring me to challenge her, but I didn't. What could I say? She knew who she was dealing with; she knew that I would have done the exact same thing.

"And if he's killed?" asked Paul, his voice dangerously flat. I looked to see him staring at Straub with worryingly unguarded dislike. She didn't miss a beat, however.

"Every precaution will be taken to avoid that possibility, Mr Winter," she said, poker face still perfectly intact.

"And if it happens anyway?" asked Paul, shifting on his feet. "You know nothing about this thing yourself, as you've already said. You're working under intense, what was the word you used, fog? You've no idea what could happen, so how the hell do you intend to 'take precautions' with something beyond your understanding?"

"The brief answer, Mr Winter, is that we don't have any other options right now," said Straub, almost absently, looking at her watch again. "The country is in chaos, and people are dying. That's the long and short of it. And off the record again, if it means risking the life of a man who, as far as we can tell, is an irreversible vegetable in an attempt to potentially stop this thing, then we are going to do that. Unless you have any better suggestions, which with all due respect I doubt seeing as we have a team consisting of the finest scientific minds in the world working on this. Now, if you have any more questions, this is your last chance to ask them." She moved her hands behind her back, and looked at us both.

Despite the situation, I couldn't help but be impressed by Straub. She was formidable, of that there was no doubt, but she was also well spoken and efficient in a no-nonsense way that was the total opposite of the way I went about my affairs. I was direct too, but I was messy and chaotic. Paul, I could tell, was less impressed.

"Just one from me," he said, that look still on his face. "What are you going to do if he is killed and it's broadcast live to six billion people? Who explains that one away? You?" Straub didn't bat an eyelid.

"It won't be a problem, Mr Winter," said Straub, shaking her head slightly.

"We're clearing the local airspace as we speak. The immediate area has been evacuated, and our men are preventing anyone from entering for the time being. We can only do so much, but I think it's enough. And I do assure you; we'll look after him. We want Caementum stopped to save lives; we're the good guys in this. Remember that." Her radio buzzed again, and Straub listened into it.

"Roger that. On my way," she said, and then lowered the radio. "Right then, gentlemen, if I can just ask you to wait here until you're sent for. You might as well get comfortable, as I'd say that you have a good twenty minutes or so until you'll be called. I'm going to ask you not to root around in here anymore, and these men here heard me ask that, if you get my meaning. If you need anything, ask my men, and by that I mean water or a toilet break."

"Hang on, though, what are you actually wanting us to—" I started to say, but Straub held up a hand.

"Sorry, Mr Pointer, I did give you a chance to ask questions, and I think I've already told you enough about what is going to be requested from you. You'll get the finer details shortly. Someone will come for you. I'll speak to you later." She turned, and the guards saluted her as she walked out of the door.

"Bitch," muttered Paul under his breath.

***

Chapter Five: The Coming of the Stone Man

***

I remember that time so well; it was so torturously dull that I couldn't forget it if I tried, while simultaneously being unbearably tense. Can you imagine? What an awful combination. *God,* it went on forever. The TV was now just news without any new footage, so it looked as if the military had in fact cleared the airspace just as Straub had said. There was speculation that something big was going down, and apparently the government had issued a statement about a 'stoppage attempt involving electromagnetism that required civilian clearance in a five-mile radius'. It was good, but I doubted everyone swallowed it. Even so, the world was in the dark.

And of course, the case was the same regarding the Stone Man in general; I look at the TV now, and try to remember a time when we knew nothing about it, when we were still living in the blessed ignorance that we'd enjoyed before that hot summer weekend over a year ago. Now we know what it wanted.

And even with that knowledge—along with the other parts that we learned the hard way—people are still going to die.

***

Paul flicked the TV off; I didn't mind. It was showing us nothing, after all, and the endless speculation was just annoying. We were nearing the twenty-minute mark, and we'd barely spoken a word, with me laid out on the sofa and Paul slumped silently in the armchair. Blackjack was not, pardon the pun, on the cards; I was embarrassed to talk to Paul after Straub gave the game away, and Paul clearly wasn't in the best of moods with me, given the silent treatment I'd received since Straub left. In fact, when he finally spoke, it wasn't to me.

"Guys, I need to use the toilet. Boss lady said I could go, so I guess one of you two escorts me?" He was referring to the guards, who looked at each other; one then turned to Paul and nodded without a word. Paul got up and walked out of the door that the guard had opened for him. The guard then followed him out, and I heard their feet heading up the stairs. As I lay there quietly, it struck me how we were already treating this house as if it were our own. Paul and I had used him like a bargaining chip in order to stay at the heart of things. But we were also trying to help; I keep telling myself that even now, but of course I'm never convinced. We hadn't treated him correctly since we arrived. There'd been no respect, but it was too late to change that.

Patrick had already been taken away on a stretcher by two men in medical-looking clothes, presumably for his adrenaline injection, or to be examined and then prepared for it. I guessed they wanted to get as much data from him as they could before the Stone Man arrived, in case this all ended with his death. The medical guys had looked at me and Paul on the way in; they'd stared at us like lab rats. Paul had given them the finger. To my great relief, once Patrick was out of our immediate vicinity, the effect of the pull was suddenly greatly reduced. I assumed it was something to do with his current catatonic state, as taking him a distance of about a hundred feet from the house—they'd taken him inside the largest tent, the one furthest away—certainly wouldn't have been enough on its own to dull the pull before. We'd been suffering from it when we were fifteen miles away.

Earlier, we'd been watching the proceedings through the window. It had been interesting, for a while. Soldiers scurrying here and there, and two tent-like canvas structures being erected in the middle of the street (after men with surveying equipment made complex calculations regarding placement and distance). It wasn't just soldiers on the streets, either; people in civilian clothes with laminated passes on lanyards around their necks could be seen every now and then, sometimes supervising the delivery of equipment into the tents and exchanging what I assumed was data by showing each other readouts on handheld tablet computers or laptops. Occasionally, one would gesture towards the house in mid-conversational flow, and I thought we'd be getting a visit; we didn't, however. There was a constant buzz overhead, loud even inside the house, of helicopters hovering, and this along with the unending stream of orders being relayed by soldiers with megaphones meant that I was glad to be indoors. It was just too bloody loud out there.

The overall atmosphere outside was clearly one of intense, fevered labour. The only people who seemed to be keeping their cool were the few stationary, rifle toting soldiers that we could see, as well as the three figures that stood outside the first tent; Straub, and two men who were clearly her superiors. They were wearing dress uniform, and looked older than her. The fact that they were so much taller than her as well made Straub look, at this distance, like a child. Even so, her demeanour didn't seem to change. Brigadier Straub was no fawning underling. I'd half-expected to see the Home Secretary or even the Prime Minister here, but I suppose you didn't introduce the top man into what could well be a highly dangerous situation, in the same way that the president and the vice-president never travel on the same plane.

I sat up and rubbed my face, suddenly feeling very tired. The long walk the day before, the drunken night's sleep, the long ride, the run through Sheffield, the drive over here, the intense stress put on my body by the crazy psychic feedback or whatever the hell it was … it had all added up. And now that the latter sensation had dulled—which had been like turbocharged caffeine hooked up to a power station—I felt like I'd just been rudely woken up, only to realise that I needed a whole extra night's sleep. I had to be careful. The last thing in the world that I wanted when the Stone Man arrived was for me to be anything other than one hundred percent. I had to be switched on and focused. *Eyes on the prize*, I told myself. *You miss a thing and Hugh Hefner is inviting some other hack up to the Playboy mansion.* I smirked at myself, but even so, the sky really was the limit, providing I didn't do something to screw it up.

I slapped my cheeks lightly, and stood up, taking a deep breath and cracking my knuckles as I wandered over to the window again. It was nearly time, I knew. I realised that the activity outside had come to a standstill, and as I saw what they were doing I knew that it was confirmation of the very real feeling in my bones; I understood that there was only about ten minutes left.

There was still noise outside from the helicopters and buzzing radio chatter, and now and then someone in civilian dress would scurry from one tent to the other, or hold up some sort of sensory device in the middle of the road. But the two lines of soldiers were another thing altogether; my first thought was of the Arch of Swords at a wedding, when the bride and groom leave the church flanked on either side by the groom's comrades. There were no swords here though, and even if there had been, the distance between each soldier and the man facing him was easily twelve feet. Plus, they weren't shoulder to shoulder with the man next to them either; there was about five feet in between each man in their respective lines. Either way, they had formed a channel to flank the Stone Man from the house over the road (which presumably would be no longer standing in ten minutes' time) right up to the end of the driveway. It was clearly an adaptation of the walking circle they had employed previously to surround the Stone Man for whatever reason. Even if I didn't already know it—if I didn't already feel it so much that I could almost *see* it, half-picturing it the same way that I could almost see Patrick through the wall of his house—it was clear that the lines of soldiers in front of me marked the Stone Man's path.

The tent nearest the house, a few feet back from the end of the driveway, now had some sort of Plexiglas covering across the front of it. I couldn't see Straub and the two men in dress uniform anymore, so I put two and two together. The perks of leadership, or simply looking after vital personnel? I didn't know, and doubted that covering was anything other than a precaution against radiation or whatever, but either way I hoped to be inside that tent when the Stone Man got here. I thought I would be.

The toilet flushed upstairs, and after a pause I heard the feet descending again. Right on cue, the radio of the guard still in the room crackled. I found out his name as he answered:

"Taylor."

As ever, I couldn't understand the noise that came back, not at a distance at least, but this time I did pick up one word that, to my surprise, chilled me rather than thrilled me.

"... *approaching.*"

Corporal Taylor looked at me and, expressionless, jerked his head towards the door. My presence was clearly requested elsewhere. Taylor opened the door, and led me into the hallway, where Paul and his guard had reached the bottom of the stairs.

"Had the call, have we?" Paul asked. Not directed at me; at Taylor.

"This way, sirs," said Taylor, gesturing with his hand towards the door, wanting Paul and I to walk in front of him. We did so, and Paul put his hands on top of his head as he walked, fingers laced together and resting on the back of his skull like a man being marched out to face the firing squad.

"Knock it on the head will you Paul," I muttered, quietly. "We want to keep these people sweet." I instantly regretted the words as soon as they'd left my mouth. I knew what would come back the other way. I was surprised when it didn't.

"That'd be a good cue for me to say 'I bet you do' or something catty like that, wouldn't it?" he muttered back, unsmiling. I didn't have a response, as Paul opened the door and stepped outside. The light had really dropped now, the sky just beginning to turn a beautiful orangey pink. From far away, we heard a distant, booming crash. The Stone Man was approaching, all right. One of the guards moved in front of us to lead. To reach the tent we had to move through the line of soldiers, but the gaps among the men were more than wide enough for us to pass through easily.

"Don't worry about it," muttered Paul, still looking straight ahead, and I felt a burden heavier than I realised slip from my shoulders. I was surprised that his opinion had bothered me so much. "I won't say I'm not disappointed, but I also won't say that you weren't right to play things close to your chest. You don't know me from Adam. Although, it does make me feel like a bit of a dick when I think about me going on in the car. You know, about saving the day and all that. You must have thought I sounded like a bloody kid."

"No, no, I didn't think that at all—" I began to protest, but at that moment we'd passed around the back of the tent and in through a rear entrance. I hadn't expected it, but I supposed it made sense to go in from the back if your

136

bomb shield or whatever was across the front. Before we were more than a few steps inside, we were searched. Paul protested, but caught my eye and stopped; he knew I was right. We *wanted* to be in here, after all, so we had to play it their way. They already had my bag and laptop. I wasn't too bothered about losing those; I had backups of my contacts, and there was nothing too personal or vital on the laptop.

Inside were several computer stations, and one that looked like some kind of satellite or radar display. The noise didn't lessen any once we were inside, either. The tent was filled with the constant chatter of personnel (mainly civilian-dress types) along with the many large industrial fans that were placed here and there to keep the computer equipment cool and working at maximum efficiency, as well as various computer alerts, update notifications and sat-phone calls ringing and pinging away. Despite the noise being so chaotic, the hurried activity going on within the tent was anything but; everyone seemed to be going about their business at pace, but with ruthless efficiency. It was impressive, to say the least.

I spotted Straub over at one long console, standing behind a seated row of three civilian-dress types. Next to her, as before, were her two superiors. We were led over to them, our guards saluting her and the other two men in dress uniform as they turned.

"Here they are," she said to the other officers, who simply nodded silently in response. Straub then addressed us. "It's almost time, gentlemen. You must be excited; particularly you, Mr Pointer," she said, without smiling. I considered the question; in a way, I still was, but now that I thought about it, I found myself feeling scared. Now the moment was here, the one I'd been waiting for that would give me the answers I so desperately wanted ... I suddenly found myself thinking about the word Patrick had used. *Disaster.* To dismiss it entirely would obviously be foolish, even if it was the word of a terrified, hysterical man, because we knew *nothing* about the situation here. He wouldn't be scared for no reason, would he?

"More nervous than anything, to be honest," I said. I waited for an introduction to the other two men, but none came.

"Who are these two then?" asked Paul, as if reading my mind and applying his own unique brand of subtlety. Straub held up a hand.

"Question time is over, remember, Mr Winter," she said, "we are now in the field and the operation is under way, and so you are expected to do nothing but give us your complete cooperation. I will say, however, that I hope you appreciate why we had to put you under observation for the time being. There are so many unknowns in this situation that we are going in rather blind ...

apart from, it seems, any insight that can be gleaned from you two. Therefore, we couldn't take any risks. You understand."

"Apart from the one you're taking with that man's life," said Paul, a tight little fake smile on his lips. Fortunately, a civilian-dress member of staff with a tablet computer in her hand ran over to show the device to the three people in charge. They looked at it, nodded, and then Straub dismissed the staff member with a wave of her hand.

"Please don't be self-righteous, Mr Winter," answered Straub, as calm and unfazed as ever, "I have given you room to provide an alternative solution to the problem, and unless I'm mistaken, you haven't managed to do so; if all you have to offer are criticisms on the people making the decisions, without being able to offer any better decisions yourself, then I suggest you reserve your judgement." I looked at Paul, and mentally winced as I waited for an angry response. To my surprise, he just looked away after a moment, seething. Straub simply nodded, concluding that the matter was done, and moved on.

"In any event, at its current rate of progress, Caementum should be here within ten minutes, and past the boundary of the contained zone within eight. We need you here, inside the command tent, from now on. Any changes, anything that you might notice from now on, you are to pass on to me, directly and immediately. Understood?"

I nodded, and as I looked at Paul to see his response, I realised that we were being watched by several of the civilian types. They were still working—the situation was far too pressurised to stop—but I caught several of them sneaking furtive glances over their shoulders, looking away from their workstations to get a glimpse of the two men who had a supposed link to the Stone Man. They'd heard about us, then; I wondered which of them were military personnel and which of them were drafted-in scientists. I thought then, as I do now, that they must have been dying to get their hands on us. If time had permitted, I'm sure that they would have.

When Paul didn't respond or turn around, Straub addressed him directly.

"Mr Winter? Is that understood?" Paul looked off into space, like an admonished teenager.

"Yes," he spat. To my absolute amazement, Straub stepped forward, reached up, and put a hand on his shoulder.

"Mr Winter," she said, and when Paul didn't respond, she said it again. Slowly, he turned his head around and down to look into her face. When she spoke, it was still with that same stern, no-nonsense manner, but her voice had softened.

"Please understand. It's good that you care. If we had another choice, I would take it in a heartbeat. I look at that man and think how I would feel if that was my husband, and I thank God that he isn't. I thank God mine's away on a bloody golfing stag weekend with his idiot friends. I know that's a human being, and I know it's a life. *But there isn't another choice.* People are dying, and I need to know that I can trust you to help us. Can I trust you?" She stared into his eyes, and Paul stood there dumbly, completely disarmed. He nodded briefly, quickly, looking down.

"Thank you," said Straub, and then instantly the brigadier was back, running the show. She turned to me. "Now, tell us; can you feel it now?"

We could. It was, of course, stronger than ever, and I knew that if I tried, I could jump into its head again and see which corner of suburbia was about to be reduced to rubble, destroyed as the Stone Man made its relentless way here. Even at that moment, there was another distant, heavy crash, this one slightly louder than before. The officers exchanged glances.

"Yes," I said, answering both for myself and Paul. "There's nothing different about that, though." I half-considered making something up to cement my and Paul's position on the inside, but thought better of it. I actually shuddered a little inside when I suddenly thought of the damage that I might have potentially caused by speaking without thinking first. It had been a foolish thought. We were pretty solid here, and they wanted us as observers, even if it turned out that we had nothing useful for them in the end.

"Fair enough. Take position by the partition over there," said Straub, gesturing to the clear panel across the front opening of the tent. "I'll be with you shortly, but I'll be coming and going; there's a lot to be done here. However, if you get a sense of *anything* at all, let us know immediately. It could be extremely important. In the meantime, however, I'll have to ask you to be quiet. We'll be giving C.I. Four his adrenaline in a few minutes, over in the medical tent. I don't know if that will affect things for you, but I'll give you a radio update the second that it's administered so that you can stay informed. These men will be on hand if you need anything," she said, nodding at our former guards who now seemed to be our gophers.

We walked over to the partition, the guards/gophers following, and stared out into the road. I wanted to reach out and touch the clear partition, but, after seeing some of the state-of-the-art tech inside the tent I decided against it. They hadn't told us *not* to touch it, but there was so much going on that I thought they might have forgotten to give the dumbass civilians the knowledge all the staff took for granted, i.e. the plastic thing is electrified/the plastic thing is alarmed/the plastic thing renders you sterile. It all seemed possible.

Instead, I satisfied myself with looking out into the street, as Paul stood next to me and shifted from foot to foot impatiently. By comparison to the hive of activity that was the tent, the street looked like a ghost town, albeit one with a pathway made of heavily armed soldiers in the middle of it. I could see the helicopters above us from this angle; Apache-looking things, heavily (and pointlessly) armed. One nearby, one slightly farther off, and another slightly farther than that. With a pang of regret, I wished that I still had my camera, but consoled myself by thinking it was a worthy sacrifice that helped us get to this point.

After a few minutes, the tension began to get unbearable. The distant crashes were becoming steadily louder, and now we could see that any new trails of smoke were coming from relatively close by. I realised that I would soon be seeing the Stone Man in the flesh, or stone, for only the second time. It was an odd feeling. Despite it being a day since I'd been in its presence I felt as if I hadn't *stopped* seeing it.

Straub came over to us, flanked this time not by men in dress uniform but some of the civilian staff. She quickly asked if we had any news, and then some civvies appeared out of nowhere to take both our blood info, pressures and samples. Just as quickly, they were gone, and the waiting began again. It felt like the Stone Man should already be walking over us by now; a check of the watch told me that only three minutes had passed. It was insane. Another brief moment of excitement arrived when the alert came over the radio—passed on to us by Corporal Taylor—that Patrick had been given the adrenaline. Paul and I looked anxiously through the panel, to try and see what he looked like when led outside, but he didn't appear. I looked at my watch. Roughly seven minutes, according to Straub's figures, until the Stone Man was mere feet away from me once more. Surely they should be bringing him out by now?

I caught myself; *bringing him out by now?* What the hell was he, a Christian to be thrown to the lions? *Bring out the condemned.* Patrick may have been a stranger, and insane upon introduction, but I had to remind myself of what both Paul and Straub had said. He was a human being. And to my eternal shame, even with that reminder, I couldn't help but feel deeply impatient that he wasn't being brought out already, that the bait wasn't in position.

A hard poke on my shoulder brought me out of my thoughts. I turned to see Paul staring at me, eyebrows raised. Again, the face of a young boy, caught in a moment of electricity. When he had my eye, he jabbed a finger in my direction, and then made a circle with his thumb and forefinger, raising his eyebrows again. I nodded back, and gave him a thumbs-up of my own along with a forced smile. Yes, I was okay … I then tapped my head and made a dismissive gesture with my hand. *Just thinking.*

Paul nodded, and then held up his hand at eye height for me to see, palm flat, fingers splayed. He was showing me that his hand was trembling.

Once the message had sunk in, he let out a sigh and began to lower his hand, but then stopped and slapped me on the chest. He'd spotted something. Paul pointed at the medical tent several feet away, as a group consisting of three rifle-toting soldiers and two civilian women emerged from the rear of it. The front of the tent, again, had a clear covering, the same as the one that we were inside. We couldn't quite see from where we were, but it looked very much like Patrick was in the centre of this group of people. They made their way over from the opposite side of the street until they reached the middle of the road, the soldiers leading Patrick by the shoulders while the civilian women carried bags containing some kind of technical equipment.

Patrick looked the same as before—sunken eyes wide open, twitching hands and face still in slight motion—but it looked like his verbal, Morse code barrage might have stopped slightly. His mouth was still moving rapidly, but his lips were relaxed and the up-and-down movement of his jaw was only slight. It seemed very much that although the adrenaline had made him mobile, it had also affected whatever speech skills that he had left. It didn't make any sense, but Patrick's brain had clearly been rewired in ways that I didn't understand. He stood there, swaying slightly on his feet, as the soldiers kept him gently upright. They weren't being rough, I noticed; that was good, even if he wouldn't be aware of the difference. Although we'd only seen ever him in rant mode or his current catatonic state, I watched him as he stood helpless and surrounded by strangers and I felt the first true stab of pity. For the first time—if only briefly—I wanted to be wrong, to watch the Stone Man wander straight by without incident and for Patrick to be miraculously healed. The thought didn't last long, but it is still of some small comfort to myself to know that it was at least there.

The soldier not holding Patrick's shoulders stepped back and let the civilian women step in, who promptly set about attaching small pieces of equipment to Patrick's body with straps. There were three devices in total, one on his arm, one on his chest, and one on his head. To this day I have no idea what they were for. Two crashes—the closest yet—sounded in quick succession, and with the exception of Patrick, all of the people there—even the soldiers—jumped slightly, before quickly refocusing and carrying on. The civilians added some fresh data into their tablet PCs and then headed back to the tent, escorted by the third soldier, leaving Patrick stood in front of his house with his two remaining attendants. Six minutes. Two more trails of smoke were in the sky by now, and the radio chatter inside our tent had increased considerably.

The street before us seemed to become very still. Everything was in place, it seemed, as far as the military were concerned, and the activity outside had stopped. As the seconds passed, time seemed to slow to a crawl, especially when all we could do to relieve the tension was watch the bait stand there in catatonic ignorance of whatever fate was smashing its way towards him. I wondered why the hell the soldiers forming the path to the house were even lined up like that, if Patrick wasn't inside the building anymore. A last minute precaution, perhaps, against anyone who might somehow have managed to get inside the secure zone? The thought seemed unlikely to me, but I supposed that they weren't taking any chances. Three more crashes, loud and close enough for us to hear the details of them—two of them were the sound of rubble collapsing upon itself in two, and the other was that of rending metal—sounded out across the clear summer evening. The sun was beginning its final descent now, but there was light and time enough yet for us to know that we would have a clear view of whatever was about to happen, despite the close smoke that was beginning to fill more and more of the sky. Three minutes. One of the helicopters hovering above moved slowly sideways, then stopped.

One of Patrick's attendants picked up his radio and listened to it, then returned a message of his own. At this point the distant noises seemed to be fairly constant; smaller crunches and bangs, with only the larger, booming sounds—buildings collapsing, presumably—standing out in the silence. The soldiers in the line stood firm, staring straight ahead, but the soldiers with Patrick—who had been given more free rein, I assumed—looked in the distance of the sounds. There was the loudest bang yet, loud enough for me to wince (I've always been protective of my hearing) and Patrick's attendants exchanged words, shifting on their feet. I wondered if that movement was from nerves. I'd have been nervous if I were in their shoes, although terrified would have been more appropriate. The only thing in the same league as being the bait was being the guy *holding* the bait. I looked around for Straub, and saw her standing farther back in the tent, overseeing the largest workstation with her two superiors and giving out orders. She looked very tense, nervous herself even; she stood bent at the waist, getting a closer look at the monitors with one hand on the back of the chair in front of her, but still seeming utterly in control. She was a professional. There was another deafening bang, and then we were inside two minutes.

"This is it," whispered a voice in my ear, and I jumped slightly. Paul was looking at me, wide eyed; those child eyes were back, but this time they weren't excited. They were scared, but not for Paul Winter's well-being. My

own heart was racing beyond measure now as well, almost like it had during the crazy, lightning adrenaline that we'd been subjected to before Patrick's collapse and subsequent removal. I could do nothing but nod at Paul, and show him my own shaking hand. There was another explosive crash, and suddenly I was blinded by dust.

It was strange, because the dust was everywhere and yet it didn't seem to be getting into my eyes. It cleared as I moved through it, and then I was out, and could see another house in front of me, getting closer. I wasn't slowing down either, and it became clear I was going to hit it. Now these few seconds had passed, I'd had time to come to my senses and realise that something had happened, that I wasn't in the command tent at all somehow, but back on the streets we'd driven through earlier today. As I crossed the street, still aiming at the house ahead, close enough now to be inside its shadow, I realised that I was back inside the Stone Man, looking out, and even through the shock of that revelation I heard a familiar sound. No, not a familiar sound; a familiar *rhythm*. A low level, pulsing staccato rhythm, like Morse code being played on a down-tuned bass guitar. As I smashed through the fence around the back garden, in my panic I wildly wondered how I hadn't heard that when I'd been inside the Stone Man before, and why I could hear it now, but already I was abandoning that thought in my desperation to get out, to get back in my own, and with that I was suddenly looking through a plastic screen once more.

I just had time to get over my second, disoriented shock inside thirty seconds, and to gulp some air frantically into my lungs as I opened my mouth to say *It's here, it's coming through now* but suddenly there was no need. With a crash of shocking volume and a huge final burst of smoke, the Stone Man smashed its way through the house at the bottom of the street, and began its final unstoppable journey towards us.

***

In my previous career—that of a nobody reporter—I'd taken a lot of eyewitness accounts, covering everything from minor public brawls to full-on explosions (the best being at a chemical factory in Dudley). The most common phrase, the one that I heard time and again was *It all happened so fast*, even when the actual incident in question wasn't that fast at all.

I never really understood what they meant until it was all over that day; standing as I was in the dark sunset of a summer evening in Yorkshire and wondering what the hell had just happened. I knew even then that it hadn't actually happened very fast at all; the Stone Man had come up the road at its own steady walking pace, and everything *else* had happened reasonably slowly. But when I think about the actual key events, they seem to play out in my mind in such a chaotic, haphazard manner that they feel like they must have been over in seconds. I asked Paul about it later, and he said he remembered them the same way.

In reality, it had probably taken around two to three minutes, and all the actual chaos, the confusion and the shouting, came afterwards as the military tried to save the day, to do anything to respond. But they were far too late.

I haven't talked about any of this—I certainly haven't described it in detail—since the day it happened. This will be extremely difficult, and believe me, if I hadn't worked my way through half of this fucking mini bar I wouldn't be talking about it now. But I said I would. I have to finish the job. I have to finish the job.

Some nights I still see that street. I can see it through the plastic shield. And while in some dreams you're powerless to stop things from happening, this isn't a dream. It's a memory, and I'm no more capable of doing anything about it today than I was then.

***

Even at such a great distance—farther than the length of a football pitch—it was incredible to see. Somehow, you still got an impression of its weight; whether that was from the cracks that appeared in the concrete under its feet, or from the heft of its body as it moved, I couldn't say, but to see that *density*, to know it was heavy stone that weighed so much and yet it was somehow bending and folding and travelling like it was made of rubber ... it was simply incredible to watch. All over again, I was awestruck, and Paul even more so; I heard him gasp for breath, and I realised that this was the first time Paul had seen the Stone Man anywhere except on the TV.

"Fucking *hell*," he breathed, his face pale and his mouth open.

As the Stone Man continued on its slow, inexorable way up the street, we could see it leaving a steady stream of dust behind itself, powder and debris that blew off its shoulders, leftovers of the house that it had just destroyed. I saw this and had a fresh revelation; despite muddy fields, the oil of destroyed cars, the rubble and plaster of demolished buildings and even the white hot fragments of exploded metal from items of various military ordnance, nothing seemed to have permanently stuck to the Stone Man. How the hell did any of that *not* stick to stone?

It would have been so easy to say its movements were robotic, when attributed to a humanoid shape with no facial features, but the fact was the Stone Man was far too smooth in its gait to be described in such a manner. It moved *fluidly*, yet it was solid and ponderous at the same time. Everything about it, from its size to its movement, said *relentless*. Unstoppable. It was awe-inspiring, and terrifying at the same time.

I snapped out of my open-mouthed trance, and tried to figure out if it was heading directly for Patrick. The Stone Man was not, of course, following the line of the street. It had come through the house at a slight angle to us, and I felt a lightning flash of excitement as it became obvious where it was aiming. It was still heading for Patrick's house, and not Patrick himself. Paul tapped me on the shoulder, and pointed frantically at the house. I nodded equally frantically, letting him know that I'd seen it. Shortly, I knew, we were going to get some answers. It was electrifying.

I suddenly realised Straub and her two superiors had moved, and were now stood a few feet to our left. They were of course watching the scene as well, with Straub listening to information from her radio, and occasionally calling over her shoulder to someone at one of the nearer consoles, asking for reports on temperature, distance, rad count, and the like. I don't know what they were hoping to find. She turned to Paul and me.

"This is it," she said, and even the unshakeable woman looked nervous now, or as nervous as I thought Straub let herself get when in uniform. Her voice was slightly breathless. "You two have been pretty quiet, but if you ever had a time to shine, it's now. Anything to report?"

Paul and I exchanged a glance, but it was Paul who spoke first.

"Nothing here," he said, shaking his head, still wide-eyed. "The pull hasn't even changed, and I half-expected that it would."

"The what?" said Straub, looking irritated for some reason.

"The pull, you know, the ... feeling, the thing that drew us here," answered Paul. Straub nodded, and turned to me.

"You?"

"I don't know," I said, not taking my eyes off the Stone Man. "Just now ... I was in it as it came through that house. I didn't even try to see where it was this time, I was just suddenly *in* there. I don't know if it's because now the thing's this close, and the shock of the noise startled me—"

"What?" interrupted Paul, but Straub flapped a hand at him and he shut up.

"Why didn't you say anything?" she snapped, looking furious now.

"It literally *just happened!*" I protested, "I mean, about thirty seconds ago, and then it was coming towards—"

"Right, right, shut up," she said, speaking rapidly. Her two superiors looked at me sternly as she spoke. "Did you get anything *new* from it?"

"Well … well no," I said, exasperated, turning to her but looking quickly over my shoulder through the plastic screen. The Stone Man had halved the distance between us by now, and seemed frighteningly large and solid; even the cracks in the floor beneath its feet had, to my eyes, taken on a more ominous appearance. Someone called out a distance from one of the workstations, and Straub quickly spoke into her radio, telling two men to stand by. I didn't get their names, but I could see it was the two soldiers stood with Patrick by the way that they both responded into their radios, and then looked again towards the Stone Man. According to the workstation people, it was 150 metres away from Patrick, but it was still heading towards the house. All signs so far suggested that it was going to totally pass him by. Then Straub was talking to me again.

"Anything at all? Anything *different?*" she urged, now quickly looking between me and the approaching Stone Man. The clear tension in her body seemed to make mine worse, as anything that made someone like Straub go into action mode meant it was time for someone like me to start running for the hills. But it wasn't me that had to be frightened. It was the poor abandoned bastard out there.

Regardless, I forced my racing mind under control and tried to think, which wasn't easy with three high-ranking members of the military standing in front of me, demanding answers, while an impossible stone juggernaut headed up the street. *Anything different?* Actually … there had been, hadn't there? That sound. That rhythm that had been quietly been playing. Was that even relevant? What the hell would that tell them? My thoughts were interrupted by a feeling that was beginning beneath my feet, one that Paul felt as well as he grabbed my shoulder in surprise. The big man's grip was painfully tight, and I realised that he was as electrified as I was.

My brain broke my shock by reminding me where I'd felt this in my feet before. Millennium Place. It was the vibrations in the floor caused by the Stone Man's feet striking the concrete. The call came out across the tent again.

"One hundred ten feet and closing."

"Well, this … well it might be nothing," I said, babbling slightly, "but there was like a, like a … quiet rhythm in there. It was very small, but it was there." Straub held up her hand, snapping her fingers over and over frantically and impatiently. A balding man in a shirt and tie tore himself reluctantly away from his station and hustled over, a younger woman in a lab coat trailing behind him. His face was flushed, either from the excitement of the situation or with annoyance at being called away in the middle of things.

"A rhythm," snapped Straub quickly, addressing this new man without taking her eyes off me, "does that match up with anything? A rhythm from Caementum." The balding man looked suddenly exasperated, looking between Straub and me, back and forth, and then at the Stone Man drawing closer and closer to the house.

"Well!" he started, and then shook his head quickly, calming himself. Even in my own shaken state, I recognized this action. This was the response of a man under intense stress who, at the worst possible moment, has been asked a question by someone who not only wants immediate answers, but wants them to a stupid question ... and the person asking is your boss. "It, it, it ... it depends entirely on the rhythm *itself*, doesn't it? I mean, technically the rad count produces a rhythm, but it's holding steady now and I'd never say it was particularly rhythmic, it's too inconsistent. Brigadier Straub, I'm extremely sorry, but unless you have something more definite this really is the worst time—"

"Tell him," said Straub, low and serious, "do it. How did it go? Do it for him. Do it now."

And then, when my brain heard the question, a funny thing happened.

Straub's request produced several simultaneous questions of my own in my head, each one answering itself and leading onto another question.

Everything clicked.

I knew, right then, what the Stone Man was here for.

How could I reproduce the rhythm? I don't know how it went.

So how did the rhythm go? It was familiar, I know that.

Wasn't it too fast for you to reproduce anyway? You couldn't do that.

I felt something roll over in my stomach, and I whirled away from Straub and the others to look out through the plastic screen. She was shouting something at me, but in my horror she became totally irrelevant.

But you've heard it reproduced before, haven't you? What is it?

I saw the Stone Man draw near the start of the line of soldiers, and then, for the first time in two days, it stopped walking. My mouth was dry, and when I tried to speak, nothing would come out.

It was a constant, rapid beat, wasn't it?

BAMBAMBAMBAMBAMBAMBAMBAM

The Stone Man raised its head, straightened, and then began to turn on the spot.

GCCAATTGAATTTGGCCCGTTAACTCGCCAATAATCCCGTTAACTCAGGCATG

Something terrible clicked, and I finally realised that the three letters that had been there all along, ever since the guy in the green vest had said them, telling me what the Stone Man wanted. I desperately wished I didn't know; what could I do anyway? It had to happen. It had to end.

Not Morse *code.*

Its turn complete, the Stone Man paused again momentarily, and then began walking towards Patrick.

I found my voice.

"It's *genetic* code," I whispered, unable to tear my eyes away from the scene about to occur in front of me.

"It's what?" whispered Paul, not hearing me, lost in the scene before him. My mouth dry, I looked at Straub as she stared intensely ahead, in control, giving orders into her radio. I realised that she had expected this all along. She had to have. The scientific minds at her disposal would have made the connection nearly instantly, unlike myself, who merely thought of a chain of Gs, Cs, As and Ts, and felt like it was a vaguely familiar reminder of something that I should know, and then dismissed it. The scientists surely worked with that stuff every day. I was just someone who'd seen genetic code a few times, in science fiction films and on the news. How could I have been expected to know?

"*You knew,*" I whispered, wide eyes on Straub and feeling the heavy fall of the Stone Man's feet vibrate through the concrete as it advanced upon Patrick. Straub's eyes darted to mine briefly, but even though she didn't stop talking into her handset, it was enough to tell me that my suspicions were correct.

"It's going for him," said Paul, grabbing at my sleeve as his eyes remained glued to the street. "It's not going to stop, it's going for *him!*" With that, he actually started to hop lightly from one foot to the other, helpless in his panic and fear for the helpless, unaware man standing in the road. It was such an effeminate action for a man of Paul's size that it would have been funny in any other situation, but it wasn't that day because I knew that he was right; the Stone Man wasn't going to stop, looming larger and larger before us and bearing down on Patrick as if to crush him. It was *here* for Patrick.

The soldiers holding Patrick clearly realised it as well, speaking frantically over the airwaves and stepping back, still holding on to Patrick's arms.

"Hold your position until further instruction," replied Straub, firm and intense, but I noticed the two soldiers exchange a glance, suggesting that doing otherwise might be an option. Who could blame them? There was an unstoppable, unthinkable stone monster bearing down upon them, come to claim the man they were holding, and its pounding, inexorable footfalls now sounded like a judgement.

The soldier said something again, more frantic now, and Straub repeated the command. On the Stone Man came, crunching pavement as it did so, and I could see both of the soldiers arguing with each other over Patrick's head.

"Hold your position!" yelled Straub, and for one of the men, those words broke the spell; her words had the opposite effect. He let go of Patrick's shoulder and began to back slowly away, holding his assault rifle across his chest. The other man screamed at him, then looked at the advancing Stone Man—now only a few feet from its goal—and seemed to visibly shrink slightly. He hesitated, and then also let go of Patrick, pointlessly aiming his rifle at the Stone Man's head as he backed away.

Incredibly, Patrick stayed upright, swaying gently on the spot. I realised that his mouth had stopped moving completely, his jaw now hanging limply open. His eyes still stared blankly ahead, seeming to look straight through the enormous stone figure that would have filled his vision, for it was now upon him.

And yet it wasn't. The Stone Man passed straight by Patrick's right shoulder, causing Paul to temporarily loosen his grip on my shirt.

"It's left him, it's left him, look, it's left him, it's left him!" he cried breathlessly, freezing halfway through his foot-to-foot motion. And indeed it had, already several feet behind Patrick and seeming to head towards the retreating soldiers. There was an enormous bang, followed by a shattering sound, and it took a second for me to realise that the second soldier, the one aiming his rifle, had pulled the trigger, the shot ricocheting off the Stone Man's head and passing through the window of a nearby parked car. The Stone Man, of course, didn't respond, and instead suddenly began to turn, bringing itself in line with Patrick's back. Paul's hand clamped down on my arm once more, and he reassumed his frantic dance.

"Look, look! Why aren't they doing anything? Why aren't they *doing* anything?" said Paul, babbling to himself. He already knew why, of course, but knowing it and seeing it were two different things. Patrick was the sacrifice. There wasn't any other choice. They had to do it. If the decision had been mine, I would have made the same one. Even Paul would, I think.

"They don't want to stop it," I whispered, shaking my head. "They knew it wanted him, and they want it to take him. They need it to happen so it can end." My breathing was fast and shallow now, horrified yet—to my disgust—excited. Of course it was exciting. Don't judge me for that. All the other stuff, fine, but don't judge me for being excited. You would be exactly the same. I was there. Even if you don't think you would be, you would be. I know.

The Stone Man walked up right behind Patrick … and stopped. As Paul and

I held our breath, I realised that the tent around us was almost silent. Everyone, from the science teams to the radar operators to the medical staff to the commanding officers, knew that this was the moment of wait-and-see. And don't think there was anyone there that wasn't excited, either. I could feel it, the air hot and heavy with breathless anticipation. The pause continued, almost for a full minute. No one spoke. All you could hear was the movement of air, from hushed human breathing to the mechanically pushed kind coming from the workstation CPU fans. The silence then broke as a cry went up from one of the workstations.

"*Temperature drop!*" they yelled, meaningless to Paul but not to me. I'd felt a severe drop in temperature around the Stone Man before; it had been just before the Stone Man started walking for the first time.

"Unit one, stand by," said Straub into her radio, referring presumably to the line of soldiers by the house. I could no longer see Patrick's guards, who had retreated out of my sight line. I never found out what happened to them. I'd like to think that they were treated leniently. How could they be trained for that? As I was straining to see their retreat, the cold hit us suddenly, washing into the tent and making nearly everyone gasp either in surprise at the incredible change or as a physical response to the sharp drop in temperature. This time, it was even colder than it had been in Millennium Place; it was like walking out of the sun into a meat cellar. Something new was about to happen. Patrick, meanwhile, was still oblivious to everything, but still miraculously upright.

The Stone Man lowered its arms to its sides and stood still. Its head then lowered slightly, as if it was inspecting Patrick's neck, but even when lowered its head was still clearly visible high above the top of Patrick's. This was due to a combination of the Stone Man's imposing height, and Patrick's short stature. Patrick looked like a child, dwarfed by his abuser. It lent the whole scene even more of an air of impending doom; the giant, literally stone-faced hunter, poised behind its helpless and vulnerable prey. The air around us continued to drop, and yet I didn't think that the goose bumps breaking out on my skin were entirely due to the temperature.

Then even the deafening rattle of the low-flying choppers was drowned out by the most awful, cacophonous drone. It was so loud that it hurt, and everyone around me, even Straub, clapped their hands to their ears. I could see the mouths of the people inside the tent open wide in pain, their eyes screwed tight as they attempted fruitlessly to shut out the noise. It was like the sound of a rusty iron gate being wrenched open, but at a much lower pitch; it was like the roar of a tiger with a torn throat, turned all the way up to eleven. And it continued, getting louder.

Yet still I watched through squinting eyes, having to see, yet not wanting to at the same time. Of course, the sound was coming from the Stone Man, but then we began to see why. It was changing. Its chest was slowly beginning to protrude, but not all of it. In fact, as I watched, I realised that it was just two small sections in the centre line of its chest, side by side, and they were perfectly straight, symmetrical sections at that. The farther they extended, the louder the sound became. It was almost unbearable, yet the shapes extending out of the Stone Man's chest continued to grow. They were rectangular, upright like monoliths, about five inches wide and at a combined length that covered the distance between roughly where the Stone Man's collarbone would be and the top of its 'stomach'. Their front surfaces were perfectly flat. As these strange segments of the Stone Man's chest continued outwards—exactly matching the rest of it in colour and texture, free of any join lines and so seamless as they appeared that you could believe that they had always been there—they merged together, meeting into middle of its chest and forming one wider rectangle, free now of any line to suggest that they had ever been anything but one piece. Those of us who were still able to watch could see that the top of this new rectangle was at the same height as the base of Patrick's skull, and covered an area that followed all the way down to in between his shoulder blades.

I could see Straub yelling something pointlessly into her radio, the words drowned out by the roar of the Stone Man as the extension touched the back of Patrick's neck. I expected his head to be slowly forced forward, but after a few seconds, I realised that it wasn't, even though it was clear—from the continuing movement of the texture that covered the Stone Man's surface—that the chest piece was still moving forward. How was that happening? The answer soon became clear.

To my horror, I realised that this extending part of the Stone Man's chest was burrowing into Patrick's neck and upper back. As it did, Patrick's now-lazy verballsation of his genetic makeup instantly stopped. His eyes flew open, his body jerked upright as if electrocuted, and Patrick began to scream.

To this day, I desperately, desperately hope that it was a reflex action, some kind of automatic defence mechanism perhaps, and that he remained as consciously unaware as he'd appeared to have been all along. I don't want him to have known what was happening. But I still hear those screams sometimes; at night, when I lie alone in the dark, and I find it hard to convince myself that Patrick didn't somehow come back to himself in his final moments, snapped out of his catatonia by unbearable pain. We could only just hear his cries through the deafening wall of sound from the Stone Man. Somehow, they managed to pierce through the noise and into my soul. The screams were high pitched and desperate, like those of a broken dog.

Patrick's arms were held stiffly his sides, his fists bunched up so hard that the veins stood out in his forearms, and the whites of his eyes were shot through with red as they bulged in their sockets. There was no blood— somehow—from the point where the Stone Man's chest piece dug into his neck, and then suddenly it all seemed to stop apart from the deafening noise. The scene was frozen before us: Patrick's neck and back impaled on the Stone Man's chest, his body taut and screaming. The Stone Man standing still, impassive, unmoved. For a moment all movement ceased, except for the silently shouting mouths of various people inside the tent, with Straub's superiors yelling right into her ear in a frenzied attempt to be heard, all of them noiseless under the audio barrage from outside. Numb with shock, I turned to see Paul pulling on his hair, screaming noiselessly at the plastic screen and hopping around helplessly on the spot. A thin plume of black smoke emerged from either side of the point where the Stone Man met Patrick's neck, and then the chest piece began to withdraw. As it did, Patrick's screams begin to choke off, and his eyelids fluttered spastically. They then closed, but he remained upright.

After a second or two, the chest piece pulled completely clear, and revealed a perfectly cauterised rectangular hole where the upper portion of Patrick's spine used to be. The hole was charred, the solidified blood lining its walls burned black, but otherwise clean. The front surface of the Stone Man's chest piece was still flat, the segment of Patrick presumably locked away within somehow. As it retracted, it split into two once more, and the roar that filled the air began to lessen until the chest piece was entirely within the Stone Man again. The surface of the Stone Man's chest was then free of any sign that anything had ever come out of it.

The second the roar died, Straub's voice could be heard, telling her units to stand by, stand by, but I wasn't paying attention. The ringing that was now in my ears was deafening, but I wasn't concerned about that in the least; I was watching Patrick, who still to my utter amazement stood upright, though his face was now slack and lifeless.

The Stone Man was immobile also, but the temperature was still close to freezing. If anything, it seemed to be getting worse, and even in all the chaos I could feel my fingertips starting to go numb. Somebody behind me shouted something about a rad spike, along with a number, and I noticed Paul crying beside me, shaking his head with his fists still tightened into his hair. For my part, I don't remember thinking anything at that point. My brain had shut down. This was all too much, too much, and the fresh explosion of activity inside the tent now felt like needles in my back. Even so, I couldn't take my eyes off that hole in Patrick's body.

There was a very sharp, stinging sensation, like the flick of a wet towel but happening simultaneously all over my skin (I would later find out that it was due to a milliseconds-long temperature drop of another fifteen degrees) and then the Stone Man vanished before our eyes without a sound. People all around me immediately started shouting. I didn't notice that it was no longer cold.

Patrick's head flopped forwards onto his chest, still attached by the now-loose flesh of his neck, and then his body flopped onto the floor like a sack of meat. A medical team rushed to attend him, and I turned away and began to vomit helplessly.

***

Chapter Six: Straub Spins a Yarn and Dangles a Carrot, Paul and Andy Say Good-bye, and There's an Unpleasant Surprise For Everyone

***

While all the resulting shouting and rushing chaos was going on, Paul and I had stood dumbly for ten minutes, not knowing what to do with ourselves, until we were suddenly and briskly escorted out of the tent and back inside the house. We sat like scolded children, stunned and trembling, until one of the soldiers' radios had buzzed and we'd then been led into the back of a waiting truck. Straub and her superiors had disappeared into the back of the tent almost immediately after Patrick's death and the Stone Man's subsequent vanishing, presumably to take charge of proceedings, and we hadn't seen her give the order for us to be moved. We didn't protest, regardless; I was still numb with shock, and Paul allowed himself to be marched along without a sound, eyes still red and head bowed low. He was almost unrecognisable.

We were driven for quite some time, maybe an hour, but we couldn't tell where to as the back of the truck was covered with tarp. It was hot in there, even though the sky was now completely darkened over, and the heat combined with the presence of the two soldiers riding with us lent the whole experience an air of heavy oppression. Perhaps if I'd been more aware at the time, I'd have properly registered the expressions on the faces of the soldiers. These were battle-hardened men, trained men, but looking back I can see how they looked just as rattled as we did.

We arrived at our destination. It was a large, nondescript building, the outside lit by a single floodlight, with nothing visible in the darkened surroundings to suggest which part of the country we were in. We appeared to have pulled up at the back entrance. To this day, I don't know where it was. I assume it was part of some military base, perhaps even a simple barracks. It certainly wasn't a high tech MI5 affair, as you might expect; once inside, the place was functional and sparse, and looked like it had been built sometime in the sixties. The long, high-ceilinged hallway that we were led into was dark, apart from a few dim sources of light up ahead that streamed out of what looked like small office windows. Some people were clearly working late, as I could hear a printer or photocopier buzzing away in the distance.

We were led into a small room—not quite what you would call a cell, as it was more pleasantly furnished than that word would suggest—lined with faded carpet, and with walls covered in sky-blue paint. There were two cheap three-seater sofas facing each other, and Paul and I sat on one each without being instructed to do so. As the two soldiers filed out, Paul suddenly lifted his head.

"My wife," he said, quietly, "she'll wonder where I am. She'll worry."

The last soldier to leave hesitated in the doorway, and looked at Paul.

"Someone will be with you shortly," the soldier said, and then left, closing the door behind him. Paul didn't argue, and instead lay down on his back. I did the same on my settee. Despite the events of the last hour, we were both so damn *tired*. We were physically exhausted.

We lay there in silence for at least forty-five minutes, listening to occasional footsteps outside and distant mechanical noises, and after a while I thought that Paul had actually gone to sleep. I looked over; his eyes were in fact open. They looked haunted.

"You okay?" I asked, without thinking. I surprised myself. I was concerned. Paul let out a slow, steady stream of air from his nose in response, then he spoke.

"God knows," he said, his voice cracked and dry. I wondered when he'd last had a drink of water, and then suddenly felt thirsty myself. I looked around. No sink. Paul fell silent again for a moment, and then looked at me.

"He didn't have anything to do with any of this, Andy," he said, his voice small and quiet. "He was just a normal guy. And they let it happen. They drugged him and led him out there like a sheep to be slaughtered. Sure, they didn't *know* he would be, not for certain, they only *thought* he would be ... but they would have done it regardless. It could have been you, or me. And I don't think anyone's going to get to know about it, either. They won't tell anyone about this."

I knew what he meant, but at the same time the thought came again: *What else could they have done? What other option was there?* I didn't voice it though. I knew, despite his disgust, that Paul didn't ultimately disagree. He just couldn't get his head around it. Instead, as always, I turned to more practical matters.

"He was chosen, Paul. I don't think it would have made any difference either way. I think it was pretty much inevitable. For some reason, it wanted his DNA or whatever ... or a piece of someone with those genes."

"So why not a finger? Or some hair? Or some fucking, some fucking *spit* or something?"

"I don't know. Who knows what they want it for. I'm not sure we'll ever get to know. It's gone."

I was wrong, as it turned out. We *would* get to know, and we would wish that we didn't.

Paul suddenly stiffened, his face twisting for a moment, and then stared at me, hard.

"Did you see it? I mean, at the end. Did you see through its eyes when ..." he gestured backwards with his head. I shook mine.

"No. I did just before, when it came up the street, but not at the very end, no."

"What ... what do you think that's all about then?" Paul asked quietly, looking slightly scared. He'd transformed, at least temporarily, back into the child again, scared and confused. I didn't think the usual, confident Paul was a front though; I thought he was simply both people, just as we all are never one person alone. Different sides of us, brought out by different situations, and we can never truly know who we will be from one day to the next. You can be one of them *more* than you are any of the others, and decide that is *you* ... but when you are caught unawares, the dice of your personality is rolled and the outcome is not given by any means.

"Well," I said, feeling more tired than ever and shifting on the sofa. I felt strangely comfortable talking about these things now, a distance between myself and earlier events beginning to form in my head. Whether it was an effect of being elsewhere, or the pull finally stopping, or even shock, I was starting to feel numb to it. "It's like I said earlier ... and I think what we've just seen confirms it. Think about it. You build the Stone Man in such a way that you can see through its 'eyes'. It's unstoppable. So you set it off, and it has one purpose: to collect ... you know ... and bring it back. Okay? And if that's what it's designed for, then it makes even more sense to have a built-in remote camera, doesn't it? As how else would you know when the job was done? How else would you know when to call it home?"

Paul nodded slowly, not taking his eyes from mine.

"And therefore you'd need to broadcast from the Stone Man to wherever you are," I continued, "just as it would need to remotely detect Patrick. And just like you and I picked up on the latter, I think I could also pick up on the former."

"Why not me as well, though?"

"Well, I had the signal clearer than you from the start. You could only pick up on me until we actually met, and touched. It'd make sense that I could pick up other things that you couldn't." Paul nodded again in response, and then lay back on his sofa.

"So ..." he said, contemplating the ceiling, "the question is ..."

"Who sent it?" I said, finishing the sentence for him. "I know. And based on everything we've seen, I reckon your idea probably isn't too far off." He looked at me again, intrigued.

"What, you think …" and just as he had done when sat in the pub, he pointed his finger upwards without a sound.

"I reckon so," I said. "Let's be honest, it's certainly a lot more credible once you consider everything it's done, all those things that are way beyond our understanding. Hell, throw teleportation into the mix and it's suddenly pretty much the *only* option." Paul was silent for a moment.

"Jeeeesus," he finally said, quiet and awed, but in a way that suggested the other Paul was coming back, the usual Paul, perhaps returning because he was needed to get through the situation. I became numb, Paul became more alive; that was the difference between us. "What the hell do you do about that, eh?"

"Right now, I think they're more worried about keeping it quiet," I said, "and will probably worry about the rest later."

"Which means we might be in trouble," said Paul, arching an eyebrow. "Especially with you being press."

"I don't think so, for two reasons," I said, propping myself up on one elbow. "One, this isn't *The X Files*, and I don't think any of those squaddies out there today were exactly black ops guys or the like. Look at Private Pike; I think they're confident that standard military disclosure agreements will keep a lid on it, so I doubt we're getting taken out the back or anything. But two, and this is the big safety net for us … they have no reason to believe that they've seen the last of the Stone Man."

"You think it'll come back?" asked Paul, bleaching slightly.

"I've no reason to believe it *won't*. And someone had enough of a reason to send it in the first place; who says they only needed to do it once? These guys need us, Paul, as long as they think the Stone Man might come back. They'll want to make sure we're keeping quiet, sure, but they need us. We're fine. Don't worry." I expected a response, but Paul didn't speak for a while. Surprisingly, he started gently shaking his head.

"What?" I asked, slightly annoyed. He turned to me.

"They needed Patrick, too," he said, quietly. "Look how he ended up."

I didn't have a response, but with perfect timing, the door opened and one of the two soldiers came back in.

"This way, please," he said, pulling his rifle against his chest to open up the doorway for us to pass through. Paul and I exchanged a glance, and then did as we were told. We were led further down the previous hallway, passing the small, fogged-out windows on the way and hearing the sounds that for all the world could have been coming from any office in the country. We were taken through the double doors at the end of the corridor, which led us into a second, much shorter hallway with only three doors in it; two on either side, and a more grandiose-looking one in the centre, with an additional guard already stationed in front of it. It was fairly clear where we were headed.

After knocking, and hearing a muffled response from within, one of our guards opened the door and led us through. We were now in the more pleasant, but no less intimidating surroundings of what appeared to be an office. Adorning the walls were several maps, and although the flooring was more luxurious (sporting what looked like an almost-new, thick blue carpet) and the several pot plants had been dotted around the room in an attempt to give it a more homely feel, the walls were still covered in the same faded paint that we'd seen in the main corridor, and the strip lighting above cast a harsh glare onto everything. A very large oak desk sat in the centre of the floor, upon which we could see several framed certificates and a few field photos of Brigadier Straub. The latter was unsurprising, as Straub herself was seated behind the desk, waiting for us. She didn't stand as we entered.

"Good evening, gentlemen, sorry for keeping you waiting," she said, gesturing to the two empty seats that were already placed in front of her desk. She turned to our guards. "Wait outside, please. You'll be called if necessary." They saluted and left, passing another, previously unseen man who was coming the other way. This guy was perhaps only a year or two older than myself, and dressed in civilian clothing: shirt and tie, black trousers and shoes, and the now-familiar laminated ID on a lanyard around his neck. His hair was slicked back, and that, combined with his old-fashioned glasses, made him appear more senior than he really was. The bags under his eyes looked dark, and his face was slightly red. This was clearly a man who had not slept properly for several days, and his breathing was slightly laboured. In his hand was a tablet PC.

"Doctor, grab a chair from over there please and join us," said Straub, picking up and glancing at a piece of paper in front of her before turning back to us. The man she'd addressed as Doctor dragged over a metal office chair and placed it next to us on our side of the desk, sitting down without looking at either Paul or myself.

"This is Dr Boldfield, head of the civilian team dealing with the Caementum investigations, and also our top scientific adviser," said Straub, nodding at the Doctor, who now looked at us and passed the nod on. We nodded back.

"He'll be needing to interview you both thoroughly," Straub continued, "and I expect you both to give your full cooperation. You will also be required to undergo some reasonably detailed examination and physical testing, although I can assure you that it will be nothing painful or damaging in any way. I won't lie, this isn't because we're going easy on you—the situation is too important for that kind of restraint—but simply because the tests don't *need* to be painful. However, this meeting right now is to bring you up to speed on what's going to be happening in the next forty-eight hours, and how you're going to be involved."

Paul and I didn't say anything in response, and waited for her to continue. Straub sat back in her chair, and held up the piece of paper she'd been examining.

"Here's the official version of events, as prepped and approved by Her Majesty's Government's PR machine. You'll both be getting a copy of this, and you'll be expected to familiarise yourself with it thoroughly. Obviously, it goes without saying that the events you witnessed are now highly classified, and that any mention of this conversation—or your original expedition—will be classed as high treason, not to mention that we will use all of our influence to make your life, effectively, over. What I have here is just the synopsis; the longer version will have all the details."

"What's it saying? The short version, please," said Paul, calmly.

"Pretty much what actually happened, with only a few key alterations," said Straub, matter-of-factly. "There's no point claiming that we know where Caementum came from, as anything we come up with could blow up in our faces if the thing comes back. Yes, that's a possibility we're fully prepared to accept," she added, not knowing that we'd already assumed as much.

"So you two will still be as you were," Straub continued, "two people who developed a genuine mental link to Caementum, except that you won't have gone to Mr Marshall on your own. The truth will be that you came to us with proof of your link, and that we took it, and you, from there."

"You're kidding, right?" I scoffed, but noticing that she'd referred to an actual name rather than saying *C.I. Four.* "You actually expect people to believe that we had a psychic connection? The public will never swallow it, even if it *is* true. You'll be a laughing stock."

Straub smirked slightly in response, and shook her head.

"Not at all, Mr Pointer. After all, *you* convinced *us*. With the right scientific data, we can prove anything, but I don't think even that will be necessary. Think about what the public has seen this week, what they've experienced. Online polls tell us that seventy-six percent of the UK already believes that Caementum was of extraterrestrial origin; do you really think they won't believe that it had telepathic abilities? It's not like we're coming out of the blue and claiming that we've discovered the world's first provably psychic man. Off the back of the last few days, it will be *easily* accepted, and our PR team's research backs that theory up completely." Her face was neutral again once she'd finished, and I have to say that I couldn't disagree with her. I wasn't going to say so though, and stayed silent. She took this as compliance, and carried on.

"We, in turn, then took you to where you believed Caementum was headed as quickly as possible. You'll notice, Mr Pointer, that this version also avoids the rather unflattering fact that you went there of your own accord in hopes of breaking a story, and that you didn't attempt to alert any authorities."

"Hold on, how could I have possibly convinced—" I started, flushed, embarrassed and angry (she was totally correct, of course, but I still didn't like it) but Straub held up a hand to cut me off.

"Of course, of course," she said, patronisingly, "but some might not see it that way, and this version of events protects you from that." Her poker face was working overtime now, but even so I thought that Straub was part of the group of people that she'd just mentioned. She carried on talking.

"And so you and the military arrived at Mr Marshall's house, wherein you identified him as the target, something which he confessed to already suspecting. He then bravely offered to go to Caementum for the good of the country, knowing full well that to do so may result in his death. He will be presented to the world as a willing hero."

There was silence in the room, and Straub sat quietly for a moment regarding us, almost as if she was daring us to argue against this plan. I continued to say nothing, and to my surprise, so did Paul. What could we say?

"The removal of body parts from Mr Marshall will not be mentioned," continued Straub, satisfied again that compliance had been achieved. "That is, quite frankly, too graphic for the public, and they don't need to know those details, but they will be told that Mr Marshall died in the presence of Caementum. However, our version will be that he suffered a fatal cardiac arrest, due to the stress of the situation. Our explanation for Caementum's journey will be that we think it wanted to communicate with him specifically, for some reason. We don't want people panicking about the possibility of a return, and stopping people from knowing that it came to harvest body parts will certainly help with that. I'm sure you agree."

"What did it remove?" asked Paul. Straub blinked in response, as if she'd missed the question. She'd been prepared to move on, but Paul had taken her back a step unexpectedly, and she missed a beat while she mentally recalibrated.

"From Mr Marshall?" she asked. Paul nodded, and after a pause, Straub gestured to Dr Boldfield to respond. Boldfield adjusted his glasses and shifted in his seat to face us, suddenly put on the spot.

"Caementum somehow removed the upper portion of Mr Marshall's spine and part of his brain stem, from just above the C1 vertebrae to the T5," he said, sounding almost impatient. Clearly, Boldfield just wanted to get out of the room ASAP so that he could get on with things … possibly including our tests. While I believed Straub when she said we had nothing to worry about with said tests, I was still happy to keep this guy waiting.

"This was obviously instantly fatal," Boldfield continued. "Any pain he felt would have been brief, from the time his skin was punctured to the moment the spinal cord was severed. We think his reaction was—"

"It didn't look too brief to me," I said sharply, but my heart wasn't in it. I was tired, and couldn't decide if Boldfield was trying to make us feel better or himself. I thought it was the latter. It hadn't been an overly slow death, but 'brief' was pushing it. I didn't have time for half-truths, and they wouldn't help me sleep better at night. "Has his family been informed?"

"Not much family to speak of," said Straub, "but yes, they have. Parents deceased, and he was unmarried. Immediate family consisted of one sister and two nephews. They were informed this morning, and have been debriefed in accordance with the official story. They'll keep it quiet until the press conference tomorrow night."

"Press conference?" asked Paul, suddenly sounding very concerned. Paul wanted nothing to do with any of that, it was clear. He just wanted it to be over.

"Don't worry, Mr Winter," said Straub, reassuringly, "the Prime Minister will be doing all the talking, and to be perfectly frank, if you don't want to be a part of it, you don't have to be. You'll still be well compensated in return for your silence, as promised … although you will be expected to basically be on call for the rest of your life, or until we find a way to end the threat. We'll sort you out an ongoing consultancy pay for as long as you're in that role, don't worry. But as for the press conference, we can wheel out anyone to display as our 'psychic' link, although I think Mr Pointer here would rather like that role, correct?" This last part was directed at me, and brought me nicely onto my current point of concern.

"So I get to give away the biggest story of my career—of anyone's—for free? And lose all credibility as a journalist in the process?" I said, folding my arms. I didn't like this at all. Yes, my hopes had been heavily dampened by our first meeting with Straub, but now I knew for a fact that I wasn't going to break the story; instead I was going to be a chump player in it. I'd be famous, but not in the way I wanted. There'd be money, but I'd been promised that anyway, and now my dreams of joining the upper echelons of journalistic history were shattered. It just wasn't the same. Had I been thinking straight at the time, I'd have been more focused on the millions I was doubtless going to make by being the guy at the heart of the biggest story in human history. But as I said, right then, sitting in that office, I was *very* tired, and more than a little petulant.

"After the press conference, Mr Pointer, you can sell your story to whichever news outlet pays the most, and I think you *know* that the fee will be astronomical," said Straub, shrugging gently. "Of course, the *manner* in which you tell your story is entirely up to you, and therein lies your chance to grab the recognition, or whatever it is, that you want. Basically, as long as you submit your report to us for vetting, you can tell it your way. Present your own to-camera piece for Fox News, write your own exclusive for the *New York Times*, the *Sun*, whoever; the story is yours. You're a professional, after all, and I think having a reporter that isn't one of their own writing the story for them will be a very trivial matter indeed if it means they get the rights." She raised her eyebrows at me, and the realisation slowly sank in. She was right. In a very short space of time, possibly even within the next forty-eight hours, I was going to be the reporter that everybody in the world knew ... and I was going to be rich. I didn't like the fact that I'd be giving a soft-soaped version, and that I'd effectively be a government lapdog, but hell, it meant I could then report on anything I wanted after this, surely! I could write my own ticket! I could finally do some real journalism, not to mention being a *fucking millionaire!*

I almost couldn't take it in, and instead felt myself becoming slightly light-headed, the room suddenly seeming unreal. In a mild panic, I jammed my fingernails into my palms, and that brought me back to reality. *That stuff can wait*, I told myself. *Now is the time to be keeping your head. You don't know what she's up to, after all, and she could be trying to blindside you. Focus, dickhead. She just wants you silent but onside. She thinks they still need you, and badly.* I took in a slow breath, sat up straight, and looked at Straub.

"Okay. Okay. Sounds appealing, I admit," I said, and found myself impressed with how together I sounded, even though my stomach was doing backflips. *A man has died, Andy*, my inner monologue said, in an attempt to maintain my calm. *Try to remember that when you're thinking about free trips to the Playboy mansion.* "So all I have to do at press conference time is stand there?"

"You may be asked to answer a few questions, but we'll keep it brief and you'll be fully prepared for any eventualities, don't worry," said Straub, but she was looking at Paul now. "Mr Winter, I take it that you don't want to be part of this? You don't have to be. We would just need you to stay quiet and out of the spotlight ... where I think you'd rather be. Am I right?" Paul nodded slowly in response, looking straight back at Straub.

"Yeah," he said, drawing out the syllable. "For my wife, you know. She wouldn't ... Plus, I know there's a lot of money potentially involved, but ... I saw ... the man died right in front of me." He paused for a moment, paling slightly as he saw it again, but then seemed to realise something. He turned to me and held up his hands; I could see that he looked as tired as I felt. "Sorry ... no offence, Andy. It's your job and someone's got to tell it I suppose, so you might as well make your money. But me ... I'm getting paid by you lot anyway, right? For being on call, and all that? Good money?" said Paul, turning to Straub.

"You'll be looked after, certainly," said Straub. I noticed she used a slightly warmer tone towards Paul than she did towards me. It annoyed me slightly, but not too much. I was still trying not to think about the incredible changes that were about to come my way, in case I started doing a naked dance on the desk.

"Then I'm fine," said Paul. "I don't want to do it."

Straub marked something on a notepad to her right in response to this, then looked at us both.

"All right then," she said, and rested her hands on the desk. "In that case, I think we're done here. Mr Winter, you'll be taken home to your wife. Try to get a good night's sleep, as we'll be picking you up in the morning at 9:00 a.m. for your examinations. The press conference is scheduled for tomorrow night, Mr Pointer, and we'll be taking you to a hotel for now, due to your current housing situation. We thought you might appreciate something other than a bunk bed. Your wake-up call is at seven; you have a long day of prep before we put you in front of the cameras. We'll sort you out some clothes, as you'll be meeting with the Prime Minister, after all." Before I could respond, Paul spoke.

"Can I tell my wife the truth?" asked Paul, slightly defensively.

"I can tell you no, Mr Winter, but let's be honest, what's said in your bedroom at night will be hard for us to hear about," said Straub, sternly. "However, if she can keep a secret then whatever you choose to tell her in private should stay that way, and we won't have a problem. I trust you remember the severity of the response should you choose to break our agreement; I would advise you not to forget it, and to remember that we may— we *may*—choose to monitor you from time to time. I did say it would be *hard* for us to hear about ... but not *impossible*. Plus, when you're deciding what you wish to tell her, bear in mind that the ... incentive we used to ensure your silence would apply to her also in the event of the truth getting out. I would think long and hard about putting her in that kind of position." She let this hang in the air for a moment, and the room was silent as both Paul and I absorbed the statement.

"Right then," said Straub briskly, wrapping things up, "Unless there are any questions ...?"

I forced my mind to focus more sharply than ever upon hearing this opening, as I didn't know if it would be Boldfield himself conducting the tests and examinations or his lackeys. If I was going to ask Stone Man questions, I wanted to do it while I had the top guy. This wasn't to do with the story—I'd be told what they wanted the world to know—as this was for my own curiosity.

"Actually, yes," I said, looking back and forth between Straub and Boldfield. "I have three. Don't worry, I think these are questions that the media are going to ask anyway, so it's nothing you're not going to have answers for. But I'd appreciate the real ones, if they're different. You might as well be honest, based on what I already know."

"Okay," said Straub. "Number one?"

"The most important one, the one that's always first. *Why?*"

"You mean our theories as to why it came?" asked Straub. I nodded, and she gestured to Boldfield.

"Well, other than the obvious," he said, barely disguising a stressed-sounding sigh and looking at his watch, "meaning the idea that it came to acquire a specific genetic sample from an individual with a specific genetic makeup, or at least one who fit within specific parameters, we don't have any one theory that's more solid than the others, frankly. Personally, I go with the study argument; that it was here to collect and return said sample for examination, but even that breaks down. Why not take the brain itself, for example, rather than the stem?"

"So you think it's extraterrestrial as well then?" Paul asked, intrigued. Boldfield looked at Straub, and she gestured for him to carry on.

"It really is the only conclusion," Boldfield said, removing his glasses and wiping them. There was fresh sweat on his brow. "Teleportation, increasing its own density and mass at will, instantaneous and directed metamorphosis of solid matter on command ... all of these things are light years beyond even the most cutting-edge work being carried out by the finest scientific minds in the world. Our *best* work is at a Stone Age level compared to this. It also explains why it may have procured that area of the spine; perhaps that is where the brain or control centre of their species lies."

"So you think the Stone Man is an alien itself?" I asked, leaning forward. Paul was doing the same.

"Who can say?" said Boldfield, rubbing his eyes now, exhausted and not enjoying the questioning, but maintaining his thin veneer of politeness. "Again, personally, my hunch is no. Everything about Caementum, including your remote visions, Mr Pointer, suggests some kind of distance-operated unit. At the very least, it's some kind of environmental protection suit, perhaps with an E.T. inside ... but that doesn't seem right to me. Of course, that last part is just my opinion. I couldn't possibly say for sure at this stage."

"Okay," I said, and held up two fingers. "Two. Why go all the way to Sheffield for it? If it just needed a specific type of DNA, or something within a certain bracket, why not find someone closer?"

Annoyingly, Boldfield looked at Straub again, who seemed to share my exasperation slightly.

"Full disclosure, Doctor, he's going to lie to the world for us, for goodness' sake," she said, twirling her finger for him to get on with it.

"Right," said Boldfield, putting his glasses back on with another sigh. "Again, this is just theory, but we believe that it was simply a matter of who it found first. Think about it. It arrives here, and begins to scan. It picks up a signal, and sets off. It doesn't matter where it is; Caementum cannot be stopped, and we now know that it can remotely prevent its target from leaving whatever area Caementum detected them as being in. If the target were to be removed from the area and die, it could just find another one."

"But that's so ... *inefficient*," said Paul, frowning. Boldfield stiffened slightly, and shifted in his seat before he spoke. I got the feeling he thought we should already understand this.

"You have to remember, Mr Winter, that we have no idea how its people perceive time. Days to us could be experienced as mere seconds to them, or perhaps they seem so long that the idea of rushing for *anything* is absurd. We don't know, so we can't apply our methods of logic to their approach. Either way, what *is* unarguable is that Caementum didn't *need* to rush. All it needs to do is pick the first target it detects, pin it, retrieve it, and then come home once the job is done. It seems to us that, for them, the retrieval itself is more important than the timescale."

I shrugged, and held up three fingers to signal my third and last question, but Paul asked it first.

"What are you doing to prepare in case it comes back?"

Boldfield smiled bitterly at this, and I had the feeling that whatever it was they were doing to prepare, he'd done nothing *but* that since the moment the Stone Man had vanished.

"At the moment—and this is exactly what the media will be told about this too, but it's the truth—we're examining some of the unusual energy and radiation patterns that we detected from it. The work that we're currently doing is all about understanding and perhaps disrupting these patterns;

hopefully, to either affect its physical integrity or to break whatever remote control that's influencing it, if any." He looked at his watch again, and then showed it to Straub with a pained expression on his face.

"Yes, yes," she said, sounding slightly exasperated. "Thank you, Doctor, you can go. Thank you for your time." Boldfield rose, nodded to us both distractedly, and then headed out of the door. Straub reached under the edge of her desk, and the door was then opened by our two guards.

"Okay, gentlemen, thank you again for your patience," she said, standing. "I'm not sure when we'll speak next and, with the greatest respect, hopefully we never will, if you understand me." She held out her hand for us to shake. We did, and so then she gestured to the guards.

"These two will sort out your transport. You'll excuse me if I don't see you out, but I'm extremely busy, as you can understand. But please, gentlemen, do let me stress this again, and I say this not only for your sakes, but frankly for those of your families: this conversation never happened." With this last statement, all the breeziness dropped out of her voice, and her face became very stern indeed. The air that seemed to have permeated the room—the one that felt like the end of a successful job interview—had now disappeared, and we were left in no doubt as to the seriousness of the situation. Again, I was impressed by Straub; although she meant it, and her warning was as serious as possible, the timing and delivery of the statement had been deliberate and theatrical. The woman knew how to have an effect.

"Understood," said Paul, and Straub nodded, holding her hand out towards the door. We left her office in silence.

Walking down the corridor to the double doors, neither of us said a word, until we found ourselves once more in the warm night air. Immediately outside there were now two jeeps, and somewhere close, I could hear rotary blades starting up. One of us was getting the aerial treatment; I assumed (correctly, as it turned out) that it would be Paul. Given the length of the unseen drive here, I thought that we had to be some distance away from Sheffield now, and thus Paul's home. I obviously wouldn't be going too far; any hotel would do for me, and tomorrow I would be summoned for media prep. *Media prep.* The words shivered down my spine, carrying a little thrill all the way. I didn't think that I'd be getting a good night's sleep, no matter how much I needed it.

"This way, sir, and you're going that way, sir," said one guard, directing us each to our relevant jeep, and talking to us a little more politely than before, I thought. Perhaps because we'd been into the inner sanctum? Either way, Paul and I caught each other's eye, realising (when we should have realised earlier) that we were about to be separated.

I found, to my complete lack of surprise, that I had no idea what to say. Were we friends now? Had we bonded? Did we even like each other? It had only been a day, but it felt like a week, and I had no concept of what the appropriate action was here. Paul seemed like a good bloke, and we'd been through a pretty damn mind-blowing experience together; we'd even had a fight, pretty much, and made up. All that meant something, surely, I just didn't know what. Fortunately, Paul came to the rescue.

"You gonna be all right?" he asked, putting his hands in his pockets and drawing his arms against his sides, taking a deep breath. The man really was tired, but the concern on his face was genuine. It was an unexpected question—I'd perhaps anticipated a more token response—and it was sincerely asked. Again, I was touched.

"Yeah, you?" I said, not really knowing what else to ask. I did actually want to know though.

"Jesus, I've no idea," he said, frowning. His eyes became distant, looking through me as he spoke. "What the hell do you make of a day like today? What does anyone make of it? And that guy. At least he wasn't married or anything … but bloody hell … there'll be nightmares, I think." He sighed, looked off into the distance, then turned back to me. "Look, get your head down tonight, get through this press conference business, and if you have a spare five minutes at any point, give me a call, all right? You on Facebook?"

It sounded like a ridiculous question, given the surroundings, and what we'd been through—it was something you said to a girl you met on a night out, or to a new friend on holiday—but it made sense. Plus, as most things seem to be with Paul, it was sincere.

"Yeah, drop me a message on there with your number, I'll send you mine," I said. "Do it quick though, I think things might be about to blow up on my account."

"Ah yes, the man of the hour," smiled Paul weakly, perhaps wondering if he'd made the right choice. God knows I would have been. In his shoes, I'd have been kicking down the door of Straub's office to tell her I'd changed my mind, dodging semi-automatic rifle fire as I did so. "Try not to get lost in it all. Listen, I think … I think I'm probably gonna need to talk to you about some of this stuff, okay? You were the only other one there, at least the only other one who saw it the same way I did. So just … just keep an eye on your phone, okay?"

"Of course," I said, realising that I'd need a replacement handset now, but didn't mention it. On impulse, I held out my hand. "I might well be the same. Take care then … and I *will* speak to you soon. Okay?" Paul nodded, and took my hand in that bear paw of his, shaking mine warmly.

"She's gonna be worried sick," Paul said as he let go, shaking his head and looking at the floor, thinking about his wife. "Can we stop at a payphone on the way?" he directed this question to the guard, who shook his head.

"Unnecessary, sir. You're going to be home extremely quickly, air transport has been arranged," was the response.

"Mm, not quick enough," Paul sighed, but it was the resolved sigh of a man too tired to argue. He gave me a lazy thumbs-up, and that weak smile again. "Take care, Andy, look after yourself. Hell of an adventure, hell of an adventure. Speak soon, mate."

Paul waved good-bye with another sad smile, and then turned to get into the jeep. I returned the wave and headed towards my own jeep, a weird feeling of sadness creeping into my bones. I've never liked good-byes of any kind, and going back to being alone in all of this was suddenly very unpleasant. As the jeeps' engines started up, I looked across at Paul, sitting in the backseat. His face was hidden in his hands, and stayed that way as he began to be driven away, but at the last minute I saw him raise one hand in my direction. His revealed face was without expression, and then he was gone, disappearing into the darkness.

I wouldn't see him again for three months.

***

A lot of what happened next you'll already know. You saw it on TV, you read the papers. You know who I am. But you won't know it from my side. You won't know how it really all went down, won't know the proper timeline of things, so I'll give you the short version here.

Was it shallow? Was it an embarrassment of excess? Would I have gotten tired of it all in the end? Yes, yes, and probably. A lot of it I'm embarrassed by, when I think about it now. But at the same time, *fuck it*; it was simultaneously the most fun and the most lonely time of my entire life. I wish it had never ended.

This is what I remember of it.

—The early wake-up call at the hotel, head pounding, exhausted from a restless night of excitement about my glorious new future. A knock at the door to deliver some toiletries and some comfort clothes for the day: jeans, a T-shirt, clean boxers and socks. Being told a car would arrive for me in twenty minutes. The buzz kicking in through the tiredness, knowing I was about to become the centre of the world. It was ... indescribable.

—The drive to a small field nearby, getting into the waiting chopper. Landing on top of a London skyscraper and being met by David, who was to be my liaison for the day, carrying a clipboard and wearing, of all things, a headset, like a TV show-runner. David doesn't talk much, is middle-aged, always wears a grey suit. Stern faced, even more businesslike than Straub, if that's possible.

—David escorting me down into the building, which looked like an ordinary office block, with people dashing here and there and working at computers in cubicles. Asking where we were, and David saying that it was a government department and not telling me anything more.

—Being taken into a blank waiting room and left alone for several minutes, then being fetched again by David and taken into a larger room with a desk and two more people, a man and a woman, whose names I never get because that is the point at which the speed of the day ramps up to ridiculous levels.

—Bullet points, diagrams, diversionary tactics for difficult questions, a list of twenty likely questions to memorise and the appropriate responses for each (there would be four questions allowed of me before the conference would be wrapped up). Q and A practice sessions, at one point occurring while a woman with a tape measure takes down my vitals for the making of my bespoke suit. I was to look good on TV. Being told to make sure I mentioned the destruction of my home, regardless of the questions, to help shore up my credibility. Protocol for meeting the Prime Minister, where to stand. Documents to sign, waivers, disclosure agreements. Realising that I don't have a phone. Asking about this, and being told I would be given one. Later, being given a Blackberry. It's not as good as my old one. Eating somewhere in the middle of all this, being brought a tray of rather nice sandwiches and juice.

—The end of an exhausting afternoon, head bursting from all the things I had to remember, and departing around 5:00 p.m. in a car with blacked-out windows that takes me to Downing Street, sitting on the backseat with big men in suits who sit either side of me, also wearing earpieces. The wait in the car seeming to go on forever, even once we'd arrived. Half an hour before showtime, being brought inside Number 10 and meeting the Prime Minister. It seems unreal, as does the whole day so far. His greeting is friendly, but short and businesslike, and then he goes back to his team of advisers. A makeup artist attends him, then me.

—The press conference on the steps of Number 10, dazzled by the hundreds of paps and journos gathered in front of us; national-level guys with faces I recognise, faces I once envied but now I know that I am about to surpass them utterly. I wear my new suit, and it fits like a glove.

—The Prime Minister delivering the PR account of the Stone Man story, with the delivery and assuredness of a pro. Then I am presented, not quite as a hero—what did I actually do in the end, even in this version of the story, other than simply being at the heart of it—but with a tone suggesting that I am very important indeed. Feeling deeply nervous as the hands go up and the voices start. I am not a TV reporter, but I handle the questions well. They are all within the list of twenty likely questions, and I've been prepared well.

Describe the mental sensation. When did you first have your vision. What do you say to people that call you a fraud. Do you think it will come back. And that's when everything is wrapped up and we're done.

—Being taken to a different hotel, under guard for my own protection, where the arrival is totally different to the previous night: a mob of press are somehow waiting at the other end, and my two burly minders bully me through them and into the elevator. They wait outside my room at night.

—Ringing flatmate Phil and getting him to gather every newspaper he could that mentioned me. Phil going nuts with questions, asking why my phone had been off, how the hell I got mixed up in this, where I'd gotten the suit from. Apparently he's been telling everyone that I was his flatmate, and I think that maybe his tone sounds friendlier than I've ever heard it.

—Lying in bed, exhausted but still browsing online, reading every online article about myself that I can find. Egotistical? Perhaps, but wouldn't you do the same in my shoes? Annoyingly, every one is merely about my account of events, with almost no assessment of me as a man. The only objective description of any note is that I was 'confident' at the podium, and one article adds the word 'local' to the word 'reporter' when mentioning my job. I wince when I read it, and silently curse the jealous little toad that wrote it.

—Being collected early the next day for my examinations, and taken to a private room in a London hospital. We start with an MRI and blood work. We do ESP tests, Zener cards and the like. Visual exams, personality profiling. Halfway through the day I meet my cabinet-appointed agent, Bryan, who will be talking to me later about various offers. He will negotiate the best deals and look after my interests, but also make sure the government's take priority, and ensure that the boat isn't rocked, as he puts it. The treasury get thirty percent, too, which stings a great deal, but I am not in a position to argue. Plus, when I hear what Bryan has to say about my potential earnings, even losing such large portions of it seems insignificant. Bryan says that so far, it looks like TV is the way to go, as expected, and that all of the networks—US, of course—are fine with me being the one to write and present it. The highest offer so far is eight million dollars, and Bryan expects it to go way beyond that. The base rate of advertising for the Superbowl is four million per ad, and my report of my experiences with a confirmed extraterrestrial will have ratings far higher than the Superbowl. Legitimate alien experience? Massive. Worth at least one hundred million in advertising revenue, if the Superbowl generates seventy-five. He expects to get me twenty million as a minimum. I'm stunned. This all has to be a dream.

—Facebooking Paul once I'm back at the hotel at night. I find that he's already added me, and messaged me with his number. *Watched your performance,* he says. *Looked good. All well this end, once she'd calmed down. Get in touch when you can. PS Love the suit.* I send him the new Blackberry's number.

—Being flown to America on day three, with government representative David and agent Bryan in tow. David still hardly ever speaks, but he's here to vet proceedings. I begin to think that David might actually be some kind of high-ranking spook. We fly business class, and I drink champagne. I pass out during the flight for several hours, and it's good, but my headache is back when I wake up.

—Meeting the producers in LA. Bryan has already told me that NBC will be paying me twenty-one million dollars. Even after the treasury's cut, I am a multimillionaire. I am wined and dined and asked to cowrite a one-hour-long script with their writing team. David insists that I am allowed to write it alone, then turn it in for editing. He also demands that we have final cut approval of the finished programme; he doesn't say it, but I know that by 'we' he means himself and his superiors. He's given what he wants, of course.

—Spending three days in a luxurious LA hotel, writing the script based on the government's timeline of events and writing Paul out of it as requested. I no longer went to Sheffield solo; I went with the military and government reps after convincing the local police that I was legit (saying exactly what was happening with the Stone Man on TV while an officer watched it on his phone in another room. Describing the cars and surroundings onscreen with no way of seeing them. This was supposedly enough for the Coventry police to grant me access to the higher-ups, who at that point, due to Coventry being ground zero for the Stone Man, were in contact with the military. Not my story, the government's.) David analyses the final product, then sends it back to the UK for assessment. With some minor edits, it is approved.

—The NBC team adapting my draft into a more suitable TV format. I am then flown back to the UK to shoot on location. David stays with me throughout the whole process, as does Bryan. I like Bryan, but I can't relax with the guy; I strongly suspect he wouldn't give me the time of day if I wasn't of use to him. David is just cold, his lined faced always stern. I try to place an exact age on him. I think fifty-five. We're granted exclusive access to the damage sites for filming. The many ruined areas of Coventry are still guarded by police, to ward off sightseers and memorabilia hunters while the city is being repaired. The government are done taking their samples too. It feels strange being back, like stepping into a past dream. It's only been a week, but it feels like months since I was last in Coventry. The city is already rebuilding, but the end is a long way off. Flattened again, as it was in wartime, and having to rebuild for a second time. It isn't fair.

—Having a trailer. Starting to drink more. Loving every minute of it but still seeing Patrick's face at night. I think about calling Paul. I don't.

—David giving me another new phone with location tracking built into it, telling it to keep it on me at all times. I think the Blackberry might already have it, but I assume this one has the same but with bells on; I don't think he means it just has conventional GPS.

—A parcel arriving from Paul. It's a present; a new Dictaphone. The one I'm using as I tell this story, in fact. It comes with a note. *To replace the old one ... and to get it all out if you need to.* I appreciate the thought.

—Calling the *Times* from my hotel to offer a piece on the growth of nostalgia cinema. They're excited—my name already carries weight—and they offer good money. The *New York Times* offers more. I start to make notes for the article. The TV special broadcasts, and the ratings are through the roof, topping the last record-breaking Superbowl. I think about buying a house, but then wonder where I'd buy it. America? I like it there. The money arrives in my account. My wealth is official.

—Flying home to the UK for a break while I finish the *New York Times* piece. I stay at the Savoy. The *NY Times* publishes my work to some minor fanfare, and it's noted in media outlets that it's my first report since the Stone Man. There are a few dissenting voices, asking why my work is now a big deal when before, I couldn't get anything into the nationals. These voices hurt.

—Receiving an invite for a big Samsung product launch in New York. I take it up, and contact David to inform him that I'll be out of the country.

—Flying back to the States (business class, again, as I AM now a multimillionaire, something I actually keep forgetting, forcing myself to look at the pricier options on menus as I don't fully realise that I can afford them) and having two weeks that I don't really remember very much about. Bryan calls with the best prices on the book offers, and they're good. He says we've kept the movie rights in all potential deals. I decide to get started, but first I ring the

New York Times again about another story, perhaps something about the current nature of celebrity. They want it, but the offer is less than before. I wonder if it's the subject matter, or my own celebrity appeal already starting to slip. I write the article, realising now is the time to begin to cement myself as a writer, and that I have to try to get the book finished.

—Finding that Paul has rang my Blackberry, but I've missed the call. He hasn't left a message.

—Being asked to come back to the UK by Boldfield for some more tests. Nothing severe, I'm told. I'm put in a room and asked to listen to some frequencies, and then am bombarded by what I assume are X-rays as they're all stood behind a thick screen while it happens. They tell me it's safe, and I don't really have any choice but to believe them.

—Bryan constantly ringing about the book deal progress, as well as giving me invites to one soiree after another in the States. I fly back, and have another crazy, shameful few weeks. I get laid, repeatedly, and at a calibre I never would have imagined. The men at these affairs are all sycophants trying to kiss my arse, or posers trying to outdo me, but I don't care. The attention is nice in any aspect, and to my amazement I'm not finding myself trying to avoid it, not trying to shy away from it like normal because *I don't have to try for the first time in my life*, I can behave how I like and they're doing all the work. There's no *pressure*.

—The *New York Times* printing my new piece. I don't think of another one after all; I'm having a good time and have a book to write. I've already made good progress.

—Feeling a tension that I didn't really know was there starting to fade as the weeks pass. I realise that the nightmares have stopped.

—Calling Paul.

"Hey, Andy! Wondered if I was going to hear from you! How's things in the world of celebrity?" He sounds pleased to hear me, but his voice is slightly thick, as if he has a cold. He still sounds tired.

"Well, I'm calling from a hotel in the Bahamas, so it can't be *that* bad."

"Poor sod. When you could be in sunny Sheffield. Or Cov."

"Yeah, I'm sure I'll get over the delightful climate here and beautiful beaches. Someone has to do it."

We exchange pleasantries, each catching up on what the other has been doing in the meantime; the paycheque from the government has come through for him, and it's good. He and his wife have used it to start up a side business—catering—ran by her, and the early signs are promising. He's told her the whole story, and she's kept it quiet. Work is going well, and their finances are good to great, and look to stay that way. His tone is light, but hollow. It's a front, and a very weak one. This is not the same man that I met in Sheffield. Again, I find myself wondering what is wrong with me; how I am so unscathed emotionally by what happened to that man in the street as he screamed before my eyes. I tell Paul that if ever he needs money—a lot of money—he only needs to ask, and it will be given. I surprise myself by telling him that he can have half, anytime he wants it. He goes quiet at this, and makes a quiet thinking noise. He then thanks me.

"I'll keep that in mind, Andy. You never know, do you ... principles are good and all, and right now I don't need it, but when the moment comes, who knows. Who knows."

He goes quiet, and I wonder what to say. He speaks first, though.

"How've you been sleeping?" The question speaks volumes.

I say not bad, better now. I ask him about *his* sleep. He sighs, and there is hidden pain in it.

"Not good, mate, not good. Pretty terrible, really. When the lights go out ... can't drop off. And when I do, half the time I have the same dream. I see it again. Boom, just like that." He pauses for a long time, and when he speaks again, he's almost whispering, the truth behind the upbeat lie coming out.

"Sometimes ... sometimes it's *me*."

I don't ask if *It* is Patrick, or the Stone Man.

—Finishing the book and sending it to the publishing editor, after receiving approval from David, of course. Flying back to New York at the publisher's expense. I have a few days drinking and ass-kissing with the New York literary set, then I get to work on the edits that I've been given by the publishers. This is when I'll be catapulted to a solid position of respect, cemented as a writer and not as a grim reality show celebrity.

-October 2nd, the day that it all comes to a shrieking end. The day that the Stone Man comes back.

***

I could tell that something was wrong from the moment I woke up. At first, I thought I was still drunk, but realised quickly that this was a different feeling. Familiar, but unrecognisable through my sleep haze. I checked the clock: *23:07*. I'd only been asleep for an hour. Last night had ended extremely early indeed for me, I dimly remembered, although it had been a pretty early start as well; six o'clock dinner reservations, celebrating someone else's book launch, a member of the squawking, butt-kissing literary party pack that I barely knew. I hadn't felt comfortable at all, spending the alternating between restlessness, irritability and even dizziness. Eventually I'd made my excuses and arrived home around 9:00 p.m., and out of frustration and petulance I'd given up on the day and taken a Xanax, managing to pass out. That made it even more odd; I should have been asleep for hours. How the hell was I awake already?

I staggered to the bathroom, my silk boxers feeling weird around my legs and groin. I'd bought them as an indulgence, and had regretted it all of the previous day. I'd spent too long in opulent surroundings, had been spoilt by the world of New York's finest hotels. Even now, if I threw open the expensive floor-to-ceiling drapes, the view from my current room would be breathtaking.

The thick shag pile carpet felt thick and warm under my feet, a sensation then replaced by the smooth but equally warm bathroom tiles (heated from underneath, of course). I pissed in the toilet and rested my head against the wall, regretting another drinking session surrounded by wannabe social climbers. I tried to remember what the hell I'd been drinking, and wondered how whatever it was had managed to get me into this messy state so quickly. As my mind slowly awoke, I remembered the answer.

Orange juice.

I'd had a night off the sauce. So what the hell was this? Why was my head buzzing so much, when all I'd had was vitamin C? The tugging sensation was in my skull, my teeth, my *skin*—

I was suddenly very, very awake, and as I jerked upright I felt the resulting head rush hit me, hard. I managed to grab the sink as I started to go dizzy, and took a moment to let myself settle. My equilibrium eventually did, if not my nerves, and I half-ran, half-stumbled back into the bedroom and turned on the TV. What time was it again? Eleven p.m.-ish local time. That meant it was ... my brain struggled to work properly, but I dragged the answer out. Around 4:00 a.m. in the UK. Sunday morning here ... but just early enough on a Saturday night for people to see it, for clubbers staggering home to know that it was there and start a full-scale panic. An hour or two later, and maybe it could have been kept quiet for a bit longer. CCTV cameras could have picked it up, then the authorities could have been quietly informed. Then the security logistics could have begun with just that bit more of a head start, instead of being one step behind the panic from the very beginning. A few lives could have been saved. Slim chances of all that, but even so ...

With a shaking hand, I pressed the power button on the remote. Of course, it was being broadcast live from the scene. I'd just had time to hope it had arrived somewhere else, but somehow I already knew that it wouldn't have. The blue strip lighting in the floor was the giveaway. Without a doubt, the scene before me was Millennium Place. This was the start of what would become known as the Second Arrival.

As it stood there, bathed both by floodlight and the headlights of the military jeeps and APCs parked impotently around it, I thought that it looked just as solid, real, and implacable as before. The Stone Man had come back.

I actually let out a little cry of dismay, and in that moment everything that had happened in the last three months felt somehow lessened, suddenly diminishing into an alcohol-fuelled fever dream. Seeing the Stone Man like this again, viewed at a distance, it was almost as if I expected Patrick to be brought forward once more, drooling and gibbering, for his date with grim destiny. The Stone Man was here, and someone was going to die. Die horribly, and without dignity.

That was besides all the others that would be killed either in crushes, panic or religious disputes. I thought that they would have started already, and as I then wondered crazily what the Internet would make of it, I realised that my phone was switched off. *Fuck.* How long had the Stone Man been here?

And how was the pull here already? It hadn't been until the morning after the Stone Man had turned up when I first felt it before, and I'd been through two physical episodes before that. Could it be I was now conditioned somehow, finding the pull more quickly and easily now I'd been tuned to it once already? My mind whirled.

I dived over to the bed in a panic, where I'd left my government-issue phone on the nightstand. It wasn't a model I'd ever seen before. I'd been given one, a small grey box as basic and functional as a phone from the early 1990s, only smaller. It was heavy, though. No camera, no Internet, but it had a startlingly long battery life, often lasting six days (helped by the fact that it was never used) but that came with a downside; it was often very easy to take charging it for granted. So far, I'd let it die twice, but after receiving no reprimands from David (or any other government spooks; I was still convinced that he was one), I thought I'd gotten away with it. However, I'd let it happen for a third time last night. As a result, I'd set it charging when I got home, but in my distracted, irritated state I'd forgotten to turn it on while it did so.

I watched it boot up, breathing hard and willing it to switch on faster. The old-school green screen appeared, and the moment that it registered a signal, a text alert pinged into life. Voicemail. Wincing, I rang it; there were twenty-six messages.

First up was Straub, pointlessly telling me to turn my bastard phone on. Then David, telling me to stay put as soon as I switch my phone on. Paul, ringing from a military base, saying that he'd been picked up already and that they'd scared his Mrs half to death, almost kicking the bloody door down, and wanting to know where I was. Straub again, now repeating what David had said. Bryan, telling me to say nothing to anyone, and to keep a low profile until I was picked up. David repeating his earlier message. Straub, audio cutting in halfway through a conversation that she was having with someone else in the room and then saying no, it's his sodding answer phone again. David—

A beep interrupted my thoughts, cutting in over the current message playing. I looked at the screen, which was now telling me that I had an incoming call. David. I answered.

"Hello?" I said, breathlessly.

"*He's here, he's here!*" shouted David, sounding astonished and talking to someone else, and for a second I thought he was talking about the Stone Man. I then realised he was alerting people around him to the fact that I was on finally on the phone. He then addressed me. "Thank God you've finally turned your fucking phone on. You were given that for a reason. I've been calling you non-stop for the last two hours."

"I'm sorry, I'm sorry," I said frantically, muting the TV via the remote and already looking around for my clothes. "I'm in New York, I'm at the—"

"We know, we know, it came up the minute you turned your phone on," he said, cutting me off with the voice of an extremely stressed man. "Stay put. There'll be a chopper arriving on the roof in ten minutes. Paul is already here, but we're behind the clock. He says he can feel the target, but he can't pinpoint the fucker without you, which rogers us entirely. Based on our previous intel, Caementum started walking within two hours last time. That time is now up, even before we have you in the air and on the way back to the UK. We have no route, no path to evacuate, and it's about to start smashing its way in a straight line. People are going to fucking *die* because *you* had to have an early night." My mouth gaped at this, half of me wanting to say *how fucking dare you* and the other wanting to curl into a ball and die myself. The responsibility was mind-blowing. I'd been asleep five minutes ago, I reminded myself, desperately searching for a way out. Could this just be a bad dream? David was talking again already.

"Just bring a UK map up on your laptop and get on with your fucking magic trick. I'll wait," David snapped. I mumbled something dumbly in response, dropped the phone onto the bed, and ran over to my laptop that was charging away on the table. Of course, I never allowed *that* thing to run out of juice. A few seconds later and Google Maps was up onscreen, showing me a full image of my home country, one large enough to work with thanks to the seventeen-inch screen. Even in my current state of panic, I was confident that this would do. The image was just to help me focus, after all, to ease the connection and to help me visualise ... but even as I raised my hand to the picture, I knew that something was different, and not because of the medium I was using. The pull was back, and deep in my skin and bones and blood, but something was missing. What was it?

I tried to focus harder, to get my mojo back, but after several minutes I had gotten nowhere. I felt cold, and something felt like it had begun to loosen in my bowels. I wanted to vomit. I couldn't make the connection, and horribly, I thought I knew why.

I was too far away.

I couldn't help, and people were going to die as a result. Feeling dizzier now, trying to block out the leaden guilt settling into my brain, I picked up the phone again with shaking hands, and my voice came out as a whisper.

"I can't get it."

"What?" asked David, his response coming out as a bark. "What did you say?"

"I can't get it," I repeated, wanting to cry. "I can't help you. I think ... I think I'm too far away."

There was silence on the other end, but only for a moment. David, like Straub, had his job for a reason. Also like Straub, I knew absolutely nothing about him, despite spending far more time in his company than hers. The guy hardly ever spoke, and even when he did he remained utterly inscrutable.

"Right. Get dressed, and call the concierge," said David, angrily dragging himself away mentally from the bollocking that he wanted to give me and already getting on with business. "Explain who you are and tell him that you need access to the roof; that building has a helipad, and the plan stays the same. Be ready. You'll be transferred from the chopper to a private jet and should be back on UK soil by eleven thirty GMT."

"You're still bringing me home?" I asked, confused.

"Yes," he snapped. "I always thought you shouldn't have been allowed out of the country, but it's not my say-so. But if you're useless at a distance, that's even more reason to get you back here. It'll probably be too late for you to be any help with the evacuation, but if you have a connection to this thing, then we might fucking well need it. Hopefully there won't be too many dead bodies by the time you arrive."

This was the most I'd ever heard him speak at once. A penny slowly dropped.

"There'll be at least one dead body *after* I get there though, won't there?" I said quietly, talking almost to myself as the blood drained from my face. I would be the huntsman once more.

"Nice," said David, coldly, taking the remark as a jab. "Though I'm not sure how that makes you feel better, you idiot. Just get in the air, get the map on your smartphone up and keep trying on the way."

I heard him hang up, and the line went dead. I thought dumbly about checking the rest of my messages, but I couldn't face it. I felt mentally numb. I had fucked up in the worst possible way. One job to do, one that *really* mattered more than anything, and I'd blown it. The only one in the world who could do it, and I was in the wrong place. If I'd at least remembered to turn my phone on while it charged it would have been better—the getting home process would have started a few hours earlier, and maybe I could have helped sooner—but I hadn't and there I was, on the other side of the Atlantic Ocean. They'd said keep it on you, and keep it charged, and I'd gotten so casual with it that I'd blown it. There was blood on my hands again, but this time, it had been painfully, utterly avoidable. I almost made it to the toilet in time, but didn't. I vomited half in and half out of the bathroom doorway.

As I sat on the floor, breathing slowly and trying to stop the room from spinning, I looked at my watch. Three minutes had passed already, and I had to be on the roof in seven. I dragged myself to my feet, holding on to the door handle, and got dressed. All the while my body was riddled with the pull ... but it wasn't the pull, I reminded myself, not really. I paused in the middle of reaching for the hotel's phone to call the concierge, trying to become more aware of the sensation in my body. I was aware of that same movement that seemed to be inside my bones and skin, but this time it ... what was it? It had no direction, it seemed. I was connected to the Stone Man again, or some kind of signal at least, but whether it was coming from the thing itself or its next target I had no idea, and had no more time to ponder it. I had to get onto British soil and narrow things down. I picked up receiver and called the concierge.

The next hour was a blur:

Getting into my brown Savile Row suit and making it up to the roof thanks to the concierge, desperately trying the map trick on the Blackberry's Maps app (I still kept it, of course; I needed a smartphone as well as the government brick with its super-GPS) but still getting nothing in response. Hearing the nagging voice in my head. *If you can't do it until you're back in the UK, how many deaths will happen because you were in America and not home in time to help? All because you had to live it up over here?*

Feeling the air blast around me as the chopper landed and took me to the airport. Walking through it all like a zombie, feeling both frantic and alert with worry yet sick and despairing, trying to hold back from descending into a full blown crying fit. The guilt ... I could barely walk.

The flight back was an endless nightmare. I remember, many years ago, being slightly late for an old-but-still-close university friend's wedding, and then realising that I was actually making up time on the drive across the country. I'd felt relief wash over me. I was going to make it after all, I'd thought, and with enough time to spare so that I wasn't going to have to burst into the church halfway through the ceremony. And then I'd hit the worst traffic jam of my life; an oil tanker had shed its load onto the M4, and all three lanes had been rendered completely stationary. And I mean completely. Engines were off, and people were walking around their cars to stretch their legs. I'd still been in my twenties, and I'd never seen such a thing before. And I can still remember the feeling—very vividly—of growing panic as I'd realised that not only was I going to be late, but that the unthinkable would happen, and that I would miss my good friend's wedding day. And as the hours had passed, and the point of no return grew ever closer—that moment after which there would be no way for me to make it, even if the wedding was delayed—I grew more and more frantic, *and there was nothing I could do to influence things.* All I could do was wait. Helpless. As time wore on, my moans and groans of frustration had turned into swearing, then shouting, then punching the roof of my car, desperate for a release.

The flight back from New York on that October day was far worse.

Two hours of constantly checking the atlas on my offline laptop, of regular calls on the plane's phone from the UK asking for an update. It could set off along any point of the compass, after all; how do you prepare to evacuate a whole country? They would have protocols in place to an extent, I knew, but they could only do so much, and besides, how do you keep a lid on worldwide religious hysteria? The last few minutes of those first two hours were agonising—as I reached that point of no return in my window of opportunity—but this time I was not sitting alone. This time I was flanked by a few secret service men, as well as soldiers In full fatigues, seated in the small, airline-style seats of the private jet. I'd gotten used to business class, and this thing wasn't far off. I assumed this transport was normally reserved for state VIPs, but even so, the luxury was wasted on me in my state of mind, so desperate was I to fix my mistake.

And then two hours became three with still no report that the Stone Man had begun to walk. As three hours became four, and the situation remained the same, hope teasingly began to creep in. Could something different be happening this time? The hope made things worse, as I couldn't allow myself to believe it. I knew that the second I thought everything might be all right, we'd get the call to say the Stone Man was walking. It was torturous beyond belief. I started to sweat, never once leaving the map screen on my laptop but still somehow getting nothing.

Four hours became five, and I thought that I was going to melt. The pull in my body wasn't getting any stronger either, I realised. I'd half-thought that it would begin to build as we neared Britain, but it didn't. I wondered dimly if it were simply that it would only increase once I was within a few hundred miles of the target, like before, and that made sense. Either way, the hunt hadn't even begun yet, and as five hours became six, the situation showed no signs of changing. I knew now that it would be just as we arrived—just as I finally started to allow myself to think that I might make it—that the Fates would reveal that they'd been waiting until the cruellest possible moment to twist the knife, and the Stone Man would begin its path of destruction just as I reached the finish line. But six hours became seven, and we were now over UK airspace, surely within detection distance of the target, and I still had nothing.

The feeling was one of both relief and nervousness. I could still help. I could still avoid the guilt ... but it didn't make sense. Was the time of my arrival irrelevant then? Had being in America and letting my phone die made no difference whatsoever, as for some reason I could no longer sense a target? Wait ... was that it? Could I simply have lost the ability to do what I did before? Or perhaps I was only able to sense Patrick?

Relief and nervousness increased on both sides. I'd be out of the loop, of no use to anyone, and it meant that they'd have no choice but to wait until its walk was begun to start mapping a route of evacuation and response ... but it also meant I'd be absolved, as I never could have been of any help in the first place. I desperately, desperately hoped that was true, of course, but at the edge of that thought my mind was already turning over something else, to my amazement. I know, you'd think that the relief would be enough after that journey of self-recrimination, but as ever, I was thinking already.

It would mean I'd no longer be one of the most important men in the world.

We landed just after 12:00 p.m., and still nothing had changed, amping up simultaneous relief and nerves further; even with both feet firmly on UK soil, I had nothing but the same throb in my bones that I'd had upon waking in New York. We'd arrived under grey skies at RAF Northolt, and were met by Straub (to my mild surprise) and David, with their escorts waiting in jeeps on the runway. I wondered what level of authority David had here, if any, and assumed he was just here in the context of being my handler. Straub shook my hand as she led us hurriedly towards the waiting jeep; David didn't offer his. He looked more miserable than ever; slightly bald on top with a decidedly Friar-Tuckish haircut below, glasses perched on his curved nose and a mouth that seemed built to remain permanently in the stiff-lipped position. As I say, I'd guessed his age to be around fifty-five, but I had no idea if that was right. It was the first time that I'd seen him without a suit, and as he was in just trousers, shirt and tie in this early October weather, he must have been pretty cold. I hoped he was.

"Any news? Anything changed now you're here?" asked Straub, as the jeep turned in a sharp semicircle and led us towards the barracks.

"Nothing," I said, shaking my head. The wind was up today, and I had to raise my voice slightly to be heard over that and the jeep's engine. "Nothing at all. I thought it might increase as we got closer, but it hasn't changed one bit. Not even now, when I'm in the country. I can feel it, I know the Stone Man is here and that there's also a target ... but that's it."

"Brilliant," sniffed David, shaking his head. "All the coke and booze have fucked the one thing about you that makes you useful."

I turned to him and glared. I had no idea what David's actual rank was, what his official title was supposed to be, and all I had was a mere suspicion of his probable spookdom. That was it. At the very least, right now, he didn't know for certain if he needed me or not. As far as I was concerned, that gave me the freedom to talk as I pleased.

"Sorry my inexplicable mental link isn't working perfectly for you, David," I snapped. "You could try some of your human rights violating shit to get it working again though? Extraordinary rendition? Waterboarding? Something classy like that perhaps? Although, with you up on your moral high horse today, wouldn't something like that rather contradict your current stance?"

I was pretty pleased with myself for that, but to both my surprise and disappointment, David smiled. I'd never seen that before.

"For you, I'd make an exception," he said, grinning, and I damn near pissed my pants. I found myself harshly reminded that this bookish-looking, miserable man could well be one of the most dangerous people I'd ever met. I tried to hide it, by simply shaking my head at him as bravely as I could, and went back to looking through the windscreen. We were already nearing the barracks.

"Okay, gentlemen, that'll do for the pissing contest," said Straub, looking at some notes on a clipboard she was carrying. "Mr Pointer, Mr Winter is waiting inside. You two will be put under escort and expected to immediately begin trying to identify Caementum's latest target, if it all there is one. Maps and a GPS system have been provided. Caementum has shown no signs of movement since its arrival, not even so much as the straightening-up action it performed within the first sixty minutes of its previous visit. Police are on alert across the country, and quite frankly we're hoping that you two together can give us, and them, a far greater head start."

"I'll do my best," I said, but I was starting to believe that my best wasn't going to be good enough. I had nothing, after all, and I'd found myself expecting that to change the moment my feet touched the UK, but it obviously hadn't happened. If physical contact with Paul didn't do anything, then I was out of ideas. A horrible thought struck me: *what if that means everyone will think I'm some kind of fraud?* I'd be the laughing stock of every scene I'd become a part of. No, worse; I'd be hated.

But there was no time to think about that, as we'd actually driven around the barracks, not towards them as I'd thought, and were now pulling up outside another, smaller building. David and Straub were getting out, and so I did the same. We quickly entered into this other building, and I now found myself inside what appeared to be a medium-sized meeting room, the sort kept plain enough so as to be adaptable to suit whatever group of people was using it that day. At one end there was a large whiteboard with a rolled-up projector screen above it, and several rows of chairs. These were empty. The walls had large windows running along each side, and behind the last row of seats were several long tables, and *these* were occupied. I'd half expected more bulky computer terminals and lab-coated scientists running everywhere, but instead there were simply several normal-looking computers, a few soldiers, and a pair of nervous-looking and laminated pass-wearing civilians. I assumed these two were the sum total of the intelligence/science personnel we were getting here, as this was clearly not the main hub of operations. I surmised that this was some sort of a quick, mobile set up arranged for the benefit of my arrival, a halfway house of information where I could—ideally—quickly get the info they wanted so they could pass it back to the actual HQ. I thought this because, behind the farthest table back, looking intently at a computer screen of his own and wearing a T-shirt that said *No, YOU'RE ten minutes EARLY*, was Paul.

Despite the situation, I was delighted to see him. He looked up as we came in, and my delight turned to mild shock. He'd lost a lot of weight since our last handshake. He was still a big man, his size standing out in the spartan room, but his eyes were more sunken, and his general facial features were more defined, his skin slightly less healthy looking. He hadn't turned into a zombie by any means, but it was clear that he had physically lessened in the last three months. He'd obviously had even more sleep troubles than he'd let on, and even darker issues than I'd suspected. It was concerning.

He grinned upon seeing me though, and then that twinkle was back in his eyes; he wasn't a complete wreck yet. He came around the table, extending his hand, and I strode over, doing the same. I got the impression that he was equally pleased to see me, but as we drew closer, I saw his expression change to one of surprised realisation. I stopped walking, surprised myself. Paul cocked his head, raised an eyebrow and pulled his hand back towards himself, where he held it up for me to see.

I understood.

"Crunch time, eh?" I said, forcing a smile as my nerves spoilt my pleasure at seeing Paul. This would be the moment when I found out either that I'd let people die, people that I could have saved ... or that I was useless, and about to become a possible figure of public hate.

"Apparently you've not been able to get anything on the guy it's here for ... any changes since you landed?" Paul asked.

"Nope. This is basically shit or bust."

Paul nodded slowly, then waggled his fingers and blew on them.

"Okey dokey," he said, taking a deep breath. "I was about to say it's good to see you, but I've got a feeling another bloody kick in the nuts is coming my way very shortly. We have to stop meeting like this."

He smiled, wry but nervous, and slowly extended his hand again. I closed the distance between us, holding out my hand as I did so, and stopped just before touching his. I don't really know why I hesitated. I was just very aware of the gravity of the moment, what hinged on it. I admit it; I was scared. Not only of the unpredictability of the situation, but frightened that nothing would happen. I could feel every eye in the room on us, from the soldiers to the civilians to Straub and David, who had hung back near the whiteboard as I'd approached Paul. Nobody said anything.

"Come on, then," said Paul, wiggling his hand. "Reach out and touch someone." But his eyes looked scared as well.

"Do you feel anything at all? I mean, have you felt anything?" I asked, almost in a whisper.

Paul shook his head.

"Nothing, buddy," he said, softly. "No visions ... not even a tingle. I've been telling them, but they've had me zooming in and out of GPS maps all day anyway."

I let out a rush of air, trying to pump myself up, but I was even more nervous now. I felt the hairs on the back of my neck stand up. Then I just thought *Fuck it,* thought somehow replaced by pure action, and grabbed Paul's hand tight, bracing myself as I did so. I closed my eyes.

There was no change whatsoever.

I opened one eye, and saw Paul doing the same. He clearly had nothing either.

"Shit ..."

His shoulders dropped, as did mine, but he didn't let go of my hand. Instead, he shook it.

"Well," he said with a sad shrug, "before things get all crazy again ... nice to see you, mate."

I nodded, and clapped him on the shoulder in a rare moment of instinctive physical contact from me—I could see that he'd meant what he said, and I wanted him to know that the feeling was mutual—but I was crestfallen. Amazingly, there was no relief; now I knew that guilt wasn't an issue, all I could think of was what I'd just become. Whatever connection I had to the Stone Man, it was now gone, or this was a different Stone Man altogether. I felt empty. I was convinced that I was probably going to be discredited, but even if that didn't happen ... I was surplus to requirements here. If there were answers to be found, they weren't going to come from me; I wasn't going to be the guy who solved the mystery. Effectively, I was nobody, because whoever *did* find out the truth, they would far outclass the guy who was there before them. They would be today's news, the new golden boy or girl, and although my money was going nowhere, I realised that what I cared about were the trappings of being a media darling. I knew it ... and I didn't care. In that moment, any thoughts of the moral implications of wanting to be a hunter again didn't even penetrate, and all I could see was my social status slipping away, potentially replaced by a newcomer. I felt panic.

You can judge me. Just remember, you haven't tried it. Whatever you might think of it, see if you get to try it, and then see if you want to give it up, however false it might be. Hell, maybe you would, maybe it's just me. Maybe I'm just a shallow prick. I don't care. You owe me, so fuck you. You all owe me.

Anyway.

I quickly tried to think of anything that was different. Could I still be in the loop, could I think of anything that had changed? If I could, I might be able to fix it. What had changed ...

I sat on the nearest table and let my legs swing, lost in thought.

"Still nothing," said Straub, and it wasn't a question. Everyone else in the room visibly deflated, and tension was replaced by angry disappointment.

"Wait, wait," I said, staring at the floor and waving a hand. "Let me think ..."

David was pulling out his radio and shaking his head.

"It's okay, Andy," he said, using a lightly sarcastic tone as he put the radio to his mouth, "we have some of the finest scientific minds in the world to do that for us, so we're all right on that front. Thanks, though." He pushed the button. "R7B, prep for helicopter pickup immediately, transport to Coventry ASAP." The voice on the other end responded, and he pointed the radio's aerial in our direction. "We're leaving in two minutes." He turned to Straub. "I think this is a waste of time. It's obviously not the same one."

"What's a waste of time?" asked Paul. I got the feeling that he'd dealt with David already today, and didn't like him either.

"Second plan, if this didn't work," said Straub, answering for David. She sounded gutted, as if she had run out of options. "Authorised when you were getting nothing on the way over here, a last-ditch check. We get you near Caementum again, see if it makes any difference. Have to try it, at least." She pointed to a door in the back wall. "There's a toilet through there, and I'd advise using it if you haven't been recently. Bird'll be ready any second, and God knows when you're going to get another chance to go."

Paul grunted, and headed towards the door Straub had pointed to. The combination of my intense nerves and the mention of the toilet loosened something in my bladder. I realised I couldn't remember when I'd last gone ... it had been at the start of the flight over. Being someone who makes a rule of never passing up a chance for a piss (you really do never know when you're gonna get the chance to go when you're in an urban environment), I held up a finger.

"Am I all right to go as well?"

I saw David scowl, but Straub ignored him.

"You're not under arrest, Mr Pointer," she sighed. "You're helping us, and this isn't a classroom, contrary to appearances. Go, but be quick."

I entered the toilet just as the cubicle door shut behind Paul, which was fine by me. I've never felt entirely comfortable stood at the urinal with my cock out next to another man. Most people seem to just accept it as the done thing, but I've always been inherently aware of the actual reality of the situation. Same as communal showers; just not for me. This is one confusing social situation where for once I feel like *I'm* the one with the problem, though.

We both urinated in silence until I felt compelled to break it.

"How've you been? I have to say ... you're not looking the same."

I small snort came from the cubicle.

"You noticed, eh?" Paul said, his voice echoing slightly off the tiled walls. "Like I said ... I haven't been sleeping well. Life at home hasn't exactly been a bed of roses, to be honest."

"No?"

"Nope. The Mrs doesn't get much sleep now, 'cos of me at night. I get ... well

... I get more nightmares now, to tell you the truth. Bad ones." He was saying it in as lighthearted a way as he could manage, but again I knew better, the truth more clear in his words than he realised. "So after a bit it started to, y'know ... frazzle her nerves a bit. Lost her patience with me after a while."

"Patience with you doing what?"

There was a pause, and a small sigh.

"I dunno ... I've not really been ... myself, so much. I've missed a lot of work. Signed myself off as sick for a few weeks. Just couldn't face going in, you know." He paused, and then continued. "I've been moping about a lot, if I'm honest. Been finding it hard to go out. She was good about it at first, but ... she gets frustrated sometimes. I suppose I don't really blame her."

There was silence again, as if he wanted me to give my opinion, but I was thinking about my own situation. I'd had nightmares, but what had happened with Patrick had clearly taken its toll far more on Paul than it had with meEven in that moment, I should have been thinking about Paul, about what he was saying, but there I was, internalising again. I pulled my thoughts together.

"Have you seen anyone?" I asked, trying to make some kind of supportive response. I was *trying*. Isn't that worth something? "Have you thought about getting hellllllllllll—" My jaw suddenly stuck, and I held that last syllable as my entire body cramped up and I fell sideways. There was a white flash as my head hit the tiles, and I heard a corresponding bang from inside the cubicle. I was dimly aware that it had come from Paul falling bodily against the plastic cubicle wall.

Something was happening, that much was clear, but at that moment in time my main concern was not swallowing my tongue. No Shaun here to jam a wooden spoon between my jaws today, as my teeth ground painfully together and spittle ran from the left hand corner of my mouth. I remember thinking faintly that I'd been very lucky; I'd been milliseconds away from zipping up my fly. If it had hit at that moment, there could have been some major complications.

My knees were drawn up into my chest, and my head and shoulders pulled down towards them so much that they touched my forehead. It was like my entire body was trying to draw inside itself, as the pull kicked into me properly with intense force. It was all over me, expanding inside my bones, and then suddenly, behind the darkness of my screwed-up eyelids, a light seemed to grow. *Here we go*, I thought, and I was right. Emerging slowly into view, I saw a face.

It hung there just like before, but just as it fully arrived it became another, then another, too quick to see anything other than a flash of skin. Then back to the first one, too fast to make any of them out, their features and outlines so faint that at the speed they were switching they just became a blur of flesh and hair. One of the faces belonged to a woman, I thought I could see that much.

I can vividly remember there being a loud snapping sound this time, and then it all passed. I was lying on the tiled floor, soaked right through to my suit with sweat, and I could hear Paul breathing heavily as he pulled himself to his feet.

"Andy?" he gasped, fiddling with the catch on the cubicle door.

"Yes, fine, fine," I croaked back, realising my throat was now sore and dry. "You see that?"

"It was crazy," he said breathily, emerging from the cubicle. Like me, his clothing was dark with sweat. "It was just this … mess … I can't really describe—shit, have you seen your eye?"

I got up shakily and turned to the mirror, and then cried out in surprise. My right eye was totally bloodshot. I looked like something out of a horror film.

"Don't worry, don't worry," said Paul earnestly, trying to reassure me. "That shit heals, I know. It'll go." I forced myself away from the mirror and turned back to Paul, noticing the change in the pull. The first time it was all over my body, but singular, focused. Today, it had been without direction, without any sense of purpose. Now it seemed different again, like it was focused, yes, but …

"Does it feel the same as last time to you?" I asked Paul, and he looked down, trying to focus.

"No …" he said, uncertain. "It's like … it's harder to pick out. Can you tell which direction it is? There's … uh … it's going different ways?"

He was right. That was exactly what it felt like.

"Something's changed," I said, and was immediately proved right as Straub burst through the door.

"What the hell are you doing?" she shouted. She looked, for the first time, as if she were no longer in control of herself. Something had definitely happened. "Get a move on! We're delaying the chopper, you have to get on those maps now and see if anything's different—" She cut off abruptly, our appearance finally penetrating her fury. Looking at my bloodshot eye, she said, "Something changed, hasn't it? Did you detect it? Can you feel it now?"

"Wait, what the hell's happened out there?" asked Paul, bewildered. It had been a very intense two minutes.

"I think we know why you weren't getting anything," said Straub, hurriedly leading us back into the other room, where both David and the two civilians were jabbering frantically into radios or telephones and hammering at computers. "It was waiting."

"Waiting? What for?" I asked, my blood running cold, but I thought I already knew.

"Backup. It's not alone. There are two more of them. And they're different."

***

Chapter Seven: Two Out of Three Ain't Bad, A Dressing Down From David, The Sergeant, and A Very Unpleasant Trip To Birmingham

***

People went nuts. If things were bad before, this time it was far worse. If had just been the Stone Man alone, it might have died down quicker, but the panic and hysteria started in Coventry and spread like wildfire. Plus, the destruction before had been immense, but now it would spread in three directions, or perhaps become one solid wall of moving implacability. The concept was terrifying.

All the Internet theorists already believed that the Stone Man had caused Patrick's reported 'heart attack', intentionally or otherwise. They said either the force that powered it, or the strange stone-like material that its extraterrestrial body was constructed out of, was fatal to whichever human it had selected, simply by standing in their presence. Some believed that whoever sent the Stone Man was threatened from afar by the existence of its particular victim, that its creators knew something about the human gene that we didn't, and that they felt that Patrick could not be allowed to breed and create more like himself. Some fringe elements believed that Patrick was really an undercover alien, tracked down and executed by the Stone Man's vengeful owners. The theories were endless.

The one unifying through line in all of them, however, was that intentionally or otherwise, to be the Stone Man's target meant death. Everyone—even the politicians, reluctantly, as they had to be—was in open agreement on this. And that fact made it even more terrible during the Second Arrival when, across both traditional and social media, an immediate and forceful cry went up around the world:

Who are the Stone Men here for, and how do we find these people?

***

We were led at a run to Paul's previous computer terminal, when an idea struck me. I grabbed Straub's arm.

"Before, I visualised it," I said, blood rushing in my veins while the pull tried to drag me simultaneously in what I now knew were three separate directions. "I could see it, walking across the map, like in a computer game. I think I might need to see the new pair to be able to do that."

Straub didn't say a word, and instead waved her hand at a soldier who'd been holding a tablet PC up for one of the civilians, waiting patiently as they barked responses into their phone. The soldier hurried over, despite the civilians' protests (these ended sharply as soon as the civilian saw that the soldier had moved under Straub's orders) and Straub took the tablet from him. She thrust it into my hands, and I saw the now-familiar shot of the Stone Man standing in Millennium Place. But as I already knew, it had brought company. Behind it, seen via the slightly grainy Internet feed being shot from above, I saw the two new Stone Men ... even forewarned, I was shocked that these were indeed different.

The basic design was the same as the original—the tapered hands, the slightly elongated head, the rough, rocky surface and the gentle bend at the waist—but most notably, these were bigger. If the original had been around eight feet, these were closer to ten. And even more curiously, they were a different colour. The original was still its dark, greyish-brown colour, a fact that was even more clear now; the small amount of dust that had been surrounding it the last time I saw it was gone. Someone or something had given it a rubdown.

The new ones—albeit in a dim, washed out kind of way—were a pale, sickly blue.

I don't know why—maybe it was their size making them appear even more destructive and unstoppable, maybe it was the colour, maybe it the was the knowledge that they were here to remove parts of someone's body, and couldn't be stopped until they had—but seeing them there, motionless in the centre of Millennium Place on that cool October afternoon ... it scared the crap out of me.

"Jesus ..." said Paul. I'd seen enough, and pushed the tablet away.

"Right, got it," I muttered, and moved over to the computer screen and sat down, feeling uneasy, but not about whether or not I could work my magic this time. I knew I could; the incident in the toilet had made that clear enough. I didn't have time to enjoy or consider what I was actually doing in my reacquired role, or think about the bigger picture involved. Already, there had been another switch, and the job at hand meant that I just had to get on with it.

On the screen was a map of the UK. The PC functions were unnecessary, I knew; even if we zoomed in, we wouldn't get a clearer image of where the target was. At this range, just like before with the normal map, I couldn't be any more accurate. We would have the rough area, and we would have to travel there, but this time we had extremely rapid transport.

"You got this?" said Paul, leaning on the back of my chair. I thought about it; it might be different with three.

"Um ... I don't know," I said, head whirling. "Put your hand on my shoulder and concentrate or something. Think of the original Stone Man. We'll do him first."

Paul did as he was told, and as he did so I suddenly froze, half-expecting the jolt like our first meeting, and with no time to warn him ... but it didn't come. It seemed that once the circuit was complete, it was complete for good. Letting out a sigh, I looked at the map as I tried to picture the first Stone Man's solid bulk in my head, mentally putting it in Coventry on the screen before me.

Almost immediately, and far more quickly than before, the monitor disappeared and I was seeing the UK from above, with the moving seas again surrounding it. It was incredible, yet effortless and natural at the same time; of *course* I could see the UK like this, it was just a question of shifting perspective. I saw that now. While I saw the Stone Man standing still, my finger—not my whole hand this time, my finger, as with Paul's boost I could be more specific—raised of its own accord and travelled north again, fast at first, covering hundreds of miles. This target was a lot further north than Sheffield. It passed the border into Scotland, slowed down around Edinburgh ... and stopped.

"Edinburgh," I whispered, and Straub immediately pointed at the nearest soldier, who started whispering into their radio.

"Can you zoom in? Get us an address?" she asked, and I shook my head and shushed her.

"Paul," I said, feeling calm and focused now. "Think of the one on the left, the first blue one. Can you see it? Focus on them?"

"Got it," said Paul, equally quietly. We were working in sync, feeling our way together. The Stone Man on the UK image before my eyes was now switched, it's larger, pale blue companion taking its place. This time, my finger barely moved.

"Birmingham," I said.

"Thank Christ," breathed Straub, "minimal damage at that range."

"The other one now, please, Paul," I said, taking a deep breath before the final attempt.

"Uh huh," he whispered, eyes still closed. The figure in the centre of the map changed, but it was barely noticeable; it was the other's twin, after all.

This time, my finger started to head northwest again ... and then faltered. It was stopping, but not because of it finding its target; I was struggling to follow the signal any further.

"What's wrong?" asked Straub, sensing that there was a problem.

"I can't ... Paul?" I said, the image faltering before me as my concentration struggled.

"I know, I know," he said, "It's like—"

And then the vision before me vanished, and my head was full of a high-pitched screeching sound. It was ear-splitting, like brass fingernails on a ridged blackboard. I screamed at the same time that Paul did, and he let go of my shoulder as I let go of my focus. Mercifully, the screaming sound abruptly stopped, but I instantly became aware that the pull had reduced. The second blue Stone Man's signal was gone.

"What the fuck ..." Paul gasped, but I knew immediately. It was obvious. Wide eyed, I turned to Straub.

"They've cut us off," I said, my voice shaking. "Their owners know."

The room was silent for a moment, with even Straub at a loss for words. This latest development implied something else; in a roundabout way, this was a form of contact. They'd responded to our actions, whoever or whatever they were. Either way—with one of the blues at least—we were out.

"The original, are you cut off from the original as well?" snapped Straub, and I already knew the answer; I still had a link to that one, at least, as strong as ever. I tried to feel for the remaining Blue as well; I had that too.

"Yeah, I've got the original, and the other Blue too. Paul?"

"Just those two, yeah," he said, shaking his head. "We stayed in there too long, I think. Like, in deep contact. Maybe if we'd come out sooner ..."

"Maybe, but anyway it's too late for that," said David, heading for the door, and speaking over his shoulder. "We still have two, and that will have to do. We've got to get you both in the air immediately and over Edinburgh so we can narrow down on the original's target. We've no idea if you're going to be able to find the target quickly, and even if you do we don't know if we can beat the blue one to its Birmingham target by the time we're done in Scotland. Let's get in the air. Agreed?" David was aiming this question at Straub, who was nodding. She began to head for the door as well, beckoning for us to do the same. I looked at Paul; he seemed to share my confusion.

"But ... you have the trajectory," I said, following David regardless. "You can't take the targets to the Stone Man, or they'll die once they leave their containment zone. We saw that with Patrick, the guy started to have a goddamn seizure once we drove him away from his house. I mean, yes, the Stone Man will kill them anyway, but who knows what happens if they die before it gets them? Does the Stone Man then move onto someone else? You can't risk the extra damage involved in that, surely?"

Straub didn't answer, as she was busy on the radio commandeering units in the north, telling them to be on standby for our arrival and giving the evacuation orders and rough trajectory coordinates. David didn't either, simply because he was ignoring me. We headed out of the building, and towards the nearest hanger and the now-familiar sound of rotary blades. Whether it was due the tension of the situation, or just anger from my dislike of David, I've no idea, but I reached out and grabbed his shoulder. I didn't pull him around to face me—I hadn't plucked up that amount of guts, for certain—but he stopped and turned of his own accord, looking pretty pissed off himself.

"You want our help, and I asked you a question," I said quietly, before he could speak. I surprised myself. It was tough guy talk, certainly far tougher than I'd ever tried on in my life. I didn't think I could intimidate David, but I thought I could let him know that I was serious, and prepared to dig my heels in even now.

"Plus," said Paul, stepping up beside me, "we haven't actually been told the plan here. I know time is a big issue and everything, but I want to know what you plan to do with the targets once the poor bastards are found. Hide them? Cover them with lead, and hope it breaks the signal? We didn't know what would happen to them before. Now we know what the Stone Men are here to do to them. What do *you* plan to do?" Paul folded his arms, and I became aware of the size difference between him and David. Not that it probably made much of a difference; I had a feeling that David had enough training up his sleeve to take down Paul with minimal effort, and then have his reporter friend for dessert.

"What do you think, Winter?" said David, angrily. Aggression seemed to be his default setting. "Don't be naïve. This isn't the time for experimentation, and the instructions have been very clear and simple: damage limitation. So that's what we're doing. People die the more time we spend pissing about, so feel free to moralise all you like, but every moment we delay risks another death on *your* conscience, not mine."

"But that doesn't even make any sense," said Paul, his voice rising to match David's level of aggression. "Andy's right. We can't move them, as you risk killing them before the Stone Man gets what it needs. You don't know what might happen. It might, I dunno, just go off wildly and never stop, you've no idea—"

"We've been planning and researching this for months, Winter, do you think we have no ideas at all?" snapped David, interrupting. "You arrogant prick. There were two radiation spikes from the Stone Man at specific points once it started walking, right? To put it in terms you'd be able to understand, these were on the long-distance frequency of the electromagnetic spectrum, meaning that they were designed to travel—guess what—very long distances.

We think either of those rad spikes might have been the point that the Stone Man somehow created the barrier, if you like, for the targets. Maybe it simply affected their minds so that they believed there was a barrier there, a belief strong enough to kill them if they went far enough past it. Maybe it was a real, physical thing, we don't know!" David threw his hands up, the nonstop tension of the day combining with his anger to animate him. "But the point is, it might mean there's a window, a chance to move the target closer. The second major spike was several hours after the first, and *that* could have been the one that actually put the barrier up, with the first being some kind of seeding signal, right? That's a long enough gap between the spikes to make it worth the effort. Plus, the original didn't become active in any sense until roughly two hours after its arrival, and it looks like it's been waiting for its buddies to get that process started again. It hasn't started walking yet. So we *might* have that extra two hours here too. We're not fucking morons, if we're wrong and the target shows signs of physical seizure, as with C.I. Four, we take them back inside the barrier. We have to *try* the first option, at least." He finished, and brought his arms against his sides sharply, causing his hands to slap against his legs. It was an unintentionally camp gesture that would have been funny at any other time. "Now do either of you two arseholes disagree with that, or can we get a fucking move on? Happy now?"

He stood glaring at us, jaw set, and we felt suitably chastised. I nodded sheepishly, not happy at being spoken to like that but shamed because he was right. Lives were at risk. We didn't have all the information, and we weren't helping. The time to challenge David was when we were presented with the whole situation, not when we knew only half of it. We should have gotten in the air first, then asked en route. I tried to ignore the more important fact highlighted by his response—that people would definitely die—by reminding myself that we would help more people live by finding the targets. It didn't really work.

The door opened behind us and Straub appeared, looking shocked that we were all still stood there. David saw her, shook his head at us and began walking again. We fell into step, and shortly after that the four of us were airborne, again with two soldiers as escorts.

Paul and I were silent during the flight, which took around an hour and half by my reckoning. David and Straub were in constant radio contact with various people, liaising with different aspects of the police and military as they scrambled to prep for the whole length of the two trajectories, the ones of which we knew the end points. We could only hope that the third Stone Man, the one also heading northwest, wasn't going much further than Birmingham;

its trajectory was, for the first part at least, the same as the other Blue. Paul and I stared out of the window, watching the UK pass below us like a toy landscape as the pull in our bodies slowly grew. Paul's nose had begun to bleed again, although he had waved off Straub's concern over it, and had been wiping it with the hem of his T-shirt ever since. I can't speak for Paul, but as I endured the physical assault, I tried not to think about what we were doing, as the creeping, nagging thoughts questioning the morals of what we were doing began to work their way into my consciousness. Yes, we were potential lifesavers, heroes if not heroic in our demeanour; but mainly we were the point men for an assassination mission, and the targets were not terrorists or guerrilla revolutionaries, but ordinary people. If Patrick was anything to go by, they already knew that their death was coming, sensing several days in advance that something had been sent to claim them, and we were as much a part of that now as the Stone Men themselves. Hell, we wanted to help them do it quicker. They'd been sent to do a murderous job by someone, and so had we. Telling ourselves that we were doing it for the safety of others didn't help, and knowing that my role in all of this made me feel important as well as guilty sickened me to my stomach. I couldn't help it though. You have to understand.

Once we were nearing Edinburgh's airspace, David finally addressed us; by this point, the shakes, racing heartbeat and light-headedness were back, nearly at the level they'd been at on the way to Patrick's.

"We're nearly there," he said. "You two need to start doing your thing, and directing the pilot. He can hear you through your headset mic. Once we're over the right street, he'll land us as near as possible. Our pickup is on standby."

We nodded—the pull was so strong that we already knew it wouldn't be a problem—but I thought it was too soon.

"We should hold on until we're right over Edinburgh," I said shaking my head. "We've been cut off by one of them, and I think it's because they knew someone actively tuned into them last time. I think we should spend as little time tuned into them as possible. Let's wait until we're right over Edinburgh." David held my gaze for a few moments before shrugging sulkily and turning away. Obviously, he didn't want to admit it, but he knew I was right. Finally, a point for me over David.

Once we were closer, I took the lead in directing the pilot, letting Paul keep his eyes shut and try to ride it out as best he could. He took this role gratefully, and I felt he'd earned it; hadn't I been the one swanning back and forth between Britain and America, having the hedonistic time of my life, while he'd been at home with nightmares and a wife who was running out of patience? It got harder and harder to speak as we drew nearer, but I gritted my teeth and got on with it, giving directions with a weak, shaking voice. I kept releasing my grip on the signal intermittently, hoping it would make me harder to spot. Either way, we remained connected, whether it was due to my approach or not. I was not cut off at any point, and we steadily homed in on the target. One thing that did concern me slightly was the fact that I hadn't flashed into the eyes of any of the Stone Men yet. Not that I wanted to, of course, and it might have been mainly to do with the fact that the original had been walking, and for a long time, before I first found myself seeing out of its head ... but I still found myself thinking, again, that they didn't like us snooping, and had taken more precautions this time.

By sheer, dumb luck, once I'd identified the street—which would later be revealed to be Lismore Avenue—there was a bowling club two streets over. Although the green would be ruined, and the current game abandoned once a military helicopter plonked itself down in the middle of it, the players would have something to talk about for years to come. It seemed that not even the televised Second Arrival could prevent the people of the Postal Bowling Club from playing on match day. Clearly the evacuation either hadn't begun yet, or hadn't reached these streets.

Straub called off the pickup as we were so close, and instructed the waiting unit to rendezvous with us on Lismore Avenue, but then took another look at myself and Paul and thought better of it. Even though it would have been about a thirty second walk, she clearly either didn't trust us to make it in our current state, or thought it would take too long.

Once the pickup team had cleared the bowlers from the green, the chopper set down and we disembarked, with Paul and I having to be helped to step down from the chopper. We were bundled into a waiting jeep, bodies shaking and teeth wanting to burst, and after the seconds-long drive we were slowly cruising along Lismore Avenue. Parked up ahead was a military APC, which we knew contained an armed unit. There was one lone soldier stood outside it to dissuade onlookers, but already we could see faces staring out from the windows that we passed. Just like before, all the military vehicles looked immensely out of place in such a suburban setting.

"Just tell us when we're outside," said Straub, gently but firmly. "Tell us which one."

On cue, we both raised our hands once the Jeep drew alongside the correct building, but it wouldn't have been necessary; it was the only house with the curtains fully drawn. Like Patrick, they clearly knew their number was up. It made the place seem creepy, foreboding. Suddenly it became the locked down house of the crazy old inventor, or of the family that no one ever sees come and go, while the strange thudding and chopping sounds come from inside.

Either way, inside that house was the man or woman we had been sent to try and take to their murderer. Even in my current state, I felt cold and sick. This was awful. Truly awful.

"Can you see where he is? Like before? Can you see where in the building he is?" asked David rapidly—he knew all the details of our previous excursion—and we stared through our tired, wincing eyes at the front of the house.

Like before, the pull had become so strong that we had that strange effect of half-seeing, half-feeling the figure inside. This time they were easier to spot. This time they weren't lying on the floor.

"He's ... sitting, right?" said Paul, looking at me.

"Uh huh," I agreed, trying to make out more of the image. "Looks like he's on a chair. He's sitting very still."

"He? A man again?" asked Straub, pulling out her radio.

"No ... no, I don't know," I babbled, frustrated with both the effort and the question. "I mean *they* are sitting then, whatever sex they are. If it's a woman though, she's a stocky one." Meanwhile, the other soldiers got busy 'evacuating' the neighbours (read: removing witnesses) and loading them onto a newly arrived truck. They were each brought out over the next few minutes, featuring the expected complainers and shouters, but they were moved without real incident and extremely quickly at that. Straub and David were silent while this went on, apart from the odd 'hold position' reminder over the radios to the other waiting men, who were now in a line along the terraced row of houses. I sat quietly and tried to ride it all out, to shut it all off as much as possible while my body rebelled against me. I thought Paul might have been trying to get my attention, but I was having none of it.

"Okay," she said, and began to raise her radio to her mouth.

"Wait," said Paul, suddenly lunging forward. "I can feel something—"

"You're done here, Winter," said David, already stepping out of the jeep and heading to the APC, from which several soldiers were already emerging and beginning to converge neatly by the house door. It looked like David didn't take any chances on the front lines. He addressed the soldier driving the jeep; whatever David's job title, it clearly held some rank. "Take these two up the street, around the block, wherever, and keep an eye on them until further notice."

"Hold on," said Straub, still seated and talking to both the soldier and David. "I have the authority on this operation." Silently, I rejoiced, loving the one-up on David even in my fragile state. She turned to Paul, but her face was, as usual, all business. She was, I noted again, a thorough professional. "What is it, Mr Winter? Be *extremely* quick." I saw David bristle, then watched as he turned to the ranking soldier stood nearby and started to bark questions.

"*We* have to go in," said Paul to Straub, meaning the two of us. He slurred his words slightly as he spoke, his mouth slower to react than he wanted it to be. "We have to make contact. There's something … Andy, can't you feel it?" He didn't make eye contact with me, and I knew why; I had absolutely no idea what the fuck he was talking about. So far, this situation was exactly the same as before in terms of the pull and the abuse my body was enduring. What the hell was Paul playing at?

"Don't try me, Mr Winter," said Straub, terse and stern. She was clearly about to end this interaction, and we'd been extremely lucky to get this much time. "If you're trying something on, you really will regret it, I promise."

"They've bloody changed something, I'm telling you *they've changed something*," said Paul, his voice rising to a shout as he suddenly leant out of the jeep and shouted at the advancing soldiers. "*Stop those men!*" he screamed. "*If they go inside, they'll kill the target!*"

"*Halt!*" shouted Straub, and the advancing men did exactly as they were told, but she grabbed Paul's T-shirt and yanked him back into the jeep, a movement that he either allowed or couldn't resist in his weakened state. With both of them sitting, he looked like a giant compared to her, but it didn't matter; her blazing eyes made me cower, and I wasn't even the guy they were being trained on. Straub, finally, had nearly lost it, and I should have known what it would take to cause this; somebody interfering with her professionalism, and at a moment when it really counted.

"You fuck with my operation one more time, Winter, and I will have you beaten to within an inch of your life!" she growled, her face inches from his. "No one will know about it, I guarantee it, and if you don't want to end up in the worst human-rights-free hellhole of a prison that I can find on this planet, so tell me right know *what the fuck you're playing at.*"

Paul didn't bat an eyelid at any of this, though. He'd grabbed my hand, hard, and was now too busy frantically pointing at the house and shouting. I'd never seen him like this. He was so frantic that he was almost whining.

"I knew it! I couldn't see it for certain until I grabbed your hand for the connection, Andy, but they've changed something! They've changed the perimeter, they've changed it! We were wrong, *the perimeter is already there and it's different!* Andy, can't you feel it? Feel *around* the house, stop trying to feel *inside* it! They've changed it just like they've cut us off from the other Blue!" He looked at Straub, his eyes wide and pleading as his trembling free hand balled into a fist. "They don't want us interfering, I don't know why but they don't! Those men cross the perimeter, *the target dies too early*, I'm telling you! Andy, tell her!"

I looked at Straub, her anger already fading, hesitation growing. This was new, it was unexpected, and at the same time it was dawning on me it was also dawning on her; the military had banked on everything being the same as last time, and it suddenly wasn't. From the very start, this was different. New Stone Men ... they should have expected more new additions to the situation. And here was one of them.

Paul whirled around to me fully and grabbed my collar with his free hand, but not hard enough to pull me towards him; he didn't have the strength.

"Feel *around* the house," he urged again, almost spitting in my eyes as he did so. "We were trying so hard to find the target, we almost missed the booby trap! They don't want us here, whatever we did with Patrick, be it the, the, the thing, the adrenaline injections, whatever, *they didn't like it!* We tainted him, don't you see, putting those chemicals in him? They want him their way or they don't want him at all! Can't you feel it? It's moving, it's moving on the floor! Use the connection!" He held up both of our hands, clasped together, and shook them in front of my face.

I was speechless, rattled utterly by these new revelations, and as my mouth gaped and I stared into Paul's eyes—who by turning to me had now turned his back on Straub—I watched one of those eyes open and close in a very rapid wink.

I got it. I couldn't believe it. *Paul, you sneaky little bastard.* On that day of unbelievable events, the thing that shocked me the most out of all them was the sheer size of Paul's balls.

He was gambling, quite possibly, with his own freedom, and banking it all on his acting skills. Looking back, I can see why he would. He'd been great. On any other day I might have frozen with the shock of it, but with all the craziness going on, I somehow found myself rising to the challenge in a way that I might have otherwise failed to pull off. I didn't have to pretend to be feeling the pull, after all; I just had to adapt the truth. I had no real idea what Paul was trying to get at, or what he was trying to achieve with this charade of his; if it turned out that he was trying to sabotage the operation, I decided then and there that I would ruin that attempt. I didn't like the idea of doing that, but I believed the operation was the best and only option, damned as we would be, and I didn't want it stopped by a possible attack of pointless principle from Paul. But I didn't think Paul *was* trying to do that. Either way—unless I definitely knew he wasn't onside with the mission—I had to back him. He was going to jail if I didn't, and strangely, in that moment, I realised that he had become my friend. It's funny, isn't it, how things only strike you in the right place and time. If that moment never comes, how would you ever know?

I looked at Straub to check if she'd seen—I couldn't help it—but I immediately looked away, encouraged by the clear confusion on her face. David was shouting something over the radio, but I ignored it and focused on the house, on the pull, closing my eyes. I was going to have to pull off a convincing performance of my own, now and under immense pressure. Paul's hand hit me in the chest.

"Try holding my hand, use the connection," he said. He sounded completely sincere. I grasped his hand, still staring at the house as intently as I could, trying to focus on the pull for inspiration without looking as if I was faking it.

"Those ... those sneaky *bastards*," I said, trying to match Paul's tone. "It *is* different. I can see it ... it's near the door ... the window ... but ... it's ... it's moving?" I hoped to God this was the kind of thing he wanted, and I had to restrain an urge to look at Straub to see how I was doing, but I knew that would blow the whole thing. I was terrified.

"The gaps," said Paul, still working the urgency in his voice. "Can you see the *gaps*?"

And that's when I got the rest of it.

Gaps in a moving barrier, and everybody would believe only we could see it.

Paul wanted one of us to get into the house for some reason. I had to make a choice then and there if I was still on board. I still didn't dare look at Straub, but I took her continued silence to mean that she was buying this. She wouldn't have let us go on this long if she didn't. And who could blame her? Our whole story before was insane, and we'd been proved right. Why would she think this was any different? She had to trust us ... or at least we were gambling that she did.

"*Yes*," I said, surprising myself at how believable it sounded; the amazement in my voice was clear to all. "I see them. It's not perfect; they must have changed it in a hurry and thought it was enough. They've put a perimeter, a different one, I feel like it's ... lethal. Maybe not just to the target, either." I heard Straub sigh, but not in annoyed or impatient way. I thought I heard dismay, frustration. I pressed on. "Someone could get in, but ... you'll never get that squad in. It's moving too fast, I'd have to guide them and ... I couldn't do it...."

"Can you get through?" snapped Straub, brief, low and efficient. That was it. We had her.

202

"I ... I think so ... but ... what if I get subdued? That guy's a lot bigger than Patrick, I can see it from here." No acting here; it was a genuine question.

"You're not both going in," said Straub. "That's out of the question. We have no idea what's in there, and if we lose you both we're screwed." There was also an edge to her voice now, a slight tone, and to this day I don't know if it meant maybe she didn't believe us one hundred percent. Straub was a very smart woman; she would have had doubts, I think.

"We have to," said Paul, "we can't see them without each other, and it might be too dangerous on our own."

"If Patrick was anything to go by, they'll be alone," I said, actually starting to believe we might get away with this. "They look big, but not as big as Paul, and I think we'll be okay. There's two of us, don't forget. And you must have some kind of non-lethal weaponry here? Pepper spray, rubber bullets?"

"And how exactly are you going to get them out?" asked Straub, angry and uncertain ... but I thought she was considering it.

"We can get *one* man through the gaps between us, just not a whole military unit. Believe me, Brigadier, the last thing I want is to go into that house," I lied, really pushing my luck but thinking it was necessary. "I've already got my money and frankly I'd rather be on a beach somewhere than dealing with half-naked crazies. I'm trying to be a real reporter and not the flavour of the month, but if you want this problem solved with the target alive or without losing half of your men, this is the only way."

Straub stared at us for a moment, and raised her radio to her mouth.

"Do we have an ID on the resident yet, over?" she said.

When the voice came back over the speaker, and I knew we'd taken another step towards getting inside.

"Williams, Henry P. Aged seventy-three, husband to Williams, Mildred R., deceased. Over."

Straub spoke into the radio, this time while still looking at us.

"Stand by. Over and out." She turned to face the APC, and to the ranking officer of some sort that David had been talking to earlier. David was nowhere to be seen, presumably inside the APC.

"Any signs of forced entry?" she called over, and was met with a shake of the head. She turned back to us, seemed about to say something, and then hesitated. She pointed at Paul. When she spoke again, she was clearly very angry, but I wondered how much of that was directed at herself for even listening to us. She shouldn't have blamed herself, if so. She had no choice, really.

"I could get on the phone to Boldfield right now, and get him to correlate any radiation spikes we've detected since Caementum One's return—and there have been a few, I'm not saying how many—but he is up to his fucking eyeballs in it right now, and it would take him time," she snapped, her voice still low and deeply threatening, her finger pointed at Paul's face like knife. "What I'm faced with is suiting you two up in stab armour—as I very much doubt that a British man in his seventies is packing heat—and sending you in to face a pensioner that you could take down even if you're physically out of it. Plus, let's face it, in terms of Caementum, or Caementum One at least, you two are the closest thing to experts we have, and you didn't screw things up when you were unsupervised. We have rubber bullets, and heat imaging sights, and the target is in the front room of the house. So, as long as he stays in that room—that's a big front window—we can even provide ranged backup, to an extent. On paper, it's all there. The risks are pretty much zero, you could say." She leant further forward, very close to us now, her lip curling with now barely concealed fury. "*If you're telling me the truth,*" she added, spitting the words out through gritted teeth. A vein was throbbing in her forehead. "So believe me, once this is over, I *will* correlate the spikes. And I'll know if you're bullshitting me. So trust me—*trust me*—if you're lying, take it back now, and I'll let this pass. But this. Is. Your. Only. Chance."

I will admit, I was the most terrified that I had been since this whole affair had begun over three months ago, and if Paul hadn't have answered first I might have confessed then and there. I'll say it. Why not? What do I have to lose? I might have done it ... I probably would have done.

"It's the truth," said Paul. His poker face was amazing. Straub turned to me. "Mr Pointer? Andy?"

I heard myself reply, my voice seeming to come from someone else.

"It's the truth. I just want to get out of here."

She stared at us for a long time, and then, not taking her eyes off us, I was sure I heard a faint sigh. She then raised the radio again.

"I need two stab vests, two helmets and two headsets up here right now." She addressed us again. "Gentlemen, tell me exactly where he is in the room and I'll tell you how this is going to go."

***

I've timed this about perfectly, I think. The booze is taking care of business very, very nicely ... excellent. Good job. I find this next part pretty hard to talk about, you see.

***

So that's how Paul and I found ourselves covered in the gear that Straub had requested, standing behind a perimeter of our own; the men and vehicles forming a rough semicircle around the entrance, about fifteen feet away from it. Straub was going through the instructions for the fifth time, her voice loud and clear through the two-way headsets we were wearing.

In a nutshell, we were to find our way through the 'gaps', and then to use the glass cutter provided to pop the downstairs window. It was the kind that extended from the front of the house, with two smaller, angled side windows and a large centre pane. We were to go in through the side pane, while Straub's men covered us via the centre. They had the target sighted through their heat vision scopes now; he was still sitting in his chair, unmoving. The warmth of his body indicated that he was still alive, a fact that I might have doubted otherwise. There was no way they could just be asleep with all the chaos going on outside, and surely they wouldn't be sitting upright, out on display in relatively open space in the middle of the room. It was confusing; Patrick had been doing his terrified best to hide when we'd turned up. Why did this person appear to be waiting? It was more than confusing, in fact; it was frightening. But if Paul was going in, then I didn't feel that I could let him go in alone.

But I'd make sure he went in first.

Once inside, we were to identify the target, and to inform him that he was being 'evacuated'. If he didn't comply, then we were to subdue him with the chloroform rags we'd been given. We asked why they just didn't stun dart him through the window so that we could bring him out; apparently, given his age, the chemical risk of direct injection was just too high. To my concern, we'd also been given extendable batons as backup. Again, overkill, but they weren't taking any chances ... other than letting two untrained civilians inside. But again, what choice did they have? Plus, as Straub had said, on paper, it all looked reasonably foolproof.

David was stood a few feet back from the group, talking on his phone and occasionally scowling at us. I tried not to catch his eye as Straub finished.

"Keep chatter to a minimum, both with the target and between yourselves. Only communicate that which is absolutely necessary. Get in, get the target, get out. Understood?"

"Got it," said Paul, as confidently as his shaking voice would let him sound. His symptoms were still bad, as were mine, and I heard the weakness in him and suddenly remembered the trouble that I'd had last time with getting in through a window. I realised Straub was looking at me, and nodded quickly. My mouth was dry and I didn't want to speak.

Straub looked us over one more time, and nodded to herself, as if to say *Well, here we go.* She had her own headset on now, and spoke into it.

"Civilian team entering the premises. All units stand by." Then, to us: "In your own time, gentlemen. Good luck."

We began to walk towards the house, to the left-hand-side front window, as instructed. I glanced over my shoulder, to see Straub holding up a set of what I assumed were infrared or heat vision goggles, and a soldier lying on top of the APC sighting through a scoped rifle. I assumed it had a last-ditch tranquiliser dart inside it in case something went wrong; even though they didn't want to use it, they would take the shot if necessary. I shuddered, and turned back to the house, where Paul stood a foot or two in front, holding out his hand behind him. I wondered what the hell he was doing, and then I remembered the setup; I took his hand, and at that moment Paul jumped backwards dramatically, acting like he'd seen something in front of him.

"*Jesus!*" he shouted. "Keep up, Andy, for fuck's sake! It's closer than I thought! Concentrate, will you?" He was damn good.

"Sorry," I muttered, and followed Paul's lead as he instructed me to get shoulder to shoulder so that we could 'move at the same time'. This also helped keep us both upright, as we were going to need to save our minimal remaining strength to get in through the window. In this fashion we pantomimed our way towards the house, bodies tense and radiating fear as we acted as if we were dancing through a moving minefield. I think we were both aware of the need to keep it realistic, but also to not take too much time about it; we'd taken up an extra ten minutes since Paul's first charade as it was. It worked, either way. At one point, when we made a sudden leap in unison, I heard several of the soldiers behind us jump slightly back. I couldn't blame them. We'd made a real meal out of this.

Eventually we reached the window, and as Paul took out the glass cutter, he spoke into the mouthpiece.

"Perimeter cleared," he said, "attempting to enter the premises. Commencing cutting procedure ... now."

Despite the situation, I raised an eyebrow at him and smirked slightly.

He looked at me for a second, and then shrugged in a *Well, I don't know, do I* kind of way, then carried on cutting the pane. After a minute or two, he'd sliced a square in it large enough for even his bulk to squeeze through. Fortunately, this time he knocked the bottom of the pane inwards so that the top of it fell outwards, dropping onto the path and not leaving a minefield of glass inside, like at Patrick's. I lunged—or rather, wobbled—forward as it fell, and actually managed to catch it. I don't know why I bothered; I just felt like any sudden noises might affect the situation. I propped the cut section of the pane against the outside of the house—the building was old and single glazed—and knelt down, lacing my fingers together for Paul's foot. I took a deep breath, and nodded at Paul. He gave me the thumbs-up, and put his boot on my palms.

"Commencing ..." began Paul, and then he caught my eye. "Ah, going in now," he said quickly, and pulled himself through the frame. It took him several breathless attempts, but he eventually made it halfway in. He managed to prop himself up on the way through, pushing past the drawn blind and using some unseen object just inside the window (at one point his weakened arms nearly gave way, but he managed to save himself) and then stood, turning around to face me and reaching his arms out. Taking his hands, I weakly fumbled my way up and inside as well, and then stage one was complete.

"We're inside," I said into the headset mic, taking in my surroundings. The room was dark, very dark, so much so that it was hard to see, but it was clearly a room that hadn't changed for some time. The amount of clutter was immense; cabinets filled with unseen ornaments, and silhouettes of large pot plants that stood out against the few sources of light that were peeking through the drawn curtains. Ferns, miniature palms. Any available surface had bric-a-brac on it, and the wallpaper was some kind of darkened pattern that I couldn't make out. Unlike Patrick's, however, it didn't smell. The surfaces all appeared to be clear, and if there was leftover food lying around, we couldn't smell it.

The object by the window that Paul had used to prop himself was an ancient TV—like Patrick's, it was turned off at the moment—and this was facing a large armchair on the other side of the room. In the armchair, sitting upright, was the dim shape of Williams, Henry P., aged seventy-three, widower of Williams, Mildred R.

In the dark, we couldn't see if his eyes were open, but we could hear him breathing; he was taking slow, deep, but trembling breaths. Maybe he was asleep after all? But before anything else, I had to know what going on with Paul. I was in deep enough already without going blindly into even murkier depths. I'd let Paul put me in harm's way, however unlikely, and worse, I knew that I could end up being shafted for treason. I put my hand over the microphone, which I knew would probably cause noise on the other end, but I thought at least Straub and company couldn't see me do it.

"*What the hell is all this about?*" I half-mouthed, half-whispered. Paul turned to me and covered his own mouthpiece, holding up his free hand in an attempt to let me know he was sorry.

"*I'm sorry, Andy, honestly,*" he said quickly, using the same barely audible voice, but his eyes were boring into mine with great intensity. "*But could you do it? Could you let them storm in here like a goddamn drugs raid?*"

"*What?*" I asked, confused, but glancing at the shape in the chair, half expecting this elderly man to get up and charge at us, fingers drawn into hooks that were aiming for our eyes.

"*We* owe *these people this much,*" whispered Paul. "*Just, just a* chance *at going out with some dignity. Those assholes out there would kick the fucking door in, sling him over their shoulders and bundle him into the back of the van!*" He shook his head at the thought, his jaw grinding. "*One way or the other, this poor bastard is going to* die *for this country, whether he likes it or not. And we're the gun dogs that led the lynch mob to him. Okay, I get that, it has to be done. But I'll be* damned *if I'm going to let them drag him out into the street without at least giving him a* chance *to walk out of their own accord. I can't fucking sleep as it is, Andy! I can't sleep! I keep seeing ...*" He stopped, his eyes wide and pleading, and then held up his free hand, taking a deep breath and looking at the floor. "*You understand. Tell me you understand.*"

I stared at him, wondering if I actually did, but Straub's interruption over the headsets saved me.

"Pointer, Winter, report. What are you doing? What is the situation?"

"We're just checking the immediate area, Brigadier," replied Paul, his eyes now back on mine. "Just checking that we're okay to proceed, so we don't run into any other unpleasant surprises."

"All right. Proceed with caution, but also with efficiency. Can you see the target?"

"We can," I replied, "I don't know if he's—"

"I can ... hear you, you know," came the voice from the darkness, and we both jumped back a foot with fright. The voice had been clear, but also breathy and trembling, like that of a man having to exercise extreme physical control. It was the voice of a man making a great, taxing effort.

"We've ... we've made contact," said Paul, trying to compose himself, hard enough in this new situation even without our nerves already being on fire.

"Roger that," said Straub, "Proceed then, gentlemen. The clock is now ticking. They've—" And she broke off, as if she was hesitating to tell us something.

"What was that, Brigadier?" I asked, pushing the headphones against my ears. Straub paused for a second, and I could hear her sigh.

"They've started to walk," she said, quietly. "This needs wrapping up, and fast. We have to get to Birmingham, as quick as we can."

Paul and I shared a glance.

"Okay," I said, but my voice was even weaker than before. "We're on it."

We moved slowly towards the armchair, our eyes more accustomed to the dark. Henry Williams wasn't speaking, but I could hear those heavy, heavy breaths; it was like listening to someone who was trying to stop themselves from being sick. As we drew closer, he spoke again, and it was like the words were being pulled out of him. It was taking a great effort for him to speak clearly.

"It's me, isn't it? They're ... here for me this time."

We immediately stopped dead in mild shock, mouths gaping like idiots. He knew ... and yet here he was. Waiting.

"Mmm ... I thought so," Henry said, sadly ... but also with what sounded like resolve. I noticed that, despite the city we were in, his accent wasn't Scottish. He actually sounded English, and well-spoken at that. Posh, even. He shifted slightly in his seat, and as he did so, he caught the light. Now I could see two things; one, that his whole body was shivering violently, and two, that he was wearing clothes of a very unexpected nature.

Henry Williams was wearing what appeared to be full military dress uniform, right down to the beret. There was even a few medals on his chest, and his sleeve bore one of the few symbols of rank that I recognised; three chevrons. He wasn't *Mr* Henry Williams, then. He was *Sergeant* Henry Williams, Retired.

And he knew what was coming, and had decided to meet it appropriately dressed.

I was so stunned by it all that I blindly tried to stick to the script.

"Sir, uh, we, we uh ... here to, uh, evacuate ..." I started, unable to meet his gaze as I fumbled my way through my words. Henry cut me off as he closed his eyes and weakly raised a hand, taking in a heavy breath through his nose as he did so. His shivers increased for a second, and he let out a little noise as he gritted his teeth and clamped them down. The shivers eventually lessened, but they didn't stop. His head slumped forward slightly, and he then shook it slowly.

"I know you'll have your ... orders, young man," he said, without looking up. He sounded unimaginably tired. "So it's commendable that you're trying to carry them out, even ... when we both know what you're saying is nonsense." The words shivered from his lips, like a man trying to speak through hypothermia. He looked at me, and squinted; I could see his facial features more clearly now. A large nose on a broad, flat face. Small eyes under thick, grey eyebrows, eyebrows that matched the few remaining bits of thin grey hair on the sides of his head visible from the point where the beret stopped. "I know your face, don't I?" he said. "The ... fellow from the television? You were with the ... Prime Minister." I nodded in response, silent, but Straub barked in my ear.

"What's he saying, Pointer? We're getting static on our devices. Get him out of there."

I ignored her, and looked at Paul for guidance, lost, mouth working soundlessly, moronically. Paul was staring at Henry, and slowly raising his hand.

"Sir ..." said Paul, "I'm afraid I'm respectfully going to ... have to ... ask you to come with us. It's ... it's for the good of the country." He almost looked embarrassed saying the last part, and I felt I needed to back him up.

"It's going to save lives," I offered, and immediately felt the same thing that Paul did. It wasn't embarrassment; it was shame. There was a dignity at hand here that neither of us possessed.

"Indeed," said Henry, nodding slowly. "I saw the whole—" Henry stopped talking and gasped, then breathed out heavily, clamping down on himself again. He then continued once his breath was back. "The whole business, on the television. Chaos, utter chaos. Families ... children mixed up in it. Dreadful business." He felt around the left-hand arm of his chair, looking for something, and found the head of his cane. "Not ... not really had a fantastic few days of it ... myself ..." He went to stand, and Paul and I darted forward.

"*No!*" Henry suddenly shouted, his voice cracking. I couldn't tell if it was from effort or emotion. Either way, we backed off, and let him stand up unassisted. It was painful to watch. The shivers, combined with his own stiffness, made a process that would be mere seconds long for Paul or myself take nearly a minute for Henry as his shaking and elderly limbs struggled to support his weight. He looked like his body should be audibly creaking, and when his head wasn't bent downwards with effort, we could see the stress of the movement standing out all over his straining face. Between the arms of the chair and the use of his cane, Henry managed, eventually, to get himself into a standing position. His expression was pained, but his stance, once upright, was as proud as he could physically manage. Sweat ran down his heavily lined face.

"Not ... normally ... that hard," he said, and looked us both up and down as he adjusted his feet.

"Knew ... someone would be here eventually," he said, nodding. "Knew this morning ... when I turned on the television ... and saw that thing. I knew that's what ... last few days had been down to. Was almost a relief ... finally knowing what it had all been about."

"What do you mean?" I asked, but my voice was almost a whisper. "What *what* was about?"

"Winter, Pointer, what's taking so long?" barked Straub's voice over the headsets, jolting us. "He's upright, we can see it, let's go! What on earth are you stood there talking for, what are you saying? Hurry up!"

"We're *coming*," snapped Paul. "We're on our way, he's just getting his breath."

Henry's eyebrows raised on his shaking forehead.

"Can't ... talk to a superior officer that way, young man," he said, sternly. "Show some ... respect."

"Sorry," said Paul immediately, nodding and holding up his hands. "Sorry. Can, uh ... can you walk?"

"I think ... if you two chaps would ... take my elbows," he said, nodding and holding them out slightly, "I should be able to, if we take it ... steady." Paul and I exchanged a glance, and then awkwardly moved to either side of him. We were having a hard time standing up ourselves, but if this guy could get himself upright then we could help him walk.

We each took hold of his elbows, and felt the violent thrumming in his limbs. It felt like trying to comfort a scared animal. Henry's body jolted again, and would have fallen had we not been there to hold him up, but this time there was no calming breath; he took a rapid series of gasping gulps of air, like someone who has jumped into unexpectedly cold water. These slowly ebbed, dying down in speed and volume, as he got himself under as much control as he could, calming back down to his previous level. All we could do was stand there and try not to panic. I had to ask the question, and hated myself completely for doing so.

"Ready?"

Henry closed his eyes tightly, and nodded. We began making tiny, shuffling, and painfully slow steps across the living room towards the front door.

"Don't like to ... cause such a scene," he said, eyes still closed as we walked. He sounded angry, but not with us. "It started ... a few days ago. Thought it was my mind ... finally going on me, the silence since ... Mildred ... getting to me."

"You felt scared, didn't you?" asked Paul, quietly. "You knew that something bad was coming, something really bad."

"Yes," said Henry, voice trembling. "Thought about the doctor ... thought he could give me something ... to give me back ... perspective ... but then that would mean another step towards a home and ... won't do it ..." I could hear Straub in the background, giving orders to the others and not talking directly to me, talking frantically about getting ready to depart, prepping separate air transport with guard for Target One and the civilian team. They were ready for us. For Henry.

"So ... I decided I wouldn't ... have it," said Henry. "Decided to ride it out ... even though I wanted to ... get under the covers and hide ... like a bloody Frenchman. But I wouldn't do it. I refused to do it ... and it got worse, and I still wouldn't do it. I watched the television ... I stood on the front porch ... that was nearly too much, but ... made myself do it a few times ... but I couldn't eat, it wouldn't stay down or ... my mouth was too dry to chew and swallow ... but I wouldn't hide." He opened his eyes, and looked into mine. The determination there was like iron. "I wouldn't hide," he repeated, and the sad pride in his expression made me believe him.

"And then ... this morning," he said, as we drew within several feet of the front door, "when I saw them ... on the news ... I knew." His shivers rose slightly, and Paul and I stiffened, but they descended again before they could get any worse. "I knew I was ... like the chap last time. They were here ... for me. And ... I was ... good lord, I was more scared than ever. Scared out ... of my mind." His eyes screwed up again, and when he spoke it was a harsh, grating whisper, but his head stayed firmly up. "*I'm so scared now, gentlemen ... and it is taking everything ... I have not to scream. I want to collapse and curl ... up.*" His eyes opened, and he looked back and forth between us as he talked, eyes wide and fierce now. "But ... as God is my ... witness ... I will not. I will *not*."

We knew he wouldn't. We knew why he was shaking so violently, why his bones felt as if they were going to break under our hands due to the sheer tension in his arms. Henry had been managing, through sheer force of will, to stop himself from breaking down into a terrified, feral state, to avoid becoming a wreck in the way that Patrick had before him ... but the effort it took, and the toll it still had to be taking on his elderly body, were impossible to imagine. Every calm and rational sentence he was producing was a Herculean task, but he kept talking, just as he kept walking towards the door and his own fate.

I see that walk at night now, in my dreams. I finally see Patrick now, too. Sometimes it's me and Paul and Patrick and Henry, all in a line, all walking towards Henry's front door, and we can't stop.

But Henry is the only one with his head up.

"So ... I thought that ... it was a case of ... whoever got here first," said Henry, eyes fixed on the door now. "You or ... them."

"It's us, Mr Williams," said Paul, his own voice shaking now. "And we'll make sure you're ..." Paul trailed off, realising the contradiction of his own sentence.

"Looked after, yes," said Henry, finishing for him generously, but everyone in the room knew the truth. We were at the front door, and I saw myself reaching for the Yale lock. I caught Paul's eyes; he didn't know what to do either. I hesitated, my hand on the metal.

"Are you ... all right?" I asked. It sounded pathetic, and it was. Of course he wasn't all right. What I meant was *Are you prepared.*

Henry closed his eyes again. He took a long time to answer, but then nodded, short and sharp. He lifted his chin, and breathed in hard through his nose. Then he opened his eyes.

"Mildred," he said. There was another long pause. "Yes. Yes, I'm ... I'm ready." I looked at Paul again, who looked terrified.

"Civilian team coming out," I said into the microphone, and popped the Yale lock.

"Roger that," said Straub, the relief clear in her voice. "Be careful on the way out, Pointer, don't blow it now." Her businesslike manner disgusted me.

"Don't worry, the gaps are ... easier coming this way, it's hard to explain," I bullshitted, not caring. In that moment, I didn't really give a fuck whether Straub believed us or not. Plus, it was mission accomplished, so what could she say? Once again, we had the lamb for the slaughter. Job done.

We opened the door to see a smaller vehicle positioned outside. It almost looked like the armoured trucks you see security firms using to pick up money from banks. I don't know where it came from. It had an open door in the rear with a ramp leading up to it, and three or four armed soldiers surrounded the vehicle. A few feet back from the doorstep, three soldiers stood waiting to relieve us of our charge.

I heard Henry's breathing quicken, and saw his chest begin to hitch and fall more dramatically. His panic didn't continue to rise any more, however; the level that Henry was maintaining himself at had just risen, but he was still keeping it together.

"We'll walk you all the way if you want," said Paul, his voice shaking properly now, struggling to exercise any control of his own. "We can take you in." Henry didn't answer; he stared at the van with his terrified eyes as wide as dinner plates and his mouth slightly open. He managed a small nod. Paul passed it on to me, and I complied. We continued with our shuffling, tiny-step-walk away from the house, and that was when I caught the faces of the soldiers.

Of course, I thought. *This is one of their own.*

As we neared the three waiting soldiers—who hesitated slightly, I thought—Paul spoke to the nearest one.

"He'd like us to take him in," said Paul, firmly. The soldier looked at him, then Henry, then myself, and finally turned to Straub, who was stood, I now saw, a few feet back from the waiting truck. Her face was ashen, to my shock, but she was still running the show, still the pro. She was on a mission. I looked for David; he was nowhere to be seen.

"Let them take him," she said, her voice coming to me both through the air and my headset. It was quiet, but hurried. Even Straub hadn't expected this. She wasn't going to let it affect her mission in any way, I knew ... but she could afford to allow a veteran a simple request. "They know their job, it's fine. Let them take him."

Henry's head turned, trembling but upright, to see where I was looking, and his eyes fell upon Straub. His right elbow began to raise out of my grip, until the fingers of his hand were touching his forehead. The street was completely silent.

Not breaking his gaze, Straub gently returned the salute. She then nodded solemnly, and looked at me, gesturing towards the truck. We walked up the ramp, leading Henry, to see padded bench seating inside, jutting out of similarly padded walls. I was glad to see that there were no restraints. At one end, a grille separated the cab from our compartment. Gently, we set Henry down on one of the benches, and as we did so the soldiers began to file in behind us, taking the remaining seats. I wondered if they would handcuff Henry for the journey. I wondered if they would give him something before the Stone Man took him. I decided that I would make sure of it; I decided that I would ask if he could be made to know nothing about it. I looked at Henry's face as he was sitting there, eyes closed and trying to control his breathing, and wildly hoped that they wouldn't be able to take him away early. I hoped that their theory was wrong, and that the real perimeters were already up, and they'd get him a mile or so down the road and have to bring him back. Then we'd have *time*. Then we'd at least have more of a chance to stop this terrible process. Somehow.

The engine started, and we had to go. We stood there dumbly, glancing at each other, until Straub's voice sounded in our ears. She was all business again, not that she'd ever fully stopped being so.

"Time to go, gentlemen. We're on the clock."

Without thinking, I grabbed Henry's hand and held it; he started slightly at my touch, but his eyes opened and he looked at me. Though his expression was terrified, to my amazement, he weakly patted my hand.

"Not your fault. Appreciate ... respect," he said, barely getting the words out, then released my hand. It was the last thing he said to us.

Paul had to pull me away, and out of the truck. We couldn't see Henry as soldiers shut the door and the ramp retracted, and then the truck was heading away up the street. The soldiers were already running towards the APC, and Straub was ushering us back into the jeep.

"I'm sorry, gentlemen, but you need to get in the air," she said, signalling the driver to start the engine. "I'm waiting here to hear if Mr Williams gets out of the immediate area. If he doesn't, I'll be taking care of things here, and someone else will be meeting you on the other end."

"Will he be awake?" asked Paul, voicing the same thoughts that I'd been having. He spoke quietly but firmly. He wasn't angry; he just wanted to know. "If he doesn't end up like Patrick, if he gets through the barrier and is fine ... will you sedate him? Does he have to be aware?" Straub shook her head at this, meeting his gaze and holding it.

"We plan to sedate all targets, at least to the point that they won't be consciously aware," she said. "It will make our job easier for us, and more humane for them. But ... gentlemen, all bets are off where Caementum is concerned, as you know. We don't know how it works. We don't know if it bypasses ..." She caught herself, and her expression hardened. "You're leaving, and right now. If Mr Williams gets through, as I say, someone else will be taking over the delivery process and I'll be joining you wherever you are in Birmingham."

The jeep began a three-point turn. We were already off onto the next part of our world-altering adventure, but I wasn't really aware of any of it. All I kept seeing was the same moment, over and over again, as Henry's uniform came into view. He'd gotten *dressed* for it, *dressed* for it, *dressed* for it. I sat with my hands limp in my lap, the pull lessening with every second as Henry travelled away from us. My head rolled limply on my shoulders as the jeep turned. Straub was saying something again, stood in the street with her own ride waiting. She'd moved on already, completely, a model of compartmentalisation and efficiency.

"Don't forget to check the outside perimeter at Target Two," she called. "You might be bullshitting through your teeth for all I know, but at least you've proved that you can be trusted to do a difficult job, one that other civilians might not have had the balls to do." She looked us both over for a second, and then continued in a voice that was only marginally softer. "That went smoothly. I know it was difficult for you. But I want it that smooth on the other end, got it?" I nodded in my seat without looking at her, staring at the floor and only seeing Henry, Henry, Henry. Paul leant a forearm on his lap and put his head on it, then waved his free hand weakly in her direction as the jeep began to pull away.

"Good luck," she called, and then we were on our way once more, to claim another member of the British public for the greater good. Nobody knew it then, of course—we all had concerns of our own—but there was something very unexpected waiting at Target Two. We would find out in less than two hours' time.

***

I found out later that their theory turned out to be right, of course. The real perimeters *weren't* up yet. They drove Henry out of there and loaded him onto a helicopter without any problem, and took him to the Stone Man. By then it had just passed the outskirts of Coventry. I didn't see it, and even though I could probably have requested to do so later—they trust me now, and some spook will definitely have filmed it—of course I couldn't watch it.

For Henry, I gather they picked the nearest securable area along the trajectory with good access, and brought Henry and the original Stone Man together. I don't know if he remained sedated. I think of Patrick's horrific screams, and I hope with every fibre of my wretched soul that Henry stayed under. On a purely practical level, I *do* know the essentials of how it went.

Part removed, Henry dead, Stone Man gone.

Just like that.

Gone.

***

I don't remember much about the helicopter ride to Birmingham. I have a dim memory of being offered water by someone, and drinking it. I remember the sensation as it trickled its way down my parched throat; it made me think of sand being washed off rocks, and I realised how dry my throat must have been. I remember hearing someone announce over the radio that the rendezvous between Target One and Caementum had been 'successful'. Straub would be meeting us once we'd pinpointed 'Target Two'. And I remember that every time I let my mind wander, it went straight to Henry's face, his wide, frightened eyes looking into mine while he said *Not your fault.*

Other than that, the main part of the trip was pretty much a blur, or at least it is to me now. I just sat there, slumped like a limp bag of meat and bones, while I tried to hold on to any sense of purpose. I tried not to catch Paul's eye the whole time. I tried to think of going back to New York, of being the main man once more, trying to take solace in the idea, but that world seemed to belong to someone else. In the remembered champagne smiles and backslaps I saw the jeering, cheering faces of the crowd in the Coliseum, baying for blood.

When I try to remember the trip more clearly now, coherent memories start around the point where the announcement came over the headphones that we were approaching Birmingham. I didn't look up, but Paul nudged my foot gently and I, at least, began to *think* about what I was doing next. I had a job to do, I knew, I just needed a second to get myself started.

Why am I here? I asked myself, and waited for a response. The discussion in my head was efficient and to the point, parts of my brain waking up under basic cognitive process.

To find Target Two.

Why?

To save people.

How?

I have to hunt them down.

Any problems with that? Think.

They have to die.

Not those kind of problems. All business. Be all business. That's supposed to be easy for you.

Okay. They cut me off last time. They spotted me watching. They might be waiting for that.

Okay. Then you wait until you're closer. Just like last time—

HENRY—

Shut up. Ask them to tell you when you're right over Birmingham, then *tune in. Keep cutting off, just like before on the helicopter over Edinburgh. Get on with it.*

I spoke into the microphone, instructing the pilot to let me know when we were positioned correctly, and then finally raised my head to address Paul. One look at his face told me all I needed to know about how he was feeling, but I couldn't let him sit this part out like before. Between the games in my own head and the now-heavy shakes, I was barely keeping it together. I *needed* help.

Silently, I held out my hand, and he took it without looking away from my eyes. He simply nodded, and then I did what I do best. I got on with things.

Some time later, through our directions, we found ourselves driving along a more affluent-looking suburban street than the one in Edinburgh. I don't recall the name. The houses were quite new, detached, each with a small garden out front. It had taken more time to get here on this occasion, once we'd identified the street, as we'd had to land the chopper a greater distance away. Word came through over the radio that Straub would be joining us almost immediately; she'd been true to her word, and had left to join us the instant

Henry had cleared the estimated containment radius. The evacuation had had more time to take effect too, and they'd done a good job; the main roads inside the city centre, at least, were far, far less busy than in Edinburgh, and our road transport had arrived fast. The motorways taking people out of Birmingham would perhaps be the opposite by now. As we headed along our short journey through the suburbs however, a police escort was needed, then provided, to get us through the thickening traffic, and Paul and I were informed that we were in areas that hadn't yet been fully swept for evacuation. Families in cars stared at us as we drove past, children staring at the army vehicles with gaping mouths. I don't think anyone recognised me. Men standing on the roadside beside their stationary cars shouted abuse at the soldiers, and at one point we passed the burnt-out husk of a four-door saloon, turned over onto its roof. The fear and uncertainty in the air was palpable.

As Paul and I directed our jeep onto the correct street, with two military transports in tow and our eyes barely open, I knew immediately that the right house was somewhere at the *end* of this road.

At such close range, I noticed, the signal felt different to the last two times. Considerably different, but I couldn't yet tell why. It was maddening ... but then I remembered that I'd find out why very soon, and suddenly the answer didn't seem important. As we drove on, I could see that we'd actually entered a cul-de-sac.

A dead end. Nowhere to run.

Paul and I hadn't spoken to each other for this part of the journey any more than we had while in the chopper, and I wanted that to continue. Nothing to do with him, of course. I just couldn't talk to him without addressing what had happened in Edinburgh, and I wanted nothing to do with that at all.

The old man. The sergeant.

I pushed it away, felt for the signal again, and that's how I found out that it had gone.

This time, when I reached with my mind for the signal, my whole body stiffened as the same painful, high-pitched screeching sound from before filled my head, and I let go, unable to take it. The cacophony was awful, like the squealing death cries of some unimaginably huge creature. I felt Paul suddenly lurch slightly in the seat next to me, and knew that he had lost it too. The previously nigh-unbearable shakes stopped dead so suddenly that their absence made me feel light-headed in a completely different way. The pull had vanished. The relief was missed in my confusion, fear and exhaustion. We'd been shut down again.

"Guys?" asked the commanding officer who'd been in charge of us since we'd left Edinburgh. I never asked his name or rank, and he never offered it. What did it matter? Straub or David or this guy, there would be someone in charge who would tell us what to do, and we would do it. That was all that was expected of us. We just had to do what we were told, and hang our consciences on the fact that we were following orders. "Which house?"

Paul and I looked at each other, confirming what we already knew, and it was Paul who responded.

"We've lost it," said Paul, quietly. It wasn't just the shakes draining him; he had nothing left. He'd gone into Henry's house to relieve his own guilt, but instead he'd made it so much worse. This time, I knew, fully, what he'd been talking about. Unsurprisingly, it had taken me twice as long as Paul—taken double the number of deaths—to feel it. Even the realisation that I was, once again, surplus to requirements held no concern this time around. "I think they've shut us down again ... cut us off from the other Blue, too. I think ... I don't know. It's one of these houses on the end. I got that much."

"*Shit*," cursed the officer, turning to look at the five houses arranged in a circle at the end of the cul-de-sac. "We'll have to go house to house. Wait," he said, suddenly whipping back around to face us, looking alarmed. He was older than me, I could see, but not by much. "What about these barriers or whatever? Did you see any of those, I mean, can you still see those?"

Paul looked at me, eyes suddenly alert, and for once I couldn't read his face. If he'd gotten the chance to blag this again, to get to go into another target's house, I'll never know if he'd have taken it, because he never *got* that chance. I do know that he hesitated to respond, at least. All I know for certain is that if he'd tried to rope me into it again, on that day, at that time, I wouldn't have gone with him. I wouldn't have been able to do it. I knew now that I could be the tracker, the finger man ... but also that I couldn't get my hands dirty again. The thought made me feel deeply ashamed and dirty, and it still does; like a grubby little blotch on my soul.

Either way, at that moment, the decision was taken out of Paul's hands as the radio squawked into life, and Straub's voice came over the speaker.

"*Straub here. Rendezvous in five minutes. Stand down and wait for my arrival, repeat, wait for my arrival before advancement.*"

"Yes, ma'am," replied the officer, looking at us as he spoke. "There's been a further development here, ma'am. The two civilian advisers appear to have lost the signal. They say they've been cut off from it."

There was silence from the other end of the radio, in which I knew that Straub would be swearing somewhere, sitting in a moving jeep. After a few moments, the radio clicked as she pushed the talk button on her end, and her voice came back.

"*Roger that. Sit tight until I get there.*"

"Yes, ma'am. I was just about to clarify the situation regarding the presence of any barriers around the building, whether or not they could still identify those."

After was another pause, during which we all sat and waited patiently, Straub's voice spoke again. This time, her words scared me to death.

"*Don't worry about any barriers. There are none. Rendezvous in five. Over and out.*"

I stared at Paul as my blood drained into my feet, and swallowed hard, my throat dry once more. She knew. She'd done as she'd promised, and it hadn't been a bluff. The only hope we had in hell of getting away with our lives intact was that her promise of swift and severe retribution had been a hollow one. Knowing what I knew of Straub, I didn't think that this would be the case. I might have been numbed to my very core by what had happened in Edinburgh, but that flat statement of Straub's—*There are none*—managed to punch through.

And Paul, to my astonishment, closed his eyes, sighed, and then began to laugh hysterically. He fell back in his seat, tears streaming from his eyes, and shook his head as he giggled like a child. And to my further astonishment, after a moment I was caught up in it and had joined him, slumping in my seat and losing it, cackling like a loon. He was right. What else was there to do? What other response was there? And it was hilarious, when you looked at it; we'd blagged the British Army, after all, and now we were busted, sat in an army jeep surrounded by the same guys that would probably be taking us to a military prison. After all that had happened, all we could do now was wait for our judgement as we sat and watched, our usefulness at an end, our bartering position totally gone. When you thought about it, the most sensible thing we *could* do was laugh. Officer no-name simply sat back in his seat and waited, ignoring our hysterics and watching the houses at the end of the street as the military transports' engines idled behind us.

We still hadn't fully subsided by the time that Straub arrived, but the sight of her certainly calmed us down. Her jeep pulled up near ours, and two additional, larger vehicles that had arrived with her drove past us and pulled up near the houses at the end of the street. One, I noticed, was similar to the vehicle that had taken Henry away. She and officer no-name exchanged salutes, and I saw that David was with her now as well. They spoke with no-name quietly, a few feet away from our jeep, and we couldn't really hear what was being said.

As we watched, Straub then listened to her radio, and seemed startled by what she'd heard. She immediately turned to David, who looked equally startled, but then waved off whatever she'd just told him and began to dial into his mobile phone. He then hurried away to make the call. Straub turned back to no-name and gave some instructions, and no-name moved away and started barking orders to various soldiers. They'd already disembarked from the transports, and had used the spare time before Straub's arrival to quickly sweep the rest of the street for civilians. I'd already assumed that they wouldn't find any; none of the houses had cars in the driveway, on a street where the average car quota for each house would have been at least two. These people had clearly all hit the road as soon as the evacuation had been announced, not waiting for the government sweep or to be taken to holding centres. One simply couldn't be subjected to that kind of thing, could one? The soldiers began to take positions outside the five houses at the end of the street, forming small teams. One house, I'd noticed—and I couldn't have been the only one who did—had the upstairs curtains drawn. None of the others did.

There was no car on its driveway, however, but the garage was closed, and there may have been one inside. Either way, I was sure that particular house was the one, and it was nothing to do with any pull or signal; it just had that air of foreboding about it. Those closed curtains, to me, said it all.

Straub approached us in the jeep, her hands behind her back. Her face was blank, as inscrutable as ever.

"Gentlemen," she said, quietly, and we nodded back, in wide-eyed silence. She turned for a moment to look at the assembling soldiers at the end of the street. "Here we are," she said, still not looking at us. "Target Two ..." She trailed off, and I could see nothing in her face to suggest exactly why. She turned back to us. "And I gather that your abilities are, for the time being at least, neutralised?"

Again, we nodded. She nodded back, the eyes in her blank face quietly reading ours.

"That's a shame. We do have some more possible options, though, options that we were quite close to bringing in when we couldn't get hold of you, Mr Pointer." Seeing our surprise, she carried on. "As you know, several others came forward after the First Arrival, and two or three accounts checked out in a similar way to yours, at least in terms of correlation with energy readings et cetera. Not as strong, or as dramatic as yours, but worth investigating, nonetheless. Of course, many more that have come forward since your account became well known in the media, but they have to be dismissed, naturally. But the few we have ... they might hold promise if, in fact, you two are cut off altogether in the event of a Third Arrival." She looked back down the street again, and audibly sighed, pausing. "I don't like being lied to, Mr Winter, and I know that's what you did. I didn't even need to check the energy readings to know; when I thought about it afterwards, it was obvious from the way you led Mr Williams straight out of his house and onto the street. You didn't even think about your story, did you?" She looked back at us now, and we still sat in silence. Was this an introductory speech before our punishment, or something else? I barely dared hope it was the latter.

"I should have seen it at the time, and it's to my great professional shame that I didn't. I, like everyone else, expected to find another target in the same mental shape as the last one. I allowed myself to be … distracted, I suppose, by what we *did* find. Rest assured," she said, turning back to the preparing units at the bottom of the road, and taking a few steps in that direction. She obviously didn't want us to see her face as she said this next part. "Even if you hadn't been 'cut off', as you say you have been, you wouldn't be going in this time. I'll be honest; despite my words in Edinburgh, and your blatant insubordination, and you *knowing* what the consequences would be … in that situation, I think it worked out for the best. I think I'd rather it went down the way it did. That *one* time."

I didn't need to ask why. My skin went cold as relief washed over me.

"Thank your lucky stars—for the rest of your lives—that it went off without a hitch up there, gentlemen," said Straub, her voice growing slightly colder. "I can write off your behaviour once—*once*—as you *are* civilians, after all, and witnessed a very traumatic incident with C.I. One that, in hindsight, you shouldn't have. I can see how that would have clouded your judgement, and I would be a liar if I said that I didn't understand your reasons. But that allowance has passed, and will not be given again. I'm not going to bother repeating myself. Try it, and see what happens. *My* conscience will be clear." The sweep units all appeared to be ready now, and so she raised her radio again, and spoke into it. "Wallace, proceed when ready."

As Paul let out a quiet but long breath of air, slumping in his seat and putting one hand to his forehead (whether this was from relief, or from dismay at seeing the beginning of another extraction, I'll never get to know) the shout went up at the other end of the road, and the units moved forward as one to surround each house. The probe had begun, and Straub stood with her back to us to watch. She seemed far more relaxed than before for some reason. Given that we were still hours ahead of the time it had taken for the second energy spike to occur, there was a strong likelihood that Target Three could be taken directly to their relevant Stone Man in the same manner that Henry had been.

Thus the second of the day's tasks could be wrapped up quickly and efficiently, and this had seemed to ease her tension while on a mission. It was a simple extraction job after all, and after two successful rendezvous (Patrick and Henry) she had to be more confident that it was a straightforward process. They must have known all the units were unlikely necessary, but they were taking no chances and it would also be a quicker way of searching several houses at once, I suppose. I almost felt compelled to remind her that there was a still a third Stone Man that we couldn't neutralise without knowing where Target Three was (*Not we,* I had to remind myself. *You're out of the loop*) and worse, we didn't know where it was going once it got past Birmingham.

As if she'd read my thoughts—so much so that it was eerie—Straub spoke without turning around. What she said was big news indeed, almost as big as the Stone Man returning in the first place, but I didn't know how awful the truth behind it would be. Yet.

"I received a report, a few moments ago, about the third Caementum, the other blue one. I assume you're interested to know." She sounded airy, almost casual. I wondered if she'd had much sleep. "It stopped moving around two minutes back. Just stopped dead. If you know anything about that, I expect you to tell us. I don't think you do—I believe you about being cut off, the dismay is plastered all over your face, Mr Pointer—but if you even have as much as a snippet of anything about that, pass it on. It could be important."

Paul and I exchanged a glance, and shook our heads at each other.

"Not me," said Paul, directing his comment at Straub. He slowly sat up, almost excited at the possibility of hope for the remaining targets, but not believing it. "What about the other one? Is it still coming?"

"Unfortunately so," said Straub, genuine regret in her voice. "The two Blue were definitely on the same path, up to a certain point at least. They were walking side by side—Coventry is a hell of a mess—but when one stopped, the other just carried on, like it had been on its own all along."

"A mistake, then?" I asked, thinking fast. What the hell could that be about? "Two of them following the same signal by accident, maybe? One realising, or its controllers realising, that it wasn't needed?"

"Possible," said Straub, watching as the soldiers—their brief attempt to communicate via megaphone to anyone inside the houses at an end—now lined up police-on-a-drugs-bust-style battering rams and opened the houses themselves. They began to file into each house quietly but efficiently. They weren't going in heavily, once the initial destruction of the houses' front doors was complete, but I was still deeply glad that we'd taken the path that we had with Henry. I wouldn't want him to see this in his home. "It would make sense.

223

My gut feeling is that it's a suicide. Someone who didn't handle the fear in the same way that Mr Williams did, and worse even than Target One. If I'm right, and they've got the job done early themselves, we get to see what that stationary Blue does next as a result. We couldn't take the risk of terminating a target early ourselves, but now it's happened on its own; we'll see then, does Caementum reset and go after someone else, in which case we have a larger problem, or does it go home like its predecessor, in which case the problem is, temporarily at least, solved? Time will tell, and hopefully soon. And we'll know what happens if the targets die early."

"If it's a suicide," said Paul, "maybe they did it for that reason. To help."

"Again, possible," said Straub, nodding, but sounding slightly bored by the exchange now. We weren't relevant any more, and our insights weren't valuable. She'd only brought it up to check if we knew anything, after all, and it was clear that we didn't. She had more important things to worry about at that moment in time. "We won't know unless a note comes up in a police report, but even that's extremely unlikely. We don't know where it was going, after all, and the number of suicides related to Caementum's appearance are comparatively sky-high anyway."

We could hear the reports beginning to come in over Straub's radio. Three of the five houses were announced to be clear, and shortly after that a fourth house was also announced to be empty. As the silence continued from the fifth house, and the soldiers didn't reappear, I began to feel uneasy. I obviously wasn't alone, as Straub spoke into the radio.

"Unit three, report," she said firmly, and after a pause the radio crackled into life. It would have been hard enough to hear the soldier on the other end as it was, due to the shaken, quiet voice he spoke in at that moment, but the screaming in the background made it even more difficult. It was a woman.

"Unit three departing ... uh ... escorting ..." The voice paused for a second, and carried on. "One civilian, escorting one civilian ... immediate medical assistance required, Carter has been stabbed, he's coming out now."

The confusion only halted Straub for the briefest of moments.

"Roger that, unit three, assistance on its way, take the civilian to transport as instructed."

Straub hurried off without looking at us again, barking orders, and Paul stood up in his seat to get a better look at the house. We were parked perhaps eighty feet away.

"What the fuck ..." he said, straining to see, and I followed his lead. As we watched, three soldiers hurried out of the front door, two holding a man up between them. The one in the middle—presumably Carter—was holding a heavily bleeding wound in his stomach, his face contorted in pain. A stretcher was already being rushed over to them, and Carter was quickly escorted away, but already the remaining soldiers were emerging behind them. You could hear their arrival before you could see it, as the screams of the woman carried far more clearly once she'd been brought downstairs. They had their target.

She was of average height and build, but even with her hands secured behind her back, it took three of them to escort her as she thrashed and screamed in their grip. She had long black hair that was frayed and sticking out in various directions, and wore what was probably her about-the-house clothing; a baggy red hoodie and non-matching navy blue jogging bottoms. From here I could see the stains on them. Her feet were bare, and her eyes went rapidly from screwed up shut to manically wide eyed, opening each time she had enough air back in her lungs to let out a fresh bellow. Her face was bright red, and her skin was slick and shiny with tears. She was the most hysterical-looking person I had ever seen. The soldiers' faces, the ones who were dragging her out of the building, were determined but also pale, as if they'd seen something awful in that house.

After she'd been taken away, and our sight line to the front door was clear again, we saw the last, remaining soldier emerge from the house. He was moving very slowly, and seemed unsteady on his feet. In his arms was what looked like, at a distance, some sort of parcel. No-name ran up to him, and we could see them talking; the officer's body blocked us from seeing what the soldier was carrying, but we could see from the back of the no-name's head that he was looking down at it. They both stood very still for a moment.

Straub approached the pair now, and we saw her gently put her hand to her mouth, but only briefly. She then took her hand away and spoke to both of the men, but we could see that she was staring at the parcel in the first soldier's arms as she did so. No-name took the parcel, and headed off in one direction, while Straub remained and spoke to the soldier. It seemed personal, sincere; she even put one hand on his shoulder briefly. He nodded, seemed to take a deep breath, then straightened up sharply and saluted her. He then began to head towards the personnel transports parked behind us. As we watched, no-name approached Straub again; the parcel was gone. They stood talking, but my eyes drifted towards the soldier who was heading in our direction. His head was down as he walked, and walking very slowly at that. Whatever had happened in there, it had clearly been deeply traumatic for him, and I didn't think it was the stabbing of his comrade.

"Jeeeesus," breathed Paul, sitting back in his seat. "Did you see the state of that soldier? I hate to say it … but that could have been us. Guess we were lucky we only went in the first time."

I didn't answer, but instead looked from the soldier to the still-talking Straub in the distance. The walking soldier was beginning to veer towards the transport on the opposite side of the street, parked several feet behind us. If I was going to do anything, I needed to do it now while it was easy.

"I'll be back in a second," I said to Paul, and climbed down from the jeep before he could reply. I sprinted across the few feet between us and the soldier, and stopped just in front of him.

"Excuse me," I said quietly, and the soldier jumped slightly at the sound of my voice. He'd been so lost in thought that he hadn't even noticed me standing there. "Andy Pointer, special adviser to the Caementum project," I said sternly, holding out my hand. I'd thought that title up on the spot, but in hindsight it probably wasn't necessary. I was world famous, after all, for the little that now seemed worth. The soldier stared at me for a second, and then took my hand in a limp handshake. He was young, very young, I could see; twenty-one at most. His face was pale, and his blue eyes squinted at me from under his blonde eyebrows. I realised he'd be staring into the sun slightly; it was getting late in the day by now, and the sun had dropped enough to be shining right into his irises. Shadows were lengthening all around us. I chanced a brief glance over his shoulder at Straub; she was still in conversation, and the two vehicles she'd brought with her were starting their engines up, one about to carry the latest extracted target to its rendezvous, presumably screaming all the way until they sedated her.

"Sorry to ask this of you, my friend, as I can tell you've had a rough experience just now," I said, trying to sound officious but sympathetic at the same time, "but I need to get the quick lowdown of what just happened while it's still fresh in your mind. It all helps, I assure you."

Dazed, the soldier blinked at me, and then turned his head in a lazy motion to look at no-name. Before he could say anything or turn back, I shut down that train of thought for him

"It's okay," I said, "I have full clearance, I assure you, and I don't think your commanding officers would be too pleased about being bothered right now. Just give me the quick rundown and we're done here."

I wasn't asking to help me make more money; I had more than enough, and I was only risking Straub's further anger when I'd already dodged a major bullet on that front. But I needed to know. Curiosity is one thing I've never had any trouble feeling.

"She ... she was on the floor," the young soldier muttered, eyes flitting in any direction other than mine. "She was upstairs, in the front bedroom. Curled up … making these little noises …" He rubbed his face quickly with his hand, and carried on, seeing it happening before him again. "She was shaking, but she wasn't responding to us. The corporal kept asking her name, trying to get her attention … and then he got in close … and her hands were out of sight, like, tucked in front of her. He shouldn't have gone in close, but it was … she was a woman in a nice house …"

He turned, and looked back for a moment, shaking his head. I checked again; Straub was still busy.

"When Carter touched her, she must have been waiting," he said, looking at the house, perhaps even at the window of the room where it had happened. "Waiting until he was right over her, because when she pulled the knife … he didn't have time to move. She buried it right in his guts. Right up to the hilt, man, and pulled it out again. You shouldn't pull out a knife once it's in you, you know. Makes it worse."

"So I gather," I said, trying to get him back on track. His shock would easily lead him off down all sorts of side avenues if I let it.

"She didn't start screaming until she'd done it," continued the solider, now turning to me with a look of confusion on his face. "Like … like she knew … she knew she'd used her only trump card, and realised it hadn't really done anything. But I could see it in her eyes, man, even before the screams, I saw her face when she stuffed that knife into Carter. She'd lost it. She was way, way gone. That was why it made sense when I saw …" His voice faltered, and he sniffed inwards through his nose.

"Saw what?" I asked. This was the crux of the thing, not the stabbing. This was what had really gotten him messed up. He looked at the floor when he spoke again.

"In the corner of the room, right next to the wall. Nobody had really looked inside it because, I dunno, we were more worried about her, and *there was no sound coming from it.* That was the thing, if we'd heard something we would have looked, but it just seemed empty. I took, like, just a glimpse, and didn't see anything at first, so we thought it was just her in the room. We thought the thing was empty because … no sound. We never thought it could have been because …"

"Because what? Wait, wait. What was empty? What was in the corner of the room?"

"The crib. The crib was in the corner of the room."

I thought of the parcel, and of the size of it, and of the second Blue Stone Man suddenly stopping walking, and hoped as an awful, sick feeling began to grow in my stomach that the connection I was making was wrong.

"After they'd taken her out, I just had a second look," the soldier said, his voice cracking as he spoke. "And, you know, no wonder everyone had missed it. The pillow covered most of the view, you see. She'd used a pillow. *That's* why it was so quiet."

I looked at Paul in the jeep, and upon seeing the expression on my face, the one on his changed from an annoyed *What the fuck are you doing* to a worried *What's happened?* I could only shake my head, slowly.

"How could she do that, man?" asked the soldier, a pleading tone coming into his shaking voice as tears sprung up in his eyes. He was looking at me for an answer. "I know she'd gone crazy, I—I mean, I mean, I know like, if this thing is coming for you it makes you freak out but, but … why do that? How do you do that? Huh?"

I thought I knew, but I couldn't say it. This was too much, and I suddenly just felt very, very tired. This whole day, this whole business … insane. Like the woman. Did she know, then? Some kind of connection between mother and child, knowing that not only was she a target but that her child was too? I think about it now—I've thought about her a lot in the time since, thought about her and Patrick and fucking *Henry*, that fucker got me the worst, fucking *bastard*—and I think that maybe her course of action wasn't insane, even if *she* was. A giant, unstoppable, stone murder machine coming for me and my child? It would only take one of us, I think, had I the chance of a say in the matter. But, again … who can say?

The soldier was scrutinising my face now as tears ran down his, a burning need for an answer written all over his expression, and I just couldn't give him one. I was so *tired*. I even nearly shrugged, a combination of fresh bitterness and exhaustion, but I managed to stop myself.

"Okay. Okay," I said quietly, patting the young man on the shoulder. His expression didn't change. "Thank you, I know that … I know that was hard. Good job. You can … carry on now. Thank you."

The soldier stood there for a second, then it seemed to penetrate that he was done. He nodded slightly, and turned to go, but as he walked away, he began to speak again, facing me and walking slowly backwards as he did so.

"Even if she thought it was right, though? Even if she thought it was the right thing to do … how the fuck did she do that? How the fuck did she *do* that?" It was a totally rhetorical question this time, but suddenly, unbidden, an answer popped into my head.

"Some people …" I started, realising that the rest of my sentence (*are crazy*) wasn't right at all. I thought about it for a second, and corrected myself.

"Sometimes … some people can just do what needs to be done."

The soldier almost scoffed, but it came out like a sob, and his forehead crinkled some more. He was several feet away now.

"*That* needed to be done?"

This time, I did shrug.

"That's not really the point, is it?"

The soldier shook his head, spat on the floor, and turned fully around as he walked away, still shaking his head. My legs felt hollow, and I staggered back to the jeep. As I fell into the seat, I was very aware that I'd only slept for an hour in at least the last twenty-four of them. The events of that horrendous day seemed unbearably heavy, even worse when looked back upon, and I was too tired to force them away. I put my palms into my eye sockets and began to breathe heavily, just to give myself something to focus on, and Paul, God bless him, gave me a moment to do so. He must have been full of questions, but he waited. A *good* guy.

Eventually, I took my hands away from my face and sat up, staring at the house.

"Is it okay to ask?" said Paul. He wasn't being facetious.

"Yes, yeah ... yes," I sighed, gently raising my hands and nodding. "Woman stabbed the guy with the wound. Blue Stone Man coming for her baby too, or she thought it was anyway. She, uh ... she decided she wasn't going to let it take it."

Paul nodded slowly, looking down the street to where Straub was talking to several other uniformed men and David, who had reappeared and seemed to be trying to butt in.

"If she was right ... that might explain one of the Blue ones stopping," said Paul. I was a little shocked. I was the brutally practical one, not Paul. But here he was, not batting an eyelid at the news, and already onto the science. He was speaking slowly, lazily, in a detached, emotionless manner, but even so it was surprising. "No suicide, but an early target killing nonetheless ... and they were walking side by side. I don't think the other Blue's target was past Birmingham. I think their targets were at the same place. Hell ... same genes, after all."

I joined him in rationalising; it was a welcome retreat, and suddenly it was easier than ever. The story was what mattered. Always the story.

"They could get the rough time of death," I muttered quietly. "Correlate it with the time the second Blue stopped. Plus, as you say ... they were walking side by side. The odds of another target being on the exact same trajectory ... pretty slim. Maybe. I dunno. The signal did feel different when we got close, did you notice that? Before it cut off? Could that be because there were two of them in the same place?"

"Mm," agreed Paul. "Makes you wonder. What do you think they'll do with the next targets, then? The military, I mean."

"How do you mean?" I asked, also realising that we both believed that the Stone Men would be back a third time, even though the Second Arrival wasn't yet over. We still hadn't looked at each other, and yet we sounded now for all the world like two dull Sunday league spectators discussing the team, rather than witnesses at the scene of an infanticide. It was shocking, yet *easy*. I was right; sometimes, some people really can just do what needs to be done.

"Well ... do they take them to the Stone Men, like Henry?" asked Paul. "Or ..." he lazily made a fist and pointed two fingers out of it, then cocked his thumb and snapped his wrist backwards with a quiet explosion sound from his lips. A child had died just recently, a few feet in front of where we now sat, and in those few minutes it was just another thing, "... right then and there?"

"Guess we'll have to wait and see what happens with that Blue that stopped," I said, and then we were silent for a while. Whether it was the weight of the day, or knowing how the other was feeling, having been party to the same awful scenes, the silence was an easy one this time. We sat that way until Straub came to dismiss us, upon which we shook hands and simply went back to our lives. Again, it would have been good to have some nice parting words, but none were needed; we weren't capable of them anyway. A shared glance and a nod of the head said it all.

Wait; 'went back to our lives'? No. We tried to, at least. Even then, before we left—Paul in one jeep, and me in another heading for the airport—I knew, and I think Paul did as well, that once the numbness of the last part of that day wore off, going back to our normal lives would not be possible.

I was right. I just had no idea how of how much so.

***

Part 3:
In the Dying Moments

Chapter Eight: Andy Returns Home, The Heavy Price of Fame and Fortune, Paul Gets Back To Nature, and Negotiations In the Dark

***

Time didn't pass quickly. It dragged, and painfully. Even though I was back in New York, and again finding myself pressed for interviews and comments on the latest Stone Man happenings (despite being left out of the government version of events this time, which I was glad of, but more on that shortly), I found that I wanted none of it. It was an unusual sensation for me, actively deciding to avoid the limelight, but I found myself doing it. I had calls from the *New Yorker* and *Times* to write pieces for them—once upon a time, these were dream offers—as my stock seemed to have temporarily re-risen in the light of the Stone Man and his associates returning, but I stalled. I just wanted to be out of the way for a while. I rented a penthouse on the Upper East Side and didn't leave for several weeks, alternating between the balcony in the day and the shared swimming pool at night. I found it peaceful in there, floating quietly in the darkness (I preferred it with the lights right down) and seeing the moonlight shine gently through the ceiling windows. I drank a lot, ordered in every night, and gained a stone in weight.

I spoke with Paul often on the phone, and he sounded even worse. If we had been numb in the aftermath of Target Two, that blessed period had worn off for us both. I'd been mildly affected by Patrick's unpleasant death, whereas Paul had been haunted. I'd now moved up to his previous level, it seemed, while he was exploring new ground. He sounded terrible.

"She moved out yesterday," said Paul, slurring his words. He'd been drinking as well. "Mother's. Gone to Mother's. Probably best, really. S'not much … not much fun around here."

"Not this end either," I replied, and I meant it, despite sitting naked in my bathrobe and nursing a scotch. There was a long pause, and that was fine, because most of our phone conversations went this way. Long pauses. Just being there with someone in the same boat was enough. "How's … work?"

"Dunno. Didden … didden go in today. Don't think'm goin' back."

"They'll fire you."

"S'ok. Fuggem."

"I'll send you some money. I'll look after you man. Fuck it, I'll send you a million."

"Ta."

He was okay for cash though, I knew. He'd been compensated again by the government for our assistance, as had I, but I wanted to. He'd *earned* that share. We both bore the burden of our guilt.

The Blue that stopped had disappeared shortly after it halted, as had the other two once their respective targets had been delivered (and the subsequent removals carried out). They'd correlated the estimated time of the child's death with the time that the Blue had stopped. All the signs pointed to the fact that killing the child had stopped that Stone Man's advance.

Of course, the general public didn't know this. I only knew because I'd spoken to Doctor Boldfield personally, once I'd been brought in again for a second round of testing. He'd been reluctant, but I reminded him that I had been granted full disclosure by his superiors, and so he opened up.

The public had been told that, again, the targets had felt their connection and brought themselves forward of their own accord, knowing full well that there was a possibility of their deaths. They were hailed as heroes, especially Target Two, who had tragically lost her daughter to cot death the day before, and bravely came forward despite her grief. Even though Target Three—the child—was not stated as being an infant. Instead, the public was told that Target Three's family 'had requested that their relative's name not be disclosed'.

Either way, this time the government admitted that their initial diagnosis of a weak heart for Patrick had been wrong, and that the mere presence of the Stone Men near whomever they were trying to communicate with—the specific people they had come to see—was fatal. They did assure the public, though, that work was being done to prevent this, and that they had made many promising breakthroughs in their research.

I used to wonder why they'd admitted that the targets had died, but given time to think about it, I don't know if they had much choice. They couldn't be one hundred percent sure that there had been no witnesses on Henry's and Target Two's (Theresa Pettifer's) streets; with Patrick, they had hours to evacuate each home—waiting for the Stone Man to come to them—while, more importantly, making sure they'd cleared the immediate area. With the Second Arrival, the whole idea was to save time, to end the destruction early, and they were operating on the assumption that the streets had been cleared by people evacuating themselves. It wouldn't do to say that the targets were just people who had been killed in the panic or whatever, if someone had footage of them being dragged screaming from their homes by armed soldiers. I often wonder, even now, what would have happened had they not lived alone. I asked Paul about this once, in another phone call. He was sober, for once.

"What choice would they have? They'd have been taken care of as well." He sounded extremely flat. I could barely hear him.

"You think?"

"Yeah. The only reason *we* haven't been shut down is because we still might be useful. We're loose ends, Andy. Dangerous loose ends. But we'll be all right until they come back again at least. Then we'll know. We'll know if the lap dogs, the *hunting* dogs, can still hunt. Or if we're people with dangerous information that are now surplus to requirements ..."

"No, no, we're done with that. We're already useless. We're cut off."

"We were cut off at the base, but we still got a good start. We might still be able to do something before they cut us off again, or maybe they'll be able to do it instantly. But if it's the latter ..." He trailed off, and then sighed. His voice was almost a whisper, but that wry humour was still there, even if it had been twisted into laughing at the bleakness he seemed to see all around him. "I reckon we'll be taken out behind the shed and dealt with, old chum," he finished.

"No way. No. I can't see Straub allowing that."

"Really? What's the one word you'd use to describe Straub overall?"

I had it instantly, but I didn't want to say it. It meant Paul might have a point.

"Professional."

I returned to New York after being in the UK for more tests, but it didn't feel like home anymore. Nowhere did, but I kept thinking of Coventry, and what it must be like since the Second Arrival. As you'll of course know, and as I mentioned earlier, they'd dug up Millennium Place after that and filled it with water, making a large man-made lake that dropped off to around six feet deep in the middle. The hope was that it would somehow disrupt whatever technology or force they were using to transport themselves in and out; appearing twice in the same spot led most to believe, including the top boffins, that Millennium Place had been the best or only place for them to appear. It wasn't much, but at this point the country would try anything.

I'd seen the footage on the TV. It was shocking, even for me, and I'd been there up close and personal the first time. The surrounding city centre had been pretty much levelled, and it hadn't really finished being rebuilt after the First Arrival. The two Blues walking together in the rain had, along with the original Stone Man, created two new paths of destruction in different directions, almost at opposing compass points, and the new damage combined with the half-finished repairs from the First Arrival made local people say enough was enough. The city centre became a ghost town, with people abandoning their homes entirely. Even the outlying areas cleared out as well—who wants to live near ground zero of a seemingly unending cycle of destruction—and the families with children were the first to leave. Once the kids were taken away, the city was doomed to a slow death. The more people left, the more businesses died, and so the exodus increased.

As far as the government were concerned, this wasn't necessarily a bad thing. They'd wanted to quarantine the city centre entirely, and once the population of the city centre had been reduced to just a few stubborn elderly folk, homeless people, and desperate looters (anything of worth was long since gone), they declared the area as quarantined and stationed guard posts around the perimeter, clearing out the last few remaining residents.

This all happened in a space of three months. The population of the city as a whole dropped from just over three hundred thousand to four thousand, scattered around the outskirts.

That was when I decided to go home.

I don't know why; I just wanted to. Being in New York was only making me worse; it wasn't my home, and what was the point of being there if I only stayed in the apartment? I just wanted to go back. I didn't want to be another one of the people who'd abandoned my city. I thought of Henry, and how he'd refused to be scared.

I wondered if it had been him who had changed things for me. Patrick hadn't gotten to me too badly, but he'd been barely human when we found him. Henry's dignity had been deeply, deeply affecting, but the realisation that it took Henry's actions to put the death of another human being into perspective—and that death, Patrick's death, had happened *right in front of me*—filled me with a self-loathing that I couldn't even begin to describe. I spent hours a day lying on my back, a bottle in my hand, staring at the ceiling and wondering what the hell was wrong with me, then drowning in a maelstrom of guilt, and then the cycle would repeat.

I even found myself, in my crazier moments, trying to flex my mental muscles in the same way that I did when I locked in to the Stone Man's pull. It's hard to describe, but it had been like a shift, a switch-flick in my brain; I wondered if maybe I could do it again, before they arrived, to catch them before they had a chance to destroy anything. It would make me the hunting dog again, the point-man for murder, but at least I could save even more lives in the process. I was desperate, desperate to find some kind of worth in myself, changing my moral stance constantly in my head in order to be able to hold it up. I had to stop thinking of the targets, think of the people, the people, the people. The logic was all there—had been there before—but it didn't help.

I never picked up on any signals, but I'd sometimes sit in the living room with an open map in front of me, drinking and flexing my mind, flexing my mind. All that happened was that I got drunk, and the black fog around me increased. So I decided that I could do all of this just as well in Coventry, and booked a flight.

I rang Paul to tell him, but he didn't really react. He just murmured an acknowledgement of my plan, and said nothing. I asked what was wrong, but meant what was *more* wrong than before. He didn't sound drunk.

"Wife's gone," he muttered. I started to tell him I already knew, that he'd told me she was temporarily at the Mother-in-law's, but then I realised what he meant. It was inevitable, I supposed. She'd been pushed far enough before, but now, he would be unreachable. People would only stick around through so much, I thought.

"Do ... do you want to come to me? Stay with me for a bit?" I asked.

"Nah. Thanks. Nah ... see you," he said, suddenly, and then the line went dead. I didn't hear from him for several weeks after that, despite calling him often.

I bought a formerly expensive house at a ludicrously knocked-down price, one that I'd always liked out on the Kenilworth Road; I didn't need to, but I wanted to. I could afford it, and the people that had simply abandoned it were overjoyed. They'd been living with friends, and I was put in touch with them through their estate agent. They'd pretty much given up on it as a loss. The place was a wreck inside, with every item of value taken and the carpets and walls torn up and vandalised, but it had a pool—a must for me now—and a fantastic garden, and it just felt welcoming. I hired some painters and decorators to fix it, bought new furniture, and by the end of the first week the place was immaculate. The teams I'd hired to fix it had charged an extra thirty percent to come into Coventry and work this close to town, which even I thought was a bit much, but it needed doing. I spent the weekdays in a Birmingham pub while they worked, and spent the evenings in a hotel at night (none were left open in Coventry, the Stone Man being the final nail in a dying local industry) and all that was fine by me. I thought that at some point I might write again, and return those calls (opportunities that had surely long since passed) but I didn't want to think about that kind of thing. The money already in the bank meant that I didn't *have* to, of course, and I continued to just piss my days away.

Once I'd moved in, I had food delivered once a week, and hired a team of two security guards to protect the place from looters, alternating shifts over twenty-four hours. They set up a little tech booth by the front door, and I had an electrified fence and gate built around the property. Yes, I'd returned home, and I might have become a drunken mess, but I would be damned if I was going to let any scum have my stuff. Plus, the country around me was getting steadily worse.

Despite government reassurances, every city—not just Coventry—was in a state of constant near-panic. I don't think it was from a fear of being 'next'—most people didn't believe they would be, any more than anyone ever really believes they're going to win the lottery—but more from a fear of losing everything, of having a Stone Man (blue or otherwise) come to their part of town and wipe it out. It made people extremely precious about their property and families, and therefore it was all too easy for some elements to fan that spark and get riots going up and down the country, particularly in more deprived areas. This led to even more people drawing into their homes, and even those in relatively quiet areas stayed indoors, watching the news for a sign or just making sure their loved ones were accounted for. The religious element, undeterred by previous violence, seized their moment and no doubt rejoiced as they drew record crowds at public rallies and events. To no one's surprise, there was more trouble with rival organisations turning up, and there were more deaths. After a short time, a temporary ban was placed on religious gatherings outdoors. Tensions still simmered, however, and the fear and mistrust throughout the country continued to grow.

It was on a Thursday, roughly four months after the Stone Men had left, that I was sitting in my back garden. It was February by then, and still cold out, but the sun had appeared in a surprisingly blue sky for the time of year, and I decided to sit outdoors. I'd been in the new house four weeks, and I don't think I'd spent any time in the expansive garden even once by then; I'd been occupied enough by moving between the home cinema, the kitchen, and the pool. Days were spent working my way through Netflix, the drinks cabinet, several porn websites and the freezer, followed by sitting on the bottom of the pool for as long as I could while holding my breath. All the while I dimly told myself that I'd get writing tomorrow, but I never did. I'd even tried once, but when faced with a blank page, my mind kept wandering to things that I didn't want to think about, and I eventually gave up. I was occupied, which was fine, and starting to become too dependent on drink, which was a vague concern, but it all kept me distracted at least. That's what I think I wanted, looking back. Either way, the surprise of the sunshine streaming through the curtains had dragged me out of bed and onto a deckchair in the garden before I'd touched a bottle, which was especially unusual that day; normally, if I woke up feeling as bad as I did that morning, I tucked straight into something strong to fight it off. But not that day. I just somehow felt that it would make me feel even worse.

It went on throughout the morning, this shaky feeling, and while I constantly thought that I'd grab a bottle and start to kill it off, somehow I never got around to it. Instead I carried on with my usual routine of films and floating/swimming, feeling more and more restless and troubled. I made myself a meal of pizza and chips (a personal favourite, I might add, that along with the booze had helped to add a second extra stone to my weight, and I would now be described as chubby) but it just felt dry and stodgy in my mouth. I left half of it unfinished, and later found myself upstairs in the bedroom, lying flat on my back and inspecting the ceiling. I couldn't lie still, but my stomach felt like it was full of lead, and I began to feel helplessly alone. I called Paul, but he didn't answer as usual, and I wondered if he were even at his old house anymore. The government knew where he was so they could get hold of him, I thought, and then found myself thinking about what would happen when the Stone Men came back. I wondered if we'd be called in anyway, despite being apparently cut off from the source, and thought that we would be. They'd have to check, wouldn't they, and I remembered Paul's ominous words on the subject.

Dangerous loose ends.

I lay there and almost hoped that we *would* be cut off, so at least we wouldn't have to be a part of the madness again. Let Straub try out her *backup options*. They could take over, see how they handled the results. Then, to my total surprise, I began to cry.

Loud, barking sobs that fired out of me in staccato fashion as tears streamed down my face, and while this went on part of me marvelled at it. I never cried, and if I did, I instantly found myself looking at it in an abstract, curious way, as if it were happening to someone else. This always had the effect of separating me from such rare feelings, and therefore ended them at the same time. It wasn't a deliberate process, and it always just happened by itself, but not today. It went on for a good twenty minutes, until my face was sore and I'd almost lost my voice. But stranger still, it didn't stop. Emotion washed through my body, and the effect was all the more dramatic on me for being someone who usually felt so little. Forty minutes later, when I was still going, mild fear came into the swirling cloud in my head, unnerved by the amount of time this had been going on for. Worse still, I couldn't seem to make it stop.

I don't know when it finally ended, either, as I woke up the next morning, face down on the bed with my eyelids crusty and sore. I didn't feel any better, either; in fact, I felt worse. I made a breakfast but I had no appetite for it, and left it untouched. I headed into the cinema room to lose myself in something loud and mindless but I couldn't relax. The surround sound—which, on a normal day could often startle me when an unexpected noise came from the rear or side speakers—today had me nearly jumping out of my seat every time such an incident happened. After crying out in fright five or six times, I gave the whole thing up as a bad idea and headed for the pool, but the nervousness didn't alleviate. I found myself jumping at shadows, and unable to shake this uncanny feeling that something was behind me, always staying just out of sight.

By the time the evening rolled around, I'd taken some herbal relaxation tablets in an attempt to calm my now tightly wound nerves, but they didn't make a dent. I started checking in with the security guard over the intercom, first hourly, then half-hourly, then every twenty minutes. He, and later his associate, did a good job of hiding their growing irritation, but even if they hadn't I wouldn't have cared. That wasn't important. I constantly checked the locks, and ended up lying awake all night with the lights on. By then, I was checking every five minutes.

By the time the sun came up, I was a red-eyed wreck, and I had developed a near-constant shake. It occurred to me briefly that, despite company checks, I didn't really know if I could trust my security guards. Once that thought had arrived, it grew infected roots, and I slowly decided that they couldn't be trusted at all. I told the current guard on duty—over the intercom, of course, and with a shaking voice—that he wouldn't be needed for the rest of the week, and that he should tell his colleague also. They'd get full pay, I assured them. I hung up before he could protest, and sat on the bedroom floor while I listened to him knock on the door downstairs. Once I heard a car engine start, I tiptoed to the window and watched his black BMW drive away. I thought it would make me feel better to watch him go, but it didn't.

I thought it might be better if I actually turned the bed onto its side and pushed it horizontally into the corner. This would, I reasoned, create a little triangle of space behind it that I could sit in, safe behind the barrier. I then thought it would be even better if I got the mattress from the spare bed and put it on top of the gap, effectively sealing me off nicely. This idea filled me with a nervous, panicked, but determined energy, and although the thought of leaving the bedroom now filled me with anxiety, I worked like a madman, fetching the mattress from one of three spare bedrooms and dragging it on its end along the upstairs landing. It was harder than I thought it would be; if I'd thought about it more clearly, I would have realised that I was weak from not eating a full meal for two days.

I sat there in the darkness of my little fort, thinking that I would finally begin to feel safe, but it only got worse. I developed a cold sweat, one that formed a fine sheen over my body at first that developed into small rivulets as the day wore on. My shakes intensified, and in a moment of clarity it finally occurred to me to wonder why this might be happening.

Why it didn't happen sooner I don't know. I assume that, looking back, it was just part of the process; the difference with *me* being that, of course, when I stopped to think about it, I *knew* what was happening. I didn't then, not fully—I was under the influence far too much for that—but in that moment it was a brief flash of thought, one that I clamped down on like a triggered bear trap. *It can't be that. It can't be that. It can't be that.* I pushed it away, clung to ignorance like a drowning man clutching a piece of flimsy driftwood.

The second night in the bedroom was hell. Shakes became convulsions, and at several points I found that I couldn't breathe, panic and fear gripping my throat and lungs and squeezing them tight, invisible hands squeezing my heart and chest. I came out the other side, but always knew there was another one around the corner. *It can't be that. It's stress. It's guilt. It's the trauma coming back. It can't be THAT.* The more time passed, the harder I had to clamp down on such ideas, but the thought was slowly prizing the my mental bear trap open, threatening to let the truth out, undeniable and devastating.

It was during the next morning, when I woke up after having passed out for just a few minutes, that I realised I was going to be sick. I tried to throw off the mattress 'lid' of my enclosure in time, but my arms were clumsy and weak by then and the mattress just folded around me as I tried to fumble it open. I threw up all over myself and the nearest wall, and, panicked even more as I convinced myself I was going to choke to death. This in turn caused a full-blown panic attack, closing my lungs up as I desperately tried to emerge from my fort. The mattress was suddenly an attacker, wrapping itself around my weakened body, determined to smother me and force me to fatally breathe my own puke into my lungs. Soaked in sweat, with vomit smeared across my face and chest, I finally made it out and over the top of the overturned bed, tumbling onto the floor and gasping in air. There was no relief, though; I was out in the open, unprotected, and my mind screamed at me to find shelter, shelter, more shelter, to go to *GROUND WHERE IT'S SAFE.*

I curled up into a ball, making noises somewhere between crying and screaming, as my mind whirled with possibilities of danger, *danger*, and as a result of that my brain reflexively reached out and flexed that mental muscle again. It remembered how it had worked before and began to test, test like I'd been doing many times a day over the last few weeks.

I locked on.

As the sudden, deafening screaming sound snapped into my mind, louder than before, finding me, filling my brain with its painful white noise, I knew what I'd suspected all along was true, just as I knew in that same moment that I was doomed.

They'd noticed us, all right. We'd caught their attention before, and then we got involved. They were ready, therefore, the next time, the second time when we came back for more, and when we stayed in there too long they not only cut us off, but they made up their minds. They'd had enough of us.

Had enough of me and Paul.

I lay there, captured, pinned like a bug, a child staring into the headlights of the oncoming train. They knew where I was, knew *me*, and in that moment—whether it was just because I was now the target, or whether it was because they wanted me to know, perhaps even gloating as I realised my punishment—I thought I knew why they had come in the first place.

I unlocked with a cry, and wept helplessly into my hands, but this was now for real. Making the connection to the source had short-circuited their influence, the illusion broken, and my mind was once more my own, but now the fear and desperation were true and came from the heart; I was going to die.

I can't really describe the feeling. Realising your own death is not only suddenly upon you, without warning, but within a few days. I couldn't accept it. It was too big. As I lay there for a long time, weeping, my mind flitted amongst so many crazy subjects. I wondered stupidly what would happen to my mortgage, and who would buy my house. I wondered who would sort out my funeral. Would anyone even attend? I even wondered what would happen to the food still in the freezer, seeing a cleanup crew grimly taking dibs on whatever choice foodstuffs they liked the look of. Then I wondered what lay after death, and if it would hurt, and if I would be even aware of the footsteps of the Stone Man as they pounded up the road behind me.

I thought of all the things I had still to do with my life, and all the things that I would be cheated out of, the injustice of it. I wept, and wept, and thought of the others, and how I'd tracked them down. Then I wondered if maybe it wasn't too unjust after all. (I don't know. You decide.)

As you can imagine, this all went on for some time. I won't bore you with it. I wouldn't be able to do it justice anyway. If you were a cancer patient, and then found out you were terminal, you'd at least have had some inkling, even if it didn't really prepare you. Or if you were waiting for test results, or had found a lump, or a badly misshapen and sore mark on your skin. But to find out you had mere days to live, with no prior warning ... I can't put it into words. I can't even try. Wait ... there is one, actually. Regret. There was a lot of that.

Eventually, after going through a million things in my head, I thought of Henry, and something snagged on that thought and wouldn't let go, kept going back to it even when my thoughts tried to move on to the children I'd never had, the ones I'd never wanted but now seemed like the biggest opportunity lost. And as I kept going back to Henry, Henry, even in my worst moment of despair the edges of an idea began to form. I didn't like it, and at first I couldn't even bring myself to think about it—it was an idea no more frightening than knowing the Stone Man was coming for me—but as the hours passed, and my tears began to dry as practicality took over, I kept going back to it, knowing it to be right and letting it take hold.

I went downstairs. Made a cup of tea. As I drank it with shaking hands, the whole thing would hit me all over again and I would burst into tears once more, but they were brief. I was still beyond terrified, and I still desperately hoped that there might be another way, but I knew there wasn't, and the determination that slowly grew in me made me functional if nothing else. I think ... if I'd been happy before ... it would have been harder, harder to move it aside and work ... but ... if I'm honest ... when I looked at my life ... I don't know. I was tired. Always tired. But I still didn't want *that.* Either way, the added pressure of time gave me no choice but to get on with things; and as I've said before, practicality has never been too much of a problem for me. If I couldn't get my head around my own impending death, then I wouldn't try. I would get on with things. I found that I could do that.

The first thing to do was to get hold of Paul. And that was not going to be a pleasant phone call.

***

Time's nearly up, I reckon. D'you know, I think I've drunk myself sober. I never thought that was really possible, but then I think the current ... situation might have more to do with it than anything else. I still haven't even had long enough to truly get my head around it, but then, I've been doing my best to think about anything else. I mean ... well ... anyway ... not yet. Not yet.

Just enough time to finish this version of events off, yes? Jesus, how long have I been here? All day, I think. I've lost track of time, and *that* will be the booze. I'm trying to think what time they arrived ... the last two times there was about eight hours in between the arrival and the time they began to walk. Big stone motherfuckers. Bastards ... you'd think I'd remember what time they turned up, as that was the moment that proved me right. As soon as the Blues came back again, they proved that I was right about the reason they were here.

***

I knew he wouldn't answer at first. He hadn't been doing so for weeks, but I was working on a hunch that, if he'd been going through the same as me—and I thought that he would have been—if I rang his phone enough, he'd have to at least pick it up to turn it off, as the sound would have driven his nerves crazy. I knew that from experience. The idea was that he'd see my number and maybe pick up. Unfortunately, his mobile was already off, going straight to answer phone. I had his home number as well, but no idea if he was still even living there, especially with an upcoming divorce. Still, I had no other options; after this it was a drive to Sheffield.

As the ringing sound came down the line, I was halfway relieved; if he was there, he at least hadn't unplugged it from the wall. Seven back-to-back but unsuccessful calls later, I began to have severe doubts. I decided to try three more before setting off in the car, but he finally picked up on the next ring. It was immediately clear that the fear still had him, that he hadn't connected and broken its hold.

"*Leave me alone!*" hissed the voice on the other end. It was choked and hoarse, the desperate tone of a madman. I struggled to hear anything of the man I knew in there. "*You fucking bastard, leave me alone, I just want—*"

"Paul, Paul, it's okay, it's okay, it's me, it's Andy," I said, interrupting and trying to sound as calm as possible, even though inside I was anything but. It almost seemed pointless, calming him down to give him such awful news, but if I was going to tell him, I wanted him to be in his own mind. He deserved that much. "I know you're freaking out, but I just need you to listen to me, okay? I know what's wrong, and I can stop you feeling that way."

"*Andy?*" said the stranger's voice on the other end, cracking with emotion at the sound of a friend's voice. I didn't know how long I had until that temporary relief twisted into suspicion and fear, turning on me as if I were an intruder, so I knew I had to be quick. "*Andy, what's happening? Oh God, what's happening to me? I can't … I can't stop feeling …*"

"I'll tell you, I'll tell you," I said in my best soothing voice, and trying not to lose my barely maintained self-control at hearing such a big man as Paul turned into a whimpering wreck. "I need you to stop for a moment for me and think, okay?"

There was no reply from the other end of the phone, except for the slightly distant sound of sobbing. It was awful to hear, but this was purely a courtesy call—no, more than that, a call made out of *respect* … and even friendship—and I couldn't listen to that for too long or I would lose all my resolve.

"Paul, I need you to listen. Come on. Please. I'll stop you shaking." I said it as softly as I could, but I couldn't keep the tremor out of my own voice. I could feel my own, real fear threatening to creep back in, and I pushed on, head and hands feeling cold and strangely light.

"*Help me ...*" the voice on the other end of the line whispered, and I nodded even though there was no one in the room with me.

"All right, Paul, I will. I need you to try something for me. You remember what it felt like? In your head, do you remember what it felt like when you tried to lock in with the Stone Men?"

The was a brief pause, then a sniff and a whimpered sound that was in the affirmative.

"Okay. I need you to try to do that in your head for me now," I said, as if talking to a child. I felt sick doing it. "Okay? I know there's no pull, but I need you to try to feel for it, just like you did before. You know what I mean, don't you?"

There was again silence on the phone. It went on for longer this time, almost to the point where I was no longer certain that Paul was still there. I began to wonder whether he was able to do it at all; he'd needed me, after all, to find Patrick's signal, but I'd thought that he would lock in without trouble now that he was the target. Correction, now *we* were the targets. I was going to speak again, and then suddenly I heard a yelp on the other end followed by the sound of the receiver hitting the floor. I heard a series of cries, and what was possibly the sound of stumbling feet, followed by silence again. He'd done it. He'd been in and out, the fear effect had short-circuited the same way that it had with me. Now his mind was his own, and he knew that he was going to die.

I sat down on the floor, sighing and rubbing my temples, and waited. Now I knew that Paul was back in himself, I didn't know how he'd react. He'd been hysterical before, but that had been inflicted by an outside influence. Now it was just him. A good two or three minutes must have passed, and still there'd been nothing from the other end. If he'd passed out, I thought, then I had no idea when I'd be able to speak to him. I couldn't make the phone ring again to wake him up if it wasn't on the hook.

Eventually though, his voice came back.

"Andy?" he asked, softly. His voice was calmer now, but still hoarse. And scared.

"Yeah."

"Did you ... have you ..."

"Yep." My lip trembled, but I would not let it give way.

"Oh *Andy* ... oh fuck ..."

THE STONE MAN

"I know. I know." I had to give a big, snorting breath inwards to hold it all in. If he wasn't giving in to tears, then neither would I.

"What ..." His voice was barely audible now. *"What are we gonna do?"*

"Well ... probably not a good idea to book any holidays, eh?" I said, the words coming from nowhere, but had to bite back a giggle that threatened to turn into hysteria.

"What are we ... what are we ..." babbled Paul, and this was the worst part to hear. This was him. This was coming from the real Paul. "Straub. We ... we'll call Straub." His voice had brightened slightly, his words coming out almost in a jumble as he clung to something that looked like hope.

"Probably the worst person to call, buddy," I said with a deep, resigned sigh. "I think we both know what her solution would be."

"Jesus ..." said Paul, his voice muffled, and I thought he was talking with his hand over his mouth. There was silence for a minute or so, and then Paul spoke again. "We stayed in too long, didn't we," he said, his voice low and resigned. "They saw us."

"Maybe, maybe," I replied. "I think they probably would have spotted us anyway. We were on their frequency, after all." I felt a burst of anger, and kicked at the nearest kitchen cupboard door. It came off its hinges with a bang, and I suddenly threw the mug I was still holding at the wall, where it exploded. It wasn't fucking *fair*, and I wanted to destroy the whole place, but I couldn't allow myself to do that. I had things to do. I took a deep breath and went back to the phone.

"What the fuck was that?" gasped Paul, startled.

"Sorry ... me. Just ... expressing my ... distaste."

"Don't do that, I'm pretty fucking wired right now, you arsehole!"

"Sorry, sorry. I'm sorry."

"No ... no it's okay. Jesus, if you don't have an excuse now ... then when do you?" Then silence descended once more. I had no idea what to say. What could I tell him? What was I ringing to actually say? I hadn't even thought about it, I just wanted to give him his dignity back and ... what? Pay my respects? Then I realised that's exactly what I wanted to do. I wanted to give Paul my respect.

"Look ... I don't know what you're going to do, Paul," I said, quietly, feeling a strange sense of calm and purpose settle into me, I had never experienced its like before. "But I'm going to ... take care of things. Early. Do the right thing here, you know? Try to stop people getting hurt."

"Uh-huh," said Paul's voice down the line. His voice was shaking again.

"Bit easier when you're saving the day by giving up other people, eh?" I said, and then the tears came and I couldn't stop them, and Paul joined me. This

246

went on for some time, but there was no shame in either of us.

"Look, look," I managed to say when we'd calmed down as much as could be expected, "I just ... I wanted to say that, what you do is up to you, and I won't judge you, or anything like that, okay? I just wanted to say that you're a good bloke, and ... none of the other stuff was your fault, all right? You were doing the right thing." The words were clogged and barely audible, more like squeaks than the manly tone I would have liked, but he understood me.

"Yes, yes," Paul gasped back. "You ... too. You're a good guy Andy, I-I like you and you're a good guy." I chuckled briefly, a grim, short bark then sent a small bit of spit flying across the room.

"I'm not, you know," I said, shaking my head sadly, "I've not really tried too hard to be one, either. I don't really like people, I think I'm pretty shallow, and all I've ever really thought about—not totally, I'm not Hitler, for fuck's sake, but most of the time—is getting ahead. And ... *ahh,* Jesus, some other stuff, and I'm sorry for all that, I really am ..." I trailed off, trying to think of the best words to describe the intentions that I'd only recently found, the sense of ... fucking *dignity* that came with it. "But this ... this I think I can do." That calm feeling embraced me, a melancholy but firm resignation that told me I could be, for the first time in my life, certain about a course of action. "This is a good thing. This last thing ... this is a good thing. And I'm the one doing it. I'm not fucking happy about it, but ... this is something *worthy.* I don't know if that makes sense to you."

There was silence on the phone.

"You're right, Andy," Paul said at last, solemn. "It *is* worthy. I just wish ... fuck me, Andy, I just wish it wasn't us."

"Yeah," I said, but I didn't add the sincere *Me too* that hovered on my lips. I thought it would somewhat take the shine off the noble point that I'd just made.

"How're you gonna ..." Paul asked, not needing to finish the question.

"I'll figure something out," I said, already having it planned. I just didn't want to talk about it, but I was going to do it in private; undisturbed and on my own terms. They wouldn't get to walk across my country and wreck it, or at least not the one coming for me. I would be long gone. It occurred to me that maybe the kid's death—Target Three, as I would only ever know her as—had maybe not been in vain. It gave us information, knowledge about how to at least stop them early. The thought didn't bring any comfort, though. I had my own death to worry about.

"Are you gonna talk to Straub first?"

"Yeah. Not just yet though. Gonna wait 'til they arrive—it'll be soon, I think, a few hours, tonight at the latest—then try the map, see if I can get anything.

Give them a head start if possible."

"Right ... the Third Arrival. Fucking thing," said Paul, his voice low. "I think ... I think I'll call Straub too. Speak to her about ... getting some help. You know. Keep it quick, like."

"Okay, mate," I said. "But look, you know, don't forget. After seven or eight hours ... after they've started walking ..."

"Yeah. Yeah. The things, the ... the barriers." He sounded sick.

"Yeah, them. Just keep them in mind, time-wise I mean. I'd, uh ... I'd best be going."

"Yeah. Yeah, okay."

"Good luck, Paul. Hope it goes ... ah, fuck, forget that. It was nice knowing y ... ah Christ, that's even worse. Sorry." Paul actually laughed in response down the line, but it was punctuated with sniffs.

"Fantastic send-off there, buddy, brilliant," he said, voice trembling even more, but I gave a sniff-laugh of my own in return. "I appreciate the thought, though," he said, "and the same to you man ... I don't care what you say. I think you're a good bloke."

"Thanks, Paul."

There was much more to say, and yet there wasn't.

"Take ... take care then."

"Yeah. Yeah, you too. Bye."

"Bye."

With a sense of finality that was nearly overwhelming, I pushed the 'End' button on the phone. That was the last time we ever spoke to each other.

***

I did start off by mentioning you, Paul, when I began recording this, and I wish to God that you could have a listen to it. I'd love to hear if I missed anything, or if I was getting anything wrong. A real shame, that.

Anyway. Time is ticking ... always is, right? Heh ... anyway. There's just a bit more to tell. Just time for a little bit more. Just a bit longer.

***

I drove back to Birmingham, after calling ahead to the hotel that I'd been staying in while the workmen had renovated the house. I didn't want to take care of business in that building; someone would hopefully live in it again someday, maybe a family, and it just didn't feel right. People died in hotels all the time, didn't they? That's what I thought, anyway. And, I admit without any shame, it would stall time quite nicely. I could have stalled until the moment they actually came back if I wanted, but I knew that would be a bad idea. The longer I waited, the longer I would have to talk myself out of it.

Everything on that twenty-five-minute drive took on an extra air of sweetness; songs on the radio—ones that I'd previously not even cared for— now sounded like masterpieces, and the inane chatter of the DJ sounded like life itself. The industrial buildings either side of the M6 now had a dark beauty to them, buildings that I'd looked at in the past and had no desire to ever see again. My vision blurred with tears many times, and I nearly pulled over once or twice as the enormity of what I had to do hit me. And then I would think of Henry, and how he'd handled things, and how he'd managed it even in the state he'd been put into, and I would tighten my hands on the wheel and carry on.

As I drove, I rang Straub. I'd rethought my previous plan, and decided to at least give her a heads-up. She needed a chance to get the wheels turning as early as possible, get units ready to scramble, even if I couldn't tell her where to scramble them *to*. For once, they would know that the Stone Men were coming *before* they arrived. All I could get right now whenever I locked in was that horrible, screaming wind that signalled my own death, and there was no way I was facing that noise again. It was like hearing the screech of a nightmarish pack of hounds as they fell upon me, and the memory of that sound made me picture teeth finding their way into my spine. I was doing more than enough for my country as it was. I would just have to wait until the Stone Men were actually here, and try to get their individual destinations if I could. I doubted it, but it was worth a try.

Once she picked up, I gave her the details. I told her to prepare for the Third Arrival, who at least two of the targets were, and what I planned to do. As expected, Straub was a consummate professional about the whole thing.

"Mr Pointer ... Andy ... I'm sorry to hear that," she said, taking a deep breath. "You seem to be ... taking it rather well."

"I wasn't exactly having the fucking time of my life beforehand, to be honest," I replied, wishing for the fourth or fifth time on that drive that I had a bottle with me and feeling deeply, deeply sorry for myself. "All that cash as well, eh? What an asshole. What a fucking *asshole*." I punched the wheel and the horn beeped, causing the driver next to me to look my way. I didn't return his gaze.

"You'd seen some awful things that you weren't trained for, Andy. And you were deeply involved with them. You couldn't be expected to shrug all that off." She sighed, and it sounded as if she was moving into a chair. It was a rare sound from Straub, one from the heart. "I blame myself for that. I should have made sure we got you counselling, or at least trauma therapy ... things were just so crazy afterward, and our first priority had to be preparing for a return. If you'd have asked ... no, you shouldn't have had to. I'm sorry, Andy. We let you down."

"Doesn't matter, Brigadier," I said, biting back more fucking tears, "I'd still be screwed now, either way. At least this way I'm in the mood for it."

"Andy," she said, talking closely into the phone, her voice softer. "Is there anything we can do? To make it ... easier? We could sedate you, you know. Then a final injection. You wouldn't feel a thing. Peaceful."

"Thank you, Brigadier, but I think I want to be on my own. I think it'll be pretty painless as it is, to be honest. I'll leave the spook phone switched on so you know where I am; you don't have to worry about me getting cold feet. I'm ..." I sighed, and realised that the sun was starting to set in the grey horizon. *Jesus,* I thought. *That is some bleak shit.* "... I'm doing this."

"You'll be a hero, Andy. We'll make sure of it."

"Yeah, yeah. Just give all my money to Coventry Refugee fund, okay?"

"Done."

"Andy ... how many are coming this time?"

"No idea. How are your new backup guys checking out?"

"Everything adds up with three of them. They know things they couldn't possibly know, with complete accuracy; we think that if we get them together, like you and Paul, we'll have another hunting unit. You're not leaving us unmanned, don't worry."

"And what are you going to tell them? About what happened to me and Paul?"

She fell silent, but only for a second.

"We'll tell them what they need to know of the truth. That you were cut off."

"I see."

"My job is to look after the country's best interests, Andy. You know that."

"Mm." A dark thought occurred to me. "Did you suspect this? Did you think this might happen? To me and Paul?"

Straub sighed again, but it was sad, reluctant one. When she next spoke, as ever, she was direct. The softness in her voice was gone, however, and the distance had returned.

"It was one scenario we anticipated, yes. We couldn't be certain, obviously, but once you were cut off we thought it might happen."

"Do tell." I wasn't even angry. Hadn't I thought the same with the others, that it just had to be done? How could I stand in judgement now that I was the one being offered up?

"There's a common factor amongst the targets, obviously," Straub said. "People within a certain genetic bracket. The Stone Men connect with them, and then hunt them down. Fair enough. And the targets seem to know on some level that they're picked, have an ability to receive the signal, or what have you. And there are those who are sensitive to it, the ones who got migraines or were sick, people perhaps on the outskirts of that genetic bracket. And on the other end of the scale are people like you and Paul, the ones who can not only receive it but *search* for it, who can tune between different frequencies. And all of those people, we theorised, must have something in common, something the Stone Men, or their masters, want. I think you yourself might have suspected that they just pick the first target they find, yes? Distance and time aren't a factor for them; their targets are going nowhere once they're pinned in place, after all."

I heard her catch her breath as she realised who she was talking to. Being Straub, the effect was only temporary.

"Sorry. That was insensitive. What I mean is, once the targets were stationary—especially once you'd been noticed and cut off—we theorised that it might be a case of them ..." She paused, the phrase *killing two birds with one stone* clearly about to pass from her lips and being caught there. "... neutralising you and Paul permanently, and—seeing as you were within the right bracket, if our theory is correct—getting what they want from the two of you as well. Of course, this could just be a simple 'hit'. They might be sending two of their Stone Men purely to take you out, and wasting one gene-harvesting trip to do so. Again, time doesn't appear to be a concern for them, so in their eyes, why not?"

"Why not indeed," I said quietly, wishing I hadn't called. I thought about how time had always been a concern for me, spending life all too aware of the ticking of the clock (at least until recent events had turned me into a bumbling drunk). And now all of my time was up.

"Can I ask you one favour, Andy?"

"Whatever the fuck you like, Brigaddy-Wiggady. I'm all yours," I replied, giddy and dead inside at the same time.

"Will you wait until they arrive? Check a map for us, maybe give us a head start? We'll have the ... replacements ready now anyway, but just in case. Help us correlate. You might not get anything, but—"

"Don't worry, Straub," I said, cutting her off and wanting to wrap this up. I'd had enough. "I'd already planned to do so. I'll let you know."

"Laura," she said.

"What?"

"My name is Laura." It should have had impact, but it didn't.

"Oh. Right. Well ... good luck, Laura."

"Good luck, Andy. Thank you. The country thanks you."

I thought about this, searched for a weighty reply, and gave up.

"No, they don't."

I hung up on her. I realised I should have added *But I'm doing it anyway* to give it a more heroic feel ... but then decided it was better without. I couldn't go to my grave with that load of cheese appearing in the headlines.

***

Once I'd checked in, exchanging pleasantries on autopilot with the woman behind the impressive foyer's desk, I thought once or twice about calling Paul again—I don't know why, I just felt compelled to do so—but thought better of it. Best to leave him to it; I'd gotten him into this, after all. But if Straub's people were correct, sooner or later they'd have gotten around to him anyway. I had more than enough guilt on my shoulders that I could give myself the benefit of the doubt on that one.

Once in my luxurious room (and dammit if I wasn't giving myself the best one), I ordered a pizza—I love them and always have—then ran a bath. I decided to eat the pizza while *in* the bath. I correctly thought that it would be great, and half of me was aware that it actually was—noticing how the taste of the food and the physical sensation of the warm soapy water on my skin combined in the most delicious way, made more so by knowing that this was my last meal, and somehow simultaneously not really being able to understand the concept—but the other half was beyond terrified, and held up only by grim determination. I took my time getting dry, watching the news channel and waiting in my fluffy, white, hotel-provided dressing gown. I'd brought the atlas in from the car.

I wondered about the future, and how the country could ever adapt to this. How we could build and rebuild while knowing that at any time it could all be taken away ... but then I thought that a culture would develop around it. If Straub's people were right, the people who were sensitive to the Stone Men— those who got the migraines and the shakes, those who passed out—would be the targets of the future. Once word got around, once people knew that the way to protect their own interests was to find and prematurely end the people that the Stone Men wanted, then I thought that people would put two and two together and watch for these physical symptoms ... and then God knows what the next step would be. I had visions of camps for potential targets, set up along lines of previous destruction to create safe channels on already ruined land. Witch-hunts carried out by frightened mobs. The country was in for an interesting few years while it worked out all the terrible kinks. But a system would come, I was fairly sure.

I thought about friends and loved ones, and realised just how few there were. I pulled out my phone and shut down my Facebook profile, after deciding against posting a final, dramatic status, one vague enough to send an ominous chill, yet indecipherable until news of my death came out and all was made clear. I wanted to, certainly—the drama of it was almost too tempting—but decided that if I was trying to do a dignified thing, then I would be dignified in all respects. Plus, deliberately vague, attention-seeking Facebook statuses are for thirteen-year-old girls.

I didn't send any individual messages or texts. I thought that it would only get me thinking twice, plus I had no idea how Straub—or more precisely, David and his ilk—were going to spin my death, and I hadn't totally decided if I would let them ... and that's when I had the idea to record this account. I had time, after all, I thought ... I had to know first though. I would know if I was right; I needed that.

I walked down through the hotel foyer in nothing but my dressing gown, acknowledging every astonished face with an insane, cheesy grin and a wave, tears flooding my eyes with near-hysteria. That was a last little pleasure, I'll admit; despite the situation, it was fun freaking people out. I headed out to the car park, grabbed the new Dictaphone from my car's glove box, and returned to my room, locking the door behind me. The catch slotted home with a heavy-sounding click, reminding me that I would not be passing through that doorway again. I hadn't lingered in the hallway, nor the lobby; I hadn't really allowed myself any lingering anywhere, or the taking-in of sights, since this whole thing began. It would have been a bad idea, but lingering in the room was different. That was my space to prepare, and I knew what would and what wouldn't be threaten my resolve.

Not long after that, towel drying my hair, I felt the world tip sideways, and my entire body broke out in goose bumps. The next thing I knew I was regaining consciousness while lying on the floor, a line of thick spittle drying on my face.

I didn't freak out, to my surprise. I wasn't totally expecting it, being both on the receiving end and, as far as I'd known, cut off, but I wasn't too surprised either. I *wasn't completely* cut off then, it seemed. I had at least enough to know when the first one turned up; perhaps all the targets had felt the same thing. Now it would be waiting for its friends, and they were what I wanted to see. I calmly—but shakily—got myself to my feet, and carried on getting ready. I rewashed my face, and had a shave. I would not be rushed.

Shortly after that (once I'd gotten into my best shirt, suit and tie, which with the money I had to spend was saying something. If I was going, I was going smartly, even if I'd be a mess after impact. *I'd* know, that was the thing) the breaking news came through on the TV, interrupting a report on the presidential election. This was bigger.

The live feed was of a sight that once would have once been familiar, but not anymore. The man-made lake where Millennium Place once stood made the whole area unrecognisable. Further back from the edge of that was the barrier, and beyond that was the usual, spaced-out ring of military vehicles. And of course, near the centre of the water and almost entirely clear of it, the head of the original Stone Man could be seen, the rest of its body concealed below the surface. Its head had no eyes, of course, but in that moment I almost felt that it was looking directly at me, searching through the TV screen and hunting for me over the airwaves.

My lip started to quiver, but I bit it, hard. I was done crying, and I would not let these things take any more from me. Not one bit. Anger grew in me, a white-hot fist of it growing in my stomach, but I would not lose my composure. I wouldn't give them the satisfaction.

Not me, fuckface, I thought. *You don't get me. This building has eighteen floors, and I'm in the penthouse. Unless you're outside waiting to catch me on the way down, good luck digging up the bits of what's left.*

This started me laughing, and this time I let it happen. I gave the image on the TV the finger, and went to inspect the contents of the mini bar.

I checked the TV; the Stone Man's backup still hadn't arrived. I stared at the Dictaphone, and decided that I'd best turn off the news, if only while I got started. Yes, all I was waiting for was the original Stone Man's Blue backup—and not to try to pick out their targets for Straub, by the way. Yes, I'd give it a go, but I had other reasons—and worried that they might turn up as soon as I turned off the set, but I figured that even if they did, ten minutes wouldn't hurt. Straub would have everyone on standby by now. So I switched it off. And ... I'm stalling, aren't I? I'm getting near the end and I'm stalling. Oh God.

Right. The last bit that *has* to be recorded, and then I'm done. This isn't an excuse, either; it needs to be done. I need to make sure Straub knows this before next time, which is stupid, because A, it probably won't make any difference, and B, if I've worked this out then I'm fucking certain that the brain trust that Boldfield runs knows it too. It's bloody obvious, for crying out loud, simple maths that a child could do, but I couldn't know for certain until the Blues turned up as well. She'll already know ... but I need to record this so I *know* that she'll know.

I could call her, but ... that's the outside world now. I'm in here. I locked the door. Ah, but that's bullshit, isn't it, Andy, and now you're stalling some more, because you already *texted* Straub a few hours ago, so you could have texted her that little piece of info as well, couldn't you, instead of telling her where to pick up your stupid tape? So why don't we, Mr peace-of-mind, cut to the chase? Hell, they should have started walking hours ago, you shouldn't have had time to get this far, so stop pushing it.

Good point me, you dick ... so it *is* just stalling. And there's even more of them this time, so maybe that's why I've had extra time, I don't know, maybe it takes longer for them to charge up or whatever.

I'm a *storyteller*. Okay? I always have been, and it's how I earned a living throughout my entire adult life. I lost sight of that a long time ago, and many other things, and this ... this is my biggest story. And I want to finish it. I want to say that I was a part of it, and that I was *here*, and I know that someone will listen to this. I just want that piece of myself back.

So. Earlier, when I said there was something I had to do? You may remember, whoever you are—Straub, if you're listening—that I said that. Well, that particular thing was sending a text to Straub, because then I had at least *one* answer. I knew why the Stone Men came to us.

Why they came to take bits of us.

I already had an inkling when I first saw those two Blues, and more so after Target Two's—no, no, Theresa *Pettifer's*—baby had died, and the last Blue stopped and disappeared. Back then, I had a number that I'd worked out in my head. It was only very, very basic maths, after all, so when I say 'worked out' that makes it sound more complicated than it was. I mean worked out *logically*, more than anything. All I knew was that when the Stone Men returned—if they came back and their total number matched the one that I suspected—then it was pretty certain my suspicion was right. A long while later, when I locked in while lying terrified on my bedroom floor in Coventry, I thought I felt something; whether it was because I was a target now, or whether it was the masters *wanting* me to know, I don't know. Either way, I thought I knew that my theory was right ... but still I had to wait for the number, to *check* the number, in order to prove it.

I thought there would be *seven* Stone Men this time.

Several hours ago, looking at the TV screen in this room, I was proved right. The original, plus six Blues this time.

Patrick's spine, taken by the original Stone Man ... but its chest had come out as two parts when it did, hadn't it? They'd then merged, taking part of Patrick's spine ... but then had separated into two parts again as it retracted. Potentially, splitting the spine.

Then, two Blues arrive. So now there's three Stone Men, with three targets this time. But one target is never reached, as the signal, the pull, is taken away. So only *two* targets are met. They're harvested, and split into two. So *four* new parts are therefore taken.

So *four* new Blues would arrive this time, along with the original and the first two Blues. Seven.

Whatever the Stone Men are—whatever they're for, whether they are the puppets of others or a race in themselves—they need us in order to make *more*.

Maybe the original is the race, and the Blues are the puppets, or whether the originals are just *fucking harder to make without the right body parts*, without the right genetic type of spinal cord to run their central nervous system—it doesn't matter. It's all speculation, and until we know where they're coming from we'll never know. The *purpose* is the same regardless.

This isn't an invasion. How could they invade by making a handful of new soldiers every few months, while we reproduce thousands of new versions of ourselves every day? They don't rush, sure; time is not an issue for them, whereas we run to keep up with it every single day before it runs out. I'm sure they laugh at us for that. But even if they kept it up for millennia, we'd always be making more of us, so they could never fully win. Plus, hell, given that long we'd probably find out a way to smash the fuckers. Besides, to invade is to enter an area for the purpose of seizing it, of taking it over and keeping it, and I don't think they're interested in that. Theirs is a long-term plan, and I expect we'll be seeing Stone Men for a long, long time. They're only interested in our territory for our people anyway.

It's not an invasion. *It's a breeding program.*

I won't be the only one to work this out of course, as I say. Far smarter minds than mine have been working on the Stone Man situation since the very first one touched down in Coventry many months ago, and they'll have figured this out too, but maybe they have a few tricks up their sleeve as well. Who knows? I can only hope so, for all of our sakes. I think there are tough times ahead for our country, either way. No reports yet of arrivals anywhere else in the world either, so I can only assume there's only one point on our planet that they can arrive at, or one point at least that is the easiest place for them to do so.

I'd better get the map and see if I can make some headway. In a way, it'll make my ... job that much easier. I mean, if I can help give other people a death sentence, it's only fair I'm prepared to do the same for myself, right?

Done. No joy. They've shut me down properly this time, it seems. That screaming ... oh, it is terrible. I will not falter before it.

I've let Straub know. Yeah ... and I'm stalling again, aren't I?

I'm not a noble man, and I haven't done many noble things. Would I be doing this if not for that arsehole Henry? I don't know. But I am doing it, at least. This one last thing.

Christ. Ah ... *Christ.* I can't do this. I can't do this. Oh Jesus.

Dignity ... for once in my fucking life. Please. Oh ...

Right. Right. I'm going to stop this recording, and then I'm done. I don't have any grand last words, and if I waste any more time trying to think of some then I might change my mind. But I *am* going to do it.

And that's the big surprise for me in all of this. When it really counts, some people can just do what needs to be done ... but it turns out I'm one of them. And I've been a coward all my life. Who knew? I've always—

No. Doing it again. I'm going.

... 'Bye.

***

Paul was sitting in the middle of a field, alternating between looking at the blackness of the sky and the blackness of his phone's switched-off screen. It wasn't really *his* phone (that was in his opposite hand, still receiving signal despite his rural surroundings, and providing his up to-the-minute news feed) to be precise; he thought of it as *Straub's* phone, the government issue one that was to be left on at all times. It had been switched off ever since he finished with his call to Andy on the landline phone.

The hours since had been spent pacing, crying, shouting at no one, sending cryptic messages to close friends and not responding to any of the concerned replies he'd received back. It wouldn't have been the first time lately that they'd had cause to send them. Paul's friends had been worried about him for many months.

After a long time, he'd had to get out of the house, to find some kind of release. He'd been nervous as he headed for the door, concerned about the barriers arriving early, but based on the timescale of the Stone Men's previous visits, he'd still felt that he had a few hours yet before the Blues arrived and they all began to walk. Once *that* happened he wouldn't be going anywhere,

257

and he wanted his freedom for as long as possible. Plus, he thought he'd *feel* any change on that front. At least, he told himself, if he suddenly got zapped while driving, then he wouldn't know anything about what would come next. *Probably a six-car pileup,* whispered a voice in his head, but he ignored it. He was a desperate man now, and that desperation was growing.

He'd headed west out of Sheffield, after wrapping himself in several layers and stopping to grab a torch as he left the house. He'd intended to be outdoors for as long as possible, and the sun was already setting by the time he'd left. Paul didn't much fancy spending his last few hours alive nursing a broken leg, courtesy of an unseen rabbit hole.

After about half an hour, he'd found himself driving through the beautiful fields around the Ladybower Reservoir. He could appreciate the area based on past experience; at the time it was far too dark to see anything outside of his headlamp beams. This would do. Driving became a pain anyway, constantly having to wipe the tears from his eyes and clear mucus from his nose, his chest heaving steadily all the while. He'd had to park the car at an almost forty-five-degree angle, as there was no space between the road edge and the steep grassy embankment. The road had been very narrow, but not too winding at this point, and with his hazard lights on in the night other drivers would have plenty of time to avoid him. Plus, what would the police do? Give him a ticket? It wasn't exactly something he would have to worry about.

As he'd got out of the car, his breath fogging in the chill February evening, he'd slipped his hands into his pockets for his gloves. He'd felt the weight of Straub's phone in there for the umpteenth time, fingered its edge gingerly.

She can wait. Bugger her. They can all wait. Half an hour, it's not much to ask.

He'd slipped on his gloves, grabbed the torch from the passenger seat, and turned it on. The powerful floodlit beam had revealed a low road barrier on the opposite side, a small ditch beyond that, and a wooden fence. Easy obstacles to clear, even for a man of his size and low fitness, and then he would have free access into the sweeping, open fields beyond. A place to sit. A place to be as much in the open air as possible, to feel himself and the earth breathe.

The thought had given him pause. What the fuck was he doing here? How had he ended up like this, desperate and wanting to sit in the mud because it somehow made him feel alive? A year previous, on the same month, he'd been celebrating his mate Rich's fiftieth. Holly had been there too, of course. They'd drank and laughed back then, and watched Mick and Jenny's kids and half-jokingly talked about some of their own. But this year, as he stood outside with the night air stinging his cheeks, he'd thought that maybe that was the last time he'd ever felt really, really good. Paul then found himself thinking how he'd had no idea what was coming. How he never could have known. How he would become another person entirely, shaped utterly by forces outside of his control and events in which he had played no part in the planning. He'd stood in the road and wanted so, so badly to go back to that past version of himself and warn him, but of course, he couldn't. The old Paul would still just get up on the next Monday morning, maybe even treat himself to a nice fried breakfast, drive to work whistling along with the radio, duck into the toilet for a cheeky half hour with that day's tabloid, and then maybe think about finally getting some work done by 9:45 a.m., blissfully and totally unaware. Unaware of the time to come when he would be stood in the dark, weeping and thinking existential thoughts and forced into planning his own suicide.

He'd set off, crossing the road barrier and the other obstacles with less ease than he'd originally expected (he was wearing bulky layers and hadn't considered the extra hassle they would cause), but still feeling a slight sense of calm as he felt his boots squelch into the soft, wet grass. The torch had lit up a path directly ahead of him; it revealed thick patches of dry shrub grass here and there, and a few small, leafless trees scattered randomly around the expanse. Up in the distance, there was the base of a large hill. A quick glance revealed that it went on in both directions for some way. He'd flicked the torch off for a second to give his eyes time to adjust to the light. Once they had, he'd actually grinned as he saw the stars above. That was what he'd wanted; to be out in the open, and for as long as he could allow it he could tell himself that he wasn't trapped at all, that all of this was his to wander around in. Just for a while.

He'd decided to walk until he found somewhere dry to sit. Then, he'd told himself, he would call Straub, and they would take things from there. He'd know, after all, when the barriers were up. He was certain he'd feel it.

That had all been several hours ago, and he'd crossed over four fields in the meantime before coming to rest on a stile. It formed a perfect seat: the stile itself forming the base, and the fence slats acting as the backrest. He'd cried a bit when he sat down, then stared off into the sky once he'd done so, thinking about, of all things, Sheffield United, and the realisation that if they ever got back into the Premiership then he wouldn't be around to see it. That had nearly set him off again, but instead, he'd had a thought that made him smirk in the darkness. Even without the Stone Men's arrival, he didn't think he'd have lived to see *that*.

Paul had been sitting on the stile ever since. He wasn't frightened of the dark; he never had been, even as a child. He'd always been one of those kids whose sense of adventure far outweighed his fear. All he'd been feeling since he'd sat on the stile was a strange sense of calm, one that only shifted into panic whenever he thought about having to call Straub. Even though he knew they'd all be walking soon, he waited. At first he'd justified it with anger (*I've done enough, it's cost me enough, and now I'm losing everything*) and then with logic (*I'll feel it when they start to walk and Straub can have a chopper here in twenty minutes, or a guy with a gun. I'm allowed this last time, surely?*) but even when he'd felt the vibration slam through his bones that let him know his Stone Man, at least—the one coming for him—had set off, the phone remained unused. After a while he'd quietly stopped trying to justify it to himself, and somehow, that felt okay to him. The more he pushed the thoughts away, he found that he felt calmer still. The only thing that felt bad was the idea of calling Straub. That brought everything back when he thought of it, and so he did it less and less. He was aware of a strong sinking feeling though, of a dropping of his chin; as Paul remained sitting on the stile and more time passed, he began to find that, for some, anything could be given up as long as it wasn't one's life. He was surprised.

He was aware of the cold, but thanks to his many thermal layers, he thought he could handle it and sit there pretty much indefinitely. The thought had great appeal; his own quiet little space, alone with his thoughts. He wondered how much space he'd have, eventually, once his barrier was up, how much room to wander and breathe (of course, though, he told himself, that it wouldn't come to that, that he'd call Straub first. Eventually. He just wanted a bit more time). He let the thought linger for a moment. Just how big was the inside area of a barrier, after all? His mind instantly skipped to his last frame of reference, going through the available evidence and finding the best piece instantly. *Patrick.* How far had he gotten outside of his house, before he ran into the barrier in a blind panic and trapped himself in the spider's web? About forty feet, maybe? Maybe fift—

Paul jumped to his feet, electrified.

Sweet Jesus, Mary and Joseph. Surely … surely …

He hardly dared to believe he might have something. Even if he did, it was so miniscule, so … so *barely there* as a chance, that he couldn't hang his hopes on it, couldn't allow himself to even consider salvation, as it would be beyond cruelty to do so and it then turn out to be wrong. He was a drowning man who had seen a small shape on the horizon, unsure what it could be and uncertain regardless that it could reach him in time. But the shape was there, nonetheless. They didn't know everything about the Stone Man, and the variables were immense, so there had to at least be a chance that he was right

...

He began to pace back and forth at speed, rubbing his face and babbling his thoughts out loud, unaware that he was doing it. His fingers twitched and his breathing became rapid—almost to the point of hyperventilating—as he checked and double-checked all the Stone Man facts that he knew, or thought he knew. He paced as he tried to poke holes in his own realisation, testing it soundly yet desperately hoping for it to pass, like a man of lapsed faith confronted with a miracle. As he did so, and his idea began to stand up more and more against it all, his feverish excitement grew, despite his best attempts to contain it.

This could work. This could really WORK!

But Straub! He would have to convince Straub to … to what? Paul realised that yes, he had the vague shape of a plan, but that was it. No logistics, no *details*. If he were to even have a ghost of a chance of convincing Straub, he would have to have the whole thing perfectly laid out, with as many variables covered as possible. He checked his watch; nearly 11:00 p.m. He'd delayed so long already, and they were walking now. He knew he couldn't wait much longer, but he had to get his story straight. His life might depend on it.

Paul turned his smartphone onto its note writing function. He began to get it all down on electronic paper with frantic hands, actually beginning to sweat despite the cold. His quivering thumbs drove him mad as he did so, and several times he had to stop and let out a scream of frustration to the night sky. His attempts to get his adrenalized body to put his mind's desires on record via a precision instrument were torture, and yet he didn't notice the small, steady flow of tears that streamed down his face and froze his cheeks in the chill night breeze. The madman's smile on his face was desperate, and his eyes were wide white-and-red circles in the dark.

Eventually, after he'd finished, and read and reread it several times while making small adjustments to it here and there, he was ready to go. He took a deep breath, and switched on Straub's phone

Even when he pushed Straub's name in the phone's contact book—the only other name in the contacts book being David's, but Paul wasn't going to be dealing with *that* guy—the call kept failing, much to Paul's nerve-rattling frustration, but the reason for that soon became clear. The torrent of texts, voice mails, and e-mails that flooded in after a few minutes of unsuccessful call attempts told him both that the phone, after being switched on, had been too busy gathering all of his waiting communication information, and that Straub and her people had been trying very hard indeed to get hold of him. He almost thought about reading some of the texts and listening to the voice mails, but decided against it, pushing forward impatiently. If there was anything in them that might actually offer him salvation, Straub would surely tell her himself straightaway ... but he doubted very much that that salvation was the content of the messages.

The next call that he attempted connected successfully, and the phone was answered on the other end after one ring. Paul waited for her to speak, and initially there was an odd silence on the other end, save for a faint rustling sound. It was a sound Paul knew; the sound of someone holding a phone mouthpiece to their chest to muffle it. He could picture Straub clearly, barking at the rest of the room to *shut the fuck up, he's on the line.*

The muffled sound lifted, and Paul could now hear machine noises in the background, but nothing else. Straub paused before she spoke, and when she did, her voice was calm, soothing and controlled ... but the effort it was taking to make it so was clear in every gentle syllable.

"Paul," she said, trying to sound warm but managing only ice cold, "we've been trying to get hold of you. Are you all right?"

"Yes ... I mean no, no ... I mean, look, I've been busy," Paul bleated, wincing at *I've been busy* despite his frantic state of mind. It was the most lame comeback possible in the face of world-changing events. "I mean ... sorry, I'm bloody sorry. This is just bloody hard to handle, all of this. I'm just ..." Paul trailed off, taking in the field around him, the starry night sky, the feeling of the cold breeze as it made his skin raise. He had to bite down on fresh tears.

Not now, Winter. This is NOT the time. Keep it together.

"Of course it is, no one's blaming you," replied Straub, and Paul thought she might even mean it, despite the stress of her own situation. After all, could anyone really blame him for not just handing himself in? Could they? "This isn't a normal situation, Paul. But you're calling me now, aren't you, and that's a start. I can only imagine how hard that alone must have been for you, so you're making a hell of an effort, and I appreciate that, I do."

Paul listened closely, thinking he heard another voice nearby on Straub's end, a whispered stream of words in the background. He couldn't make out what the words were, but he could guess. The adviser, the negotiator, listening in to the call and prepping Straub's responses for her. These were the pros, after all. Paul reminded himself to be extra aware of whom he was dealing with.

"Good, good, I'm glad, thank you," replied Paul, his voice shaking as he began to play his own negotiating game. "I ... I wanted to talk to you."

"I'm listening," said Straub, after a very telling pause, "it's the least I can do, considering ... what we're asking of you." The second pause was too short to be a thinking pause, and the words afterwards were spoken too fast. Straub had attempted to cover the fact that she had someone giving her cues, and failed. Paul decided not to let on that he knew. He took a deep breath, and tried the gamble that might save his life.

"I wanted to suggest something," he said, speaking slowly and deliberately, his eyes shut. "I know that you probably already know where I am now, and that you're also probably on your way. And that's okay, I know I've ... been taking a long time to get in touch, and that you have a job to do. I understand all that. So I'm not going to go anywhere, and I'll sit here and wait for you lot to turn up, I promise. The barriers will be up soon anyway, and I know you're trying to get to me before they do, so you can ... take care of things. And that, that, you know, that's fine too. I just want you to listen to me for a few minutes, and hear what I have to say, and then you can do with it what you like. Straight shooting, cards on the table. All right?"

There was silence on the line, except for the continued background hum of whatever machines Straub's team had working in the background. Paul began to panic a little.

"All right?" he repeated, more anxiousness in his voice than he would have liked.

"Hold on," said Straub, all business now, the false honey gone from her voice, and then the muffle came back on the line. All Paul could hear was the rustling sound in his ear, and the almost deafening thud of his heart in his chest. The muffle lifted, and when Straub came back, she was to the point.

"Okay, Winter, straight shooting. We're all ears. You have about ten minutes until our team are there, so I'd make it good. We weren't a million miles away from your position as it is, being totally honest. Our new guys—the ones who came forward—checked out. Together, they had it down to about a hundred mile radius from where you are now, and they were closing. They're not as good as you two were, which explains why it took us so long to be convinced by them, but they work at least." She caught her breath for a moment, and then, to Paul's surprise, she sighed. "That's coming out wrong. I didn't mean it that way. It was supposed to make you feel better; that we have people that can still help, that can save lives." She sighed again. "I do mean it about not judging you though, Paul. I'm pissed off it's taken you this long to turn up—and if I'm honest, I'm surprised as well—but I can't say you're a totally bad person for it. It's the biggest thing to ask of someone, after all."

"The new guys," asked Paul. "Do they know what's happened to me and Andy? As in, do they know two of their targets are the people who used to ...?"

Again, a lengthy silence.

"No," said Straub eventually, and firmly. "They don't. And I'm sure that even you'd agree it needs to stay that way. No?"

"I don't know," answered Paul, rubbing his eyes as he suddenly felt incredibly, unbearably tired. His head started to throb. "I don't fucking know." A thought occurred to him. "Andy. Have you ... where's Andy?" This time, there was no hesitation from Straub. Relaying bad news was obviously something she was more experienced with.

"He took care of things himself. He didn't want our help. I spoke to him this morning. His body has been recovered from the car park of a Birmingham hotel since; he'd jumped out of the penthouse window. He wouldn't have suffered, Paul, jumping from that height. It would have been instant. He died a hero."

The weight in Paul's stomach doubled, and he had to steady himself as a wave of nausea washed over him. He knew it was coming, but for it to be so final was too much, and almost as much was knowing that Andy had the stones to get the job done ... while Paul didn't. And even in that moment, the voice that whispered *SURVIVE* told him that it didn't matter, that he had a job to do. He tried to get his lips moving, but for a moment, nothing came out but a high-pitched, barely audible whine.

"Winter? Paul? Are you there?"

"I'm here," whispered Paul, dragging himself back to conscious function by sheer force of will. "I need ..." He coughed. "I need you to listen."

"You already said that. I know, Paul."

"Uh. Ah. Yes. Yes ... I ..."

"Breathe, take your time. This is your time."

Paul slammed his left heel into his right shin, and the sharp physical pain focused him.

"Okay. Yes. I have something I want to suggest to you," he said, breathing deeply and slowly. "I have a proposal."

***

Paul spoke for roughly three minutes as he outlined his plan, his voice shaking terribly when he got to the main point of it. Straub listened in silence throughout, giving no indication of either agreement or disagreement. He included as much detail as he could, keeping it all as realistic as he thought possible, and repeatedly emphasising the potential benefits to the whole country. His hope was that by doing so, he would give his plan more weight, and not just be seen as an attempt to save his own skin.

Once he'd finished and his breath was held in his throat, all he could hear down the line was the continued steady hum of machinery. It hadn't changed during the entire phone call, as seemingly relentless and unending as the Stone Man's pursuit. He waited for Straub's response. He would shortly find out whether his life would end in the next few minutes, or if he would, in fact, receive a stay of execution. The latter wouldn't mean salvation—at least, not for sure—but it would mean a *chance*. The thought of it was like an adrenaline shot.

Straub finally spoke.

"Give me a moment," she said, and Paul could read nothing in her voice. He was left alone in the dark for a full minute as the muffle went back on, and when she came back all she said was:

"I'll call you back. Stay there."

The line went dead and Paul stared at his phone's now-returned home screen with his jaw hanging slack.

It wasn't no. It wasn't no. They might actually go for it.

The minutes passed, and Paul continued to stare at the screen, his gaze unmoving as he hopped slowly from foot to foot and waved from side to side like a catatonic patient. He only looked away once, to the west, as he thought he heard the sound of several approaching helicopters.

The screen changed, and Straub's name appeared. Paul's hand moved so fast to hit 'ANSWER' that it was barely visible in the dark as it did so.

"Yes?" asked Paul, simultaneously ashamed of the desperation in his voice and yet too desperate to truly care.

"The barriers," said Straub, her voice inscrutable, "are they up? Can we move you?"

Paul hesitated, torn between giving a foolish, instinctive lie as a response and the need to actually check. This held for a moment, then sanity prevailed, and he marvelled at his own temporary *in*sanity, at how close he'd come to screwing everything up.

"I don't know," he replied, before quickly adding, "but I'll check, I'll check." In his desperation, he hadn't thought that they'd want to move him, his plan being based on stuck where he was. His mind raced, seeing sudden cracks in the plan that might mean its failure, but he quickly realised that it made no difference. Where he was, or elsewhere, it didn't matter. But did he really want to risk being moved and have the barriers appear while in transit? That would be disastrous.

"Wait," he said, holding up a hand to halt someone who wasn't there. "I'll find out, but you can't move me. If you want to try this, if you want to try my idea, it has to be here. The barriers could go up en route. Yeah, you'll have me and can finish me off at your leisure, but you won't get to try this out, and this could be the answer to the whole thing. If you're gonna move me, you might as well send the hit squad and get it over with."

"Winter, do you realise what you're suggesting?" replied Straub. The tone wasn't aggressive, was still matter-of-fact. It almost sounded as if she was testing him. "The amount of damage that would happen in the meantime, leaving you there? The potential loss of life, directly or indirectly?"

Paul took a deep breath, and pushed his luck.

"Are you seriously telling me that your boys in the back room didn't think of something similar already?"

Straub sighed, and there was impatience in it.

"Yes, Winter, but in an entirely different scenario," said Straub, but Paul thought she didn't sound too certain in her response. "Not with a target stuck up north, for starters. We were talking about a completely controlled, purpose-built environment, right in the middle of bloody Coventry, right at Ground Zero, and in a scenario where a target was detected early enough to be moved into that area. Operatives specially trained and prepared for the exact procedures involved, supplies already in place, and most importantly the whole thing would be out of the eyes of the media. And besides, the whole thing wasn't to even be tabled again unless other protocols we've been developing failed first, *multi-billion pound* development protocols at that."

"And have they failed?"

There wasn't an answer for a moment, but when it came Paul felt his fresh hope shatter.

"They have, Winter, and the remaining protocol in that instance was immediate elimination of identified targets. Preparation was to begin *after* that, straight away, for the next arrival. I'm sorry. We're talking about the lives of six against … well, who knows. The decision isn't a difficult one." Despite her words, Straub did actually sound sorry.

Just before blind panic set in, something clicked in Paul's head. It had taken a moment or two to register, but Straub had just given something away.

"The bloodhounds," he said in a near-whisper. "The new guys. Did they get everyone?"

"Pardon?"

"The targets. You said the lives of *six*. There should be seven. Did they get all the targets? They didn't, did they?"

That silence again, but only briefly.

"No," admitted Straub. "They were … disconnected before they could get the seventh. It would seem our friends elsewhere have gotten more efficient at detecting interlopers. Presumably they've learned to be on the lookout since you two."

Hope gently raised its broken head once more, wincing and barely alive, but still clinging on.

"And replacements," he said, his breath quickening again, "how many reliable replacements are coming forward? Obviously, whoever you have at the moment will be next, but unless you have seven of those guys at the moment I think you lot are shagged for knowing where the next lot of targets are when the big stone bastards come back. Right?"

"What's your point, Winter?" snapped Straub, and now her temper was showing. Straub seemed to be someone who thrived on pressure, but she was only human. "More people will come forward. By the looks of things, if this pattern continues, we'll have months to find them, and we're planning our own widespread recruitment tests. We'll get them."

"But you don't *know!*" shouted Paul, desperation and hope combining to take his voice to a crescendo. "Those fuckers could come back and you could have *no one*, and they'll tear up half the country tracking down their people. And the one chance you had to try something out, the last chance to have your target and *experiment*, with enough time before the Stone Man is right on him and you have to blow their brains out at the last minute to stop them being caught ... you're choosing to put a bullet right up that last chance's arse. And even better, I'm right in the middle of fucking nowhere!" He shouted this last part to the field around him, throwing his free arm out wide and turning on the spot. "This is the best case bloody scenario! Yes, it won't be planned, it'll be done on the fly, but you have *some* prep, don't you? You can adapt, can't you? Can't you?"

When the response wasn't immediate, Paul found that he couldn't take any more. All pretence dropped away, and the tears came straight away, as he thought of his wife, his life, even Andy.

"Aren't I owed a bastard chance?" he sobbed, wheedling and pleading and not caring, thinking only about his losses and the unfairness of it all. "I mean ... haven't I been useful? You know things now, thanks to me and Andy, right? Haven't I done something worthwhile?" Paul buried his face in his free hand, and cursed himself as he played his dirtiest hand. "Isn't *Andy's* death worth something? His, his ... self fucking sacrifice? He was a good servant, right? He'd want you to try."

"That won't wash with me I'm afraid, Winter," replied Straub, her voice shocking Paul with its coldness. "Andy did an extremely brave thing, and a great service to his country, but as much as I respect that, I have a service of my own to perform for the *same* country. And while I sympathise greatly with your plight, at the same time you waited for an awfully long time to get in touch with us, knowing what might happen in the meantime. And I notice that you only really seemed to do so once you had this plan of your own to help the country … and coincidentally, to also possibly help yourself."

Paul wanted to scream *you bitch* at her, but he couldn't, both because the possible saving of his life was in her hands, and that her words had weight, so much awful weight. He stood instead in silence, and waited for her to continue.

"But I will discuss it," she said at last, and in a quiet tone Paul hadn't heard her use before. "If a similar plan hadn't already been talked about, one that could be adapted without too much planning, well, I wouldn't even bother wasting my breath. But lucky for you, it has, and despite my strong reservations over your recent actions, your past work has saved lives. On balance, you're owed enough for me to at least ask the question. And it makes some sense. I'll call you back," she said with another sigh, this time with a slightly sad-sounding one. "I might be a while. Our men will be with you very shortly anyway."

Paul heard her move away from the phone, about to hang up, and then he screamed down the line.

"*Wait!*"

"Jesus, Winter, what?"

"Will I speak to you again? I mean … I mean … either way?"

His trembling voice made clear what he really meant. With the reality this close, in the now much louder noise of the oncoming choppers—their lights now visible in the near distance of the night sky—he found that he couldn't say it.

Straub hung up.

Shortly afterwards Paul was seated in the back of a parked helicopter, one that was floodlit by a searchlight mounted on the side of its twin, both standing side by side in the now partially lit field. He'd been handcuffed, but not roughly so, and there had been a minimum of shouting and pushing. It was almost as if they'd been instructed to treat him with a degree of respect, or at least gentleness, and he thought that his clear willingness to cooperate upon their arrival might have helped matters. He had volunteered himself, after all. Either way, sitting and waiting while armed men stood by, ready to execute him should the order go out, meant that Paul's mood was far from relaxed. Despite the cold, the inside of his clothes were damp with sweat.

They can't risk it, surely he thought to himself, and realised that he believed it, too. *Now the bloodhounds are useless for next time, they can't get rid of me before trying this out. I'm much, much farther away than they'd like ... but surely they need to try out all possibilities, even if the cost is high? Surely? They need to experiment now that everything else has failed?* He was desperate, he knew that, the word not enough to describe the frantic terror inside of him, but he didn't think these thoughts were delusional.

Out of nowhere, a radio was handed to him.

"She wants to talk to you," said the surprisingly posh-sounding voice from inside the balaclava, the one covering the head of the soldier who had appeared in the helicopter doorway. All of these soldiers were clad in black, from the top of their heads to the tips of their boots. He pushed the radio into Paul's hand, and walked away, leaving him in the care of the men seated either side of him and the two standing outside the chopper. Heart pounding like a lead piston, Paul lifted the radio to his ear. When he spoke, his throat and mouth were so dry that his voice was barely more than a croak.

If she's calling ... there's a chance.

"Hello?"

"Find the barriers," said Straub's voice, tinnier over the radio's speaker than on the phone. "We need to know how much room we have." Paul barely heard what Straub said next as relief washed over him, but he forced himself to concentrate despite the voice screaming about time, blessed *time* in his head. "I'm not going to lie to you, Winter, if seeing this thing through means we end up turning you into a vegetable like Patrick Marshall, but you stay alive so we can see if it works or not ... well ... we'll do it. While your continued life is paramount to us in terms of this experiment, your state of mind is not. You need to understand this."

"I do, I do," said Paul, not caring and thinking only about what was next, how long it might take to either get an answer, or for them to decide enough was enough and pull the plug. Months, or years? The rest of his life? It didn't matter, it was *time*, and Paul was aware, in that moment, of just how much had gone out of him in that field. He was someone else now, and that was better—to his thinking—than the alternative.

"At the same time," Straub continued, the background noise wherever she was far louder now, alive with activity as things were already getting under way. Straub even had to raise her voice slightly. "If we can keep you conscious and aware, and still have the operation working at an efficient level, we would rather do that. We may need to be able to instruct you, and have you able to respond to us; we have no idea what this thing may bring up, after all. So we would rather keep you *compus mentis*, so to speak. But you do need to be aware that the prime factor for this experiment to work is keeping you alive, and if that means taking you just past the barrier, then we will." Paul's delirious optimism caught that remark this time, the repetition finally breaking through. That would be the same as death, the death of his mind if not his body. *But that might not happen, might not NEED to happen*, said the voice in his head, and with that he was away again, not listening.

"From what I gather, the people at the very top were split about this, but it was the Prime Minister's call and he's approved it," said Straub, unaware. "Operation Paquirri is now officially under way. But you need to find the barriers, Paul, for your sake. If you can't, then we're still going ahead with this and that will almost certainly mean you entering into a permanently vegetative state. We'd rather not have that, as I say—it benefits us for that not to be the case—but we're doing it anyway. So find the barriers if you can, and do it fast; very shortly that field and the surrounding area are going to become incredibly busy and loud, so if you need to move around and concentrate, you need to do it now. Do you think you can do that?"

"Yes, yes," gibbered Paul, almost weeping with relief even though he had no idea if he could find the barriers or not. He thought he could, though. He'd been cut off one way, but as he still had enough of a connection to the Stone Men to know he was a target, to feel them start to move, then he thought he could find the barriers. He thought that maybe even Patrick and Henry could have, if they'd have known what they were looking for. *If Patrick hadn't been running in a blind panic, he could have felt it too*, thought Paul. *Like running into a glass door. At speed, not checking, you wouldn't even know it was there. But if you'd gone slowly, feeling as you went ...*

Once Straub had signed off, Paul was escorted out of the helicopter by two of the soldiers, and shortly after that he found himself wandering around the nearby immediate area, surrounded by torchlight and concentrating with all of the willpower in his body. It was a fresh terror for him, like being forced to walk through a minefield. He didn't truly know how it worked, after all; was merely touching a barrier enough to render him catatonic? Or would he have to try to break through it for that to happen? Would he be able to feel it beforehand, sense that he was drawing near? Was it even there yet, even though the previous evidence said that it should be? Paul moved forward with shuffling, terrified steps, feeling with his mind and his hands, and constantly waited for the shock that signalled the end of his consciousness.

He found that, unlike his previous time in the darkened field, he could find the willpower required of him. His body screamed at him to stand still, and abject fear pleaded with him to stay rooted to the spot, but he continued to walk forward blindly even though it might have meant his end. If asked, Paul wouldn't have called it bravery, however. His life depended on him risking it, and the act would save only himself. Fear conquered by greater fear of something worse is still *fear*, and he didn't know if there was a name for great undertakings that come as a result of it.

Paul had learned this, just as he had learned a great deal about himself in the last twenty-four hours. He knew that this was just something he could do, and that it was fortunate for him that he could.

Eventually, as he continued to walk and concentrate so hard that he had a violent headache, Paul felt the beginning of a shift in his head, and a slight tingle in his fingertips. He went only slightly farther, enough to confirm that he wasn't imagining it, and then stopped. He wasn't going to risk any more than that. It was close, very close, and he didn't know where the exact tipping point was. He didn't want to find out the hard way.

"There," he said to the soldier to his right, and gestured on the floor with his foot. As the soldier stepped forward and thrust a small metal stick into the ground, Paul couldn't help but think how the man that had just taken instructions from him could just as easily have been instructed by someone else to put a bullet into his brain. He pushed the thought away and began to walk in a straight line, away from the stick in the opposite direction to the way he'd come. His thinking was, if the barrier area was really small, he might push farther if he had to, but would he need to? The walk from where they'd set off—next to the parked chopper's landing gear—had been roughly forty feet. The choppers had landed as close to where he'd been standing as they could, and at the time he'd moved about ten feet away from the stile that he'd been sitting on. Paul did the rough maths as he walked:

So the helicopters were what, ten feet from me? And I'd been sitting on that stile for hours, and the barrier had probably gone up during that time ... so that would make the stile and fence the line through the middle, as that's where I was when it went up. So me about ten feet from the fence, and the choppers ten feet from me, and the barrier edge forty feet further out than that ... that's sixty feet. Roughly.

Paul reached the fence again, relaxed on this side of it, and climbed over the stile, tensing as he did so. If the barrier was a circle, or even a square, he had roughly another sixty feet to travel to the opposite edge, but he was taking no chances. His hands went out, and he began his shuffling, nervous walk again, but with slightly less fear this time, knowing (to an extent, he couldn't be certain) that he would have enough warning, that he should sense the edge of it before hitting it.

Eventually, the tingle came into his fingers and mind, and he breathed a sigh of relief and pointed at the ground with his foot once more. As the soldiers ran a rope between the two metal sticks, crossing the fence to do so, Paul looked at the distance he'd covered. He thought to himself that the sticks were placed at about an equal distance apart on either side of the fence. He realised dimly that the fence would, of course, have to be bulldozed away.

A short time later, after Paul had outlined the perimeter completely, the measurement came back: 133.6 feet on all sides. The perimeter was a square, after all.

They'll play it safe, thought Paul, *and that's fine by me. They'll operate on far less than that, allow for error. Operate within a hundred feet, something like that? Is that enough? That's a big area, isn't it? One hundred feet?*

As he stood in the field, breathing hard with his heart feeling like it was beating in his throat, he watched the eight soldiers work (with the remaining two doing watching of their own, their eyes on him). The others were beginning to lay down markers, carrying out the extremely preliminary stages of what would become a mammoth operation to prepare the area in time. Already, the air was starting to fill again with distant noises—blades in the air and engines on the roads—and, far off, lights were again appearing in the sky, but many more than before. Unknown to Paul, the Prime Minister had thrown his weight behind the plan; the government response would show this, and it was already beginning. Paul tried to slow his breathing in order to calm himself, as he realised that he wouldn't be doing anything now for many hours. How long did it take the Stone Man to walk to Sheffield last time? And how long had it already been walking? He didn't know, but he was pretty certain that he had a long time to wait, and for most of that he would be out of the way; they would need to not only clear the *barrier* area of any obstacles, but secure the *surrounding* area. He wondered what they'd tell the media, and realised that they'd probably have to put some kind of cover over it as well, to guarantee blockage of any views from above. With Patrick, he guessed there hadn't really been time for anyone to secure satellite footage, but this ... barring any surprises (*you don't know what it's got up its sleeve, Paul*) could go on for years, and that would mean interest.

He started to take slow, deep breaths, and after a few minutes, if only for a moment, some of the old Paul—a stranger in his new life—came back, and he chuckled gently as he thought about the amount of work involved; all just to enable what was effectively an idiotically simple plan. The preparation of the area, land rights, media suppression, food and water supply chains, man hours, power, surveillance, security, funding ... an immense amount of management, preparation and paperwork all to carry out a fundamentally basic, idiotically simple task.

The old Paul shook his head, and even though afterwards he went away and didn't ever really come back again, he continued to chuckle quietly in the dark, a condemned man laughing at the absurd.

***

Chapter Nine: Execution

***

Paul looked at his watch for the third time that minute, and then went back to staring towards the large opening in the metal wall over one hundred feet away. Inside the hall—a construction that would be best described as hangar were it not for the absence of aircraft—it was relatively silent; none of the personnel were talking, of course, and the main sound was the hum of the industrial space heaters and various computer stations that lined the walls. The jeep's engine was also ticking over—had been since he'd been put inside it—but it was a finely tuned machine, and so the noise from it was minimal. There was the odd burst of radio crackle now and then, with updates that had been coming more and more frequently since the last hour had begun, but Paul was sure that if he were closer to the command tent in the far corner—the only separate structure within the hall itself—he'd be able to hear plenty. From outside, Paul could hear the increasing and dropping whirr of distant helicopter blades as several of them exchanged positions far overhead, and the odd shout as various members of personnel called to one another, hurrying and bossing. Regardless, the lack of interior sound, combined with the horrendous anticipation, was maddening. No one had spoken to him directly for the last two hours, ever since he'd been put into place, and he hadn't seen Straub again since she'd arrived. Even then it had been at a distance, and Paul was certain she'd deliberately avoided his gaze. His only usefulness was as bait now, after all.

Make the most of it, the voice in his head said, cynically. *You don't know what that sodding thing's gonna do once this all starts.* The voice had a point, Paul had to admit. There were absolutely no certainties as far as the Stone Men were concerned, even with all the research and analysis that had been going on around the world for the last year. They were operating on the basis of mere assumptions, assumptions based only on what they'd seen so far and the small number of notable energy readings they'd managed to obtain. Those assumptions were now the thin, brittle surface that Paul's life rested upon. Little comfort indeed, and even if all the prior theories were correct, they were no guarantee that his plan might yield any results.

As if it were the last thing he'd ever see (*probably is,* the voice added), Paul took in his surroundings again, trying this time to see the finer details, the intricacies of the clumps of dirt in the floor, the beauty of the mist haze surrounding the electric lights in the ceiling, the imperfections of the thin metallic walls. He failed. It still looked like a big metal barn.

The floor had been landscaped, at least as much as possible in the time available. The total, flattened area, levelled off to create as even a surface as they could, was a square at least three hundred feet across. Paul guessed they wanted room to manoeuvre should the need present itself. The corrugated ceiling was very high—for reasons Paul couldn't guess at—standing at least one hundred feet. Though the winter sun was fully up outside, and Paul could see the grey, cloudy sky through the hastily-erected hall's opening, the light inside was far brighter and warmer. A few jeeps were parked along the western wall, and at the end of the row—presumably in case an opportunity should present itself, despite being useless in the past—stood a tank. There were even two cameras, manned by a three-man crew, stationed at opposite corners. These weren't courtesy of the media, Paul assumed; these were for the purposes of posterity and research. Being as cut off from the world as he was (*cut off again,* the voice said), he had no idea what the actual media knew of this, whether they were too busy covering the seven directions that the Stone Men had taken or whether they'd gotten wind of the operation occurring across two fields in Sheffield. He thought the latter was likely. The Stone Man coming for him would be close by now, he thought, and even if the media were just following its path they would have come across military interference and tried to find out why. Plus, securing the field would have taken some kind of interaction with the land owner—even if just to tell him that his field had been commandeered—and at the very least people living nearby would have noticed several army convoys, parades of earth-moving vehicles, and several helicopters hovering above.

Had there been a local evacuation? Paul had no idea. He'd been given a sedative and put under guard while they'd worked tirelessly through the night and into the next day (he'd been so tired by then that, despite all the adrenaline, his body was ready for it) so he hadn't seen the actual process, but he'd heard the back end of it as he'd woken up. He hadn't been allowed out of the tent that he'd been placed in for several hours after, but once he'd been led out for briefing and preparation he'd seen the small village of tents and plastic outhouses that had sprung up magically overnight. One or two members of personnel, even soldiers, had caught his eye for a moment and looked hurriedly away. Being bait might be contagious, after all.

The sight of the hall itself as they'd approached had been impressive indeed; not necessarily for its size, but for that fact that this huge, grey, thin-walled fortress (if that wasn't a contradiction in terms) had sprung up overnight, squatting in the middle of the landscape like an ugly metal wart.

As he passed through its giant sliding doors (opened by manpower rather than machinery) and into the small command tent that stood inside, he'd felt a moment of claustrophobic panic and his breath had locked up in his chest. It felt like being dragged underground.

He'd sat patiently, and listened as his own plan was relayed back to him by men he didn't recognise—even David wasn't there, perhaps busy cleaning up other elements of the current Stone Man situation—and nodded at the appropriate moments. When asked if he had any questions, he had only two:

"What's been arranged for when I need to sleep?"

"No solid plans for that part yet, as all resources have been directed towards preparing and securing the area prior to Caementum's arrival. This will be addressed shortly."

"How long, based on any info that you have, do you expect this operation to continue?"

Glances were exchanged.

"Currently? Indefinitely."

He'd been led out to the waiting Jeep, which then drove to the far end of the hall and turned to face the entrance. That had been two hours ago, and he'd been left pretty much alone since, apart from his silent driver and the two armed guards accompanying them. During this time, seen at a distance, Straub had made her arrival in the hall, flanked by her own small entourage. Paul liked to think that her lack of communication had been due to being too busy, but he didn't really believe it.

Paul thought that the restraints weren't necessary—his ankles were bound to the seat—but he could understand why. They didn't know if he was going to panic, even if this was all his idea. Now they were committed to it, they needed him under control.

And now, with the time ticking away, he realised that his shirt was sticking to his back. He'd lost several of his layers before this all started—the inside of the hall was warm enough—but he was still sweating fast.

This will work. This will work. Those things don't care about time. They expect all their prey to run straight into the web. Why else would they build the buggers so big? They're designed to intimidate. Faceless. Unstoppable. Big.

More time passed, and the distant radio chatter changed from intermittent bursts to a constant stream.

Soon. Oh Jesus, it's almost here.

A squad of armed soldiers jogged into the hall in formation, and lined up along opposite walls, facing inwards. Through the entrance, Paul could see more and more people scurrying back and forth, final preparations beginning. After all, if the plan worked, they would have more time than ever to study the

Stone Man.

I don't want it to be the original. It will be worse if it's the original. I've seen what it does.

A shout went up from outside, and almost at the same time the helicopter noise from above increased dramatically and stayed there, the choppers moving closer and assuming position. That was when Paul thought he felt the first heavy thud pass through the floor.

Wait, it's here? It's already that close? Oh fuck. Oh fuck.

Suddenly, the radio chatter stopped almost altogether, and the only time it was heard was when short bursts of unintelligible info came through in regular but spaced-out intervals. Paul thought it sounded like some sort of distance countdown. During this time, the thuds continued, gentle and barely felt at first, then growing (to Paul's ears) into a solid, ground shaking series of dull booms.

This went on for what seemed to Paul like half an hour, but was in actual fact only six minutes. At the end of that time—and for the first time—Paul saw one of the soldiers inside the hall pick up his radio and send a message of his own. He was standing, Paul saw, nearest to the entrance and at the end of the line of men flanking the eastern wall. Paul heard his response, even at a distance, undistorted by radio noise.

"Visual confirmed."

Paul stared frantically out through the open double doors, squinting to see any movement. All the running back and forth outside had now stopped, and were it not for the helicopter noise, Paul could almost believe that there was no one there. In his sight line to the outside world, there were no temporary structures, as obviously they'd calculated the Stone Man's approach and wanted it clear. Now there was just the field beyond, seeming to stretch away for as far as he could see.

And then (at first, he thought he was mistaken, the faint suggestion of movement on the horizon seeming like a trick of the light, something incorrectly seen through a heat haze, a trick that then became more and more solid and proved to be something else) far off, a slowly rising dome came into view, small at this range but unmistakable. It continued to do so as it came up over the crest of the slope, becoming a head. Then a pair of shoulders, a barrel chest, a waist. The surface of its body was a greyish brown.

It's the original.

It continued to rise into sight as it came, emerging slowly, its incredible size having impact even at this distance, something huge brought up from below like the remains of a sunken ocean liner. Now Paul could see its legs, see the feet come down in perfect rhythmic sync with the vibrations in the floor. It was the Stone Man, and it was there for him.

Reflexively, despite everything, Paul jolted from his seat, all thought gone from his mind but the unstoppable urge to run. Before the awestruck soldier next to him could move, he was up and his hands were on the edge of the jeep's door. In a millisecond he would be swinging his legs up and over and then he would—

Clank.

The forgotten handcuffs on his ankles reached the full length of their extension, and jarred his legs back as he made to leap from the vehicle. His hands slipped on the jeep edge, previously supporting his entire bodyweight, and his suddenly unsupported chest went crashing down onto the metal. The pain was intense and immediate, and all of his air shot out of him, causing the world to go temporarily grey as his guard hauled him back inside the jeep. The guard's radio was blaring, but Paul couldn't make out the words as he tried to get air back into his lungs, eyes goggling and breastbone screaming. Two sets of hands gripped his shoulders now, but Paul barely felt them as he gasped and wheezed, staring out through the windscreen at the giant figure as it approached.

Whoever had calculated its trajectory had done their homework correctly. The oncoming Stone Man was almost perfectly framed by the huge doorway, a grim picture before Paul's eyes that contained an image of relentless pursuit. The vibrations through the floor began to feel like distant war drums, and as Paul began to take on sweet, blessed air once more, he tried to dig deep and steel himself for the intense test of nerve that was about to begin.

You aren't being fed to it, the voice said. *You're not like Patrick. They're not just going to hand you over, and they aren't going to double-cross you. They wouldn't have bothered building all this shit for starters, especially when all they had to do was pull a trigger and end the problem. They're committed to this. Their main concern is keeping you alive, that's the whole point of this. You don't know what it's going to do once the plan is in motion, but you have some more time, at least. You have to relax. It WANTS you to be scared. Don't let it win. Don't let it win.*

Paul nodded to himself, and knew the voice was right, knew its words were true and wise, but those words didn't change anything. His heart still pounded like it was going to burst in his chest, and his breathing, now restored, continued in and out of him in ragged gasps.

The Stone Man had reached the doorway now, and Paul now noticed that at some point, several of the soldiers flanking the walls had broken away from the lines and were now clustered around each of the giant sliding doors either side of the entrance. The hurried nature of the construction had meant that motorised doors hadn't been installed. As the Stone Man passed through the entrance, its surface brightened, caught by the bright interior ceiling lights; the effect was startling, looking as if it had become more powerful, lit from within somehow, now that it was within reach of its prey. Wide-eyed, Paul caught the faces of the personnel within the hallway, soldiers and civilians alike. All had paled slightly, or stood with their mouths agape.

Once the Stone Man had moved ten feet farther inside the structure, the doors began to slide inwards as the soldiers pushed. For the first time since its appearance, Paul looked away from the Stone Man and looked at the landscape outside, a task made more difficult now by the fact that the Stone Man was directly in his path, taking up more of his line of sight. Even though the view beyond the doors was grey, cold, and unwelcoming, Paul watched his view of it shrink to a sliver as the doors slid home, and felt a fresh surge of desperation. He didn't know when, if ever, he would see it again, and as the doors banged to and the soldiers began to bolt them shut, the feeling of loss became a certainty. If being brought into the hall had been like being dragged underground, the sound of the closing doors was like the first shovelful of earth landing on top of his coffin.

"Stand by."

The voice came over the radio, and Paul wasn't sure if it was Straub's. The Stone Man had closed the space between them considerably, becoming immense in Paul's sight line, and the only way Paul could tell the difference now between the heavy thuds of the Stone Man's approach and the hammer blows of his own heart was the sheer speed of the latter.

The size of the Stone Man was mind blowing. At this range Paul was able, despite himself, to marvel again at the fluidity of its movements, the way such immense, heavy stone limbs could hinge and flex upon themselves like rubber, free of creases and join-lines. It was magic made solid, dark magic, evil intent given physical form.

Is it though? Is it not just doing its job?

The Stone Man was now within fifty feet of the jeep, and Paul realised his fingers had buried themselves in his seat padding up to the second knuckle. His right heel began to kick against the rubber mat in the footwell.

Forty feet. With bulging eyes, Paul glanced at the soldier in the driver's seat, who was sitting and staring stoically ahead, the only evidence of his own discomfiture being the two lines of sweat than ran down the side of his face. He held the radio to his ear with one hand, waiting for the order. Paul wanted to scream *NOW* at him, and only managed to not do so through sheer force of will.

They had to run this. He had to let them.

Thirty feet.

"Stand by."

Paul's kicking heel became a stamping gesture, his foot looking for an accelerator that wasn't there.

Twenty feet.

It's too big to be real. This can't be real. This whole thing is a nightmare. This whole thing has been one long fever dream. I'm in a coma, I'm already dead, OH GOD GET ME OUT OF HERE—

Ten feet.

"Clearance."

"Roger," replied the soldier, in a thinner voice than his facial expression would have led one to expect, and pressed his foot onto the accelerator as he turned the wheel. The jeep's engine gently roared, and the vehicle swung out and to the left, away from the Stone Man's path and towards the yellow plastic strip that ran along the floor upon the western side of the hall. Paul had been right about them operating well within the barrier limits; the strips that ran in a square around the hall were only roughly one hundred feet apart in both directions. Once the jeep reached the strip—the time it took to do so was almost two seconds—the driver drove them quickly along its length. Paul's head swung wildly behind him, watching the Stone Man; was it still moving? With the bouncing, rapid movement of the jeep, he couldn't quite tell. The driver swung them around, the jeep spraying earth from the dirt floor as it did so, ending up facing the south wall, but already the driver was reversing quickly in the opposite direction. The jeep backed neatly into the northwest corner, and stopped. The whole procedure had taken less than five seconds.

Paul let out a breath he didn't know he'd been holding, giving a small moan of both relief and despair as he did so. The first part—the very first time—had now worked. Even though everyone had expected it to, the temporary relief was immense. But what would happen now? All eyes were on the Stone Man.

It was already beginning to turn, its right shoulder leading its body, the head staring straight ahead as it did so. There was no sense of urgency, or of recalculation in its movements. It was simply continuing to follow, and Paul felt a brief, infinitesimal flicker of hope.

That's it, he surprised himself by thinking. *This way.*

Once it had completed its relatively slow about-face, the Stone Man recommenced walking again, this time heading towards the northwest corner of the yellow square where the jeep waited. Paul's hope and confidence immediately died a harsh death, so much so that he briefly wondered if the fear, the intense anxiety and desperation, weren't projected from the thing at close range in a similar way as they had been from wherever the Stone Man came from in the days before its arrival; the same intense fear that he and Andy had broken the circuit of when they locked in—

Is that its insurance policy? Paul wondered. *Is that how it makes sure that its targets charge into the barrier once it gets close? If Andy and I hadn't locked in before they got here, if that hadn't somehow broken the effect, would I be going insane with the urge to run by now, as opposed to just shitting myself?*

It was a thought he didn't have time to ponder further, as it was nearly time to move again. The countdown came over the radio once more, verbally closing the distance as the Stone Man did so physically. Paul had visions of those arms suddenly extending longer, reaching from its body—just as its chest cavity had when it took Patrick—and plucking Paul from the jeep, the handcuffs around his ankles gouging into his bones until the chains holding them snapped, and then Paul would be drawn towards the Stone Man, where its chest would begin to open once more and Paul would be turned in the air, his spine now exposed—

Ten feet.

"Clearance."

The engine rumbled again, and Paul felt his blood run cold for only a millisecond as the tyres spun helplessly in place, before catching hold and propelling the jeep away to the Stone Man's right this time, running along the eastern wall before turning and parking in the southeast corner.

They all watched, everyone in the hall, as the Stone Man went through the same procedure once more—the slow turn over the same shoulder—as it prepared for another approach. This time hope flared brighter in Paul's heart, but even with that feeling came balance.

It was working. They'd have to see, they'd have to give it time, but it was working ... yet if it *stayed* working ... could he ever get used to this? He didn't know, but if he'd been right all along, he would simply have to.

It's not programmed for this, he'd said to Straub, in his frantic, desperate explanation. *I don't think this is in any of its presets or whatever. They obviously know us to an extent, know our base urges and instincts, maybe because they think in a similar way in some respects, I don't bloody know. But I think with them ... that's it. They operate in straight lines.*

The Stone Man completed its half-circle, and was beginning to head towards them once more.

Look at the way the Stone Men operate, he'd said. *They think route one, the simplest procedure, as time taken doesn't bother them, right? They don't bother with contingencies, because for them, the logical solution should work every time. That's why they just build the unstoppable creature and set the bugger off, waiting for the results because, as far as they're concerned, that should take care of everything. But, if we don't run blindly into the barrier ... they don't know what to do.*

The rhythmic pounding through the floor, like the ticking of the second hand on the universe's biggest clock, shaving away precious, precious time with every step.

So what happens if we don't run? What does it do? If nothing else, Straub, you need to know that. But regardless ... if you're ever going to have a chance to beat these things, you need time as well. Time to study them, time to try out more of your crap on them without having to worry about innocent civilians and falling buildings. Right? So what if, and I know this is just a bullshit theory, but at the same time we've seen nothing to suggest that it's got anything else in its bag, but ... what if all it can do is pursue? What if we just keep the fucker moving, and chasing, indefinitely? Hell, what if we do that and after a while, after weeks or months, the bastard just runs out of juice? There's so much we could learn, and being totally honest, it might mean you find something out that can save my bloody life, or it breaks down before it can get me. So, what I'm saying is, if I can find out how big the barrier is, and if it's big enough to work ...

"Clearance." Paul's hand gripped the door handle as the jeep lurched again. He didn't know it then, but that hand movement was something that, in time, would become as automatic as breathing.

... why don't we just let it chase me for as long as we can?

As the jeep swung out to the left again, and Paul's premature conviction that his plan might bear some kind of fruit grew, he also had a sudden, clear, but fleeting thought. It was pushed away almost as soon as it arrived—he didn't really have any choice now, regardless—but part of it still caught in his mind, and over the many months ahead it would grow steadily, causing him greater and greater unease.

In that moment, he'd briefly seen the plan working, and what it might mean if he really could be kept moving indefinitely. Being here in the hall, doing circuits of this tiny space in Sheffield for the foreseeable future, with no idea of how long that might be. Paul knew that there were three possible-to-likely outcomes to all of it: either they stopped the Stone Man, or it stopped itself, or they eventually decided to pull the plug on the whole thing and shoot him in the head. He was prepared for any of those, he thought, or at least as much as anyone could be.

But there was a slim chance of a less likely, fourth outcome.

For some reason, he couldn't decide how he felt about the possibility; because if it remained in their interests to keep him alive, they would do so, with the experiment continuing in that tiny, windowless, sightless place. An experiment that could potentially run for years, if they saw fit, with no end in sight. And Paul didn't know how long that would be bearable, and then thought of the alternative, and decided that the alternative would always be worse, of course it would. But he looked at the walls, and the closed doors, and the approaching Stone Man, and knew that it was all because of his choices; then he had to remind himself again that the alternative would always be worse, always be worse. It was a thought process that would go around in circles in his mind many times, reaching the same conclusion with less and less conviction in the years to come, but for now Paul's fingers gripped the door handle tighter; the Jeep swung, and began to back into the opposite corner once again.

***

They said I should record something on this. I don't know what the bloody hell they expect me to say.

Testing. Testing. One, two. Hello. Hel-LO.

Part of the therapy, allegedly, helping me to externalise, I think he said, but it all sounds like bullshit to me. Personally, I think they just want it for future reference, part of the big picture or whatever. It's not for my benefit, that's for sure. I don't think they're really too bothered about my mental health, and I don't think they really ever have been, to be honest. As long as I can follow instructions, I don't think they'd give a monkey's arse if they found me shitting into my hand and wiping it on the wall.

You hear that? You don't give a toss. I know you don't. I'm not an idiot. I don't know why you want this pissing recording, either. The fucking camera gives you enough Big-Brother-is-watching-you jollies, I'd have thought, but apparently not. So I will externalise, but not for you. I'm going to record this, and then wipe it. Stick it up your arse.

Ah ... balls. I don't know. Maybe I'm being too harsh. Maybe I'm having one of my bad days. Some days are certainly worse than others. A lot worse. I thought today was one of my 'good mood' days—that's why I finally thought I'd give this a go—but maybe I was wrong.

They don't *have* to send the therapist, I suppose. And they didn't have to make this cabin so nice. It could have just been a bed and a TV. But it's like a little flat, albeit one on wheels, and I even get to cook my own meals, have my own fridge. I even get beer, and decent beer at that, albeit in limited qualities. Hell, they even managed to soundproof it a bit, so in terms of noise, you wouldn't really know you were moving.

You can feel it though. You can always feel it. The guys doing the driving are good, really good, and even when they change they keep the rhythm the same. And that can't be for anybody's benefit but mine, after all. They know I'm used to the rhythm of it. I told the therapist. They know I'm used to grabbing the handles on the turn, the reverse, the brake; if I'm honest, for some reason I have a bit of a sense of pride in my doing it without thinking, at the perfect time, just before it happens. They send the physio in too, twice a week, to check I'm okay and work the kinks out of my back.

My knees and hips worry me though. I think it was in the twenty-third month when I first noticed the ache in the right, and that's since started in the left too. I only get it if I'm standing, obviously, when even the grab handles can't really make a difference to the momentum on your knees. I try to sit down most of the time now, unless I'm working out on the multigym. I'm in the best shape of my life, of course, but it's typical that I'm stuck in a fucking box. Either way, the new cabin can't come quick enough. Exactly the same as this one—strangely enough, I hope it is, anyway—but the new one is fitted with some kind of gyroscopic base, super suspension, I don't know, but basically I'm told it should cancel out eighty percent of the momentum. I'm not holding my breath though. They've been talking about it since we passed the one-year mark, when they saw it might be a long game after all. I think it must have taken them all of the second year to decide that it definitely was. *Then* they started to budget for it. Whatever. As I say, they're more worried about their 'research' than the poor bastard at the heart of it.

They let me get my food orders in though, within reason, and one day a week they go through the same rigmarole; drop off units at either corner, handing bags over, me taking them in before we move again. Usually takes about half an hour to get the shopping in. Even now though, they have a guy waiting at either end with a tranquiliser gun. I *think* it's a tranquiliser gun. I've tried to get the names of the soldiers I deal with regularly, and they're friendly—I think they think I'm an all right bloke—but they've always politely refused or changed the subject. I think overall, the military trust me more now, but who knows? Maybe they think I'm starting to go a bit twitchy. They could be right, I don't bloody know. I hope not.

They top up the water for the shower cubicle and the sink, the taps, the lot of it, and it's pretty impressive how they do it. The drivers are very good, as I say. They hook up the hose to the mini-tanker and drive together as a unit until it's done. Got to be good at your job to do that, I reckon.

I'm allowed TV on demand, but no news and no live footage. Films are okay as well, but I don't get the Internet, and that was a major problem for me at first. Now I can barely imagine having such a luxury. They let me request hobby materials, too. It's almost laughable that I asked for a load of craft stuff first, thinking it would pass the time. It just went bloody everywhere. Maybe I'll try again once the gyro stuff is built in. That'd be great if it worked. I started on a few language tapes too, but it was hard to stay motivated when I don't know if I'll ever get to use it. They send me porn as well, and I don't even have to ask. That was a pleasant surprise.

The first two weeks were the worst, though. In the jeep. That was bad. Really bad. I couldn't even sleep. Then they got me into a van with a mattress in the back, and that was almost like heaven for a while. I don't know why they left it that long to switch me over. Nerves? Expecting something fancy from the big bastard at any moment? I don't know. It took them a month to get the cabin sorted. Everything was done on the fly, everything, and to be fair to them, I didn't think they thought it would work anyway. They must have expected it to end out of the blue, and when it didn't, my needs were low on the list when they were scurrying around trying to see what they could do next. I shouldn't really blame them, but I do. Ah ... do I? Jesus, I don't know. I used to be able to see it from their point of view easily, but it's been three years now and it's hard to keep perspective.

The window is almost a bit of a piss-take though. What the hell is the point? I keep the curtains closed most of the time now. In the early days I used to check—literally, every few minutes—that Caementum ... shit ... I mean the Stone Man was still following. It took a good seven or eight months before I stopped. Now I just keep the curtains drawn.

I don't know what they told the media. I don't know what they've told my family. I've asked if I can have visitors, but I'm not allowed. The therapist, the physio guy, they're my visitors, and although the therapy is obviously one way, Tony the physio is a chatty guy. If I ask about stuff I'm not allowed to know about, he tells me straight out that I know I'm not supposed to ask about that and changes the subject. I think he'd tell me more if the guard wasn't there when he visits, or if the camera wasn't on. Discussing anything from before my time in here is okay, anything going on in the world after that is out. Apparently it's better for me, Dr Palmer says—said it several times actually, especially the time I got a bit wound up when he said it, like, and they had to board my cabin and put me out—but I disagree. Especially because ... well, never mind. I don't know how good that camera is. Not that I have to hide things from the 'Bad

Guys'—I don't think they are the bad guys, they have a job to do and are doing it—I just don't want to get anyone in trouble. Before I came in, there was a recession on, after all, and jobs were hard to come by. That might still be the same.

Anyway. The people I actually deal with in here are kind, is what I'm trying to say. The rules they're enforcing are for good reasons, I believe that. They do keep me abreast of *some* developments, I will give them that. Straub has even visited four or five times, and that was a surprise, even a pleasant one, I dare say. She lets me know what they've tried, and learned, and even though it's usually a thinly disguised story of failure, they have made some headway towards understanding its 'molecular structure'. She struggled a bit with some of terminology herself (she's no scientist, after all), but from what I can gather the thing is made up of nothing they've ever seen before on earth. They're only just beginning to get their heads around it because it goes against so much of what they already know, but she won't tell me if they have any idea about how they can use that info to shut it down. The term 'classified' makes me wince whenever I hear it now.

There are theories about why whoever sent them might be wanting to make more Stone Men. The general consensus is that they aren't amassing any kind of army to invade us with. Why would they need to? After all, they could just send three or four and wait for them to smash our infrastructure to smithereens. One of the more popular ideas, I gather, is that they are some kind of workforce.

Strange to think of them as anything other than murder machines after what I've seen, and how I'm living, but there it is. Based on their 'indestructibility, wedge-like hands and seeming ability to control their own mass', Straub tells me that lots of people think their main function—other than to come here and reproduce more of themselves—would be as earth movers, perhaps for dangerous work like channelling rivers, or simpler stuff like preparing land for construction. Lots of people have asked how they built the first one if they need parts of us to build more, but more people have replied with the fairly obvious answer; they don't necessarily *need* us to build more, but maybe our parts make it *easier* to build more, or to build the bigger, blue Stone Men that might have other functions that we haven't seen yet.

I don't know how I feel about those ideas. It makes their masters, or even them, into something else in my mind. I think of them as, I suppose, evil. *They* are the bad guys. But thoughts like that suggest something else; that they think of us simply as cattle, a means to an end. We've been seeing it all along as some kind of sinister master plan, but this might be something basic to them, something that they've been doing for centuries, coming from wherever they are and going to other places like ours and creating ... what, Stone Men, other things, other workers, other helpers? Whatever it is that makes their place function. It might be as common to them as working out the council budget for the year.

I don't like all that though. It makes it harder to hate them. Whatever the reason, they come here and they scare people into their gruesome deaths. Fuck their reasons. I hate them.

Ah ... I don't like using this thing. It makes me think of Andy. They let me hear his recording, after I kept asking for months and months. They did a few assessments beforehand. It was a hard listen, very hard, but I was glad I did. There were things on there he wanted me to hear. I heard them, mate. I liked you too. I don't blame you for getting me into this. Which you did, by the way, but anyway.

I don't regret not taking Andy's way. I don't regret it at all. He was a hero? Good. Good for him. I mean that. But let's see who saved more lives in the end, eh? *That's* what counts. He was brave? Absolutely. Incredibly brave, or at least I think so. He didn't sound so sure. And did I delay, did I hesitate, did I risk lives because I was too scared to do the right thing? Fuck it, yes. I can say that. Enough years have passed. The therapy is about keeping me sane in here, but we've talked about the past as well, and I've come to terms with it. I was scared. Who the fuck wouldn't be? But here's what I *did* do, what I *did* have.

I thought on my feet. I thought of a solution. And here I am, and as bad as it gets—and sometimes it does get very bad—I'm still pretty sure it's better than the alternative (ask me again, if I'm still here in ten years, and see what I say then, but for now I'm pretty sure). And thinking of that solution not only kept me alive—and let's be honest, let's be *really* honest, that was why I thought of it, anything else that comes of it is a bonus—but might well mean we figure out how to beat them. So Andy might well have been the braver man, but I might be the guy who made the difference, and I was the 'coward'. So what the hell does that mean then, eh?

And for me, personally, what's come of it? I might be saved yet. I might get to live *and* go free, while Andy's in the ground somewhere. I'd have been rewarded, and what would that mean then? The brave man dies and the coward lives, how does that work?

Yeah, okay, it might still go the other way, especially as ... actually, sod it, I'm gonna delete this anyway, but hang on ...

Right. I've made it look like I've finished and I've gotten into bed, so they can't read my lips. If I talk quietly, they shouldn't hear me under the duvet, and this is being deleted anyway, but I need to say this out loud. For me.

Tony slipped up last week. Just briefly, and he moved on, but it's been a different physio that's come back since. Told me Tony was on holiday, but I don't know. Anyway, the last time he was here, Tony was chattering away about traffic where he lives—he has a tendency to rant sometimes, Tony, I don't think he realises that he does it—when he said that his wife was in the car with him.

"She says to me I shouldn't complain," Tony said to me, "as it's not as bad as it was a few years back. She says I should remember what it was like, back when we kept having all the bother every couple of months—" Then he suddenly stopped dead, and the pause was only very brief, but I looked to my right, at the guard—obviously, Tony was stood up behind me, working on my back, but I could see the guard's face all right, a young guy—and he was glaring at Tony, but not even angrily; more like he was worried too. He didn't want to get in trouble either, and they both knew the camera and mic would be on. Then Tony had started talking again, rounding off the story by talking about football traffic. The change was quite smooth, but the way the guard had looked at me afterwards—and then looked away suddenly—told me that something had nearly been given away. And I still haven't decided whether it's good or bad news for me.

See, I think 'the bother every couple of months' were the Arrivals. And I think that, since 'it's not as bad as it was' when they were having the 'bother', that says to me there hasn't been another Arrival since the last one. I think that, since we've caught the original one here, and effectively have it stuck in a loop with me, it's somehow gumming up the works. I don't know, maybe they have to have them all back before they can start again, or maybe—and I think this is more likely, seeing as it was always the original that turned up first before the others came—that they need it back to make the system work, like it's the linchpin or something. Or maybe they've just given up and moved on elsewhere, worried that we're figuring them out or that we're just too much trouble. I haven't a clue. But either way, I think from the government's point of view, the situation is this:

As long as they keep the original here, and following me, the others don't come back. And I think that, unless the research yields some results soon, that will stay as the bottom line. And what that means for me, I don't really like to think.

But better than the alternative? I still think so. I *think* I still think so. For now, at least, I'm here. There's air in my lungs and blood moving in my veins. I still want to keep it that way.

***

Paul paused for a moment, breathing slowly, then pushed the 'STOP' button on the Dictaphone. He looked as if he was going to start recording again and add something else, but then he pushed the 'DELETE' button instead.

Throwing back the duvet, Paul sat up in bed and swung his legs over the edge, rubbing at his face. He looked up into the upper right-hand corner of the cabin, at the small black camera lens, and gestured at the bed behind him. He then shrugged, put his face to his flattened hands to mime sleep, and then shrugged again. It wouldn't look out of the ordinary; he often mimed things to it throughout the day, even though they could hear him. He didn't like to talk to it for some reason.

He got up, reaching for a grab handle as the cabin turned, and walked the few feet to the sideboard. Grabbing a mug out of the rubber holder, he clicked the button on the kettle, and sighed gently as it boiled. While he was waiting, he pushed the button on the CD player, and music began to play through the surround sound speakers embedded in the walls. A thought occurred to him, and for the first time in many months, he reached for the curtains that covered the small porthole window in the nearby wall.

As ever, if he really wanted to see it, he would have to flatten his head against the glass. They'd deliberately placed it so that he would see as little of that particular view as possible, but he'd learned that he could see it if he tried. The best time to do so was always on the turn. He remembered again how Straub had told him of one report, a bright spark of hope that said there'd been a drop in some of the energy readings; but the dip had only lasted a few days before everything had returned to normal. Even so, they were sure it meant something, but Paul didn't dare to believe it.

He pulled back the curtains and pressed his face to the glass. The Stone Man was still there, of course, walking steadily after him. Just as it had always been.

*

IF YOU ENJOYED THIS BOOK, PLEASE A STAR RATING ON AMAZON; LUKE SMITHERD IS STILL SELF PUBLISHED AND COULD USE ALL THE HELP HE CAN HE GET ...
AND IF YOU DID ENJOY IT, YOU MIGHT LIKE TO TRY OF ONE OF LUKE SMITHERD'S OTHER NOVELS, **IN THE DARKNESS, THAT'S WHERE I'LL KNOW YOU.**
HERE, AS A **FREE BONUS***, IS THE BEGINNING CHAPTER OF THAT VERY BOOK!*
(ALSO, READ ON PAST THIS THE EXTRACT FOR THE AUTHOR'S AFTERWORD, A FEW NOTES ABOUT THE CREATION OF **THE STONE MAN***, OR VISIT LUKESMITHERD.COM WHERE YOU CAN SIGN UP FOR THE 'SPAM FREE BOOK RELEASE NEWSLETTER' SO YOU NEVER MISS A NEW RELEASE)*

IN THE DARKNESS, THAT'S WHERE I'LL KNOW YOU

By Luke Smitherd

Chapter One: An Unexpected Point of View, Proof That You Can Never Go Home Again, and The Importance of the Work/Life Balance

***

Charlie opened his eyes and was immediately confused. A quick reassessment of the view, however, confirmed that he was right; he suddenly had breasts. Not very noticeable ones, perhaps, but when he'd spent over thirty years without them, even the appearance of a couple of A-cups was a real attention grabber. As he continued to look down, the very next thing to come to his attention was the material covering them; a purple, stretchy cotton fabric, something he had never worn, nor had he ever harboured any plans to do so. As he watched his hands adjust the top, he came to the most alarming realisation of all; those weren't his hands doing the adjusting. The giveaway wasn't in the slenderness of the fingers, or the medium-length (if a little ragged) fingernails upon their tips, or even in the complete lack of any physical sensation as he watched the digits tug and pull the purple top into position. It was the fact that, while they were clearly stuck to the end of arms that were attached to his shoulders (or at least, the painfully skinny shoulders that he could see either side of his head's peripheral vision; his shoulders were bigger than that, surely?) they were moving entirely of their own accord.

He was so stunned that he almost felt calm. The bizarreness of the situation had already passed straight through *this is crazy* and out the other side into the utterly incomprehensible. Charlie stared dumbly for several seconds as his mind got caught in a feeble loop, trying and failing to get its bearings (*What ... sorry, what ... sorry,*

WHAT ...) While, in that moment, he never really came any closer to coming to terms with the situation, his mind did at least manage to reach the next inevitable conclusion: this wasn't his body.

The loop got louder as these unthinkable, too-big-for-conscious-process thoughts instantly doubled in size, but got nowhere (*WHAT* ... *WHAT* ... *WHAT THE FUCK*). All Charlie was capable of doing was staring at the view in front of him as it moved from a downward angle, swinging upwards to reveal a door being opened onto a narrow hallway. A second doorway was then passed through, and now Charlie found himself in a bathroom. He wanted to look down again, to see the feet that were carrying him forward, to help understand that he wasn't doing the walking, to aid him in *any* kind of conscious comprehension of his situation ... but he quickly realised that he couldn't affect the line of sight in any way. The viewing angle was completely out of his control. Instinctively, he tried to commandeer the limbs that were attached to him, to move the arms like he would have done on any other minute of any other day since his birth, but there was no response. There was only the *illusion* of control; the moment when one of the hands reached for the door handle at the same time that he would have intended them to, as he reflexively thought of performing the motion simultaneously. What the fuck was going on? *What the fuck was going on?*

The crazy, unthinkable answer came again, despite his crashed mind, even in a moment of sheer madness—what other conclusion was there to reach?—as he saw the feminine hands reach for a toothbrush on the sink: he was in someone else's body—a woman's body—and he was not in control.

Incapable of speech, Charlie watched as the view swung up from the sink to look into the plastic-framed bathroom mirror, and while he began to notice the detail in his surroundings properly—tiny bathroom, cheap fittings, slightly grubby tiles, and candles, candles everywhere—the main focus of his concern was the face looking back at him.

The eyes he was looking through belonged to a woman of hard-to-place age; she looked to be in her mid- to late-twenties, but even to Charlie's goggling, shell-shocked point of view, there was clearly darkness both under and inside her green eyes (physically and metaphorically speaking) that made her look older. Her skin was pale, and the tight, bouncy, but frazzled curls of her shoulder-length black hair all added to the haunted manner that the woman possessed.

All of which Charlie didn't give a flying shit about, of course; thoughts were beginning to come together, and his mind was already rallying and coming back online. While Charlie would never describe himself as a practical man, having spent most of his life more concerned with where the next laugh was coming from rather than the next paycheque, he had always been resourceful, capable of taking an objective step backwards in a tight spot and saying *Okay, let's have a look at this.*

While he was beyond that now—had he been in his own body, that body would have been hyperventilating—he was now aware enough to at least think more clearly. As the woman continued to brush her teeth, Charlie watched, and thought the one thing to himself that instantly made everything else easier:

This is probably a dream. This is fucking mental, so it's got to be a dream. So there's nothing to worry about, is there?

While he didn't fully believe that—the view was too real, the surroundings too complete and detailed, the grit and grime too fleshed out and realised—it enabled him to take the necessary mental step back, and put his foot on the brake of his runaway mind a little.

Okay. Think. Think. This can't actually be happening. It can't. It's a lucid dream, that's what it is. Calm down. Calm down. That means you can decide what happens, right? You're supposed to be able to control a lucid dream, aren't you? So let's make ... the wall turn purple. That'll do. Wall. Turn purple ... now.

The wall remained exactly the same, and the view shifted downward briefly to reveal an emerging spray of water and foaming toothpaste. The woman had just spat.

Right. Maybe it's not quite one of those *dreams then, maybe it's just a very, very realistic one. Don't panic. You can prove this. Think back. Think back through your day, think what you'd been doing, and you'll remember going to bed. What were you last doing?*

He'd met the boys, gone for a drink—excited about the prospect of one turning into many—the first night out for a little while. Clint's mate Jack had been over from London too, which was both a good excuse and good news for the quality of the night. They had ended up on a heavy pub crawl, and somebody had said something about going back to their place ... Neil. That guy Neil had said it. And they'd gone to Neil's, and then ...

Nothing. Nothing from there on in. And now he was here. As he felt hysteria start to rise, escalating from the panic that he already felt, Charlie frantically tried to put a lid on it before it got badly out of control.

You passed out. You had some more to drink and you passed out. That's why you can't remember what happened at Neil's, and this is the resultant booze-induced crazy dream. So wake up. Wake your ass up. Slap yourself in the face and wake the fuck up.

Charlie did so, his hand slamming into the side of his head with the force of fear behind it, and as the ringing sting rocked him, he became aware that he suddenly had a physical presence of his own. If he had a hand to swing and a head to hit, then he now had a body of his own. A body inside this woman's body? Where the hell had that come from?

There'd been nothing before, no response from anything when he'd tried to move the woman's arms earlier. He'd been a disembodied mind, a ghost inside this woman's head, but now when he looked down he saw his own torso, naked and standing in a space consisting of nothing but blackness. Looking around himself to confirm it, seeing the darkness stretching away around him in all directions and now having a body to respond to his emotion, Charlie collapsed onto an unseen floor and lay gasping and whooping in lungfuls of nonexistent air, his body trembling.

His wide, terrified eyes stared straight ahead, the view that had previously seemed to be his own vision now appearing suspended in the air, a vast image the size of a cinema screen with edges that faded away into the inky-black space around him. Its glow was ethereal, like nothing he'd ever seen before. How had he thought that had been his own-eye view? It had clearly been there all along, hanging there in the darkness. Had he just been standing too close? Had something changed? Either way, there was no mistake now; there was just him, the enormous screen showing the woman's point of view, and the black room in which he lay.

Charlie pulled his knees up into a ball and watched the screen as he lay there whimpering. That slap had hurt badly, and instead of waking him, it had added another frightening new dimension to the situation. He was terrified; he lay for a moment in mental and physical shock, and for now, at least, everything was beyond him. The words that he feebly tried to repeat to himself fell on deaf ears—*it's a dream it's a dream it's a dream*—and so he lay there for a while, doing nothing but watch and tremble as the woman made a sandwich, checked her e-mails on her phone, and moved to sit in front of her TV. She flicked through channels, thumbed through her Facebook feed. As this time passed—and Charlie still watched, incapable of anything else for the time being—he came back to himself a little more. He noticed that, while he was naked, he wasn't cold. He wasn't warm either, however; in fact, the concept of either sensation seemed hard to comprehend, like trying to understand what the colour red sounded like. Thoughts crept in again.

You can't actually be in her head. You can't actually be INSIDE her head. People don't have screens behind their eyes or huge holes where their brain should be. You know that. You haven't been shrunk and stuffed in here, as that's not possible. So this ... HAS ... to be a dream. Right? You have a voice, don't you? You can speak, can't you? Can you get your breath long enough to speak?

Charlie opened his mouth, and found that speech was almost outside of his capabilities. A strange, strangled squeak came out of his throat, barely audible, and he felt no breath come from his lungs. He tried several more times, shaping his mouth around the sound in an attempt to form words, but got nowhere.

Focus, you fucking arsehole. Focus.

Eventually, he managed to squeak out a word that sounded a bit like *hey* and, encouraged by that success, he tried to repeat it. He managed to say it again on the third try, then kept going, the word getting slightly louder each time until something gave way and the bass came into his voice.

"Hey ..."

With that, the ability to speak dropped into place, even if getting the hang of it again took a real physical effort. He at least knew *how* to do it now, his mind remembering the logistics of speech like a dancer going through a long-abandoned but previously well-rehearsed routine. He looked out through the screen with sudden purpose, determined to find out if she could hear him.

"Hey ... *hey* ..." he gasped, his lips feeling loose and clumsy, as if they were new to his face. Charlie sat up, hoping to get more volume behind it, more projection. He thought he had to at least be as loud as the TV for her to hear him, if she was capable of doing so at all.

"*HEY*," he managed, but there was no external response. Charlie's heart sank, and he almost abandoned the whole attempt. After all, it was easier and more reassuring to resign himself to the only real hope that he had; that this truly *was* a dream, and thus something he could hopefully wait out until his alarm clock broke the spell and returned him to blessed normality. Things might have turned out very differently if he had, but instead Charlie found the strength to kneel upright and produce something approaching a scream.

"*HEY!!*" he squawked, and fell back onto his behind, exhausted. Staring at the glowing screen before him, dejected, Charlie then saw a hand come up into view, holding the remote control. A finger hit the mute button.

Charlie froze.

The image on the screen swung upwards, showing the white ceiling with its faint yellowing patches marking it here and there, and hung in that direction for a second or two. It then travelled back to the TV screen, and as the hand holding the remote came up again, Charlie realised what was happening and felt a fresh jolt of panic. Without thinking, he blurted out a noise, desperately needing to cause any kind of sound in an attempt to be heard, like a fallen and undiscovered climber hearing the rescue party beginning to move on.

"*BAARGH! BA BA BAAA!*" Charlie screeched, falling forwards as he almost dove towards the screen in his clumsy response to the images upon it. The hand hesitated, and then the view was getting up and travelling across the living room and down the hallway. It looked like the woman was going to look through the spyhole in her front door, and as she did so, the fish-eye effect of the glass on the huge screen made Charlie's stomach lurch. He still saw the fairly dirty-looking stairwell outside, however, and realised that the woman was inside some sort of apartment block.

Charlie stared, trying desperately to pull himself together, and assessed the situation. She could hear him then; but she certainly didn't seem to be aware that he was there. So she could be as unwilling in all of this as he was?

It'sadreamitdoesn'tmatteranywayit'salladreamsowhocares—

He didn't believe that though. He just couldn't. There had to be some sort of explanation, and he couldn't be physically *in* her head, so this was ... an out of body experience? Some sort of psychic link?

Charlie surprised himself with his own thoughts. Where the hell had all of that come from, all of those sudden, rational thoughts? True, he'd been confronted with something so impossible that he didn't really have much choice but to look at the available options, but ... was he suddenly adjusting again? When this all started, he didn't even have a body, but one quickly appeared. Was his mind following suit? He was still trembling, his shoulders still rising and falling dramatically with each rapid, shallow in-breath of nothing, but his mind was at work now; the shock had seemingly been absorbed and moved past far more quickly than it should have been, he was sure. Would he be this rational already if he were in his own body? Whatever was going on, being here was ... different. He felt his mental equilibrium returning, his awareness and presence of mind growing. He was scared, and he was confused, but he was getting enough of a grip to at least function.

You have her attention. Don't lose it.

He opened his mouth again, got nowhere, reset himself, then tried again.

"Lady?"

The view jerked round, then everything in sight became slightly farther away, very quickly; she'd spun around, and fallen backwards against the apartment's front door. The view then swung sharply left and right to either side of the hallway, looking to the bathroom doorway and then to the doorway of another, unspecified room. Charlie assumed it was a bedroom. He tried again.

"Can ... can you hear me?"

The view jerked violently. She'd clearly just jumped out of her skin, her fresh adrenaline putting all of her physical flight reflexes on full alert. It was a dumb question to ask—she obviously could—but even with his growing sense of control, Charlie's mind was still racing, his incredulity at the situation now combining with the excitement of finding that he could communicate with his unsuspecting host.

It was clear that she was terrified, and Charlie realised that he couldn't blame her. She was hearing a voice within the safety of her home when she'd thought that she was by herself, and Charlie could only guess what it sounded like to this woman. Did his voice sound as if he were right behind her, or was she hearing it actually coming from the inside of her head? Charlie couldn't decide which would be worse.

Get a grip, man. Of course she's going to shit herself when you start talking to her. Just ... try and think, okay? Think straight. You have to get out of this. You need her to talk to you; you need her if you're ever going to get this sorted out. Get a grip, get control, and think smart.

"Please, it's—" He didn't get any further as the jump came again, this time with a little scream; it was a brief squeal, clipped short as if she were trying to avoid drawing attention to herself. Charlie jumped with her this time, startled a little himself, but pressed on. "Please, *please* don't be scared. I'm shitting myself here too. Please. Please calm down—" The second half of this sentence was lost, however, disappearing under a fresh scream from the woman. This time it was a hysterical, lengthy one that travelled with her as she ran the length of the hallway into the living room, slamming the door behind her. Charlie heard her crying and panting, and watched her thin hands grab one end of the small sofa and begin to drag it in front of the door. The scream trailed off as she did so, and once the job was done, the view backed away from the door, bobbing slightly in time with the woman's whimpering tears and gasping breath.

Charlie was hesitant to speak again; he knew that he simply had to, but what could he actually say without sending her off into fresh hysterics? The answer was immediate; nothing. There was no way to do it easily. She would have to realise that she was *physically* alone at least—and safe with it—and the only way to help her do that was to keep talking until she accepted that there was no intruder in her home.

Not on the outside, anyway.

"I need your help," he tried, wincing as the view leapt almost a foot upwards and then spun on the spot, accompanied by fresh wails. "Please, lady, you're safe—" The cries increased in volume, to the point where he had to raise his voice to be heard. In doing so, Charlie realised that he now had his voice under complete control. And wasn't the blackness around him a fraction less dark now, too? "Look, just calm down, all right? If you just listen for two seconds, you'll find that—"

"*Fuck oooffff!!*" she screamed, the volume of it at a deafening level from Charlie's perspective. He clapped his hands to the side of his head, wincing and crouching from the sheer force of it. It was like being in the centre of a sonic hurricane. "*Get out of my flat! Get out of my flaaaaaaat!!!*"

"Please!! Please don't do that!" Charlie shouted, trying to be heard over the woman's yelling. "Look, just shut up for a second, I don't *want* to be here, I just want to—"

"*Get out! Where are you? Get out!! Get oooouuuuuttt!!!*" she yelled, ignoring him, and as the view dropped to the floor and shot backwards—the living room walls now framing either side of the screen—Charlie realised that she'd dropped onto her ass and scooted backwards into the corner, backing into the space where the sofa had previously been. Frustrated, terrified, in pain and pushed to his limit (it had been one hell of an intense five minutes, after all) Charlie let fly with a scream of his own, hands balled into fists over his throbbing ears.

"*JUST SHUT THE FUCK UP FOR A SECOND!!*" he screamed, and whether it was from using some volume of his own, or because her own screams were already about to descend into hysterical, terrified and silent tears, the only sound after Charlie's shout was that of the woman's whimpers. The view still darted around the room though, trying to find the source of the sound, a source well beyond her sight.

Charlie seized his moment. At the very least he could be heard, and *that* hopefully meant he could start talking her down. She was more terrified than him—of course she was, at least he'd had time to get used to the situation whereas she'd just discovered an apparently invisible intruder in her home—but he had to get through to her while she was at least quiet enough to hear him. Hysterical or not, she had ears, even if he appeared to be currently standing somewhere in between them.

"Look, I'm sorry for shouting like that, I just need you to listen for a second, okay? Just listen," Charlie said, as soothingly as his own panicking mind would allow. "I'm not going to hurt you, okay? Okay? It's fine, you're, uh … you're not in any danger, all right?"

"Where … where are you? *Where are you?*" the woman's voice sobbed breathlessly, small and scared. Her thinking was clear from the confusion in her voice; she was finally realising that she should be able to see the person talking to her, that there was nowhere in the room that they could be hiding. Charlie thought quickly, and decided that it was best to leave that one for a minute. He'd only just got her onside, and didn't want to push her over the edge.

"I'll tell you in a second. I'm, uh … I'm not actually in the room, you see. You're alone in the flat, and you're safe. You're fine. Okay?" She didn't reply at first. The sobs continued helplessly, but Charlie thought that they might have been slightly lessened, if only due to confusion.

"Wha … what?" she stammered, the view swinging wildly around the room now. "Your voice … what the fuck … *what the fuck is going onnnnnn ….*" And then she was off again, the hysterical screaming coming back at fever pitch. Charlie stood in front of the strange, glowing screen, his hands at his ears again while she bawled, blinking rapidly as his mind worked. After a moment or two, his shoulders slumped and he sat down. There was nothing he could do but wait, and let her adjust. His own breathing was beginning to slow further, and he was finding acceptance of his situation to still be an easier task than he thought; while it was no less mind boggling, his panic was dropping fast, and unusually so.

It's being in here that's doing it. It has to be.

Either way, he let her have a minute or two to calm down. Eventually, he stood and began to pace back and forth in the darkness—illuminated dimly by the unusual light of the screen—while he decided what to say next. His frantic mind kept trying to wander, to seize and wrestle all the aspects of the situation into submission, and failed every time.

You don't like the dark. You don't like the dark! Don't think about it, don't think about it … think about … wait … there's no breeze in here, no echo. It really is a room of sorts then, a space with walls on all sides?

He looked out into the darkness, looking for walls, and saw none; there was only seemingly endless blackness. Charlie thought it would be best not to go exploring *just* yet. Instead, he tried to control his breathing, and quickly ran through a mental list, double checking his actions and decisions of the previous few days before his night out:

Went to work. Did the late shift. Argued about sci-fi films with Clint. Helped Steve throw the drunk arsehole out that had started slapping his girlfriend. Went home, stayed up and watched a film because I had the Wednesday off. Met Chris in town—

And so it went on. By the time he'd finished a few minutes later—while he was no clearer about what had led him to be inside this woman's head—he told himself that he really *did* feel more capable of beginning to deal with things, and less frightened; in the absolute worst case, even though he didn't believe this to be the *actual* case, this situation was real, and had to be resolved. If he'd got in, then he could get out, and if this was the *best*—and more likely—scenario, where this was all just a dream, then he would wake up and all would be well.

Yeah. And if I had wheels, I'd be a wagon.

Charlie took a deep breath, and decided to speak again.

"Are you okay?" he said. The view jumped again, along with a fresh scream.

For fuck's sake.

"Look, we're not going to get anywhere if you keep doing that," Charlie said, not being able to keep the frustration out of his voice. "I'm sure you're a smart person really, so just knock the screaming and shit on the head and we can work together to sort this all out, right? For crying out loud, if I'm not *there,* I can't exactly do anything to you, can I? I know you're scared, and I know this must have been a hell of a shock, but I'm not exactly a million dollars myself right this minute. So, please … come on. Just … have a minute, sort yourself out, and then we'll … then we'll carry on," he finished, shrugging his shoulders in annoyed impotence. He knew that he was perhaps being a little harsh, but he couldn't help thinking that he had a bit of a flake on his hands here. Being scared was one thing, but a complete collapse like this was another.

Don't be a dick, Charlie, he reprimanded himself. *You don't know what she's been through before now. You might be squatting in her head, but you don't know anything about her.*

It was a fair point. She seemed to respond better to his last outburst though, and the sobbing was now drying up into skipping little breaths. She wasn't responding to his annoyance, Charlie thought, but it might have been the honest approach that got through. Sometimes people just appreciated it.

"Your voice ..." she said, and her own was steadier, but uncertain. "Where—" She hesitated, seeming to try and find a different question to ask, something else to say that would stop her from repeating herself. She gave up. "Where are you? Where ... where *are* you?"

She's not going to drop that one. Would you, in her shoes?

Again, a fair point, and Charlie decided that the honest approach had seemed to work before.

"Look ... okay, I'll tell you," he said, trying to find words to describe the impossible, "and I don't understand it in the slightest myself, but it's ... it's pretty heavy shit, okay? I mean, well, I don't mean heavy as in serious, as I've no idea what *it* really is, but I mean heavy as in ... hard to get your head around. It's ... *weird*. And we can't be having any of the freaking out stuff you were doing earlier, okay? I need you to work with me. Okay?"

Silence.

"Okay?"

Another pause, and then the view nodded quickly; a rapid, brief up and down motion that would have been barely noticeable to an outside observer, but seemed to Charlie as if her flat had been caught in an earthquake.

"Okay," she replied quietly, her voice breathy and small.

"Right ..." said Charlie, speaking slowly and trying to prepare each word carefully. "I don't know how this has happened, or why, but the last thing I remember is being on a night out with my mates, we were out in ... wait ... hang on, where is this? Where do you live?"

"Huh?"

"Which city? Which city are you in right now?"

"Coventry."

"Jesus! That's where I live!"

"... okay."

In the brief pause that followed while she waited for him to continue, his mind grabbed the thought and filed it away for later. It might be relevant. Maybe they'd been somewhere in the city, been *through* something, something that caused a connection ...

It's a dream, remember? This is down to cheese and too many pints, or a bad kebab.

He dragged his wandering thoughts back on track, and continued.

"Anyway, *anyway*, we were out in Cov, and then we went back to someone's house, and then, I don't know, I must have fallen asleep or drank too much or whatever, but somehow ... *some*how ..."

He stumbled, tripping at the vital hurdle.

"What?" she asked, the view still scanning around the room, as if hoping to find the answers there.

"Ah ... ah *fuck* it, look, I, I, I woke up or whatever and here I am, in your fucking head. I don't know how I got here, and hell, I might be gone in the next five minutes for all I know, but I'm here, I'm in your head, here I am. That's it."

Silence again. Then:

"You're ... you're what?"

"I'm in your head. I'm standing here, in front of this, this ..." He waved his hands in front of the immense, ethereal screen before him, taking it in as yet another rapid flicker shivered across it. These had been happening constantly; later he would realise that this effect was due to her blinking. "This screen thing, okay, and everywhere else in here it's just black, and I'm stood here, completely ..." he trailed off, looking down at his genitals and deciding that it would probably be best not to mention the nakedness to a scared woman who is stuck in a flat on her own, "... completely without any idea as to what's going on."

Silence again. Then:

"A screen ... there's a screen in my head?" she asked. "What ... what screen, what the hell are you talking about?"

Charlie rubbed at his face, angry now, both with himself and her. Of course she didn't get it, it was un-gettable, but she wasn't even coming *close* to understanding and he was doing a lousy job of explaining it. He needed to get the important facts across if they were ever going to move on, and spare her the more intricate details. He needed a different approach.

"Look, don't worry about that, forget it, forget it. Listen. Right, okay, I'll start again. My name is Charlie. Charlie Wilkes. What's yours?"

There was a long, uncertain silence.

"Minnie," she replied, her voice shaking again. She was about to go any second, he could tell.

Talk her down.

"Are you scared to talk to me?" asked Charlie, as tenderly as he could manage. "You don't have to be. Talk to me. What's your surname? You might as well get used to talking to me, you know, as we need to talk to sort this all out, yeah? Come on. What's your surname?"

"I don't ... I don't like to ..." the tears were coming again, and Charlie knew he needed to stop this fast before she lost it.

"It's okay, have a second—" he began, but she cut him off, her voice rising.

"If I talk to you ... it'll get worse ... I think it's finally happening, I think it's finally happened and you're not real and I'm going cra-ha-ha-*haaaAAAAAAA*—" and then she was gone, wailing again ... but this time it was different. This time the screen went black and the sobs became muffled, turning into the low, mournful cries of someone who has given up. She'd dropped her head into her hands or onto her forearms, with her eyes squeezed shut as she cried, cutting off Charlie's view of the outside world. He realised in that moment why her earlier reaction had been so severe; this was someone not entirely comfortable in their own mind, someone already scared of finding voices in their head or visions of things that aren't there. He didn't have time to dwell on that, however, as he realised that Minnie's eyes being shut meant that he was now swallowed by total darkness. Terror came rushing in, threatening to take him and ruin the small amount of progress that he'd just made.

"Minnie, trust me, you're not going crazy," Charlie said, raising his voice almost to a shout to be heard over her noise. "I know it *sounds* crazy, this whole situation is crazy, but I promise you I'm the real deal! Okay? My name is Charlie Wilkes, I work in a pub—Barrington's, you know Barrington's?—I support the Sky Blues even though I never go to the Ricoh, I grew up in Oxford, I moved here, what, ten years ago? I like, ah, I like movies and books, uh, I like, I like music ... *shit,* who doesn't, okay, I like cheese, and I hate getting up early! The last film I saw was *The English Patient* on Blu-Ray, the, uh, the last thing I bought from the shop was a Pepperami and a can of Sprite! My favourite place to eat in Cov is the Ocean Restaurant, and I didn't vote last election day because I forgot to get to the polling station in time ... okay? Is any of this getting through to you?"

"... you're not real ..."

"I *am!* I promise I am! Look, if I wasn't real, right, and you were genuinely going crazy, don't the voices in crazy people's heads tell them to go and kill people, shit like that? Tell them that the government is run by lizards, and that they're Jesus come to, to, I dunno, stick forks in their asses? Well I'm not saying any of those things!"

Ease off, for God's sake. Don't start attacking her again.

"Look. All *I'm* asking you to do is listen to me. That's it. That's it. You know what, absolute worst case, you've gone nuts and you have a voice in your head. But it's not a nonstop voice, look, I can be quiet if you want, listen." Charlie stopped talking for a good thirty seconds before speaking again. "See? And I'm not nagging at you to do bad things. So it's not that *bad* of a bad thing, worst case. And best case ... I'm telling the truth, and you and I can figure this out together. Okay? So just, you know, chill out for a moment, take a nice deep breath, and let's talk."

***

THE STORY OF CHARLIE AND MINNIE CONTINUES IN **IN THE DARKNESS, THAT'S WHERE I'LL KNOW YOU**, *AVAILABLE NOW ON AMAZON!*

Author's Afterword from the original Kindle Edition:

(Note: at the time of writing, any comments made in this afterword about the number of other available books written by me are all true. However, since writing this, many more books might be out! The best way to find out is to search Amazon for Luke Smitherd or visit www.lukesmitherd.com ...)

Well, here we are at last. The 'Difficult Second Novel' is finally finished. Admittedly, it should have been finished about eight months ago, and I'll get to why in a second, but before any of that, I have something far more important to say.

Thank you.

The support I've received from complete strangers who have read my first book, be it by e-mail, tweets, nice reviews on Amazon (vital!) or even financial means has been an extremely nice surprise. At the time of writing, there are currently a combined total of 33 positive reviews on the Amazon US and UK kindle stores, and the fact that somebody took the time purely to say that they enjoyed my work (and to encourage others to check it out) never fails to absolutely make my week. The downside is I'm left continually checking the site for new reviews at least five times a day. (Needy? If you only knew how much.) But seriously; I can't stress enough how important those reviews are to me both personally and to the continued progression of any kind of writing 'career' that I might have. So thanks a million, all of you, it really helps me keep going with this. Speaking of the first novel, YES, I know there were a lot of typos in the first version that went up, so I checked, and reposted, and STILL people said there were typos, and I checked and reposted, and STILL people said there were typos ... so I did a fourth draft and left it. I basically read too fast to notice my own mistakes. Look, make me a millionaire and I'll hire a goddamn copywriter, okay?? Sigh ... just do me a favour though please? If you're gonna mention typos in your otherwise very nice review, just don't put it in the freakin' review title (I'm looking at you, Ms Janet Farley ... but while I'm here, thank you so much for your very kind words ;-))

Okay, so some of you that read *Physics* (and if you haven't ... hint, hint, again ***author's note from the future: since I wrote The Stone Man, I've written several other books. I would suggest *In The Darkness, That's Where I'll Know You* first, then *WEIRD. DARK.*, then *A Head Full Of Knives, then He Waits,* and finally *The Physics of the Dead* as a recommended reading order if you're thinking of working your way through my bibliography so far ... okay, now I'll hand you back to my past self. Hmm. Strange**) may have been wondering where the hell this book has been, seeing as I signed off the last one by saying I was going straight into writing the next.

Well, to be honest, it was all a matter of logistics.

The nature of the book you've just read—things having an impact on a national scale, military and government involvement, evacuations, religious mania—depended on the logistical side of those things being *believable*. By now, you'll have probably made your own mind up about how successful I was in addressing those things, but it was something I initially found immensely intimidating. I had to decide what would actually happen—*realistically*—in a scenario that no government on earth would have prepared for, and how much of that would actually be seen by a man chasing a fantastical stone creature across the country. And I didn't have the faintest clue where to start ... so I kept on putting it off. I even ended up writing a load of plot notes for my next novel *instead of doing the same for the actual book I was supposed to be working on.* Something you should probably know about me—and this is going to sound like a bad joke but I swear this is true—I bought a book about overcoming procrastination and I never got around to finishing it. Honest injun.

Eventually, slowly but surely, I started to piece things together, including military research (difficult when performed in the context of a purely imaginary situation) and had enough to at least get started. Along the way, there were lengthy pauses whenever I got to a bit that meant more large-scale planning, but eventually the thing was completed. Funnily enough, Straub was never intended to be a woman; one e-mailer pointed out that, while they'd enjoyed my first book a great deal, they thought there was a lack of female characters.

Now, while I've never subscribed to the theory of writing characters specifically to appeal to a wider demographic—I write what I feel is correct for the story—I found myself thinking, well, *could* Straub be a woman? And a quick Google search told me that, at the time of writing, the highest ranking female officer in the British army was a brigadier. And, so far as I could tell, a brigadier could realistically be the person operating at the level Straub was in the story, and so, a woman she became. I wouldn't have done it if I didn't think it would benefit the story, and I really think it did. But what do you think? Get in touch at lukesmitherd@hotmail.co.uk and let me know. Incidentally, if there's any military stuff that I've blatantly fudged, please don't just post things slagging it off, instead let me know *how* I've gotten it wrong so that I can correct it.

The story as a whole started off as an image in my head and a question; the image being that of a huge stone figure, emerging from the sea and passing through a crowd of people as if they were made of butter, and the question being 'what would a nation do if that figure was there to claim the life of one man, and was causing great damage in the process?' I don't know where those thoughts came from—they'd been there for a long time, a couple of years maybe—but I knew there was a story in it. It just needed drawing out. So, following the same process I used when I finally got round to bashing out the plot outline for my first novel, I figured out what the hell was going on with that big stone bastard, and what it was actually there for. And what you've just read is what you got as a result.

Y ou probably noticed them earlier than I did (if you read the last book) but it was only once I was nearing the end that I noticed some of the similarities between this story and the last; two men, thrust together into an extremely bleak situation, ending up trapped within a boundary that may mean their doom. The one major difference with the other book being, I guess, that they're already dead (don't worry, that's not a spoiler; there's a clue in the title.) Angela says that she sees a lot of myself in Andy—the few good bits, I mean—but I'd like to think that if a man offered me a bed and shelter for the night, I wouldn't fuck his wife. I've recently put myself forward for reasonably extensive testing regarding Asperger's, ADHD and the like (see: major procrastination issues, above) and various other minor neurological hiccups (I always feel like I have brain fog a lot of the time, and am so frighteningly easily distracted) and it was my experience and reading about all of that that made me inject some of that into Andy. I didn't want to have him dwell on it any more than someone that actually has the condition would, but both as a plot device and a way of explaining some of Andy's social views, as well as his shortcomings (and I'm not saying that Asperger's makes you a bit of an asshole, that's just him) it fitted very nicely for me. He turned out all right in the end, I think; a lot that was as a result of the experiences he'd been through, but where his guts came from in the end … well, that's the question, isn't it?

I hope I managed to make the Stone Man as scary for you as I wanted him to be. For me, he's that thing from your dreams that's chasing you down while you're having to run away through treacle. Except this time, he's not in your dreams, he's coming right down your street, and worse, *everyone wants him to get you.*

The key scenes that I was the most excited about writing were, as you could probably guess, Patrick's death, the boys meeting Henry, and Paul's reflection at the end. I enjoyed those very much, even if I actually felt pretty sad writing the first two.

The ending only changed as recently as a month or so ago, however. I was on a plane to New York (I really wanted to finish the book there, so that I could write this bit and sign off with 'Luke Smitherd, Brooklyn, New York, October 2012' and sound like some kind of porn star jet-setter … rather than a guy who had blagged a cheap holiday by going to visit a mate who lives there) when, settled in nicely by a pint of cider, a shot of Sambuca and a vodka and orange (nervous flyer), it suddenly occurred to me that the *original* ending (having Paul's situation clearly resolved at the end of the book) not only meant that the whole thing petered out a bit, but didn't sit quite right for me thematically. I decided that leaving his fate ambiguous felt much better, but if you want to know what I think eventually happened to Paul, **I've put a quick summary of the original ending on the very**

last page. It's not that different at all—a simple answer to the question 'Did he get out or not?'—but if you're someone who'd like to leave it as is, don't skip to the very last page. If you aren't, it's all there for you.

How do I think this book compares to the last one? I think it stands up pretty well. I don't know which one I prefer more; Angela prefers *The Stone Man*, and while I think this one is more exciting, I can't decide which is the better story. Both books have a strong element of *What's going on* that drive them, and while I think the mystery element of my first novel is stronger and more complex (**author's note from the future: but I would go for my first novel last, for certain. It really pays off if you stick with it, but it has a slower start that needs working through, and I wouldn't want to lose you by the second novel of mine that you read! I think by the time you've worked your way through to it, you'll know my style and will enjoy it more. Ok, back to the past self *again*.**) By the way, if you were to recommend either of those two books to a friend, I would suggest they start with this one.

The release of this second book is very exciting for two reasons; one, obviously I want to know what people make of it, but two, I'm extremely interested to see what happens with its initial sales. You see, once enrolled in the Amazon Kindle Store KDP Select program, you can list your books for free for five days every three months. This is a great feature, and really helped get the book out there … I *think*. That's because, over the two times I've been able to list it for free, I've had about 5,000 to 6,000 downloads in total. Great, you might think, and so did I … but then a friend pointed out quite reliably that, in a nutshell, those are quite likely to be piracy bots, downloading it for repackaging and various other nefarious functions.

Plus, let's put it another way; say a lot of those were legit downloads. Okay. But as far as I can tell, when these downloads happened, there's no way for Amazon customers to say 'Alert me when this guy releases a new book.' So I don't know if there's a load of people out there *desperate* to read new stuff by me (Hey! It could happen!) that haven't been in touch with me, so I can't tell them that this book is out, and so they won't *know* about this new book coming out. So after all of this. I really can't wait to see what actually happens when this book hits the virtual shelves (Prediction: disappointment).

All of which leads me nicely onto something else I wanted to mention. I'm currently unpublished by conventional means, and so I'm currently trying to build my own 'fanbase' if you like, and maybe give this whole self-published-online thing a bit of a go, and maybe even see if I can't eventually even make a living out of this (Hey! It could goddamn HAPPEN!). And, along similar lines, I like to support other people trying to carve their own creative career path. I think it's only fair if I'm asking people to post star ratings/reviews—brief or otherwise—to help me out. So as an avid listener of podcasts, I've always tried to leave star ratings/reviews for the ones I like, to help out guys and girls who are trying to build their *own* following.

And then a funny thing happened; I found out that a lot of the podcasts I listen to are made by people that have already achieved an impressive degree of success. This is because either the ones I like happen to be by British people I know of already (I KNOW these guys have made it 'cos they're on the BBC) or US podcasts where I don't know the hosts from Adam. And from the way their podcasts are produced, I've always thought they were being made in their bedrooms or something ... then over time I've found out that they work for Comedy Central, or have their own radio show, or are staff writers for David Letterman. And that doesn't mean I don't still support their work—I do—but it got me thinking that anyone that reads my stuff doesn't really know anything about me.

Hell, I've even bought cheap Kindle books thinking that I'm helping out a fellow unknown whose work I might like ... and then found out they have five books already in print with major publishing houses. (And then I get into a jealous rage and feed my Kindle to the dog.) So here's who *I* am.

I'm thirty-jfahgfasdjdgjhg, currently live in Coventry with my girlfriend and two dogs, I work as a self-employed musician/singer (available for hire, by the way) and am unpublished. I have no media connections, literary or otherwise, and when it comes to getting ahead in the writing game, I am relying *entirely* on the support of those who like my work when it comes to getting it out there.

(This is the crawling, begging part. Yes, yes, I know. Let's just get this over with, eh?)

If you've enjoyed this book, please do at least one of the following, listed here in order of priority:

1. Put a nice review and star rating on Amazon. A sentence, even! That'll do!! (**Author's note from even further in the future (April 2015): since writing THE STONE MAN, it has gone on to achieve a great number of reviews. This has been great, and has meant that I can now class myself as a full time writer ... but now it has so many reviews that most readers now don't think I need the support of good reviews for that book. Sooo, despite good sales, reviews have dried up and the only people leaving reviews are the ones that really hated it and have to let people know ... this means that the books review score has taken a real kicking. So if you were thinking of leaving a nice star rating ... I will kiss you when I see you if you do, and if you really don't want me to kiss you I promise that I will at least *think* about not kissing you.)**

2.   Mention it in a Facebook status or tweet about it (with a link.)

3.   Recommend it to a friend.

(Common response you will get from friends in this situation:

"I don't have a Kindle."

Your Response: "Aha, but the Kindle App is free, turning your smartphone or tablet into a perfect eReader."

Their response: "Oh … well, I only have an Android smar—"

You: "It's on the Android store too."

Them: "Ah. Um. Well … these days, I don't have much time to re—"

You: (Pulling out blunt object) "Buy. The bastard. Book.")

4.   Add me on twitter (@travellingluke) or Facebook (Luke Smitherd Book Stuff)

5.   Visit www.lukesmitherd.com and put yourself on the Spam-Free Book Release Newsletter mailing list. You will NEVER be spammed, and this will ONLY be used when there's news about an upcoming book, so let's face it, you're hardly going to be inundated …

Seriously, though; you guys doing any of those is a MASSIVE deal to me. As long as I know people are enjoying my stuff, I'll keep making it. So if you want to read more, click the button marked '5 stars' on Amazon. (Or four, I *suppose*. Jeez.) As for the future, this time I am going straight into writing the next one (spare me your cynicism! It's happening, right??) and it's going to be one of two novels.

One is a book-length story (working title *Everyone Is Your Killer*) that was the other story I prepped while I should have been prepping this one. It's about 70% plotted, I have the ending, and I just need to work out a few of the finer details so it's ready to go. The second is, to my own surprise, an anthology book of short stories. I have a list of about seven story ideas that I don't think will make long enough books, so I'm thinking 'Why not follow the lead of one of my writing heroes and release a book of short stories in between every few novels?' Don't worry, they'll all be along the unusual, slightly twisted lines of my previous work. Or maybe you should worry, I don't know. Although I'm reliably informed that the better option is 'Be Happy'.

But. I'm putting an actual, no foolin', chiselled-in-stone deadline on the next one. The date today—before I go back and redraft the whole thing—is the 20th of November 2012. I'm aiming to have this published online by the end of the month. Then it's Christmas, always a very busy time of year in my line of work, and then we're obviously into 2013. So … I'm saying to you that the next book will be finished by … hmm … right, no later than the end of June 2013. There. And you know what, don't be surprised if it's up a few months earlier than that (of course, the best way to find out release date news would be to be updated as it happens, and you know what to do to find out about *that*.)

One thing a few people suggested I add—and I feel pretty uncomfortable mentioning it, to be honest, but I'd probably be stupid not to—is a PayPal address for donations, seeing as the book price is so low. Well, on one hand, as far as I'm concerned, the fact that you paid even a tiny amount for this book makes me very happy indeed ... but, at the same time, if you WANT to send me a couple of bucks, then who am I to stop you, eh? You can PayPal it to lukesmitherd@hotmail.co.uk if you feel so inclined, and if not, you're still my favourite reader. You, reading this, right now. You're the best one.

In the meantime, thank you very much for purchasing, and reading, and I sincerely hope you enjoyed it. If not, I'm sorry it disappointed, but thank you anyway for giving it a chance (just go easy on the review, eh? Or even better ... just, y'know, keep it to yourself? Please?!?) See, I think I'm starting to get into a bit of a groove now with the practicalities of the whole writing game, and I think that maybe ... *maybe* ... I'm starting to get the hang of it. We'll see.

Speak to you soon, and remember, enjoy yourself. It's later than you think.

Stay Hungry,
Luke Smitherd
Findern,
Derby,
November 20th, 2012

***

Luke Smitherd Book Stuff on Facebook
www.lukesmitherd.com
@travellingluke
@lukesmitherd
lukesmitherd@hotmail.co.uk

Author's Afterword, Paperback Edition

I'll keep this short and sweet because the original afterword *almost* said it all. *Almost*, because the guy writing back in 2012 couldn't possibly know what would happen since the book was first released, could he? (Disappointing answer: not a huge amount, to be honest, but still *something*.) The majority of it still counts: still self-published, still need reviews, still would like people to either join the Spam-

Free Book Release Newsletter over at www.lukesmitherd.com (which now exists!) like like Luke Smitherd Book Stuff on Facebook, follow me @travellingluke on Twitter.

But there's been a few other minor bits happen since then, so they need mentioning.

Least of all...the release of the edition that you currently hold in your grubby mitts! This is the first Print-On-Demand version of any my books, and also the first one to be professionally proofread. Yeah, I sprung for it. I used the excellent Diana Cox over at www.novelproofreading.com, and I can't recommend her enough. Her rates are half those of most other people providing a similar service, so if you're thinking of getting some pro proofreading done, go see her. It's worth mentioning that she didn't proofread this bit however, just in case I'm making her look bad.

Being able to sell a physical copy of this book is very exciting, although I doubt it'll have a huge impact on sales; even now it's passed the 100 review mark, sales of TSM are still only around 100 copies a month, even when priced at a mere seventy-odd pence (about 99 cents in the US.) However, I do have to say a huge THANK YOU to everyone that took the time to leave a review. I seriously would have quit by now if not for the support of you folks, so thank you. But either way, a paperback is far easier to share with friends, so please do so; at the very least, it'll burn easily when there's a blackout and they need light to read their proper books by. Plus, a paperback can be recommended to everyone, ebook-phobes or otherwise, so if you felt like oh, I don't know...plugging it on Facebook or whatever? Ah, just a thought (*cough*do it*cough.)

Since TSM was released, I've written a novella (*The Man On Table Ten*) and a novel in four parts (*The Black Room* series) which, when collected together, is the longest single story that I've produced. These will be available in physical form eventually (TBR as a single volume, and TMOTT collected together with the next few novellas that I write) but that'll mean getting those suckers proof read professionally as well (people are a lot more forgiving of typos when they paid less than a buck for the book, and I have to charge a certain amount for print-on-demand or I lose money with every book sold!) and it'll take a while for the trickle of sales to cover that cost. In the meantime, if you have a Kindle, or a smartphone or tablet PC (for which you can get the free Kindle app) why not check those out? Let me know what you think via lukesmitherd@hotmail.co.uk .

It's worth mentioning that, as it says on the cover, that TSM went to number one on the Amazon free horror bestseller chart during its allowed-once-every-three-months-for-five-days free listing on the Kindle store, which created a lovely spike in sales (on all of my books at the time, strangely enough ... the eternal mystery of the Amazon store listing algorithm) that I thought was the beginning of the good times. Needless to say, when the inevitable happened and it all slumped back down to pre-free listing levels I felt most embarrassed, and had return the champagne to the store and spend many hours trying to find where all of my clothes had landed.

I'm still ploughing onwards with the whole self-published bit though, writing new stuff and starting to look at a more focused approach to book promotion. I may even—now the book has been correctly proof read—prepare myself for all the crippling rejection and pursue the (deep breath) traditionally published route, too.

We'll see. For now, at least, I'm slightly further forward than I was in 2011. If One is publishing your first completely unknown ebook, and Ten is global literary megastar, then I'd say I'm still about a Two, maybe a a Two Point Five. Obviously that's not as high as I'd like, but I think how the me in 2011 would feel to be at even the low level that I am now, and I know that he'd go apeshit with delight. So I count my blessings.

Either way, if you've bought this paperback edition as your first taste of my work, then a sincere thank you from me, as I know it would have cost a fair bit more than the Kindle edition, and that's a good wedge of cash to spend on an unproven writer like myself. Thanks a million. And if you've already bought the Kindle version and bought this version *as well*, then you...ahhhhhh, you are my kind on lovely. Thank you so much.

Oh, by the way; established Smithereens, which would *you* rather see in paperback form next? TPOTD, or TBR? Let me know, and I'll see what I can do about making it happen.

Thanks so much for the support; please keep it coming.

Stay hungry,
Luke Smitherd,
Earlsdon,
Coventry,
September 19th, 2013

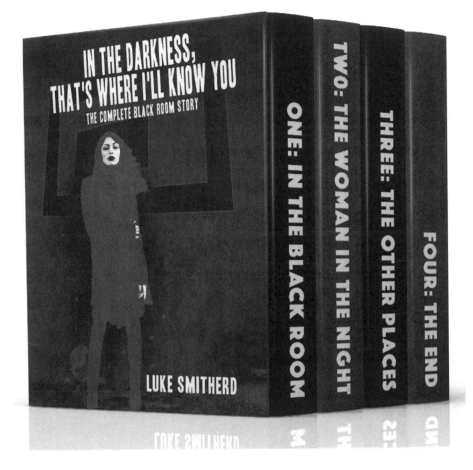

Also By Luke Smitherd:
IN THE DARKNESS, THAT'S WHERE I'LL KNOW YOU
FROM THE AUTHOR OF THE AMAZON UK #1 HORROR BESTSELLER, 'THE STONE MAN', COMES A NEW MYSTERY TO UNRAVEL...

What Is The Black Room?
There are hangovers, there are bad hangovers, and then there's waking up inside someone else's head. Thirty-something bartender Charlie Wilkes is faced with this exact dilemma when he wakes to find finds himself trapped inside The Black Room; a space consisting of impenetrable darkness and a huge, ethereal screen floating in its centre. Through this screen he is shown the world of his female host, Minnie.

How did he get there? What has happened to his life? And how can he exist inside the mind of a troubled, fragile, but beautiful woman with secrets of her own? Uncertain whether he's even real or if he is just a figment of his host's imagination, Charlie must enlist Minnie's help if he is to find a way out of The Black Room, a place where even the light of the screen goes out every time Minnie closes her eyes...

IN THE DARKNESS, THAT'S WHERE I'LL KNOW YOU starts with a bang and doesn't let go. Each answer only leads to another mystery in a story guaranteed to keep the reader on the edge of their seat.

Also By Luke Smitherd:
The Physics Of The Dead

What do the dead do when they can't leave...and don't know why?

The afterlife doesn't come with a manual. In fact, Hart and Bowler (two ordinary, but dead men) have had to work out the rules of their new existence for themselves. It's that fact-along with being unable to leave the boundaries of their city centre, unable to communicate with the other lost souls, unable to rest in case The Beast should catch up to them, unable to even sleep-that makes getting out of their situation a priority.

But Hart and Bowler don't know why they're there in the first place, and if they ever want to leave, they will have to find all the answers in order to understand the physics of the dead: What are the strange, glowing objects that pass across the sky? Who are the living people surrounded by a blue glow? What are their physical limitations in that place, and have they fully explored the possibilities of what they can do?

Time is running out; their afterlife was never supposed to be this way, and if they don't make it out soon, they're destined to end up like the others.

Insane, and alone forever...

Available now on Amazon

Also By Luke Smitherd:
An Unusual Novella For The Kindle
THE MAN ON TABLE TEN

It's story that he hasn't told anyone for fifty years; a secret that he's kept ever since he grew tired of the disbelieving faces and doctors' reports advising medication But then, he hasn't touched a single drop of booze in all of that time either, and alcohol loosens bar room lips at the best of times; so on this fateful day, his decision to have three drinks will change the life of bright young waitress Lisa Willoughby forever...because now, the The Man On Table Ten wants to share his incredible tale.

It's afterwards when she has to worry; afterwards, when she knows the unbelievable burden that The Man On Table Ten has had to carry throughout the years. When she knows the truth, and is left powerless to do anything except watch for the signs...

An unusual short story for the Kindle, The Man On Table Ten is the latest novella from Luke Smitherd, the author of the Amazon UK number one horror bestseller The Stone Man. Original and compelling, The Man On Table Ten will leave you breathless and listening carefully, wondering if that sound you can hear might just be *pouring sand that grows louder with every second...*

Available now on Amazon

Also By Luke Smitherd:
A HEAD FULL OF KNIVES
THE LATEST NOVEL FROM BESTSELLING AUTHOR LUKE SMITHERD

Martin Hogan is being watched, all of the time. He just doesn't know it yet. It started a long time ago, too, even before his wife died. Before he started walking every day.

Before the walks became an attempt to find a release from the whirlwind that his brain has become. He never walks alone, of course, although his 18 month old son and his faithful dog, Scoffer, aren't the greatest conversationalists.

Then the walks become longer. Then the *other* dog starts showing up. The big white one, with the funny looking head. The one that sits and watches Martin and his family as they walk away.

All over the world, the first attacks begin. The Brotherhood of the Raid make their existence known; a leaderless group who randomly and inexplicably assault both strangers and loved ones without explanation.

Martin and the surviving members of his family are about to find that these events are connected. Caught at the center of the world as it changes beyond recognition, Martin will be faced with a series of impossible choices ... but how can an ordinary and broken man figure out the unthinkable? What can he possibly do with a head full of knives?

Luke Smitherd (author of the Amazon bestseller THE STONE MAN and THE BLACK ROOM series) asks you once again to consider what you would do in his latest unusual and original novel. A HEAD FULL OF KNIVES is a supernatural mystery that will not only change the way you look at your pets forever, but will force you to decide the fate of the world when it lies in your hands.

Available now on Amazon

Alternative Ending Synopsis

(Aha! Hello there. Bet you weren't sure if this was back here after all, what with the plug for the other book on the previous page and all. I did say the *last* page, didn't I, and this is the last one. So here it is. It's basically the same ending, as I say, but with a definitive answer as to what happens to Paul. The last part was going to be told from his perspective, same as in the story, but after the fact. The conclusions he reaches at the very end would be the same, but from the point of view of a man looking back on it all, rather than a man inside it. I hope you'll agree that this version just isn't as punchy as the other one, and feel, as I do, that this is more of a petering out than a solid finish. Reading it back now, I'm not that keen. Either way, you might want an answer, so here it is.)

Paul begins his time inside the hall/cabin, and we learn that he spends the next ten years inside it. During that time, no more Stone Men appear. His life within it continues just as he describes it in the existing version, and while it takes its toll on him, he remains mostly sane, until one day the Stone Man suddenly stops following, mid-stride.

Wild with excitement—to the point of hysteria—he is restrained and sedated, and that is where the third person account ends. The story picks six months later, with Paul recounting the events that occurred after that from a beach in Australia.

He explains that it took the government scientists a fortnight to confirm it definitively—being extremely concerned about physical contact for obvious reasons—but they pronounce it dormant. Also, once shut down, the discover they can dismantle it like clay, and gain a new level of understanding of its physical properties now that they can examine it up close. Stone Man research takes a leap forward, and while the whole hall project is kept covered up, Paul is given a generous military pension and moves to Australia, where he promptly fakes his own death. He finds city life extremely daunting, despite his initial attempts to immerse himself thoroughly in it, and moves out to the coast, finding the quietest town he can. He spends his days fishing and living with various pets. He is a very different man now, unsure even of who he is or what his values are, and wonders if he'll ever know. However, he takes great delight in buying and trying all the products and innovations seen in films he's observed over the last ten years.

Eventually, he decides to get his thoughts out about the whole thing, and records his own account. The trigger for his doing so is made clear when he mentions the latest development; a new Stone Man has arrived in Coventry. He mentions the various media/military theories behind it (signal interference meant they couldn't send another linchpin while the other one was still here and active/it took that long to finally build another one to replace the essential original, a theory that gives credence to the 'genetically matched human parts make it easier to build new ones' theory) and talks about the rival Aeschliman and Numajiri teams; both groups of scientists who have been developing their own deterrents against the Stone Man in the last few months. Both claim to have created an infallible weapon that can break down the cellular structure of the Stone Man, thanks to the work of the last few months' post-Stone Man dormancy. Paul believes them, but decides he doesn't really care either way. As he looks across the waves, and feels darkness in his soul, he remembers the view from the cabin window, and begins to think to himself. We then sign off in the same manner as the original ending.

Printed in Great Britain
by Amazon

ISBN-13 978-1482643473
ISBN-10 1482643472

First Published Worldwide 2012
Copyright © Luke Smitherd 2012

All characters in this publication are purely fictitious, and any resemblance to real people, living or dead, is purely coincidental.
Proofreading by www.novelproofreading.com

Books By Luke Smitherd:

<u>Full-Length Novels:</u>
The Physics of the Dead
The Stone Man
A Head Full Of Knives
*In The Darkness, That's Where I'll Know You – The Complete Black
Room Story*
WEIRD. DARK.

<u>Novellas</u>
The Man On Table Ten
Hold On Until Your Fingers Break
My Name Is Mister Grief
He Waits
Do Anything

For an up-to-date list of Luke Smitherd's other books, his blog,
YouTube clips and more, visit <u>www.lukesmitherd.com</u>

For an up-to-date list of Luke Smitherd's other books, his blog,
YouTube clips and more, visit www.lukesmitherd.com